How ~~Not~~ To Catch a
ROCKSTAR

CASH & THE SINNERS

Also by D.E. Haggerty

Chapter 1

Aurora – a woman who thinks she has everything under control

AURORA

"Come on. Come on," I mutter as I dance in front of the stupid automatic doors at the emergency room.

The doors finally begin to open and I force myself through the gap. My purse gets caught – Ugh! I don't have time for this! – and I tug on it until it flies through the opening and slaps me on the thigh.

I ignore the pain and run to the nurse's station. "Jett Peterson," I gasp out. "Where is he?"

The nurse purses her lips as she fiddles with her computer. "There is no Jett Peterson here," she finally says.

"But I was notified—"

I slam my mouth shut when I realize of course there's no Jett Peterson. Jett would never use his real name. Duh. The groupies from *Cash & the Sinners* would have the hospital surrounded in no time while they screamed the drummer's name.

And it would be my job to get rid of them, manage the press, and ensure Jett wasn't bothered. It's not as if their manager, my boss, would handle any of the work.

I clear my throat and try again. "Do you have an Evel Knievel?"

Since Jett is an adrenaline junkie, he often uses the stunt performer's name when he's incognito. How it's incognito to use the name of a stuntman who's been dead for over a decade is beyond my comprehension. But it usually works.

The nurse consults her computer again. "He's in exam room three."

"Thank you," I say as I hurry toward the exam rooms.

I wish I could say I don't know where exam room three is, but this is not my first rodeo at the hospital with Jett. Not even close. I hope he hasn't broken any bones. Despite what he thinks, he can't go on stage with a broken arm.

The doctor is exiting the room when I arrive. I stop him.

"Doctor." I flash him a smile. "How is he?"

"He has a concussion and several contusions but no broken bones."

No broken bones is good but a concussion is not.

"How severe is the concussion? Will you be keeping him overnight? Does he need any additional tests? Does someone need to stay with him? Does he have any memory loss?"

The doctor's eyes widen at my rapid-fire questions. Like I said. Not my first rodeo.

"It's a mild concussion but we need to keep him overnight for observation."

I frown. Jett is going to lose his mind when he hears he has to stay overnight in the hospital. For someone who thinks it's fun to jump out of perfectly fine airplanes, he has an aversion to hospitals. The emergency room is okay, but put him on a bed and wheel him toward the elevator? He loses his dang mind.

Could this day get any worse?

"We'll need a private room and a service elevator to transfer him upstairs."

The doctor sighs. "I guess he wasn't lying about being a rockstar."

"Sorry."

"I'll send someone over to help with the arrangements."

"Thank you."

He walks off with a scowl on his face and I face the door. I straighten my back and gather my courage for another encounter with Jett the man who has a smile and a laugh for everyone but me. To me, he's an asshole. He makes me question my decision to remain the personal assistant for *Cash & the Sinners* at least twenty times a day.

The band's manager, Mike, has offered me other bands to assist numerous times. I've turned him down each and every time. I've got the rest of the band members properly trained. I don't want to start all over again.

Here goes nothing.

I push through the door and march into the room. I skid to a halt when my eyes land on Jett lying in the hospital bed. My heart thuds in my chest and my breath hitches. The man is a jerk but he's a mighty fine jerk.

His shirt is off, showcasing his toned chest and abs. How I long to lick every inch of those hard muscles. I would outline his tattoos with my tongue while my hands explored every inch of him. I fist my hands before I reach for him.

I may long to spend nights tangled up in sweaty sheets with him, but Jett has made it perfectly obvious what he thinks of me. *Not much.*

"Aurora!"

His shout has me lifting my gaze to meet his. Those piercing blue eyes I want to drown in are currently filled with warmth. How I wish they were filled with warmth because he's happy to see me. He's not. He wants something.

He winks at the nurse cleaning his forehead. "She's here to spring me out of here."

And there you have it. The reason he appears happy to see me.

"No can do. You're here for the night."

His eyes narrow at me and he scowls.

I motion toward his head. "You have a concussion."

He bats his eyelashes and sticks out his bottom lip. A lip I long to bite. "But I hate hospitals."

The nurse steps away from him and I gasp. My feet hurry to him before I can order them to stay where they are.

I lift his hair to study his wound and nearly moan when I feel how silky it feels. Great. Another item to add to the list of 'things I fantasize about on Jett's body'. I force those thoughts out of my mind. No drooling over a rockstar when he's got a big gash on his forehead.

"You have stitches."

"Didn't Nurse Luna do a wonderful job of stitching me up?" He winks at the nurse again, and I drop my hand.

What am I doing? No touching Jett.

Luna giggles. "You were an excellent patient."

"He's had enough practice," I mumble under my breath.

"Nurse Luna doesn't think I need to stay in the hospital overnight." Jett wiggles his eyebrows at her and she practically swoons.

"He can stay with me. I promise I'll watch over him all night long."

"No can do. The doctor says you have to stay overnight for observation."

"But I would have a nurse to personally take care of me," Jett pleads.

Luna giggles. It's obvious what her idea of caring for Jett means.

Rockstars are a pain in my ass. Why did I beg Mike to hire me again? Oh yeah, no one else would give me a job straight out of college and with no experience.

I cross my arms over my chest and stare Jett down. "And what happened the last time you left the hospital with a nurse?"

He smirks. "I had an excellent time."

"And?"

He huffs. He doesn't want to admit to what happened in front of the nurse.

"And?" I push because pushing is what I do best.

Jett glares at me but he can't hold my glare for long. Not to brag but I have the best 'stare down a rockstar glare' there is. I could probably teach classes and make a million dollars. Except most people don't want to stare down a rockstar.

"The paparazzi found out where I was and rushed the house," he finally admits.

"And what happened to your companion?"

He ducks his chin. "The press wasn't nice to her."

I nod to Nurse Luna. "And now you understand why I can't allow him to go home with you."

"Can't allow him?" She snorts. "You're not his keeper."

I kind of am. But if the paparazzi don't scare her, it's time to try another tactic. I whip a non-disclosure agreement out of my bag. "I'm going to have to insist you sign this."

Her nose wrinkles and she steps back.

I shake the document at her. "Sorry, honey. It's nothing personal, but it is mandatory."

She snatches the paper and reads the first line. "Non-disclosure agreement? You want me to sign this?" she asks Jett.

He shrugs. "The pleasure of doing business with me."

"But it says I can't tell anyone about you." She flips through the pages. "I can't post a picture of you on social media. I can't even tell my friends I had sex with a rockstar."

I hold out a pen. "It's standard boilerplate in the industry. I'm sure you understand."

She throws the agreement at me. "No thanks." She marches out of the room.

I wait until the door shuts on her before addressing Jett. "What happened?"

"You were being your usual bitch self."

I lock my muscles before I cringe at his use of the word bitch. It's not the first time he's called me one. And it won't be the last. Being a personal assistant to a rock band is full of fun times.

I point to his forehead and repeat my question. "What happened?"

"It's no big deal."

I sigh. I determine what's a big deal and what isn't. Not him.

"Was the press there? Did anyone notice you? What kind of media circus am I dealing with?"

He crosses his arms over his chest and I bite my bottom lip as I imagine—

Stop it, Aurora. You are not ogling the man when he's in a hospital bed. Correction. You are not ogling the man. Period. End of discussion.

"All you care about is your job. What about me and my injuries?"

I snort. "Considering you just tried to pick up the nurse, I think you're fine."

He grins. "She was pretty hot, wasn't she?"

Luna was blonde and had legs up to my neck. In other words, we have nothing in common. I ignore the twinge of jealousy in my stomach. I've had enough experience ignoring it by now.

"She was definitely your type," I mutter as I pull up the entertainment news on my phone.

I should know better by now than to ask the universe if things could get worse.

Chapter 2

Jett – a rockstar who doesn't mind a broken bone or two but hates hospitals

JETT

"Where have you been?" I shout at Aurora when she enters my hospital room despite knowing she spent the night curled up in the chair sleeping next to me.

When she wasn't on her phone or computer working that is. The woman works entirely too hard. The word fun doesn't exist in her vocabulary.

She startles and nearly drops the coffee cups she's carrying. Her light green eyes flash with pain before she blinks and it's gone. I ignore the guilt gnawing at my stomach for causing her pain. It has to be this way. I have to push her away.

Aurora Sharpe has relationship, white picket fences, and babies written all over her. I don't do relationships and I am never falling in love and having children. In fact, my bandmate Gibson and I have a pact to never fall in love.

I scowl. Gibson broke our pact when he fell for his country girl, Mercy. He can break our pact all he wants. I'm not falling in love. Ever.

Aurora stomps to the bed and slams a coffee down on the tray in front of me.

"Getting the supreme asshole of the universe his coffee," she snarls.

"Thank you," I say as I pick up the coffee.

"Did it kill you to say thank you? Should I phone the doctor to make sure you're not having a heart attack?"

I hold her gaze as I raise my hand and flip her off.

"One day you're going to give someone less tolerant than me the finger and they're going to break your finger right off of your hand."

"You?" I snort. "Tolerant? Did you forget what the word means?"

Anger flares in her eyes and her lips purse. Damn. How I want to pull her into my arms and feel all her fire up close. Taste those puffy pink lips of hers and discover for myself how they taste. While I thread my hands through her curly blonde hair as I devour her mouth. I bet her hair is as soft as silk.

I'd haul her body to mine. Touch all of those curves I've been imagining for years for myself. Aurora is a tiny thing. At a few inches over five feet, she's nearly a foot shorter than me. I bet she'd fit perfect tucked into my shoulder.

I shove those thoughts into the hole they live in. Aurora Sharpe is a woman you invite home to meet your parents. Too bad for her I don't have any family.

She opens her mouth to respond to me, but her phone beeps and she glances down at it instead.

"You're a workaholic," I mutter as I sip on my coffee.

I nearly groan as the taste of the caramel latte hits my tongue. This is not a hospital cafeteria coffee. I'd ask where she got it, but Aurora would never tell me anyway.

She hits send on her message before answering me. "Being a hard worker is nothing to be ashamed of."

"I work hard." Play hard? Work hard? Same thing.

She raises her eyebrow but before I can respond, the doctor enters the room.

"Can I get out of here?" I ask.

He flips open my chart and studies it for a few moments. I tap my fingers on the tray while I wait. Aurora reaches over and grasps my wrist to stop me. My skin warms where she touches me. I wonder how her touch would feel on other parts of my body. I clear my throat before I end up visibly excited in a hospital gown.

"Patience is a virtue," she sings.

"Good thing you're not the singer of the band," I grumble.

I'm lying. Aurora's voice is angelic. She should dump the PA gig and join a band. But she won't. Aurora's made it perfectly clear what she thinks of musicians.

She rolls her eyes. "Be polite."

"Ahem." The doctor shuts the chart. "You can go home today."

"Yes!" I pump my fist.

"But," the doctor waits for me to calm down before continuing, "you'll need to be monitored for the next few days. There's always a risk of your concussion worsening."

I grin. "I have someone in mind."

"You're not contacting one of your hussies," Aurora hisses. "This is serious."

"I'm not making Gibson fly to California from Winter Falls to be my babysitter. He's 'busy.'" I nearly choke on the word busy. I still can't believe Gibson is in love. Maybe Mercy's a witch and put a spell on him.

Aurora flicks a hand at me. "I'll handle everything. I always do."

The doctor hands her some papers. "Here are his prescriptions. The nurse will be here shortly with the discharge papers."

Aurora gives him her smile. The one she uses to get her whatever she wants. "Thank you, doctor."

He nods before leaving.

Aurora throws a bag, I didn't notice she was carrying, at me. "Get dressed."

I waggle my eyebrows. "You don't think I look hot in this?" I start to stand. "Maybe I should walk around and let you decide."

I was wearing the board shorts I had on for the surfing competition when I arrived at the hospital yesterday. But since they were covered in blood from my wound – head wounds bleed like a bitch – I ended up in a hospital gown.

"No," Aurora croaks as her cheeks darken. "Put on some normal clothes." She whirls around. "I'll wait in the hallway."

"You're hurting my ego, sweetheart!" I shout after her retreating figure.

She slams the door on me but not before giving me the finger. I chuckle as I dump the clothes on the bed. Jeans and a t-shirt. No underwear. Aurora knows I don't wear any, but I'm surprised she didn't bring a pair anyway. She doesn't 'approve' of my commando ways.

Once I'm dressed, I walk to the door and open it. "Can we leave now?"

Aurora holds up a hand to quiet me. "Okay. Thank you. Got it."

She hangs up the phone before scanning me. She frowns when she notices my bare feet. "Don't you have a pair of shoes?"

She doesn't wait for my answer before barging into the room. She opens the cupboard next to the bed and rummages through it. "It's like herding cats," she mutters as she pulls out a pair of flip flops and throws them at me. "Put those on."

I want to argue – arguing with Aurora is one of my favorite things to do, after all – but I don't want to walk barefoot around the hospital floor any more than she wants me to. Broken bones and concussions are fine. Infections are not.

A man enters the room with a wheelchair.

I pump my arm. "Time to blow this popsicle station."

I saunter toward the door but Aurora clears her throat. "Ahem." I ignore her. "Get in the wheelchair, Jett."

"Jett?" The nurse's mouth gapes open. "The hospital rumor mill said you were here but I didn't believe it."

"Here we go again," Aurora mutters before marching to the nurse. She gives him the smile and he's dazed for a moment. "Steve, is it?"

His mouth gapes open as she continues to dazzle him with her smile.

"You understand why we can't let anyone find out the drummer for *Cash & the Sinners* is in the hospital."

"I do?" His response is more question than answer but Aurora plows forth.

"I appreciate your understanding. It's very helpful." She whips a publicity picture of the band out of her bag and hands it to me with a marker. "Jett's going to sign this picture for you, and I'll send a band t-shirt over for you."

"Gee, thanks," he says as I hand him the signed picture.

I grin. "Always happy to meet a fan."

Aurora pats Steve's arm. "Thank you for your help." She taps the handlebars of the wheelchair. "Get in, Jett."

When I go to protest, she narrows her eyes at me. "Fine," I grump as I settle in the wheelchair.

She begins pushing me into the hallway where three of our security team are waiting. I shouldn't be surprised. Of course, they're here. Our security team is pretty much glued to our asses. Except when we're in Winter Falls.

The inhabitants of the small town in Colorado where my teammates have settled down don't care about our fame. In fact, they drive anyone out of town who dares to bother us. It's pretty awesome to walk around a town without worrying about being recognized. Too bad it's also boring.

The security team escorts us to the service elevator and through the back hallways to the rear entrance where a car is waiting for us.

I settle in the backseat and Aurora sits next to me. I sigh and lean my head back. I can finally breathe now that I'm out of the hospital. The antiseptic smell in hospitals makes me queasy. Which is saying something since I'm the one tasked with cleaning the toilet on the tour bus.

"Great, just great," Aurora grumbles.

"What now?" I murmur but don't bother to open my eyes. "Are we there yet?"

"Nope. And it's going to be a while."

"Why? What's going …"

The question dies on my lips when I open my eyes. There are fans gathered at the gated entry to my house.

"How did they know I'm in town?"

Aurora purses her lips. "Someone from the hospital must have notified the press." She leans forward and taps the driver on the shoulder. "Initiate Plan B."

"Which hotel is Plan B?" I ask.

She scowls. "Not a hotel."

"Whatever." I shrug. Wherever it is will be fine. I might give Aurora a hard time, but the woman knows how to do her job.

Chapter 3

Shoebox – an item slightly smaller than Aurora's apartment

AURORA

We stop in front of my apartment building. Here goes nothing. Jett is going to have a hissy fit when he realizes where he's staying. But I can't have him being interrupted by screaming fans when he has a concussion. He needs peace and quiet. And it's my job to give it to him.

Stan, the security guard, jumps out of the passenger seat and opens the door.

"Let's go," I order Jett when he doesn't move.

"This isn't a posh hotel," he mutters as he steps out of the car and scans the area.

There aren't any posh hotels in my neighborhood. It's not a horrible neighborhood per se. But it's certainly not posh by Jett's standards.

"Nope. It's my apartment," I say as I follow him out of the car.

Stan escorts us into the building and up to my apartment. I unlock the door for him and he checks there are no randy fans waiting to jump out from behind my Ficus plant.

"You're good, Ms. Sharpe."

I roll my eyes. "I've told you to call me Aurora a million times."

"Old habits die hard, ma'am."

I slap his shoulder. "And now you're making me feel old."

Jett growls behind me. Stan clears his throat. "I'll be patrolling the building and grounds."

He nods to Jett before leaving the apartment. And now Jett and I are all alone.

All alone in my apartment where there's a bed. My stomach dips and excitement rushes through me at the idea of Jett in my bed. Of him completely naked and lying there waiting for me.

Speaking of Jett, he hasn't moved away from the doorway. His nose wrinkles as he scans my apartment.

"This is your home?"

Welp. There's one surefire way to rid myself of any inappropriate excitement.

I glare at him. "Don't be an ass."

"I'm serious, Aurora. Doesn't Mike pay you?"

I roll my eyes. "Of course, he pays me. I don't work my ass off for free."

"Maybe you should ask for a raise." Says the man who's tried to get me fired more times than I care to count.

"I earn more than any other of the PAs in the firm." Because I'm worth it.

"Mike is obviously not using his cut of our royalties to pay his assistants."

I'm not destitute. I make a decent wage. But San Diego is one of the most expensive cities to live in in the United States. And I still have a ton of debt from grad school. Add one plus one and you end up with an apartment the size of a shoebox.

"Not all of us are rich rockstars who can buy flip-flops that cost more than what some people earn in a month."

He studies his feet and his brow wrinkles. "They're flip-flops."

He has no clue how expensive those flip-flops are. It's adorable. No. Wait. What am I thinking? It's not adorable. It's infuriating. Frustrating. Makes me want to pop his clueless head like a big, fat zit. Pop!

"You can go to a hotel or back home tomorrow. For today, it's important you have peace and quiet. No fans. No stunts."

He grimaces. "What else is there to do?"

Me?

Knock it off, Aurora. No one is doing anyone. Rockstars you work for are off limits. Especially rockstars who hate you for unknown reasons.

I hold up the bag of painkillers. "You'll probably pass out after you take these."

"I'm not taking any drugs."

"They're not recreational drugs. They're painkillers."

"Still." He shoves his hands into his pockets. "I promised my bandmates I wouldn't do drugs anymore."

What is he talking about?

"Oh yeah. The mushroom incident."

His cheeks flare and he ducks his chin. I wasn't on the tour bus when Jett decided to try mushrooms, but the story is the stuff of legends. Apparently, he took off all of his clothes and attacked the driver to let him off the bus because it was trying to murder him. I would kill for a video of the incident.

"I don't think Cash, Dylan, Fender, or Gibson will have a problem if you take some painkillers."

Cash, Dylan, Fender, and Gibson are the other members of *Cash & the Sinners.* Usually, the five are as thick as thieves. But Jett obviously doesn't want them to know he crashed and burned at the surfing competition. I can use this to my advantage.

"Shall I message them to ask what they think?"

"No." He shakes his head but then grimaces.

He's obviously in pain and I won't have it. I dig through the bag of medicines for his pain pills. I remove one before filling a glass with water. I shove the items at Jett. He holds up his hands and backs away.

"I don't need any painkiller."

"Liar. Your face is pasty white and you have brackets around your mouth. You're in pain."

"I can muddle through it."

I shake the pill at him. "Take the pill or I'm calling the band."

"Go ahead."

How cute. He thinks I'm bluffing. I'm not. I don't have any problem contacting the band.

Jett may be daring and adventurous but he's also prone to accidents. I've lost count of the number of times I've had to delay a concert because he broke a bone. And since the band is one big family, they won't let him forget about his mishaps. No, they'll rub in his klutziness the way a family does.

My stomach clenches at the idea of family. Something I no longer have. But I ignore the emptiness. I'm used to it by now.

I set the glass and pill on the side table near the door and dig my phone out of my pocket.

"Fine," Jett growls before snatching the water and swallowing the pill.

"Was that so hard?"

He waggles his eyebrows. "I've swallowed worse."

I barely hold in my eye roll. "What are you? Five-years-old?"

"I'm thirty-one but I can pretend to be younger if it floats your boat."

I nudge him toward the sofa. "Go sit down and get comfortable."

He settles on the sofa and glances around. "What do you expect me to do? Watch television?" He nearly gags at the word television.

"What's wrong with television?"

"It's boring."

"If you believe tv is boring, you, my friend, have been watching the wrong shows." I pick up the remote control. "Be prepared to have your mind blown."

He snorts. "Unless you're going to do a strip tease for me, I doubt my mind will be blown."

My entire body goes up in flames at the idea of doing a strip tease for Jett, but I force the excitement away. Good thing I'm used to ignoring my body's wants and needs when he's around.

"I need my pole to perform my act, but it's gone. The neighbors complained when I blasted *I See Red* while I practiced."

I bite my tongue to stop myself from laughing when he visibly gulps. "You have a pole?"

"Doesn't everyone?"

He holds out his hand. "Give me your phone."

"No. You have your own phone."

"I can't exactly order a stripper pole to be delivered to your house with *my* phone."

"As if you can get a workman out here to install a pole within a day."

"Damn," he mutters. "You owe me."

I plop down next to him and switch on the television. "Which is why I'm going to introduce you to Thomas Shelby."

"Who's Thomas Shelby?"

"Duh. The leader of the Peaky Blinders."

"I have no idea what you're talking about."

"Be nice and I'll start the show at the beginning for you."

"I'm always nice," he says in a deep voice and those flames return to heat my body from the inside out.

"Really?" I raise an eyebrow. "Do I need to remind you of the time the police wanted to arrest you because you wouldn't stop mouthing off at them?"

"It was a misunderstanding."

"A misunderstanding? You didn't mean to tell the officer to stick his baton up his ass and fuck himself with it?"

"He was harassing a woman. He wanted to arrest her without any evidence because of the color of her skin."

I frown. I hadn't heard this part of the story.

"And when I asked him politely to explain what his probable cause was to search her car, he said I was an asshole and told me to mind my own business."

"Why didn't you tell me all of this? I could have had the incident investigated."

He shrugs and glances away but not before I notice the blush on his cheeks. Is he embarrassed about being kind? No one should be embarrassed about doing a good deed.

I change the channel to my favorite streaming station. Jett groans.

"Behave and I'll order take-out from the Mexican place you like."

He perks up. "The one the rest of the band won't let me order from?"

"As long as you promise to stay out of the master bathroom."

He holds out his hand. "You have a deal."

I shake his hand and sparks ignite when his calloused hand touches mine. I inhale a deep breath and force thoughts of how those calloused hands would feel roaming over my body out of my mind.

"You're not so bad, Aurora Sharpe." He winks. "This might be the beginning of a wonderful friendship."

"As long as you don't expect me to kick women out of your hotel room for you."

He waggles his eyebrows. "What about men?"

I throw a pillow at him. "You're bad, Jett Peterson."

"Being bad is fun. You should try it sometime."

Would it be bad to throw myself at him? My body tingles and my stomach flips at how *bad* we could be.

Off limits, Aurora. Off. Limits.

Chapter 4

Sex dream – the perfect excuse Jett's been waiting for

JETT

I inhale as I slowly wake. The smell of jasmine fills my lungs. I love the smell of flowers. The first flowers I ever received were backstage at a concert. Since then, the smell reminds me of the band's success and how all the shit in the past was worth it to get where I am now.

I snuggle into my pillow. The pillow is soft and warm. Hold on. My pillows aren't soft and warm.

I force my eyes open and am met with a bundle of curly blonde hair. Huh? I don't remember taking a woman to bed. And I certainly don't remember letting her stay in my bed. I don't sleep with women. I have sex with them.

There's only one woman I want to sleep with. One woman I will never allow myself to sleep with. I inhale a deep breath and the scent of jasmine surrounds me.

Aurora.

Aurora always smells like jasmines. It's probably one of the reasons I'm obsessed with the scent.

But why is she lying in my arms? How did I end up in her bed?

Memories of falling off my surfboard surface. Ah yes. Now I remember. I was released from the hospital, but Aurora didn't want me at my house or some fancy hotel. She wanted me to have peace and quiet.

So, she brought me to her house to take care of me. Pain slices through my chest. No one's ever taken care of me before. I've always taken care of myself. I've never had anyone I could rely on.

I can't get used to it. I can't depend on anyone. Not when they'll get tired of me and my hijinks in a few months and get rid of me.

I debate rolling away and walking out the door but Aurora squirms against me and my cock takes notice. It always notices when she's around. How she hasn't seen I'm hard whenever she's in my presence is a miracle.

I tighten my arms around her and enjoy the feeling of her soft, warm curves in my arms. If this is the one and only chance I get to have her in my arms I'm going to enjoy it.

"Jett," she murmurs.

"What?" I ask.

"Jett," she sighs and rubs her legs together.

I tuck her hair away from her face. Her eyes are closed and she's writhing against me. Is little Aurora having a sex dream about me?

I should probably wake her up. I should probably get out of this bed.

She throws her leg over my hip and draws me near until my cock is pressed against her core. My cock – already hard from being in bed with the object of its desire – presses against my jeans. No way in hell I'm walking away now.

But I'm not having sex with a woman who's asleep. I kiss her eyelid.

"Aurora. Wake up."

"Mmmm," she mumbles as she rubs herself against my cock.

I grit my teeth before I roll her onto her back and bury myself in her. I'm not fucking her when she's not aware of what's happening.

"Aurora, you need to wake up, feisty girl."

"Don't wanna. Having the best dream."

"Wake up and I'll make your dreams come true."

Her eyes flip open and she stares at me. "I thought I was dreaming."

"No need to dream, feisty girl. I can make your dreams a reality."

I expect her to snort or push me away the way she usually does when I'm an arrogant ass to her. But she doesn't. She bites her bottom lip and studies me from beneath her lashes.

Holy shit. Does Aurora want me the way I've always wanted her?

My cock pulses against my zipper. It's on board with this development. I decide to try my luck.

I tuck a strand of hair behind her ear and trail a finger down her neck. "This doesn't have to change anything."

"You won't hate me in the morning?"

"I could never hate you."

She opens her mouth – probably to argue with me – my feisty girl does love to argue. But she slams it shut again and nods.

"Okay?" I ask.

She nods again.

I palm her neck and draw her near. "I need to hear the words, Aurora."

"What words?"

I grin. Only my feisty girl could make me grin while we're in bed and my cock is about to explode.

"I'll settle for 'Oh Jett, I can't resist you any longer'. Or how about 'Ravish me, Jett. I'm yours for the taking'?"

She snorts. "Ravish me?"

I tweak her nose. "I will make you come so hard you forget to breathe."

Her breath catches. "Promise?"

"All you have to do is say yes."

"Yes," she sighs. "A million times yes."

I pause. I didn't expect her to say yes. I was teasing. My cock presses against my jeans. It's not teasing. It wants to be buried deep in my feisty girl's body.

"This changes nothing between us," I say but don't give her a chance to answer before I slam my mouth down on hers.

She tastes of flowers and the forbidden. I've always been a sucker for the forbidden. I nip her bottom lip. "Let me in."

She opens up and I thrust my tongue into her mouth. I don't get a chance to explore before her tongue is pressing against mine. Dueling with mine for supremacy. I should have known my feisty girl wouldn't be a silent participant in bed.

I growl before I wrap an arm around her waist and haul her to me. Her breasts press against my chest. Not good enough. I want to feel her naked skin. I want to explore every curve she has. This is my one and only chance, and I'm not wasting it.

I roll her over until I'm looming above her and wrench my mouth from hers. Her pink lips are swollen from my kiss. I want to see those lips stretched around my cock while I plunge into her mouth. But first.

"You're wearing too many clothes."

I kneel and grasp the hem of her t-shirt. She lifts her arms with a sultry smile and I don't hesitate to accept her invitation. I whip the fabric off of her leaving her in a white bra. The bra strains to contain her breasts. It's a losing battle.

I drag the cups down and her breasts pop out.

"Pretty," I murmur as I trace her nipple with my finger. It immediately pebbles and hardens. "And responsive."

She wraps her legs around my hips. "Are you going to stare at my chest all day or are you going to ravish me?"

I respond by kneading and pinching her breasts until she's writhing beneath me. She arches her back and shoves her chest into my hands. I got you, feisty girl.

I snake my hand down her chest to her pants. I unsnap them and drag the zipper down exposing her plain white panties. I'm used to women wearing all kinds of sexy lingerie for me but it's not the packaging I'm concerned with. It's what's inside I want to discover and explore.

"Are you wet for me?"

Aurora bats her eyelashes at me. "Why don't you find out for yourself?"

Feisty. I love it.

I shove her pants down her legs leaving her in her white panties and bra. Such a pretty image. I debate grabbing my phone to snap a picture, but I don't want to give Aurora the chance to change her mind.

"What are you waiting for?" Aurora says and widens her legs.

I can see the wet spot on her panties and groan. "No idea," I mutter before ripping her panties away.

I plunge two fingers in her and moan at how hot and wet she is. She groans as she begins to ride my fingers.

"There you go, feisty girl. Take what you need."

Her head snaps forward and she meets my gaze. "What I need is you."

I continue pumping in and out of her. "You have me."

"Not your fingers."

I smirk. "You want my cock, feisty girl?"

"You did promise."

"I don't need to use my cock to make you come." I press the palm of my hand against her clit and her mouth gapes open as her eyes widen. "You'll come on my hand first. Then, on my cock. Maybe later in my mouth."

Her walls tighten around my fingers. Someone enjoys dirty talk. Good to know since I'm a dirty talker.

"Your pussy feels warm and wet against my fingers. I can't wait to bury my cock inside it."

Her walls convulse around me. "I'm... I'm..."

"Come for me, feisty girl. Come all over my hand and I'll give you my cock."

Her hands fist the sheets as she moans, "Yes."

I watch her face as pleasure hits her. It's the most beautiful thing I've ever seen. I put that look there. Satisfaction fills me.

When her climax wanes, I pull my fingers from her pussy. "Look at me, feisty girl."

Her eyes snap open and I stick my fingers in my mouth. She tastes spicy and forbidden. Two tastes I'm addicted to. "I can't wait to taste your pussy. To put my tongue in you and feel how hot you are for me."

Her eyes flare. "What are you waiting for?"

I place a hand over my cock. "I thought you wanted my cock first."

She licks her lips. "I do."

"Unless you can't handle any more."

Her eyes sparkle. "I can handle more. And I need the chance to trace all of your tattoos with my tongue."

Damn. This woman is my equal in bed. Too bad this is the only chance we'll ever have to be together.

I shove those thoughts away. I've got better things to think about now.

Chapter 5

Running away – a skill a certain rockstar has perfected

AURORA

I sigh as I wake up. My body is sore in all the right places. The best places. I stretch my arms toward the ceiling and the sheet falls down revealing my naked chest.

I usually hate sleeping naked but what's the sense in putting on clothes when someone's merely going to tear them off of you once he's had time to refuel anyway? I have my flaws but I'm always sensible.

I roll over to reach for Jett but frown when I notice the other side of the bed is empty.

"Jett?"

I strain to hear a response but am met with silence. Hmmm… Maybe he's in the kitchen and can't hear me.

Except the kitchen is five steps from the bedroom and the walls in this apartment are paper thin.

I get out of bed and quickly don a pair of sweats and a t-shirt before going to find the rockstar. It takes approximately five milliseconds of searching to realize he's not here.

What an asshole. Yes, Jett the drummer of *Cash & the Sinners* is famous for kicking women out of his bed. But I'm not some crazy fan or groupie. I'm his PA and – I thought – his friend.

We laughed and joked all afternoon yesterday while watching television. Afterwards, we ordered food from the Mexican place he loves and realized we're both secretly in love with the dodgy restaurant.

Ugh. I shouldn't have given in and had sex with him. But how could I resist? The man is sex on a stick. He's been my wet dream for practically ten years. There was no chance I was resisting. Especially after I woke up from dreaming about him to find him in my bed – his cock hard and willing.

I pick up my phone. I'm going to give the man a piece of my mind. Assuming he answers. He never answers when I call. Not even when it's for a band event.

Band event? Oh no. Aurora Sharpe get your head in the game. Jett is out in the world without supervision. I dial Jett's personal security.

"Good morning, Ms. Sharpe," Stan answers.

"It's Aurora," I respond without thinking.

"Ma'am, how can I help you?"

"You're never going to call me Aurora, are you?"

He chuckles. "Probably not."

I open my mouth to speak but pause when I realize I don't know how to ask Stan where Jett is without coming off as a complete idiot who slept with her client last night.

"Did Jett get off okay this morning?" I ask with my fingers crossed.

"He did, ma'am. I got him to the airport for his flight."

I blow out a breath. "Great. Thank you."

I start to hang up but Stan clears his throat.

"Is there something else I should know about?"

"Well, ma'am." He pauses. "I want you to know he's not worth your tears."

Welp. I guess I don't need to wonder if Stan knows what happened last night.

"My tears? Why would I cry over Jett?"

"I'll let you have your play but if you ever need someone to talk to, I'm here."

"You are entirely too nice, Stan."

"Don't tell my wife," he mutters and hangs up without another word.

I set my phone down before making my way to the kitchen. I need coffee. Lots and lots of coffee, to deal with the ramifications of what I've done. What *we've* done.

Jett and I were already at loggerheads most of the time. I don't think I improved the situation when I practically begged him to have sex with me.

I moan and drop my forehead to the kitchen counter. I'm such an idiot. Every PA of a rock band knows not to get involved with a member of the band. It's the first and most important rule of band management. And I blew the rule to smithereens.

I hope Mike doesn't fire me when he finds out. And I do mean *when.* The band manager has his finger on the pulse of

D.E. HAGGERTY

all gossip revolving around celebrities. He'll sniff out the truth soon enough.

My phone rings and I lift my head to glance at it. *Mike calling.* Awesome. Just awesome.

"Where the hell is Jett?" Mike asks the second I answer the phone.

Don't I wish I knew.

"What do you mean?" I ask as I rush to open the band's agenda on my phone.

"Don't toy with me, Aurora. I'm not in the mood. I've got a hundred fans waiting to meet him."

I read today's agenda item. *Fan Meet and Greet at Bertie's Recording Studio.*

Crap. *Bertie's* is in Winter Falls in Colorado. We're in San Diego several states away.

I really dropped the ball here. I forgot all about the event when I brought Jett home from the hospital. I didn't bother to consult my agenda. Some PA I am.

"According to his security, Jett boarded his plane on time," I hedge since I have no idea what plane Jett boarded or to where.

"He better be here soon or I'll have your ass in a sling."

I gulp. Mike's threatened to fire me more times than I can remember. The man has a temper.

Usually, I don't worry about it since I rarely make mistakes. But this time I made the biggest mistake of them all.

My phone beeps with a message.

> *Sorry, Aurora. Last night should have never happened.*

I grit my teeth as my anger flares. Thanks for the reminder, asshole. He couldn't have said he had a good time but it couldn't happen again? Nope. He has to make our night together out to be a mistake.

Where are you?

I don't expect him to respond. He never does to me.

"I've messaged him, but he's not responding," I tell Mike now.

"He's not responding to me either. Where the hell is he? You were supposed to be watching over him while he did this stupid surfing competition thing."

"I'm not his babysitter."

Mike grunts. "Think again, Aurora. Think again."

"I'll let you know if I hear from him."

"I'll make some calls." He hangs up without another word.

I'm not offended. I'm used to it. Mike doesn't know the words hello, goodbye, thank you, or please for a start. At least he doesn't use them with his assistants. With the bands he manages, however? He can kiss ass all day long and often does.

I'm dialing Stan to ask him if he knows what flight Jett was on when a message pops up.

He's here.

I blow out a breath and set my phone down. Crisis averted. For now. There'll be another one soon enough.

Soon enough?

The next crisis is here. Its headline is already written. *Band's PA sleeps with band member causing chaos in the band.*

Causing chaos in the band? *Please, Aurora. You are not that important.*

Yes, I handle every little thing the members of *Cash & the Sinners* need but I'm not irreplaceable. Anyone could do my job.

Especially since all of the members except Jett are now in serious relationships and no longer need me to find them condoms at 4 a.m. or smuggle a woman out of a hotel room.

Time to update my resumé.

Chapter 6

Ignoring you – a skill Jett excels in

JETT

Where are you?

I ignore Aurora's message. The same way I've been ignoring the messages from the band's manager, Mike, for the past hour as I drive from Denver to Winter Falls.

This fan appreciation day is the perfect way to avoid Aurora. I probably should have woken her up before I left but she knows me. I'm not the kind of guy who stays.

I'm also not the kind of guy who sleeps in the same bed with a woman after having sex with her. But I couldn't help myself. Feeling Aurora's curves against my body was heaven. I've never slept as well as I did with her in my arms.

The driver pulls to a stop in the alley behind *Bertie's Recording Studio.* I reach for the door, but he stops me.

"Let me check the area first."

I scowl. "This is Winter Falls. Nothing bad happens here."

"There are over a hundred fans waiting to meet you," he reminds me.

Fine. I flick my hand for him to go ahead and do his thing.

He returns a few minutes later and knocks on the window. "You're all clear if you aim directly for the back door."

Despite his words, he accompanies me to the back door and through the studio until we reach the sound room. The door to the live room where my bandmates are waiting is open, and Mike is bitching at the band.

"Love has ruined all of you," he mutters.

"Love hasn't ruined me," I declare as I saunter into the room.

Gibson, the rhythm guitarist for *Cash & the Sinners* and my best friend, rushes to me. "Where have you been?"

He slaps me on the back and I wince.

"Are you hurt? I told you the surfing competition wasn't a good idea."

I smirk. "It wasn't a good idea. It was an excellent idea."

He rolls his eyes. "Did you finally find a woman to lower her standards for you?"

"Don't be jealous I'm winning."

Gibson and I have a bet going about who can sleep with the most women. Even though Gibson stopped sleeping around when he met Mercy, he's winning. He can get a woman to drop her panties in two seconds flat.

And I haven't been sleeping around as much as I pretend. Not when there's only one woman, I want to bury myself in. I shove those thoughts away. Aurora and I had our fling. It's over. I don't do permanent, and she's got wife-material written all over her.

"What the hell, Jett?" Cash asks. "We were worried about you." Cash is the lead singer for *Cash & the Sinners.* The name kind of gives it away.

"With good reason." Dylan waves toward my head. Dylan is the lead guitarist for the band. He's also the peacemaker. It's funny he thinks he can stop us from causing hell. His efforts only make me want to cause more trouble.

Gibson steps closer to study my face. "What the hell happened? And why didn't you contact us?"

I waggle my eyebrows. "I had company." And I didn't want them to give me a hard time about getting hurt yet again. Getting hurt is my superpower.

Gibson crosses his arms over his chest and glares at me. "You still should have contacted us."

"It was fine. One night in the hospital was all."

"You were in the hospital and didn't let us know? What the hell, Jett? I'm your emergency contact. I should have been informed."

Aurora is actually my emergency contact, but I don't want to bring her name up. They don't need to know what Aurora and I got up to. Since they've all fallen in love – gag – they've become matchmakers. Nobody's matchmaking me.

"Do I need to repeat myself? I wasn't alone."

Fender grunts. Fender is the bass player for the band. He's also in competition for the grumpiest person alive. Love has mellowed him somewhat but he's still a grump.

"What happened?" Dylan asks.

"I hit my head."

He sighs. "I can see you hit your head. How did it happen?"

"I fell while surfing. I got a new scar and a concussion as a participation prize."

"Are you trying to break the record on how many concussions a person can get?" Gibson asks.

"Nah. I don't play football."

"If you're done gossiping, can we start the meet and greet?" Mike checks his watch. "Which is now officially thirty minutes off schedule."

"I thought Aurora was the one who had a hard-on for schedules," Gibson jokes.

Aurora. Damn it. I really screwed things up with her. I wish I could be what she needs. But I can't. There are no picket fences in my future. And there certainly won't be any children. I don't know how to be a dad.

Mike ushers us forward and we line up behind him. We walk through the sound room. "Ready?" He doesn't wait for an answer before opening the door.

Immediately the crowd starts to chant. *Sinners! Sinners! Sinners!*

I throw my hands in the air in the sign of the devil's horn. "Who's ready to meet and greet me?"

Women rush toward me and the security team forms a circle around me to protect me from being crushed.

"Shouldn't you take it easy after your concussion?" Gibson shouts.

A woman bats her eyelashes at me. "I can take care of you. I'm a nurse."

I ignore the gurgle of disgust at the idea of any woman other than Aurora touching me and waggle my eyebrows. "I always did enjoy playing doctor."

I spend the next 90 minutes pretending not to be repulsed by the idea of touching another woman while signing autographs on all parts of women's bodies.

I glance over at Gibson and notice he has his hands raised as he steps away from a fan who's eating him with her eyes. "Not interested."

"He's boring now because he has a girlfriend," I holler over at them.

Naturally, the press hears. The paparazzi aren't allowed at our meet and greets but there's other press in attendance to document the day on social media and in news stories. They begin to bombard Gibson with questions.

"You have a girlfriend?"

"Who is she?"

"Does she live in Winter Falls?"

I should have kept my big mouth shut. I know better than to give the press information about our private lives. I'm an asshole.

Mike claps his hands to gain everyone's attention. "The band members will not be entertaining personal questions today."

This is new. Normally, Mike jumps at the chance to use our personal issues to gain press coverage. And he doesn't bother to contain his glee either.

I go to stand with the band who have gathered around Gibson.

"I spoke to him this morning," Cash mutters. "We don't need a repeat of what happened with Virginia."

Virginia is Dylan's fiancée. She's also a shy librarian. When the paps surrounded her, she had a panic attack.

"Or Leia," Fender grumbles.

He has nothing to worry about. His fiancée wasn't intimidated by the paps. She chased them out of town with a shovel.

A reporter points at my forehead. "Can we ask how he got the new scar?"

I grin. They can ask me questions about my injury all day long. Anything to get their attention off the women my bandmates have fallen in love with. Those women are part of our family and need to be protected.

"You noticed? How sweet."

"What happened?" Another reporter shouts.

"All I can say is you can't fight off a shark with a punch to the nose. It's an urban legend."

"You fought with a shark?"

I shrug. "I'm sworn to secrecy."

Gibson chuckles. "Did the shark make you sign an NDA?"

"They're called sharks for a reason."

The DJ from the radio station out of Denver sponsoring today's event stands on a table to gain everyone's attention. "I hope you enjoyed the first portion of today's event. If everyone will proceed to the door, the limos are ready to drive us to lunch."

We retreat to the recording studio while the fans and press leave.

Gibson sighs in relief. "I'm glad we're done."

I scowl at him. "You used to enjoy these events. But since you've been dating Mercy, you're boring."

"I'm not boring for not wanting to sign a woman's pubic."

It takes effort but I keep my scowl on my face. I don't want my bandmates to realize I'm not as excited about the female fans as I pretend to be. If they sniff out my obsession with Aurora, they'll nag me until I give a relationship with her a try.

They don't understand. I can never be in a relationship with a woman.

Chapter 7

Tuna salad – not the problem in this story no matter how much Aurora wishes it were

TWO MONTHS LATER

Aurora

"Damn him!" I shout as I slam my phone on my desk.

The receptionist chuckles as she sets a plate on my desk. "Which Sinner has your panties in a twist now?"

Thank goodness for Dani. Dani and I are the only people in the office who don't swoon every time one of our rockstar clients appears. I think rockstars are assholes. She thinks rock music rots your brain.

She's also a grandmother who's been married to the love of her life for thirty years. She has no interest in our famous clients. Except to look at. They're pretty eye candy according to her.

I roll my eyes. "Jett. Who else?"

She sighs. "I pity the woman who falls for him. He is not a rockstar who wants to be caught."

My heart clenches at her words. Because she's right. I've known Jett for ten years now. I know exactly how he feels about love and commitment.

And yet, I can't help myself from wanting the man. From obsessing about him. I fell for Jett the first time he sauntered into a room and smirked at me with those piercing blue eyes.

Unfortunately, crossing the line and getting naked with each other hasn't cooled my obsession one bit. Instead, it's intensified. I swear when I'm lying in my bed at night, I can still smell his scent on my pillows and feel his heat surrounding me.

Obviously, my infatuation is a one-way street. Jett hasn't answered one phone call since our night together. He's never been very communicative but this is ridiculous. I can't do my job if he refuses all contact with me.

Dani nudges the plate toward me. "I brought you one of the sandwiches left over from Mike's meeting."

"You're an angel. I didn't have time for breakfast this morning."

I snag the sandwich from the plate but as soon as the smell of tuna salad hits me, my stomach protests. I drop the sandwich to clutch my middle.

"I think I'm going to be sick," I mutter.

I breathe deeply through my nose to settle my stomach but inhaling brings the tuna smell back. My stomach gurgles, and I spring from my chair to sprint for the bathroom. I barely make it to a stall before I lose the contents of my stomach.

Dani pulls my hair away from my face and rubs my back as I heave into the toilet. "There, there," she murmurs. "Let it all out."

When there's nothing left in my stomach to purge, I collapse on the floor of the restroom. "I don't have time to be sick," I whine.

Dani hands me a wet paper towel. "Are you certain you're sick?"

I point to the toilet. "Did you miss the part when I puked my guts out?"

"You were perfectly fine until you smelled the tuna."

"Maybe the tuna was bad."

"As if Mike would ever allow any food that isn't fresh in one of his meetings."

I stand and straighten my clothes. "What are you trying to say?"

She pours me a glass of water and hands it to me. I rinse my mouth with the water a few times before she responds.

"Could you be pregnant?"

"P-p-pregnant?" I sputter. "I can't be pregnant. I would know if I was pregnant."

She cocks an eyebrow. "You just threw up because of the smell of tuna."

She's right. Oh no. Am I pregnant? I can't wait to have children. I've always wanted a family. Ever since… I cut off those thoughts. I have enough going on without digging through my pathetic past.

"I can't be pregnant."

"You haven't had any sex at all in the past months?"

My body heats as I remember the only sex I've had in the past six months. Being with Jett was everything I ever imagined it would be and more. The way he touched me as if he cherished me. The way he took care of me afterwards.

Until he snuck out in the morning. My fantasies of him didn't include him being a bastard.

I shove thoughts of Jett out of my mind. "I always make the man glove up."

"Gloving up isn't always enough," Dani says. "Condoms can break or be expired."

"Expired?"

"Condoms have expiration dates."

Shit. Shit. Shit. How long were those condoms in my nightstand? I'm not in the habit of bringing men back to my apartment. In fact, I can't remember the last time it happened before Jett. Was it years?

"I need to go home."

I sprint toward the door but Dani shackles my wrist to stop me. "You need to calm down."

I glare at her. She should know better than to tell a woman to calm down.

"You can't go busting through the offices appearing stressed. The other PAs will latch onto your behavior as an excuse to try and steal your clients. They're all gagging to rob you of *Cash & the Sinners.*"

Damn. I nearly forgot this office is a den of vipers. I'm usually left out of it because I don't engage in petty gossip but all the other women need is the slightest of excuses to attack me.

I inhale a deep breath and force my body to calm down. It doesn't work. I'm in full freak out mode but at least I'm not running out of the bathroom screaming.

"Can you tell Mike I'll be working from home for the rest of the day?"

She drops her hand. "Of course." She leans close to whisper. "And let me know if there's anything I can do."

I hope I don't need her help. I hope I'm freaking out for no reason.

While I drive home, I try to convince myself I'm overreacting. I'm not the overreacting type but maybe this one time is an exception. I mean come on. What are the chances I finally have sex with the man of my dreams and he impregnates me? This isn't some cheesy dime store romance novel.

Despite being ninety-five percent certain I'm suffering from some twenty-four-hour stomach flu, I stop at my local pharmacy to buy a pregnancy test.

I blow out a breath as I study the rows and rows of pregnancy tests. They all claim to be the 'best' and the 'most accurate'. Not all of them can be the best.

Normally, I'd thoroughly research my options, but I don't think the owner of this store will appreciate me sitting down in the aisle for an hour to google the best pregnancy tests. I grab five tests instead. One of them has to be the most accurate.

The elderly cashier giggles when I set my purchases on the counter. "Oh dear, we've all been there."

I can safely say I haven't been here in my thirty-three years of living. I expected the first time I took a pregnancy test to be with a loving partner. Not freaking out about an accidental pregnancy.

"These are on the house," she says as she stuffs a few candy bars into the bag with the tests.

I try to smile my thanks but I don't think I manage when she pats my hand in sympathy.

I arrive home and dump my purchases and bag on the floor before racing to the bedroom. I rip open the nightstand drawer. The entire drawer flies out and clatters to the floor. The contents spill out and I dig through the scarves and hairbands for the box of condoms.

"Expiration date. Expiration date," I mumble as I study the box.

"Fuck a rockstar," I mutter as I fall to the floor. The condoms expired a year ago.

I guess I need those pregnancy tests after all. I shove to my feet and go in search of the bag I dropped somewhere when I arrived home.

I dump the contents on the vanity in my bathroom. I grab a candy bar and rip it open. I sniff but the smell doesn't make me gag. Good.

I devour the bar as I line the pregnancy tests up. Once they are all properly prepared, I begin.

By the time I've taken all of the tests and am waiting for the results, I've finished two chocolate bars. I open the third and final one as I watch the clock tick down.

When the alarm sounds, I wipe my hands on my pants and inhale a deep breath. But when I go to check the results, my eyes snap closed.

Come on, Aurora. You're not a chicken. You've faced down crowds pulsing with anger when a concert was cancelled. You can handle a little test.

"I am not afraid. I am not afraid," I chant as I slowly open my eyes to peek at the tests.

Pregnant.

Pregnant.

Pregnant.

Pregnant.

Pregnant.

Elation fills me. I'm pregnant. I'm having a baby. I cradle my stomach. My dreams of having a family are finally coming true.

But then I remember.

I'll be doing this alone. Jett doesn't want children. He hates children.

Maybe I shouldn't tell him. If he's going to abandon the baby, anyway, maybe it's better he doesn't know.

I glance down at my stomach.

"Welp. It's me and you against the world now, Little Bean."

Chapter 8

Thanksgiving – an excuse for your friends to invade your house and stick their noses in your business

JETT

"Happy Thanksgiving," Indigo greets as she nudges her way past me into my house.

Indigo is Cash's fiancée. They were high school sweethearts who lost their way but they recently reconnected when Cash rented Indigo's grandmother's house.

I try to shut the door behind her but Virginia and Leia follow her inside.

"What's going on?" I ask as I grab the dish from Virginia's hands. Virginia is Dylan's pregnant fiancée. He'd kill me if I let her carry anything. Not even a casserole dish.

"You have the best oven …" Indigo shrugs.

"And? Who cares about my oven?"

"She means we've decided we're having Thanksgiving at your house because no one thought you'd show up at Thanksgiving dinner at anyone else's house," Leia explains.

Leia is Fender's fiancée and she doesn't beat around the bush or play games. Unlike Indigo who thinks she's a spy.

"Leia!" Indigo screeches.

Leia shrugs. "What? He'd figure it out sooner or later."

Indigo sticks out her bottom lip. "But it's more fun to mess with him."

"Where's Isla?" I ask since I have no interest in listening to them bicker.

Isla is Leia's daughter and she's a hoot.

Leia rolls her eyes. "She's on the phone with her boyfriend."

"Boyfriend?" I scowl. "She's twelve. She shouldn't have a boyfriend yet."

"You remind me of Fender." She sets her dish on the counter and crosses her arms over her chest. "No daughter of mine will have a boyfriend before she's twenty-five," she mimics Fender's grumpy voice.

"I happen to agree with Fender on this one."

"On what one?" Cash asks as he strolls into the house as if he owns it.

The rest of the band members follow him. Except Gibson who's away at rehab. Don't get me wrong. I'm glad he's dealing with his alcohol problems, but I worry. I know how hard it is to stay clean in our world. I frown.

Indigo points at my face. "And now you know why we didn't think you'd show at Thanksgiving, pouty face."

"I do not have a pouty face."

"Do you need a mirror, Uncle Jett?" Isla asks as she bounds into the room.

I pick her up and spin her around. "What's this about you having a boyfriend?"

She rolls her eyes. "You remind me of Dad."

Fender grunts. He isn't actually Isla's dad. Her dad took off when she was a baby and Leia raised her as a single mom. But Fender fell in love with the little girl while he was falling in love with Leia. He's adopting her now.

I set Isla on her feet and she pats my arm. "I'm sorry you're missing Uncle Gibson today."

Everyone freezes at her words. I guess they planned to avoid speaking about our fifth band member today. No fucking way. Gibson is a member of this family whether he's in rehab or not.

But Gibson isn't the person I'm missing and can't stop thinking about. No, I'm worried about Aurora. Who is she spending the holiday with? Or is she alone? Maybe she's working. She works too hard.

I want to pick up the phone to call her. I miss the sound of her voice. I miss the twinkle in her eyes when she teases me. The smile she uses to get her way. I plain miss her.

Which is why I've been dodging her calls. I don't want her to get attached to me. I'm not the man for her. I'm not the man for anyone. I'm a lone wolf. Always have been. Always will be.

"Where's Mercy?" I ask. Their mouths gape open. "What?"

When no one will answer, I direct my gaze on Leia. Fender growls and stands in front of her. "Leave her alone."

Leia peeks out from behind him. "I'm fine, grumpystiltskin."

"I got this one." Virginia walks forward. Dylan scowls and goes to stand behind her.

My bandmates are pissing me off. They're my family. I would never hurt their loved ones.

"Leia and Virginia aren't in danger from me," I growl.

"But Mercy is?" Cash asks.

I rub a hand down my face at his insinuation. His correct insinuation. I haven't been very nice to Gibson's girlfriend. In my defense, I was reeling from the whole Aurora thing and keeping it to myself.

"I'll apologize to her," I mumble.

"Good." Indigo grins. "She'll be here soon with Old Man Mercury."

Old Man Mercury is the reason she ended up in Winter Falls. The grumpy old man is her uncle. It's hilarious watching her try to tame him.

Virginia shoos us to the living room. "Watch some basketball while we finish preparing the food."

Dylan kisses her nose. "Thanksgiving is for football."

"Shouldn't we be helping?" I ask as we settle on the sofas around the television.

I've never attended a family Thanksgiving before. The band is usually on the road during the holidays. But I don't think we should sit here and do nothing.

"You're cleaning up," Leia declares as she hands out beers.

"I don't need no help!" a man shouts outside.

I stand. "Old Man Mercury is here."

I open the door to Mercy trying to help her uncle up the stairs to our porch. I take over from her and she gives me a shy smile in thanks. Damn. I guess I've been an asshole to her.

"I don't understand why I had to come to Thanksgiving dinner," Old Man Mercury mutters as I help in the house.

Mercy sighs. "Because you can't be left on your own, Uncle Mercury."

"And we're all at today's celebration," Sage says as she follows us inside.

I glance behind her. Sage is never alone. And she isn't now either. The rest of the gossip gals – Feather, Petal, Cayenne, and Clove – are with her as are two elderly men who I've seen around town but have yet to meet.

The gossip gals isn't a derogatory name I made up. The ladies are proud to be gossips. And they're delighted with the nickname. They proudly wear t-shirts with the gossip gals written on them in sparkly gold paint.

"Did you invite the entire town to my house?" I ask Indigo as I help the gossip gals set their dishes on the kitchen counter.

"I didn't invite the gossip gals."

Sage snorts. "No one needs to invite us. This is Winter Falls."

This is Winter Falls is what she says when she has no excuse for her actions. It kind of makes sense since Winter Falls is totally fucking crazy. There are pagan festivals, naked men walking squirrels, and hippie bars for a start.

What you won't find here is many cars – or, at least, not cars with combustion engines. Winter Falls prides itself on being the first carbon neutral town in the world. Instead of cars, everyone gets around on bikes and golf carts.

Feather pats my shoulder. "We don't usually celebrate Thanksgiving in Winter Falls."

I know better than to ask why. Most questions are answered with PowerPoint presentations and end with a quiz. I wish I were joking.

"But for you we will." Cayenne winks.

"For me?" I motion to the house. "I think you mean for the band."

"Uh huh," Clove agrees but I have a feeling she's placating me. Placate away. I do not want to know why they claim to be here for me.

Petal shoves a man toward us. "This is my husband, Orion." She indicates the other man. "And he's Sirius."

Fender hands each man a beer and they hurry to join us in front of the television.

I can't help studying them. What would make a man stay with a woman for decades? What kind of love and devotion do you need to stay together for that long?

I have no clue. Before moving to Winter Falls, I'd never met a couple who'd stayed together for longer than a year or two. Are they happy, I wonder. Or do they resent their partner and wish they were free.

"Touchdown!" Dylan shouts and I return my attention to the television. There's no sense worrying about how couples work. I will never be part of one anyway.

The television abruptly shuts off. "Dinner's ready!"

At Indigo's announcement, everyone stands and makes their way to the dining room. I can hardly believe my eyes. The plain table is no longer plain. It's been decorated for the holiday with leaves and candles and I don't know what.

"It's a good thing we came to your house, Jett," Leia says as she sits down. "Our dining room table does not seat seventeen people."

"I'll buy a new table," Fender says.

She slaps his shoulder. "I wasn't angling for a new table. Stop throwing your money at me."

He grunts in response. Which means he's going to spoil her whether she wants him to or not. I still find it hard to believe he fell in love after what happened with his bitch ex-girlfriend.

"Now," Sage says once everyone has a plate full of food and is ready to dig in. "What are we going to do with you, Jett?"

My brow wrinkles. "Do with me?"

"What happened to being subtle?" Clove asks.

"Subtle doesn't work with rockstars."

Petal sighs. "This is going to be my favorite project."

"Project?" I scan the room for a clue as to what the gossip gals are up to now.

"They want to find you a girlfriend," Leia fills in.

Cayenne purses her lips at Leia. "You weren't supposed to tell him."

She waves her fork at me. "He's going to figure it out for himself once you start parading women in front of him."

I drop my fork and lift my hands in front of me. "I don't want a woman."

Feather waggles her eyebrows at me. "The parade of women leaving your house in the morning says otherwise."

There isn't a parade of women leaving this house. Not since Gibson fell for Mercy has there been. I don't bring women here.

Hell, I haven't slept with another woman since Aurora.

Aurora. Why can't I get her out of my mind? We had our one night together. It's all I have to offer her. I can't give her more. I'm not capable. I don't know how.

"Don't blame Gibson. He's not here," Mercy says.

Indigo wraps an arm around her shoulders. "He'll be home soon."

Mercury pats her hand. "Gibson's a good egg."

Mercy stares at her uncle. "Don't you go being nice to me. I don't know how to handle it."

He chuckles before glaring at Sage. "Leave the boy alone. If he doesn't want a wife and family, it's his choice."

Sage sticks out her bottom lip. "But he won't be happy all alone."

"Who do you want to match him with?" Leia asks and I glare at her. She shrugs. "I'm serious. There aren't any available women your age left in Winter Falls."

Sage studies me. "Maybe a woman from outside Winter Falls."

Does she know? Does she know I'm obsessed with Aurora?

It doesn't matter. I'm not acting on my obsession. Not again. The first time was a mistake. A mistake I can't get out of my mind but a mistake, nonetheless.

And I know how to learn from my mistakes.

Chapter 9

Surprise – can be good or bad but will almost always cause your heart to want to beat out of your chest

AURORA

I sigh as I cross the border into Winter Falls. Although the band members of *Cash & the Sinners* live here, I haven't visited the town yet. I don't need to be in the same town as them to be their assistant, although I do travel with them when they are on tour.

I notice the sign for *The Inn on Main,* the only place to stay in town, and turn left into the parking lot. I'm surprised by how few cars there are considering the owner claimed she was fully booked except for one suite.

Whatever. It doesn't matter. Mike is paying for the room anyway. I convinced him I needed to be in Winter Falls since the band has settled here.

I walk to the entrance of the bed and breakfast. It reminds me of a Southern plantation with its big columns and wraparound porch. It's cute. What I've seen of the town thus far is cute. I can understand why the band wanted to settle here.

Except Jett. He's not going to settle anywhere as boring as a small town. His words. Not mine.

I enter through the front door and scan the area. It's as adorable as the outside. The entry is wide with a small reception desk off to the side. To the other side is an entry to a cozy looking sitting room. In front of me is a small seating area with cookies and coffee.

I eye the cookies and my stomach rumbles in response.

"Help yourself," the woman at the reception desk says. "I'll be with you in a minute."

Don't mind if I do. I study the cookies. There's a variety. Chocolate chip, oatmeal raisin, and something with nuts. I pick up an oatmeal raisin. Oatmeal is healthy, isn't it?

I bite into the cookie and moan. Holy cow, this is yummy.

The receptionist giggles. "I have the same reaction whenever I eat a cookie from *Bake Me Happy*."

"This cookie can bake me happy anytime."

"I'm Ellery, the owner of *The Inn on Main*, and you must be Aurora."

She holds out her hand and I wipe the cookie crumbs on my shirt before shaking hers.

"Sorry, I've been driving for days."

"You're fine." She glances around me. "Where's your luggage?"

"In the car, I didn't feel up to dragging it inside."

"Let me show you to your room. I'll have someone deal with your luggage while you get settled."

Her words are music to my ears. I've been schlepping my suitcases in and out of motels for three days. I'm ready to spend more than eight hours in one place.

We climb two sets of stairs before we reach the attic.

Ellery opens the door to the sole room on this floor. "The executive suite. It's my favorite room. The bathroom is through there. You have a bathtub and a separate shower. You'll find extra bedding in the closet but with the fireplace, you should be warm enough."

Fireplace? I somehow missed the large fireplace across from the bed. There's a comfy looking chair in front of it. This place is nearly as large as my apartment in San Diego. It's definitely nicer.

"You said you'd be working while you're here?"

I nod.

"There's free Wi-Fi and if you need a printer, let me know. There's also a kitchenette but breakfast is included in your nightly rate."

The kitchenette isn't much. A two-burner stove next to a sink with a cupboard above it. It'll do for now.

"You can also eat at the diner or the brewery. They're both open for lunch and dinner."

I'll skip the brewery since I'm not drinking for the foreseeable future, but I'm eager to try a small town diner. "Thank you."

"I'll leave you to settle in. I'll have your luggage sent up."

I cross to the bay window with its view over the town. Main Street stretches out in front of me. There aren't any cars on the road but I didn't expect any. Not after the number of times Jett complained about the 'crazy environmental rules' in Winter Falls.

Stores line the street. Judging by the names I can read – *Naked Falls Brewing* and *Electric Vibes* to name a few – the town is as quirky as I expected. I'd love to settle down in a small town. I have no desire to remain in San Diego where I can barely afford my rent and don't know my neighbors.

And with Little Bean on the way, I'll need a bigger place. Now is the perfect time to make a change. Maybe Winter Falls is the change? I don't know. I haven't decided what to do about the future yet. But I have six months to figure things out while my apartment is being sub-leased.

I rub a hand over my stomach. My baby bump isn't very noticeable since I'm a curvy girl anyway, but I can't stop myself from touching the area. It's really happening. I'm having a baby.

As I watch Main Street, I notice a large group of people gather near several long tables set up around the square. I wonder what's happening. Is this one of those pagan festivals Jett told me about?

"Knock! Knock!" Ellery hollers before entering and placing my suitcases next to the door.

"Do you know what's going on?" I point outside to the town square.

"It's a town celebration."

"To celebrate what?"

She frowns. "You're not a reporter, are you?"

I bark out a laugh. "Nope. And I hate the press more than you do." I clear my throat. "I'm actually the personal assistant for *Cash & the Sinners.*"

Ellery studies me. "How do I know you're not lying and you're actually one of the paparazzi? We kick all of those out of town. No hotel refunds."

I dig out my phone and scan my pics until I find one of me with the band. "This good enough?"

"Wow." She says as she studies the picture. "They look young here."

"It was during their first tour. I've been their PA from the moment they signed with their current manager." She hands my phone back to me and I scroll through the pictures to find a more recent one. "This was a few months ago."

"You look hot with a guitar."

"Too bad I can't actually play one. I didn't get a job at a managing firm as a gateway to fame. Mike hired me because I don't take crap from anyone." Including Jett, the supreme asshole of the universe.

"Good for you." Ellery motions to the window. "The celebration is for Gibson. He got out of rehab today."

"Today?" I consult my agenda. "He's not supposed to get out for another five days. I better go speak to him and find out what's happening."

I grab my coat from the bed where I threw it. "This job never ends."

"Tell me about it," Ellery mutters.

I say my goodbyes and hurry out of the inn and down Main Street to where the party is happening. I don't think a party is a good way to celebrate being sober but what do I know?

I scan the area for Gibson but my gaze gets stuck on Jett. He's not alone.

My mouth gapes open at the vision in front of me. Jett is playing with a girl. I'd guess she's around thirteen. As I watch, the girl touches him and yells *You're it.* Jett bounds away but stops after a few steps to check she's keeping up.

I rub my eyes. I must be seeing things. The Jett I know absolutely does not want anything to do with children. It's why I've kept things secret from him for this long.

But the guilt started to eat at me. Whether or not Jett wants to be a part of this baby's life, he has the right to know about Little Bean. I just hope he doesn't destroy me in the meantime.

Enough about Jett. I'll deal with him later. Gibson is my current priority. I spot him making out with a woman on the sidewalk. She must be Mercy.

I've been looking forward to meeting her. Too bad our first meeting will involve me yelling at her boyfriend for busting out of rehab early.

I march toward them.

"What the hell?" Jett's shout has me stopping in my tracks. "What are you doing here? Are you stalking me?"

"Wow. How big is your ego? I'm not stalking you. I'm the PA for the band or did the bump on your head give you amnesia?"

The rest of the band and their partners gather around us. Awesome. An audience.

"You won't be the PA any longer if I can help it," Jett grumbles.

He couldn't have hurt me more if he stabbed me in the heart with a rusty knife. What an asshole.

Where's the man I spent a few days with in San Diego? The one who laughed at my jokes? The one who became obsessed with *Peaky Blinders*? The one who showed me how gently he could make love to me?

I force those thoughts away. I know better than to search for the man Jett showed me when he was injured. *That* man is an illusion. The real Jett is a complete and utter asshole.

I throw my arms in the air. "Not this again. How many times are you going to try and get me fired?"

He doesn't respond. Probably because he's too busy staring at my bump.

"Are you pregnant?"

I place a protective hand over my stomach.

"You are. It better not be fucking mine," he snarls.

"It's yours, asshole!" I yell.

He opens his mouth to speak but then must think better of it. He snaps his mouth shut before whirling around and stalking off without saying another word.

My breath catches and tears well in my eyes. I knew he wouldn't handle my being pregnant with his baby well, but this is worse than my worst nightmares.

I whirl around and rush away. I can't face the rest of the band now.

Chapter 10

Father – not a word Jett wants associated with him

JETT

I stomp to my house. I must be sleeping. This is some kind of nightmare. Because it can't be true. Aurora can't be pregnant with my child.

She can't be. I *always* glove up. I never, ever slide into a woman without a condom on my dick. No matter how much Aurora tempted me, I didn't enter her bare.

But I saw the proof for myself. Her little baby belly didn't lie.

A sliver of possessiveness snakes through my chest. The baby is mine. I shove the thought away. I can't have a child. I can't raise a child. I can't be a parent.

Did Aurora show up in Winter Falls to drop this bomb on me? I didn't realize she was cruel. She knows I don't want children.

I reach my house and fling my door open but when I try to slam it shut behind me Fender grunts.

I glare at him. "What are you doing?"

Gibson pushes his way in front of Fender. "I think you mean what are *we* doing."

I growl but it doesn't stop Gibson, Fender, Cash, and Dylan from invading my house. Great. The band's all here.

"Shouldn't you be at your sober celebration?" I ask Gibson.

"As if I'd be anywhere else when you're having a crisis."

"I'm not having a crisis," I claim, despite my heart hammering in my chest and the sweat gathering on my brow.

He cocks an eyebrow and crosses his arms over his chest.

"I don't want to talk about it."

"What don't you want to talk about? How you slept with our PA or how you got her pregnant?" Cash asks.

Gibson snorts. "We don't need to discuss why he had sex with Aurora. We all knew it was bound to happen sooner or later."

I frown as my bandmates nod in agreement with Gibson.

"Why are you confused?" Cash asks.

"Sparks flew whenever you and Aurora were in the same room," Dylan continues.

"Because Aurora is the most annoying and irritating woman in the world," I lie.

Gibson smirks. "You only found her irritating because you wanted to sex her up, but she was off limits."

Fender grunts.

Great. All of my bandmates think I have a thing for Aurora. I mean I do have a thing for Aurora. But I can never have her. She deserves someone better than me. Someone who knows how to make a family with her. Someone who will love and cherish her. I don't know how to do those things.

"I don't want to talk about it." I'm starting to sound like a broken record.

"Tough shit," Cash mutters as he makes himself comfortable on the sofa. Everyone else joins him.

"I'm serious. I don't want to talk about it."

Dylan rolls his eyes at me. "It's cute you think your opinion matters."

"You didn't hesitate to get all up in our business when we were falling in love," Gibson points out. "It's your turn."

"It's not my turn. This isn't some rockstar love story. I'm not falling in love."

"But you are having a baby," Fender grumbles.

A baby? I can't have a baby. I can't be a father. Father? My stomach hollows out. I think I'm going to be sick.

Dylan presses a can of ginger ale into my hands. "This helps when you're feeling nauseous."

I don't bother to argue with him. There's no use denying I feel sick when I'm gagging. I slowly sip on the drink. When I'm certain I'm not going to lose the contents of my lunch, I settle into a chair across from them.

"What happened?" Gibson asks.

I glare at him. I'm not discussing having sex with Aurora with anyone. Not even with my best friend. What happened between me and Aurora is private.

He waves his hand. "I don't need the details." His face pales. "I don't want the details. I consider Aurora a good friend. I don't need to know what the two of you got up to behind closed doors."

Cash clears his throat. "What's done is done. Aurora is pregnant with your baby."

"But I always glove up," I argue.

"Accidents happen. You know this better than anyone." Gibson waves toward my forehead where a faint scar is still visible from my fall from a surfboard.

"The question isn't how this happened," Cash says. "It's what are you going to do about it."

Move to a foreign country and pretend it isn't happening?

Dylan wags his finger. "You can't run away from this."

"What if I want to enter the Iditarod Trail Sled Dog Race? Entry fees are non-refundable."

Gibson waves his phone at me. "You're shit out of luck. It doesn't start until March 3rd."

Crap. I rack my brain for another extreme sports competition held in November or December. There must be something.

"Enough."

I startle at Fender's shout. Fender isn't much for shouting. His grunts and grumbles are usually enough to scare people. He has no need for shouting.

"You are not abandoning the mother of your child while she's pregnant."

"Maybe the baby isn't mine."

The thought has me clenching my hands as jealousy fills my stomach. Has Aurora been having sex with other men? Has she forgotten all about me? Does she not care about me?

I shove those thoughts away. I'm not allowed to be jealous of her with other men. Not when I've avoided her calls for the past three months.

"Can I slap him?" Gibson asks the room. "I want to slap him."

"You can slap him after I punch some sense into him," Fender grumbles.

"I want in on this," Cash adds.

Dylan stands in front of me. "No one will be beating Jett up today."

"Why not?" Gibson pouts. "He deserves it."

Dylan sighs. "He may deserve it but hitting him will accomplish nothing."

"It'll make me feel better," Gibson says.

Dylan points at him. "Did he hit you when you were out of control?"

"He poured water on me."

Cash stands next to Dylan. "This argument is getting us nowhere."

But it does have everyone's attention averted from me. Go ahead and argue all you want. I'll sit here and pretend to be invisible.

Cash slaps me upside the head. "Ow." Guess I'm not invisible after all. "What did you do that for?"

"Dylan said I can't beat you up. Slapping doesn't count."

Gibson jumps to his feet. "I'm next in the slapping line."

Dylan frowns before nudging Gibson away. "Enough. This fun and games isn't helping Jett with the situation."

"There is no situation. I can't be a father. End of discussion." I stand and walk toward the stairs.

"Get back here," Fender growls. "We're not done with this discussion."

I glare at him. "Just because you want to be a father doesn't mean everyone else does."

"Want has nothing to do with it. You *are* going to be a father. You need to deal with your shit if you want to be part of the baby's life."

"Maybe I don't want to be part of the baby's life."

He crosses his arms over his chest and glares back at me. "You'd be happy for there to be a child of yours running around the world who you have nothing to do with?"

"You'd abandon your child?" Gibson adds.

"It's not…" I begin but I can't continue the lie. I can't claim it wouldn't be abandoning my child. "Of course not," I snarl.

I would never abandon my child. Not the way I was. But I can't be a father either. I don't know how to be a parent. I don't have the first clue how to raise a child. How to teach him or her the ways of the world.

"But I can't be a dad," I murmur before bounding up the stairs.

This time my bandmates don't try to stop me. I'm not naïve. They're not done pushing me on the subject. My bandmates are the pushiest people I know. They don't let me get away with shit.

But I need time to figure out what to do. To wrap my head around the idea of someone having my child.

And not just someone. Aurora. The woman I wish I could have but I can't. I can't chance hurting her. I won't.

Chapter 11

Friends – come in all sizes and packages

Aurora

I throw myself on the bed at the *Inn on Main.* I knew Jett wouldn't handle becoming a father well but I didn't expect him to claim the baby isn't his and march off without another word.

What did I ever see in him? Why in the world did I harbor a crush on the man for ten years? He's an asshole. The supreme asshole of the universe. I should get him a t-shirt with those words on it. But first I need to concentrate on mending my broken heart back together.

"Housekeeping!"

"Go away!" I shout and immediately regret my mean tone. I'm not a bitch. "No thank you."

"Housekeeping!"

"No thank you!"

"Try the door."

"Is it locked?"

"We can't break into her room."

"Ellery said we could."

"Ellery didn't say we can break in."

"Open the door already. We can't leave her alone."

Ugh. I know who those voices belong to. Those women are not going anywhere. They're as pushy as their partners. And the members of *Cash & the Sinners* put the word pushy on the map.

I roll off the bed with a groan and make my way to the door. I fling it open. Indigo, Virginia, Leia, and Mercy immediately force their way into my room. Except for Mercy, I've met all of the girlfriends of the band members of *Cash & the Sinners.*

"Hi! I'm Mercy. I'm Gibson's girlfriend."

I shake her hand. "It's nice to meet you. It appears you're fitting in well with the rest of these hooligans."

She grimaces. "Sorry for barging in here, but I didn't think you'd want to be alone."

"Shouldn't you be with Gibson celebrating his release from rehab?" I ask because I don't want to admit she's right. I'm always alone. Working as a PA for a band that doesn't understand the concept of working hours doesn't exactly give a girl much time to make friends or have a social life. And I have no family.

"He's with the rest of the band dealing with Jett."

I rub a hand over my stomach at the reminder of my baby's father. *It's okay, Little Bean. We'll be fine on our own.*

"Oops. Should I have not mentioned his name? I'm sorry. I have a tendency to blurt things out when I shouldn't."

I wave away her concern. "You're fine. It's not as if I can avoid the asshole considering I'm the PA for his band."

"And?" Indigo asks. "How long are you in town for? Are you planning to win Jett back? Are you going to stay the PA for the band after you have the baby? Curious minds want to know."

Virginia snorts. "Curious? I think you mean nosy."

"Give the woman some space to breathe," Leia orders before addressing me. "I'm sorry. Indigo thinks she's everyone's best friend."

"Not everyone's," Indigo corrects. "Just the fiancées and girlfriends of the band."

"I am not Jett's girlfriend."

She waggles her eyebrows. "But you are having his baby."

Leia shoves her. "Knock it off, Ms. Nosy. She isn't going to give you details no matter how much you beg."

Indigo opens her bag and digs out a container. "But I have Mac 'n Cheese."

My stomach rumbles. I haven't had anything resembling a healthy meal for the past three days as I drove from San Diego to Winter Falls.

Leia snatches the container from Indigo and hands it to me. "Here. This is yours. This is not a bargaining chip. It's yours."

Indigo sticks out her bottom lip. "I was negotiating."

I open the container and the smell of cheese wafts out. My stomach rumbles again.

"Here," Virginia hands me a fork before guiding me toward a chair. "You need to eat."

I glance at her belly which is bigger than mine. "What about you? You need to eat, too."

She waves away my concern. "I already ate but I will sit in your armchair in front of the fire and rest my feet."

"She's going to fall asleep," Indigo says in a whisper shout as Virginia makes herself comfortable in the armchair.

I settle at the desk to eat while Indigo, Mercy, and Leia sit on the bed across from me.

"Are you going to sit there and watch me eat?" I ask as I fork cheesy yumminess into my mouth. I moan when the taste hits me. This isn't some store bought macaroni and cheese. This is homemade.

Indigo shrugs. "Maybe."

"We're here to let you know we're on your side," Virginia says with her eyes closed.

I freeze with my fork poised in front of my mouth. "My side?"

"We women need to stick together," Mercy claims.

I can't be hearing this correctly. These women aren't here for me.

"But Jett is in the band. I'm just the PA."

Leia snorts. "Oh please. You're not Yoko Ono. No one's worried about you breaking up the band."

"I always did think Yoko got a bad rap," Indigo mutters.

"But I'm the outsider. Shouldn't you be defending Jett?"

No one's been on my side in a long time. My hand trembles at the reminder of how I used to have people on my side. Of how I had the perfect life. Until it was stolen from me. I set my fork down and place my hands in my lap before they notice how affected I am.

"Jett has the band on his side," Indigo says.

"I doubt they're on his side with this," Leia mutters.

"But you don't know what happened. Maybe I trapped Jett. Maybe I catfished him. Maybe this baby is some elaborate scheme to catch a rockstar."

"Exactly," Virginia says. "You've been working eighty-hour weeks for ten years for the band. Answering to their every beck and call for a decade is all part of an elaborate scheme to catch a rockstar. Nifty plan."

"We're on your side," Indigo repeats.

My side? Are they really on my side?

"No one's been on my side in a long time," I choke out before bursting into tears.

Indigo's the first to approach me and wrap me in a hug. But she's not the last. All four women gather around me and hold me tight.

I allow them to comfort me. I can't deny I need it. I'm having the baby of a man who loathes me. I'm allowed to have a small pity party.

Indigo pats my back until my tears cease. "Welcome to the club."

"What club?"

"We're all members of the shitty mother's club," Mercy answers.

"I'm not a member of the shitty mother's club." I wipe the tears away from my eyes. "I had a wonderful mother and father."

"Had?" Indigo asks.

"Ignore her," Leia says. "You don't have to tell us if you don't want to."

"But if you do." Virginia squeezes my hand. "We're here for you."

"They're nosy and pushy but I couldn't ask for better friends," Mercy says. "They've been my rocks for the past month while Gibson was in rehab."

I scan their faces. None of them appear eager or nosy. They look concerned for me.

The concern has me crumbling. I'm not used to people being concerned for me. Mike doesn't care if I work myself into an early grave. And the other women at the management firm would scratch my eyes out if they thought it would give them the chance to work with *Cash & the Sinners.*

I collapse in the chair. "My parents were the best. They were so in love and happy. I was an only child and they doted on me. They gave me everything I ever wanted and more. I was the luckiest girl alive. Until I wasn't."

My heart races as memories of the past flash through my mind. I inhale several steadying breaths before I can finish. "My parents died in a motorcycle crash when I was fifteen."

"Oh no," Mercy cries.

"There was a pile up on the highway. Some idiot was driving down the wrong side of the highway. They never had a chance."

I force those memories away. Of not being able to say goodbye to my parents. Of knowing they died in horrific pain.

"What happened afterwards?" Indigo asks

Virginia slaps her. "Stop pushing her."

"Sorry," Indigo apologizes.

"It's okay." I dig my nails into my thighs as I remember the after. "I didn't have any other relatives and ended up in a group home."

The group home wasn't the worst. I've heard horror stories about other homes. But all the other girls already had their friends and I was the newcomer. The newcomer who was drowning in grief and had no one to comfort her.

"I lasted for two years until I managed to escape. I got early admission into college and moved into a dorm."

"The name of our club is hereby officially changed. It is now the shitty childhood club." Indigo points to me. "And you are our newest member and my new bestie."

"Has anyone ever told her she's crazy pushy?" I ask the room.

Virginia moans. "All the time." Her phone beeps and she glares at it. "Dylan is wondering where I am and how I am. I better get going before he sends the cavalry after me. He's a bit overprotective."

I ignore the pain those words cause. I would do anything to have the father of my baby be overprotective of me during my pregnancy. Considering Jett's reaction to the baby, my wishes will remain unfulfilled.

I follow the women to the door. "Thanks for coming to check on me."

"We got you, girl," Indigo says.

Leia squeezes my shoulder. "I was a single mom. I know how terrifying it is. I'm here for you. Whatever you need, you call me. You understand?"

I nod.

"You're not getting it yet, but you will," she mutters as she leaves with the rest of the women.

I close the door behind them and lean against it. I'm not entirely certain what just happened but I think I gained some new friends and allies.

"What do you think, Little Bean? Are you up for having four crazy aunts?"

Chapter 12

Blabbermouth – when someone runs his mouth without thinking

JETT

I hum as I exit the stage. The fans are screaming for more even though we already played one encore. Yes! I twirl my sticks in the air. I'm ready to play as long as needed. Playing music is the one surefire way to get my mind off of Aurora.

Aurora.

I haven't spoken to her since she dropped the baby bomb on me. Despite her being around and arranging everything for this concert. It helps that she's avoiding me as much as I'm avoiding her. Every time she walks into a room where I am, she snarls before whirling around and leaving.

"Who's ready for a second encore?" I shout.

Cash grimaces. "My throat can't handle anymore."

"Fender can sing the song he wrote for Leia. The fans will love it."

Gibson studies me. "Wow. He's not gagging at the thought of a love song. Our little boy is growing up."

"Don't make me shove these sticks up your ass."

He chuckles. "There's the Jett we all know and love."

Dylan steps in between us before I can hit Gibson. The peacemaker strikes again. "We agreed on one encore."

I drum my sticks against the wall. "But I'm ready for more."

"Excellent," Mike says as he walks into the room. Aurora follows him inside. She glances my way and scowls before looking away.

I frown at what she's wearing. She has on a baggy shirt to hide her pregnant belly. Why the fuck is she hiding my baby? Is she embarrassed to be carrying my child?

I squeeze the back of my neck. What the hell am I thinking? I'm not claiming the child. It's *her* child and *her* problem. I'm not getting involved.

Fender's question echoes in my mind. *"You'd be happy for there to be a child of yours running around the world who you have nothing to do with?"*

I'm not any closer to an answer to his question than I was when he asked it a week ago.

"The venue wants to add two more concerts," Mike announces.

Cash scowls. "We're not performing two more concerts."

"This was supposed to be a one off," Gibson says. "Besides, we're doing the weeklong tour in two weeks."

"And I need to get home to Virginia," Dylan adds.

Mike purses his lips. "The lot of you have become difficult since you've found love."

"Become?" Aurora snorts.

Mike ignores her. He always ignores her. I frown. He shouldn't be an asshole to her. She works hard for the band to make sure we have everything we need while on tour. And while not on tour as well.

A roadie rushes through the door. "Here are those extra posters you wanted," he says and drops a box into Aurora's arms.

Dylan rushes forward and snatches the box from her. "You shouldn't be carrying heavy boxes in your condition."

"What condition?" Mike glares at Aurora. "Are you sick?"

Aurora clears her throat. "I wouldn't use the word sick."

"Out with it. You know I hate women who play games with me."

She glares at him. She doesn't take shit from her boss any more than she takes shit from us. It's probably why she's lasted in her job as long as she has.

"I'm not playing games, asshole. I'm pregnant."

"You're fucking pregnant and didn't tell me!"

"It's not your baby. Why would I tell you?"

"Because I'm your boss. I need to know if you can't do your job."

She taps her clipboard with her pen. "Am I not doing my job now? Did I not set this concert up in record time?"

She did. We cancelled all concerts for the foreseeable future when Gibson went into rehab since we didn't want to pressure him to hurry up and get sober already. But since he's out of rehab and doing well, the band's back to promoting our latest album with concerts.

Mike leans close and gets in her face. Aurora doesn't budge. She glares at him with such venom on her face, I'm surprised our manager doesn't crumple to the floor in agony.

"And will you be able to do your job when you're as big as a house? Will you be able to chase after roadies when your feet are swollen?"

"I'll let HR know you think I'm as big as a house."

"Fuck HR. I'm the boss here."

Aurora rolls her eyes. "Yes, you made things abundantly clear when you used Gibson's stint in rehab to gain publicity for the band despite anything I had to say."

Gibson growls next to me. I clutch his arm to stop him. Aurora needs to handle this situation for herself or Mike will never respect her.

"Who's the father?"

"None of your damn business."

"It's one of the band members, isn't it?"

Aurora flinches. It's miniscule but Mike doesn't miss it. The asshole doesn't miss a thing.

"Which one?"

"What part of none of your damn business don't you understand? Is it the word business?"

Fuck. I can't let Aurora get a verbal smackdown from Mike because of me. I step forward.

"It's mine."

Mike's eyes widen to a comical size. "You're having a baby? You? Mister Never Wants Children and Will Never Settle Down?"

"Yep."

"Are you in love with each other?" He nearly gags on the word love.

I get it. The idea of love makes me feel nauseous as well.

"It was an accident."

Aurora flinches at my words. I rub a hand down my face. I can't keep calling the baby an accident. I don't want it growing up thinking it was a mistake.

I step toward her. I need to make this right. I need to apologize. But she sends me a glare and I halt.

"We're not in love. We're not involved. It's business as usual," Aurora declares.

I swallow my growl at her words. It is not business as usual. How can she act as if her carrying my baby means nothing to her? As if *I* mean nothing to her?

"Nonetheless you fucked one of my clients. It's ground for immediate dismissal," Mike says.

"You're not firing Aurora," Cash declares.

Mike scowls at him. "She doesn't work directly for you. I can fire her if I want to."

"Fire her and our relationship is over. You'll no longer be the manager of *Cash & the Sinners*," Dylan declares.

Fender grunts in agreement.

"No. No. No. No." Aurora holds up her hands. "I'm not letting Little Bean cause this uproar."

Little Bean? She has a name for our baby?

Cash places a hand on her shoulder. "You're not causing the problem. Mike is."

HOW TO CATCH A ROCKSTAR

"Mike's an asshole," Gibson mutters.

Mike slaps a hand on his chest. "I'm the asshole who got you a record deal. I'm the asshole who helped you get to the top of the charts. I'm the asshole who's made you millionaires."

"And Aurora's the woman who's done all the work while you took all the credit," Dylan says.

Aurora's eyes widen. "I didn't do all the work."

Mike studies our faces. He's not a stupid man. He's not letting his cash cow go. I can practically see him calculating whether Aurora is worth arguing over.

She's worth everything. Too bad I can't tell her she is.

"Am I understanding this situation correctly? You'll fire me if I fire Aurora?"

We nod in response.

"Fine. You can keep your little assistant. But tell me this." Mike glances between Aurora and me. "Is this why Aurora moved to Winter Falls? Because she can't stand to be away from Jett?"

I freeze. Aurora moved to Winter Falls? I thought she was merely visiting. I thought she came to tell me about the baby and would leave.

"She's never needed to be near the band before," he presses when no one answers him.

"I didn't move to Winter Falls," Aurora says.

"Good." Mike's grin is evil. "Then, I will no longer be paying for the fancy hotel you're staying in. If there's nothing else." He flounces out of the room before anyone has a chance to respond to him.

As soon as the door's closed behind him, Dylan approaches Aurora. "I'm sorry. I didn't realize he didn't know you're pregnant."

She waves away his apology. "It's fine. He was bound to find out when I showed up to work with a baby strapped to my back."

I frown. She's not working with my baby strapped to her back.

"Will you go back to San Diego now?" Cash asks.

I hate the idea of Aurora being several states away from me but it's probably for the better. I'm no good for her anyway.

She shrugs. "I guess."

Her eyes glaze over as she listens to someone over her headphones. "Be there in a minute," she responds to him.

"I don't have time for this now," she says as she rushes off.

"What are you going to do?" Dylan asks when she's gone.

"What do you mean?" I ask although I know exactly what he means.

"It's time to step up or step out," Fender grumbles.

"Are you going to let Aurora live in San Diego when she's pregnant with your baby?" Cash asks.

"It's better this way. I'm no good for her."

"Abandoning your child is better for her?" Fender growls.

Pain pierces through my heart at the idea of *my* child growing up thinking it's been abandoned. I know the feeling. It never leaves you. It haunts you.

Gibson squeezes my shoulder to the point of pain. "You need to get over your shit and latch onto your chance at happiness. Don't let her get away from you."

"Did going to rehab turn you into a love guru?" I ask since I'm not discussing how I can never reach for happiness with Aurora.

"Nope. Falling in love with Mercy did."

His smile is full of happiness. I've known Gibson for over a decade. He always seemed happy. But now that he's really, truly happy, I realize he was never happy before. He was hiding a boatload of pain under those smiles. Not any longer. He drank the Kool-Aid and found happiness.

Good for him. But his situation is completely different. He had a loving mother and father growing up. I didn't. I had no one. I wouldn't know where to begin with treating Aurora right.

And Aurora deserves someone who can shower her with his love. Someone who can be sweet and gentle with her. I am not that man.

Chapter 13

Gang up – when four women decide what you're going to do and you get no choice in the matter

AURORA

I open the door to my hotel room back in Winter Falls and screech to a halt at the scene in front of me. Indigo, Leia, and Mercy are scrambling around the room opening and closing drawers and throwing stuff into suitcases.

It's been a long ass day and all I want to do is sleep until my head isn't foggy anymore. Based on this scene, I don't think sleep is happening anytime soon.

"What in the hell is going on in here?"

Virginia groans from the armchair in front of the fire. "I was sleeping."

"Come on. Hurry up and help," Indigo orders as she opens a drawer and stuffs the clothes – *my* clothes – into a bag.

"Help what? Why are you packing my things?"

"Duh. You're moving."

I drop my bag and collapse on the desk chair with a sigh. "I wasn't planning on checking out this very second. I need a good night of sleep before I start the drive back to San Diego."

Leia snorts. "As if you're driving back to San Diego."

"I can't fly. I need my car."

Mercy jiggles a set of keys in front of my face. "By the way, I gave your car a tune-up while you were away."

I snatch the keys from her. "Thank you. Send me the bill." Fingers crossed I can afford to pay it.

She rolls her eyes. "You're not paying."

"I'm too tired to argue with you about this now. I'll pencil in a disagreement with you for tomorrow afternoon."

"Can I use this?" Leia picks up the suitcase I dropped by the door.

"Can someone fill me in as to why you're kicking me out of my hotel room before I fall asleep?"

"We're helping you," Indigo says.

"Is she always this mysterious?"

Virginia grunts. "Don't tell her she's mysterious. We'll never hear the end of it."

I focus on Leia. She's the straight shooter of the group. She'll fill me in. "What's going on?"

"Isn't it obvious? We're helping you pack your stuff to move."

"Leia," I growl.

"We don't have time for this. The guys will be home soon." Indigo drops a suitcase near the door. "Is the car ready, Mercy?"

"Ready and waiting."

Indigo glances around the room. "Did we get everything?"

"Ellery will let us know if we forgot something," Virginia mumbles from where she is once again falling asleep in front of the fireplace.

Leia steps out of the bathroom. "Nothing left in there."

"Come on." Indigo motions me toward the door. "We don't have much time."

"I'm not going anywhere. I'm beyond exhausted. Do you know how it feels to be stuck in the middle seat on a four-hour flight? The guy on my left fell asleep on my shoulder and proceeded to fart for the entire flight while the guy on my other side decided to show me what man spread means."

Mercy's nose wrinkles. "Why didn't you fly on the private jet with the band?"

"Mike doesn't want me getting used to creature comforts."

Such as a nice hotel room. Meanwhile, he charges every expense he can to the band as part of his management fee. I've got news for him. Thinking about the band while getting a massage does not make the massage a business expense.

She scowls. "Mike's an asshole."

I can't argue with her there. "Yep. But from what I've seen, all music managers are slimy assholes."

Leia holds out her hand. "Come on. Time to go."

I ignore her hand. "I'll leave in the morning. I need some sleep before I begin the drive to San Diego."

"You're not driving."

I raise my eyebrows. "Are we doing a road trip?"

Virginia moans. "Oh god. Please no. I need to pee every five minutes. It would take us forever to reach California. Speaking of which." She hauls herself to her feet and hurries into the bathroom.

I allow Leia to help me stand. "Why won't anyone answer a direct question? Usually, I can count on you to be honest with me."

"I promise to be honest with you as soon as we reach our destination. But we're on a deadline here."

"Whatever," I mumble and allow her to lead me out of the room, down the stairs, and out of the inn.

She snatches my car keys from my hands before nudging me into the passenger seat of the car.

"At least I don't have to drive."

"Don't worry. We're not going far."

Leia follows Mercy's car as we drive out of the Inn parking lot. But we don't turn to leave town.

"Where are we going?" I ask as I glance around.

I haven't had much time to get to know Winter Falls since Mike started pressuring the band to go on tour the second Gibson got out of rehab. Not surprising since he nearly lost his mind when they cancelled their earlier tour for Gibson to go to rehab. He thought they should hire a replacement guitarist. Told you the guy's an asshole.

"Not far." Leia pulls to the side of the street and parks in front of a large house.

"Is this an Airbnb? I didn't find any in Winter Falls when I searched."

"All will be explained once we're inside the house," she claims.

I blow out a breath and follow her out of the car. She grabs two suitcases but when I try to snatch one from her, she glares at me. "Pregnant women do not carry their luggage."

"I guess you're coming on tour with me from now on then," I mutter.

I follow her as she climbs the stairs to the veranda. The door to the house is already open and she walks right in.

I don't get a chance to look around before she's urging me upstairs. "The bedroom's on the second floor."

Mercy, Virginia, and Indigo are already in the room. Mercy and Indigo fly around the room emptying my suitcases while Virginia lays down on the bed.

"Don't worry," Mercy begins. "I replaced Gibson's old mattress."

"Is this your house?" I ask.

"Not unless you happen to find an old man clogging the toilets up."

She is not making things any clearer. "I didn't believe this whole pregnancy brain thing was real, but it's real all right. I have no idea what's going on. Did I miss a memo?"

Leia clasps my hand and leads me to the rocking chair in the corner. She presses me in it.

"This is Jett's house."

I gasp and try to stand but she blocks my escape. "I'm not staying in Jett's house."

"And we're not letting Mike, the asshole manager, kick you out of Winter Falls," Indigo says.

"But I can't live with Jett. We'll kill each other within minutes." I rub a hand over my belly. "He doesn't want our baby. You're going to make me live with the man who got me pregnant but now is ignoring the situation? I thought you were my friends."

I feel tears well in my eyes. But I sniff and suck them up. I don't have time to cry. The band will be home any minute now. I need to get out of here before Jett returns.

Ah, now I understand the reason for the urgency. "You think if I'm all settled in the house when Jett arrives, he won't freak."

"I'm betting he still freaks," Mercy says.

"He's definitely going to freak," Virginia mutters.

"But he won't be able to do anything about it," Indigo says. "Since you have nowhere else to go."

I scowl at her. "I am not a charity case. I can return to my apartment in San Diego."

Leia raises an eyebrow. "The apartment you sub-let?"

Damn. I forgot about sub-letting my apartment. I was convinced Mike wouldn't mind paying for a hotel room for six months. I should have known better. The man who gets manicures every two weeks for himself doesn't spend money on things that don't benefit him.

I force a nonchalance I don't feel. "I can stay at the Inn."

Maybe not in the executive suite but there must be cheaper rooms.

Indigo shakes her head. "No can do. Ellery's booked up for the Christmas holidays."

I throw my hands in the air. "There must be someplace to rent in Winter Falls."

"It's a small town. There's one apartment building and there are no vacancies."

I rub a hand over my face. "I'm too tired to deal with this. I'm certain I can come up with another solution after a bit of sleep."

"The band agreed you'd stay here," Indigo says.

"The band agreed?"

"Yep. They think it's handy having you nearby."

"Jett knows about this? He knows his baby mamma is going to be living down the hallway from him?"

She cracks her knuckles. "Yeah."

"She's lying," Virginia says from where she's lying on the bed with her eyes closed. "She always cracks her knuckles when she lies."

Indigo gasps. "You're not supposed to tell anyone."

"She's going to figure out Jett didn't agree when he gets home anyway."

A car door slams outside. Crap. Time's up.

"I'm out of here. Fender will flip his lid when he realizes I left Isla alone. She's twelve. She can be left alone for an hour. But Fender thinks his precious daughter should be wrapped in bubble wrap and protected from every possible hurt." Leia waves as she leaves the room.

Indigo follows her out. "Cash is home."

Virginia shoves to her feet. "I better get home before Dylan sends out a search party. I'm not joking. He once couldn't reach me for five minutes and called the police. My phone battery was dead. And now I have to carry a charger *and* a power bank with me at all times." She waves as she trudges out of the room.

"Mercy?" Jett shouts. "Why is your uncle's car parked in front of my house?"

"Time to face the music," Mercy sings before pulling me to my feet and dragging me out of the room.

"We dropped Gibson a—"

Jett stutters to a halt when he notices me standing behind Mercy.

"I helped her move in," Mercy says before bounding down the stairs. She kisses Jett on the cheek before rushing out the front door.

"Traitor!" I shout after her.

"What the hell are you doing here?"

Oh goodie. Jett has recovered his ability to speak and he's in a delightful mood.

Chapter 14

Pity – an emotion Aurora wants nothing to do with

JETT

"What's going on? Why are you here?"

My fingers itch to touch Aurora. To pull her into my arms. To feel her curves. To smell her flowery scent. I glance at her belly. At the reminder of the last time I gave into the temptation to touch Aurora, I fist my hands.

She flaps her arms. "I don't know."

I narrow my eyes on her. "You don't know?"

"I arrived back at the Inn and my girls were packing up my stuff and somehow I ended up here."

"You can't stay here." I won't be able to resist her if she lives in the same house. I'll give into temptation and no good can come from me giving into temptation.

She rolls her eyes. "Obviously."

"Good." I nod. "We agree."

"I'll figure out a plan tomorrow." She yawns. "I need some sleep. Between Mr. Farter and Mr. Manspread, I didn't get any sleep on the plane."

I hate seeing how tired she is. Is she getting enough rest? Shouldn't a pregnant woman rest more?

"Why didn't you travel in the jet with us?"

She chuckles. "Maybe because Mike the asshole would lose his ever-loving mind if I did."

My brow wrinkles. "Mike doesn't let you travel with us?"

"The 'management' and the 'talent' should never intermingle."

"But Mike travels on the jet with us all the time."

"Mike does whatever the hell Mike wants including billing the band for massages." Her eyes widen. "Crap. Don't tell anyone about the massages. No one else knows. If it leaks, he'll blame me and fire my ass." Her shoulders slump as she rubs her belly. "Although, he's probably going to fire me anyway."

"I won't let Mike fire you." I realize what I said and backpedal. "I mean the band won't."

She grins. "Thank you but you know sooner or later Mike's going to find an excuse to fire me and there's nothing the band can do about it."

"We'll fire him." I'm not letting our manager fire Aurora when she's pregnant with my baby.

My baby? I can't have a child. I can't be a parent. I don't know how to be one. I force those thoughts away. I've got other issues to deal with at the moment.

"Where will you go? Will you return to San Diego?"

She rubs her forehead. "So much for figuring this out tomorrow," she mutters before raising her voice. "I can't return to San Diego. I sub-let my apartment."

"You sub-let your apartment?"

"I thought I'd be in Winter Falls for a few months. I can barely afford my rent as it is. I wasn't about to pay rent for a place I wasn't living in."

"What about your parents? Can you live with them?"

Grief flashes in her eyes before she blinks and all emotion is wiped away. I scowl. I don't want her green eyes empty. I want them twinkling with humor or burning with passion. Passion as I spear her hair with my hands and devour her mouth.

My cock wakes up from its deep slumber. I clear my throat and force thoughts of Aurora naked in my bed tangled up in my sheets out of my mind.

"No, I cannot."

She whirls around and marches toward the stairs. I stop her with a hand on her wrist.

"What aren't you telling me?"

She growls at me. "What aren't I telling you? Am I somehow obligated to reveal all my secrets to you? I'll be out of your hair in the morning."

Panic hits me. I can't let her go. I can't have her, but I can't let her go.

"I'm sorry I pushed you. I shouldn't have asked about your parents. I fucking hate it when people ask about mine."

She sighs. "It's not a secret what happened to my family."

The implication is clear. It is a secret what happened to mine. Mike has worked hard to keep my past out of the headlines. I figured as one of his assistants, Aurora knew about my past but maybe she doesn't.

"You don't have to tell me if you don't want to."

"You should probably know since you're the only family Little Bean will have besides me."

I swallow. "The only family?"

"My parents died in a motorcycle crash when I was fifteen."

Tears well in her eyes. She sniffs to stop them but one escapes. I use my thumb to wipe it away.

"I'm sorry, feisty girl."

"It was a long time ago."

I cradle her face with my hands. "Time doesn't matter."

"I miss them. I miss them every day. But I especially miss my mom now. I have so many questions and she's not here to answer them."

The tears she was holding back begin to fall down her face and I haul her into my arms. I rub my hands up and down her back as she sobs.

She's breaking my heart but there's nothing I can do. I have no pretty words for her. I have nothing to offer her but my body.

She melts into my arms, and I lift her and carry her to the sofa. I arrange her in my lap as she continues to sob.

"I'm sorry," she says into my shoulder.

I brush her hair away from her forehead so I can see her face. "For what?"

"For crying all over you. It's the hormones, I swear. I'm not usually a crier."

"There's nothing wrong with crying."

She snorts. "Except it's weak."

I squeeze her neck. "There isn't a weak bone in your body."

"I don't usually talk about my parents."

"I get it." And I do. I never talk about my past to anyone. My bandmates know but we never discuss it.

She studies my face for a few moments. "You do, don't you?"

"Yep." I tweak her nose.

"Anyway, now you know why my little bean won't have any family."

"Any family? What about the rest of your family?"

She shrugs. "Don't have any."

"But what happened to you when your parents died? You were fifteen. You weren't old enough to be living on your own."

"I went into a group home where I pretty much took care of myself."

I wince. I know how it feels to be ignored in a group home.

"How long were you there?"

"Two years until I got early admission into college."

Two years isn't too long but it probably felt like forever to a girl who came from a loving home and just lost her parents.

"I'm sorry," I say since I have no idea what else to say.

"Sorry I got early admission into college?" she teases.

My shoulders sag as the tension leaves me. My feisty girl is back. Nothing can put her down for long.

"You can stay here." The words escape my mouth before I realize what I was going to say. But the words feel right.

Maybe I can't have Aurora. Maybe I can't be the partner she needs. Maybe I can't be the dad her child needs. But I can provide her with shelter.

Her eyes widen. "You're sure? This isn't you feeling sorry for me?"

"I know better than to feel sorry for you. If I showed you any pity, you'd skin me alive before parading my skinless body around the town."

Her nose wrinkles. "Sounds bloody. I'd prefer to sell your organs to the highest bidder. Baby needs a college fund."

As if I'm going to let anyone else pay for the kid's college except for me.

I set her on her feet. "I assume the girls put you in Gibson's old room."

She nods.

"Good. He has his own bathroom."

She kicks out her hip and plants a hand on it. "Are you afraid to share a bathroom with me?"

"Well, yeah. You need at least an hour to dry your hair in the morning."

"Whatever," she mutters before flouncing away. She stops at the top of the stairwell. "Jett?"

I glance up at her. "Yeah?"

"Thanks for letting me stay." She pauses. "But if you tell anyone I had a crying jag in your arms I'm going to find out how black market organ sales work."

I salute her. "Gotcha."

I wait until she disappears before collapsing on the sofa. My dick is excited the object of his desire will be living across the hallway from us. I frown down at it.

No leading me into temptation. Did you forget what happened the last time?

My dick doesn't care how Aurora's pregnant. It wants what it wants. Join the line.

Chapter 15

Eggs – the perfect way to ruin an awkward morning

AURORA

I stretch as I slowly wake up. I haven't slept as well as I did last night since—

I cut those thoughts off. I will not be spending my time reminiscing how it feels to have Jett in my bed. Jett naked in my bed. Jett above me. Thrusting into me.

Good job cutting those thoughts off, Aurora. A plus for effort.

Fine, I won't think about how Jett is as a lover. I'll think about how sweet he was last night. How he held me while I cried. How he listened to my sad story but didn't pity me.

Ugh! I slam my fist into the mattress. I'm falling for Jett again.

I'm such an idiot. The man gives me five minutes of attention and boom! I fall for him.

My phone rings. Great. It's Mike's ringtone. Welp. There's one surefire way to get my attention off Jett for a while.

"What do you need?" I ask as I answer the phone. There's no sense in bothering with pleasantries with Mike. He doesn't understand them.

"Where are you?"

Sleeping across the hall from Jett. I nearly giggle at how his head would explode if I said those words.

"Why are you asking? I'm not picking up your dry cleaning again. We discussed this."

He never listens when I speak but I still try.

"I told you to check out of the hotel in Winter Falls."

Oh no, he didn't.

"You told me you wouldn't pay for the hotel room. Whether I check out or not is my decision." The asshole is unspoken but clear to hear.

"Ah ha! You are in Winter Falls."

"You caught me. Guilty as charged."

"Good. I need you to…"

I sit up and put him on speaker so I can take notes on all of the gazillion things he needs me to do. Typical Mike. His temper is quick to rise but it's also quick to fizzle out.

I hang up the phone and sigh. I would rather spend the next ten hours lying in this comfortable bed but I've got work to do.

I throw on some clothes, grab my work bag, and go in search of somewhere to work since the mattress is entirely too soft for me to concentrate when I'm lying on it.

All the doors upstairs are closed so I make my way downstairs. I didn't get a chance to study the house last night but wow. Holy cow.

The downstairs is an open concept kitchen/living room/dining room with vaulted ceilings, hardwood floors, and tons of light pouring in from the numerous windows.

It's clearly a bachelor pad, though. If I lived here, I'd add some color with a few pillows and maybe an accent wall. And plants. This place definitely needs plants.

The kitchen, however, is perfect as it is. Especially if it includes the rockstar currently standing there. Without his shirt on.

I nearly falter at the sight of his wide shoulders and lean back muscles covered in tattoos. Tattoos I've licked every inch of. My mouth goes dry and I bite my bottom lip as memories assault my body.

"G-g-g-ood morning." I clear my throat and try again. "Good morning."

Jett glances over his shoulder at me and grunts. The rockstar drummer is not a morning person.

"Why are you up?"

He rubs a hand over his jaw and his bicep muscles flex with the movement. I never realized drummers had such well-defined bodies before I met Jett. Now I understand why my co-workers want to bag themselves a rocker.

"Phone woke me."

"Sorry. Mike doesn't sleep much. And he doesn't care what time it is when he rings you."

He grunts again before turning around to pour his coffee. He holds up a mug. "Want one?"

"No caffeine allowed." I motion toward my belly.

He freezes for a second before apologizing. "Sorry. I can get some decaf."

I can't help the laugh from escaping. "You're going to buy groceries? You?"

"Hey. I know how to buy groceries."

"Coulda fooled me."

I set my bag on the dining room table. "Is it okay if I work here?"

"Go ahead. I mostly eat in front of the television anyway."

My stomach rumbles reminding me a mini-bag of pretzels on an airplane does not constitute a meal.

"Do you want eggs?"

"Eggs? As in raw eggs?"

He grimaces. "Who eats raw eggs?"

"Do you know how to cook eggs?"

"I can scramble eggs."

"And you have eggs?"

Normally, I ensure the refrigerators of all the members of the band are full when they arrive home from a concert tour but since all but Jett now have partners, I've stopped.

He opens the refrigerator and gasps.

"What? What's wrong? Do I need to phone a cleaner?" I dig my phone out of my bag.

"No cleaner needed. The refrigerator is stocked." He raises an eyebrow at me.

"Don't thank me. I was too busy getting railroaded into moving into a house with you last night to worry about filling the refrigerator."

And crying my eyes out over my parents' death but I am never discussing how I melted into Jett while sobbing. Never ever.

"The refrigerator fairy strikes again." He grabs some butter and eggs.

While he cooks, I settle at the table. I set up my laptop, my tablet, and my phone and begin writing a to-do list for the day. I haven't managed to finish the list when Jett sets a plate down in front of me.

"Order's up!"

"Thanks," I murmur before I inhale the scent of eggs. My stomach clenches and gurgles. Uh oh. I slap a hand over my mouth and jump from my chair before sprinting toward the bathroom.

I barely manage to flip the toilet seat up before I'm losing the contents of my stomach. Jett pulls my hair away from my face and gathers it on my neck as he rubs a hand up and down my back.

I finally finish throwing up and lean my head against the toilet. "Ugh." Jett places a warm wet washcloth on my neck and I moan. "Feels good."

"Are you done?"

"Good god, I hope so."

"Do you need a doctor?"

"A doctor? Why would I need a doctor? Throwing up is perfectly normal when you're pregnant. Not a fun normal but normal nonetheless."

"You threw up a lot. And you haven't eaten. Maybe we should go to the doctor anyway. Just to be certain nothing's wrong." His words jumble together as his eyes fill with panic.

I grasp his hand and squeeze. "Jett, I promise throwing up is perfectly normal. There's no need for a doctor."

He stares at me for a long moment. "If you're sure."

"I am."

He helps me to stand. "But you need to eat something."

I roll my eyes. "Okay, Mom."

He escorts me back to the dining room. I halt before I get too close to the smelly eggs. He rushes forward and grabs the dish. He throws the eggs down the garbage disposal.

"How about some toast?" He twirls around the kitchen a few times. "We must have a toaster here somewhere."

I giggle and point to the toaster next to the stove. "You mean that one?"

He blows out a breath. "There it is. One slice or two slices? Never mind. Two slices."

He rushes around the kitchen finding bread and jam and making toast while I return to my work.

"Do you want to do a sniff test before the plate gets too close to you?" he asks as he approaches the table.

"Why?" I narrow my eyes on him. "Did you use egg butter?"

He rears back. "Egg butter? What the hell is egg butter?"

"I'm teasing you. Toast and jam is fine."

He sets the plate in front of me but he doesn't leave. He stands next to me as if waiting to rush me back to the bathroom for another round of emptying my stomach.

I pat his hand. "I'm fine, Jett. Don't be a worry wart."

He scowls. "I'm not a worry wart."

"Sure, you aren't." I shove the toast into my mouth and groan as the strawberry flavor hits my tongue. I didn't realize I was this hungry. I devour the toast in record time.

Jett doesn't move from his spot standing guard next to me the entire time. I let him be. I'm too busy making love to this toast to be bothered.

When I finish, he picks up my plate and carries it to the kitchen.

"I'll run next door. Maybe Leia has decaf coffee."

I don't get a chance to protest before he's hurrying out the back door – still without a shirt. I sigh as I watch him.

This is not good. I don't know how to resist a sweet and caring Jett. But he's made himself perfectly clear. He doesn't want a relationship. And he most certainly doesn't want a child.

I rub a hand over my stomach. "It's okay, Little Bean. Everything will be okay."

Now to convince myself of the same thing.

Chapter 16

Snowfall – sometimes cold but always sweet

JETT

"Aurora," I whisper as I tiptoe into her room.

She's sleeping on her side with the covers pulled up to her nose. The only part of her body exposed is her curly blonde hair. Hair I happen to know feels like silk when I fist it in my hands as I bury myself in her.

My cock perks up. It doesn't care how Aurora's pregnant with my child and all the problems her pregnancy brings. It wants a repeat of what happened in her apartment in San Diego. Come what may.

I inhale a breath through my nose and blow it out as I order my cock to calm down. There will be no repeats.

No matter how much I long to have my hands on her curves again. Or to feel her warmth surrounding me. It's not happening.

Aurora deserves someone who knows how to be a partner. Who knows how to be a parent to her child.

I am not that man.

"Jett," Aurora murmurs as she rubs her legs together.

Is Aurora having a sexy dream about me? I knew she missed me as much as I missed her. I knew her prickly outside was hiding a soft inside. I knew she didn't hate me.

I'm nearly to her bed before I realize I can't act on my wishes. I order my feet to stop.

"Aurora," I call again.

Her eyes fly open. "What? What's wrong? Is someone injured? Are the police on the way? I hope there isn't a fire. Is there a fire?"

"Nothing's wrong. There is no fire."

She narrows her eyes on me. "Are you sure? The last time you said there was no fire, I had to pay the hotel an obnoxious amount of money to keep the 'fire' out of the news."

I roll my eyes. "It was a few scorch marks. The hotel exaggerated to extort money out of us."

She sighs. "If there's no fire, what's wrong?" She reaches across the bed for her phone. "Who do I call? Police? Doctor? Lawyer?"

I snag the phone from her. "There's no one to call. I have a surprise for you."

Her eyes light up and I want to give her surprises every day. "A surprise?"

"But you need to get out of bed to get it."

Her brows rise. "You're certain this surprise isn't how much blood I can mop up without throwing up?"

I scowl. I never want to witness her throwing up again. One time was one too many. "Are you having morning sickness more often?"

She throws her covers off revealing miles and miles of skin. Skin I've touched with my hands, with my tongue. Curves I've felt beneath me while I pounded into her.

My cock twitches. It remembers how good it felt to be inside of her. I clear my throat and turn away before she realizes the effect she's having on me. Aurora might not hate me but she won't appreciate me drooling over her.

"What's this surprise?" she asks again.

"It would hardly be a surprise if I told you, now would it?"

She sighs as she shuffles to me. The tension in my body releases when I notice she's now wearing a robe covering her naked skin.

"Okay, but I need my phone if I'm going to prevent a PR disaster."

"Have a bit of faith," I say as I lead her out of her bedroom.

"A bit of faith?" She snorts. "Sell that line to someone who hasn't worked for you for a decade."

"We aren't that bad."

"And I don't have a lawyer in each state in the continental United States on speed dial."

"You can't have forty-eight people on speed dial."

"I don't have forty-eight people on speed dial. I also have doctors and newspaper editors and PR spin doctors and—"

I cover her mouth with my hand. "Stop. You make it sound as if we're troublemakers."

She bites my hand and I release her. "Because you are."

"You get caught stealing a sign one time," I grumble.

"Considering you had the hots for the bartender, I think you wanted to get caught."

I wrinkle my nose. "I didn't think she'd call the police."

"You ripped the sign off of the wall creating a gigantic hole. And you forgot to unplug it and somehow managed to short out her electrical system. Of course, she called the police."

"Things didn't exactly work out the way I intended them."

"Ya don't say."

"Be nice or I won't show you your surprise."

"You got a pregnant woman out of bed in the middle of the night. I am getting my surprise."

Is waking a pregnant woman bad? Should I have let her sleep? I should probably do some research about pregnant women. Not because I'm claiming this child as mine. But because Aurora is pregnant and living in my house. It's common courtesy is all.

She elbows me. "Where's my surprise?"

Ah yes. The surprise. I motion down the stairs.

Once we're in the foyer, I place her boots near her feet. "Put those on."

"Why? Are you kicking me out in the dead of night? Are you hoping none of your bandmates will notice? Did you steal my phone to stop me from calling for help?"

I begin to roll my eyes but stop when I realize she isn't joking. She seriously thinks I'd kick her out of the house. Damn it. I'm not a complete asshole.

I cradle her face with my hands. "I'm not kicking you out, Aurora. I may not be happy you're pregnant. I may not know what I'm going to do about this child. But I'm not kicking you out."

She searches my face for clues I'm lying. I drop my guard and let her see everything. My conflict about the baby. My desire to have her in my arms. My fear I can't be the man she wants. She gasps and I slam my guard back up.

I kiss her nose. "You're safe with me."

She blows out a breath. "Okay. I'm trusting you here."

My heart pounds in my chest. She trusts me. *Me.* The man who doesn't deserve one ounce of her trust. Warmth spreads through my body and a smile spreads across my face.

"Now. What is this surprise?"

There's my feisty girl.

I wrap a blanket around her shoulders and nudge her toward the door. She appears confused but she doesn't fight me. I open the door and she gasps.

"I know you've seen snow before. I'll never forget the time we got snowed in and ended up spending the night on the floor of the airport in Detroit."

She cringes. "I got gum in my hair."

"But the first snowfall of the season is special."

"It's beautiful," she murmurs as she steps off the porch into the front yard.

She throws her arms out and twirls around as she giggles. It's a beautiful sight to see. A sight I'd love to see every year with each first snowfall of the winter season. I shove those thoughts away.

Now is not the time to contemplate what I will never have. Now is the time to live in the moment. And if there's one thing I'm good at, it's living in the moment.

I jump down the porch into the front yard.

"Can you catch a snowflake on your tongue?" I don't wait for her to answer before tilting my head back and sticking out my tongue. "There. Got one."

"You have the maturity of a five-year-old."

I bow. "Thank you. Last week you said I was four. I'm maturing."

"As much as a boy stuck in a man's body can mature."

I wiggle my hips. "But what a body it is."

She shoves me. "Man child."

"Can a man child do this?" I ask before doing a cartwheel.

She holds up six fingers. "Six out of ten."

"Six? I can do better."

This time I do a roundoff. When I land on both feet, I raise my hands in the air before bowing.

Aurora claps. "Better. Definitely a six point two."

"A six point two? I'll show you a six point two," I mutter before attacking her ribs.

She giggles as she tries to push me away. "Don't. I'll pee my pants."

I freeze. "Do pregnant women have bladder issues?"

"Nope. But I got you to stop, didn't I?"

I go after her again but she flees from me. I give chase. Of course, I do. I will always chase Aurora.

"Caught you," I shout as I reach her. She slaps away my hands and I realize she's freezing.

"Time for some hot chocolate," I declare as I drag her inside.

"Hot chocolate? You have hot chocolate?"

"*We* have hot chocolate."

I settle her in a chair in the dining room before continuing to the kitchen. I open the refrigerator and pull out a jug of milk and a bottle of squeezable chocolate. I raise the items in the air for her to see. "Tada!"

She whistles. "Good job."

"You're patronizing me but I'm okay with it. I am an international sex symbol after all. I'm used to being objectified."

She giggles as I heat the milk in the microwave. When it's finished, I set the mug on the table in front of her.

She cautiously picks it up and blows on the liquid before taking a small sip. Her eyes widen in surprise. "This is actually good."

"You should never underestimate, Jett the hot chocolate maker." I pretend to twirl my cape around before sitting across from her.

She giggles again and my heart warms. I want to make her happy. I want to hear her giggle every evening as we sit across from each other at the dining table. I want to spend my life finding ways to make her laugh.

But it isn't to be. I'm not the man for her. No matter how much I may wish it otherwise.

Chapter 17

Chocolate cake – as good an excuse as any other to skip work

AURORA

"Ding dong, ding dong," Indigo hollers as she enters the house.

I quickly finish typing my email and hit send before facing her. "Making the sound of a doorbell isn't the same as knocking."

"Why would I knock?"

"Because this isn't your house."

Her nose wrinkles. "I'm confused."

"You don't understand what personal boundaries are, do you?"

"It's not as if you're banging Jett and I'd walk in on the two of you getting it on, is it?" She bites her lip and waits for my answer.

"You're shameless," I mutter as I return my attention to my work.

She plops down on the chair opposite me. "Come on, bestie. Give me something here. Does he stare at you with longing in his eyes? Has he accidentally ended up in your bedroom in the middle of the night?"

"How do you accidentally end up in the wrong bedroom in the middle of the night?"

She shrugs. "No idea. But if anyone could manage it, Jett could."

She can fish for answers all she wants. I'm not telling her how he woke me up the other night to show me the first snow of the season. It's none of her business.

A girl rushes into the house. "Come on, Indigo. I want to go to the festival."

"Isla, have you met Aurora yet? Aurora, this is Leia's daughter, Isla."

Despite living next door to Leia and Fender and their daughter Isla, I haven't had a chance to meet the girl yet. I haven't had much time to get outside period. Planning a concert tour within a few weeks is nearly impossible. But I'll manage.

"Hello, Isla, it's lovely to meet you. I'm Aurora."

"Are you Jett's girlfriend?"

"I am not."

Her nose wrinkles as she studies me. "Why are you living with Jett if he isn't your boyfriend?"

"How much time you got, kid?"

She giggles. "You're silly."

"Isla!" Jett shouts as he bounds down the stairs.

"Uncle Jett!"

"Are you ready for the festival?"

She nods.

"Wonderful. Your chariot awaits."

He picks her up and puts her on his shoulders. "Hurry up, Indigo and Aurora. We can't miss the festival," he shouts as he zooms out of the house with Isla on his shoulders.

"Jett is Isla's favorite uncle," Indigo declares and I realize my mouth is gaping open.

I know Jett spends time with Isla. It would be hard to miss since she lives next door. But I didn't realize the affection they have for one another. Why is Jett determined not to have a child when he obviously loves children?

"Come on." Indigo stands. "Time to go."

I motion to my work spread out on the table. "I don't have time."

"It's Saturday afternoon. You can have a few hours to yourself."

I snort. "You haven't met my boss."

She shivers. "Mike's an asshole."

"Ah, you have met him."

She hauls me to my feet. "I'm not accepting no. It's nearly Christmas. You should be allowed to enjoy the holidays."

I frown. I haven't enjoyed the holidays since my parents died. But I'm not getting a choice here since Indigo is literally dragging me out of the house.

Virginia, Leia, and Mercy are waiting on the porch with an elderly man.

"This is my uncle Mercury," Mercy introduces. "Ignore everything he says. He's a crotchety old man."

"Dang youngsters, think they can push me around," Mercury grumbles as he approaches me while leaning heavily on his cane.

I hurry to help him but he swats me away. "I don't need no help."

I hold up my hands. "Of course, you don't."

"She's sarcastic like you, Mercy. She'll fit right in."

Indigo claps her hands. "Are we going to this festival or what?"

"Or what," Mercury says.

"I can stay home with Mercury," I offer.

Mercy wags her finger at me. "Nice try. Virginia's old boss is on her way."

"I think you mean former boss," an elderly woman says as she climbs the stairs to the porch.

Virginia sighs. "Aurora, this is Gratitude, my *former* boss."

I shake her hand. "It's lovely to meet you."

She rakes her gaze over me before nodding. "The pleasure's all mine." She snaps her fingers at Mercury. "Let's go old man. I have a bet to place."

"A bet to place? On what?" I ask but no one answers me as we watch Gratitude and Mercury leave.

"Where's Isla?" Leia asks.

"Jett has her," Indigo answers.

Leia rolls her eyes. "Of course, he does. Those two are inseparable."

"They are?" I ask. "Jett hates children."

She shrugs. "He adores Isla."

"You ready?" Cash shouts from the front lawn next door where he's standing with Dylan, Fender, and Gibson.

"We're coming," Indigo shouts to Cash.

I decide to try and sneak away but I don't manage to step toward the door before Indigo captures my arm and draws me away from it.

"You'll have fun, I promise."

"How do you know?"

"It's a Winter Falls festival. They're always a ball."

"What's the festival for?"

"It's Yule."

"A Christmas festival?"

Virginia groans. "You did it now."

I look around the group as we walk toward downtown. "Did what?"

"Trust me. Yule isn't Christmas. I got a lecture from my uncle when I mixed the two up this morning," Mercy says. "For an old hippie, Uncle Mercury is sure opinionated."

"Okay," I give in. "Yule isn't Christmas. What does one do at a Yule festival?"

Indigo threads her arm through mine. "There are presents and crafting and a yule log cake contest."

I perk up. "Yule log cake as in chocolate cake?"

"Let's find out. The booth is set up in front of *Clove's Coffee Corner*."

"I miss coffee," I complain as we near the café and the scent of coffee wafts through the air.

Virginia sighs. "Me, too." She rubs her belly which is bigger than mine since she's due several months before me. "But think of the reward."

Dylan slings his arm around her and kisses her hair. "A little girl who looks exactly like you."

She gazes up at him with love in her eyes. "Or a little boy with your blue eyes."

My stomach sours as jealousy hits me. I want what they have. I want a partner who looks at me as if he can't live without me. A partner who worries about me. A partner who wants me to have his baby.

Speak of the devil. Jett joins us tugging Isla behind him. She has chocolate smeared all over her face.

Leia groans. "What did you do?"

"It wasn't my fault," Isla declares. "Rudolph started it."

Fender growls. "Who's Rudolph?"

Leia elbows him. "Not the important part."

I turn away from them before I become jealous of a domestic squabble. I notice the tables of log cakes set out and make a beeline for them.

"Here." The woman standing next to the first table hands me a scorecard. "Write down your scores in each category and return your scorecard to me when you're finished."

I study the card. "Neatness, creativity, attention to detail, difficulty? I don't have a clue about any of those things. All I care about is taste."

"Score however you want. We don't judge in Winter Falls."

"Except everyone is literally judging the best cake."

"Good point."

I start with the first cake and pick up a small slice. I shove it into my mouth and moan. I don't care if I have to work all night long to make up for skipping work this afternoon. This cake is worth it.

Jett sidles up to me. "You decided to join in on the fun?"

I snort. "I didn't have much of a choice."

"Good. You work too hard."

I roll my eyes. "I'm putting together a week-long concert tour and I was given less than a month to prepare. Of course, I'm working hard."

His gaze falls to my stomach. "Maybe you should hire an assistant?"

"I am the assistant."

"I'll speak to Mike about it."

"Good luck with that," I mutter as I stuff another piece of cake in my mouth. Holy cow. This one is even better. I couldn't help myself from moaning if I wanted to.

Jett's eyes heat as he stares at me devouring the cake but he clears his throat and the heat disappears. Good. I don't need any reminders of what I can't have. Trust me. The sex dreams are enough of a reminder.

"I'm serious. It's ridiculous how much you work. Mike doesn't pay you enough as it is. I'll discuss this with the band."

I should bristle at his words. How much I work and how much I earn isn't any of his business. He's made it clear he doesn't want *me* to be any of his business.

But I don't. Nope. My stupid heart pounds against my chest as I stare up at him.

How am I ever supposed to get over Jett when everything he says and does makes my heart tether stronger to him?

Chapter 18

Kiss – not the way to avoid temptation

JETT

"What are you doing?"

Aurora startles at my question. The mug in her hands tips over and the contents spill onto the counter.

"Damn it." She grabs a towel to mop up the mess.

"I got it." I snatch the towel from her and shoo her to the dining room table. She heads for the sink instead and sticks her hand under cold water.

"Are you hurt?" I don't give her a chance to answer before shackling her wrist to study her hand. It's red but there aren't any blisters forming.

"It's fine. The water wasn't boiling."

I place her hand under the water again. "Is this one of those pregnancy things? You prefer cold tea?"

She snorts. "No, this is one of those 'I fell asleep while making tea' things."

"Why aren't you in bed if you're tired and falling asleep?"

She taps her chin. "Let me think about this. Why oh why would I be awake in the middle of the night if I don't need to be? What could possibly be the reason? It couldn't be because I have a boss who doesn't understand the concept of office hours, could it?"

I growl. "You put up with too much crap from him."

"Have you forgotten how it feels to be an employee? How you have to listen to your boss? How he can order you around?"

"But he should appreciate you and how much work you do."

"I am pretty awesome."

I chuckle. I don't know how she does it, but Aurora always makes me smile.

"I am going to speak to him about your workload. I already spoke to the band. They agreed with me."

She narrows her eyes until they're tiny slits of anger. "Are you trying to get me fired?"

"No. I'm trying to ensure your workload isn't too much for you."

She pokes me. "And you know what's too much for me, do you?"

I capture her hand before she can poke me again. "You're pregnant. You shouldn't be running yourself ragged."

She growls. "What do you know about it?"

I feel my cheeks heat, but I keep hold of her hand. She's vibrating with anger now. I'm not letting her go.

"I've been doing a bit of research. Stress isn't good for the baby."

She yanks her hand away from me. "What do you care about the baby? You won't claim Little Bean anyway. You've made it perfectly obvious you want nothing to do with us."

"Wrong."

I don't give her a chance to respond before I slam my lips down on hers. Her flowery taste mixed with a bit of mint hits me and I groan. This is what I've been missing. This is why I've been antsy and couldn't settle. I needed this. I need her.

She sighs and I slip my tongue into her mouth. I thread my hands through her hair and tilt her head until I can dive in deep. I need to memorize every single inch of her. I need to embed my taste in her until she craves me. Only me and no one else.

I can't have her – not forever – but I want my taste imprinted on her. It's an asshole move but I can't help myself.

She wraps her leg around my waist and rubs herself against me. There's my feisty girl. I hitch her leg over my arm to open her up and punch my hips. My hard length hits her core and she moans.

Damn. I've missed the sound of her little moans and growls and sighs when we were together. I want to hear them all. I want to memorize them.

She leans back against the counter and something thuds to the floor.

She jerks away from me and glances down at the floor where her tea mug is shattered near our feet.

"Stay here," I order as I lift her up onto the counter. "I'll clean it up."

She crosses her arms over her chest and huffs. "I'm pregnant. I'm not helpless."

I kiss her nose. "Let me do this for you."

I find a broom in the closet and quickly sweep up the shards of ceramic. I throw them away before prowling toward Aurora.

"Now, where were we?"

She holds up a hand. "You were explaining how I was wrong to think you don't care about this baby." Her hands move to protect her stomach. The defensive move has me growling.

"I'm not an asshole. I care about the baby."

"But you don't want him."

I freeze. "Him? You know it's a him?"

"No. It's too early. But I can't call a baby it."

"No, you call him Little Bean."

"Because he's about the size of a coffee bean."

"You do love your coffee."

"It's an essential ingredient to the happiness of life." She hops off the counter. "Now, if you'll excuse me."

I stop her. "Are you running away from me?"

Her brow furrows. "Running away? What would I be running away from?"

"A discussion about our baby."

"*Our* baby? Since when is Little Bean our baby?"

I crowd her until she's trapped against the kitchen counter. I slam my hands on the surface on each side of her to keep her right where I want her.

"Little Bean has been *our* baby from the first moment he was conceived. From the first moment I sunk my cock into you and felt your heat surround me."

Her eyes dilate until the green is no longer visible. She swallows and I inch forward until there isn't any room between the two of us. Until her breasts press against my chest. Until I can feel her taut nipples poking me.

She clears her throat and her eyes fill with challenge. "He's not, though. You don't want to claim him. You want to pretend he's not yours."

"I can't be the father this baby needs."

"Why not? Why can't you be the baby's father? What are you afraid of?"

Too many things to enumerate. But I'm not telling her my sad story.

"I will never abandon him. He'll want for nothing. I'll support him in all the other ways that matter."

She shakes her head. "You don't get it. The only way that matters is being his parent. Money doesn't matter. Kids don't care about money. They care about a loving, stable environment to grow up in."

I squeeze her hip. "I don't have anything to give."

"Liar," she lashes out. "You have a ton of love to give. I see how you are with Isla. How sweet you are with her. How protective you are of her. You're worth more than your money."

I falter for a moment. Is she right? Isla and I are good friends. But therein lies the problem. We're friends. I'm not her parent. She has Leia and Fender to help her grow up.

"I'm not the parenting kind."

"Said by every coward who ever lived." She pushes against my chest. "Move. I want to get down."

I don't want her to go anywhere. I want her here in my arms where she belongs. But I will never trap Aurora. Never force her to stay somewhere she doesn't want to.

I step back and she hops down. "I understand my pregnancy was a surprise. I wasn't exactly expecting to get pregnant from a rockstar who doesn't want children. But I will not allow you to pick and choose the parts of parenthood you want. You're either all in or you're out."

Pain lashes through me. "I can't be all in. I'm sorry. I can't."

I wasn't built to be a dad.

Her shoulders slump and I want to reach for her. To pull her into my arms and tell her I lied. But I can't. I didn't lie. I can't be all in with this child.

Aurora isn't down for long, though. She inhales a deep breath and straightens her back. My feisty girl can't be defeated. Even by me.

"Thanks for your honesty." She shuffles away from me. "I'm going to bed."

"What about you?" I holler after her. "Do you want this baby?"

She glances over her shoulder at me with a soft smile on her face. "More than anything in this world. Me and Little Bean will be a family."

Considering she lost her family when she was a teenager, I can understand her desire for one. She knows how it feels to be part of a loving family and wants to recreate it with the baby.

I don't know what a loving family is. I've never had one. I'm not in a hurry to try and create something I don't know how to be a part of.

But no matter what Aurora says, I will never let the baby suffer. I might not be his dad but he will have everything his little heart desires.

I watch Aurora walk up the stairs. Too bad I can't have everything my heart desires. But it's better this way.

Chapter 19

Gossip gal – an elderly woman who wouldn't know what privacy is if it walked up to her and introduced itself

AURORA

I sigh as I sip my coffee. I set the cup down next to my computer and begin scrolling through my emails. Out of the corner of my eye, I notice Jett swipe the mug from the table.

"What are you doing?"

He pours the coffee down the drain. "You shouldn't be drinking caffeine. It's not good for the baby."

At the reminder of Little Bean, I reign in my temper. "I'm allowed one caffeinated coffee a day," I say between gritted teeth.

"It's best not to have any caffeine at all."

"How the hell do you know? Are you the pregnancy police?"

"I've been reading up on pregnancy."

He has? Is he worried about Little Bean? Me?

What am I thinking? He's made it perfectly clear he doesn't want to claim this baby as his. I will not allow him to go all overprotective on me when he doesn't want this child. It's a double standard and I won't stand for it.

I place a hand over my bump. "This isn't your baby, remember?"

"Like hell, he isn't."

"Jett," I growl.

"No." He interrupts before I have a chance to remind him of our conversation. "I told you I will be there for this child in any way I can. Making sure you're both healthy is something I can do."

"But you can't be a parent to this child?"

He doesn't hesitate. "No."

"I—"

I'm cut off by the doorbell.

I start to stand but Jett glares at me. "Sit down. I've got this."

I roll my eyes as I follow him to the door. It's cute he thinks he can order me around. Has he not learned anything in the ten years we've known each other? Little Bean doesn't change anything.

A group of elderly women are waiting on the porch for us.

"Good morning," one of them greets before plowing past Jett into the house. "Aurora," she addresses me.

My brow wrinkles. "How do you know my name?"

"This is Winter Falls." She winks.

"I don't understand how the name of the town is why you know my name."

Jett sighs. "It's a small town thing. Everyone knows everything. And these ladies," he motions to the five women who are now standing inside the house, "lead the charge."

"I guess I better know what your names are then," I say.

"I'm Sage," the first woman who entered the house says. "I'm the leader of the gossip gals."

My brows rise. "Gossip gals?"

She grins. "It's our honorary title."

"They're very proud of how much they gossip," Jett explains.

Gossiping is nothing to be proud of in my opinion. At work, the women use gossip to tell tall tales about people and turn the group against whoever they're jealous of. It's exhausting. I stay out of it.

Sage doesn't contradict Jett. Geez. I hope gossip in a small town is less petty than in an office environment.

"This is Feather. She's your source for ice cream and sexy book ideas."

"Interesting combo," I mutter.

"Petal can provide you with sexy candles."

Petal winks at me. "Let me know what you prefer – massage candles or wax play."

"I think I'm good." And officially scared of an elderly woman but I'm admitting to nothing.

"Clove owns the café – *Clove's Coffee Corner,*" Sage continues her introductions.

Clove nods to my stomach. "Don't you worry, I have decaf coffee and plenty of herbal teas as well."

"And, last but not least, there's Cayenne. She used to own the yoga studio."

"But I can still do the splits. Let me show you." Cayenne walks toward the middle of the room.

"I believe you!" I shout before she hurts herself.

"What are you doing here?" Jett's voice drips with suspicion.

I elbow him. "Be polite." I motion toward the living room. "Would you like to sit down? I can make coffee."

"You're not having more coffee," Jett insists.

"And here I thought you enjoyed having your balls where they are. Obviously, I was wrong."

He pales and moves a hand to cover his crotch.

Petal claps. "Oh, this is going to be my favorite project."

Sage rolls her eyes. "They're all her favorite projects."

"What project?" I ask. "Are you referring to the baby? Are you midwives?"

Jett crosses his arms over his chest and glares at the women. "I believe they're referring to their desire to matchmake me."

They want to match Jett? My stomach sours at the idea of him with another woman. I'd have to find somewhere else to live. No way could I live in the same house as him while he parades his girlfriend in front of me.

"But they know damn well I'm not interested in having a partner," he continues.

My jealousy disappears. Jett doesn't want a partner. He doesn't want a family. He doesn't want Little Bean. Not in the way he deserves to be wanted. I place a hand over my belly.

"Why'd you get Aurora pregnant if you don't want a partner?" Cayenne asks.

Jett's face turns bright red and I have to bite my tongue before I laugh at his embarrassment.

"It was a…" He clears his throat. "Her pregnancy wasn't intended."

I smile at him. I don't want the baby to think he was an accident. Accident doesn't sound very nice. Unintended sounds somewhat better. Happy circumstance is how I refer to my surprise pregnancy.

"You have to admit it's the perfect opportunity for you to become a couple. Having a baby together. Raising a child together," Sage says.

I would love to be a couple with Jett. I would love to raise this child together. But it's not going to happen. Jett has made it perfectly clear he doesn't want me.

Oh, he wants me in his bed. But nothing more. And no matter how much I'm tempted to climb his naked body and use it in the million different ways I imagine every night, I won't.

I won't complicate the situation further by having sex with him again. Things got out of hand the other night. I had a weak moment. But I've fortified my walls since then. I won't let him tempt me again. I know better.

Jett wraps an arm around my shoulders and brings me near. "Whatever happens between Aurora and me is private. It's not fodder for your gossip or a reason to start a bet."

I nearly melt at the protective tone of his voice. Jett's protecting me and my privacy. The move is as sexy as the heat in his blue eyes before he kisses me.

So much for those fortified walls. All Jett has to do is say one sweet thing and I'm ready to swoon.

"Bet? What bet?" I ask before I decide to hell with risking my heart and carry Jett off to the bedroom for some very satisfying naked time.

"The residents of Winter Falls will bet on anything but their favorite thing to bet on is their matchmaking projects."

"We have an excellent track record," Sage says.

"All of our projects have been successful," Petal claims.

"And now you want to match Jett with me?" I need this to be absolutely clear before I go bat shit crazy on them.

Feather sighs. "You are an adorable couple. And I do love a good work romance."

"Enough." Jett growls. "There will be no matchmaking of Aurora and me. There will be no betting. There will be no following us around to spy on us. You won't stress Aurora out. She's pregnant and she doesn't need your shenanigans added to the things she has to worry about."

And now I really do swoon. I can stand up for myself. I've been doing it since I was fifteen. But a man standing up for me? Worrying about me? Protecting me? It's the sexiest thing I've ever experienced. Even better than naked, sweaty time with Jett.

How the hell are my fortified walls supposed to survive an onslaught from protective Jett?

"We'll back off." Guessing by the gleam in Sage's eye, she's lying.

"Why?" Petal pouts. "We're going to ruin our perfect record."

Jett glares at the group. "I'm serious, Sage. If I notice any of you with your binoculars trained on this house, there will be consequences."

"Hold on. Binoculars? You're serious about them spying on us?" I glance around the group of women who are old enough to be my grandmother. All except Sage appear innocent.

"I'm a bird watcher," Clove declares. "I use binoculars for bird watching."

Jett snorts.

Sage smirks as she studies Jett who is now standing slightly in front of me as if to protect me from them. "I think our work here is done." She snaps her fingers. "Gossip gals, move out."

Feather frowns. "But we haven't asked her to sexy book club yet."

"Sexy book club?" And here I thought these ladies couldn't surprise me anymore.

"She doesn't have time for sexy book club," Sage declares as she herds the women out of the house.

"What just happened?" I ask once the door is closed behind them.

"You just had your first introduction to small town living."

Huh. Jett didn't snarl when he said small town. I thought he hated living here.

"Don't worry. I'll make sure those women don't bother you. I'm late to meet up with the band. You okay?"

"Why wouldn't I be?"

"There's my feisty girl." He kisses my cheek. "I'll be home later. Try not to work too hard."

I stare after him as he leaves. If he doesn't want to be in a relationship with me, he needs to back off. I'm not going to be able to resist him if he goes all protective on me. I won't want to resist him.

But resist him I must. Little Bean and I don't need a man who has no staying power.

Chapter 20

Out stubborn – it's not a contest but if it were, Jett would win

Jett

Aurora leans forward to ask the driver, "Can you drop me at the commercial terminal?"

We're nearly at Denver International Airport to start a week-long tour. We'll be hopping to four different cities – Minneapolis, Atlanta, Vegas, and Nashville – before returning to Winter Falls in eight days. Just in time for Christmas.

"You're not flying commercial," I insist.

The thought of Aurora, pregnant with our baby, squeezed between two people in the back of an airplane for several hours has me clenching my teeth. She should be comfortable. She should be with me. Where I can keep an eye on her.

"You know Mike's rule. No flying with the talent on their private jet," she mimics our manager's voice and I nearly laugh at her feistiness. But I don't. This is a serious discussion. I won't be distracted by how cute she is.

"I have no fucks to give about Mike's rule."

She rolls her eyes. "Whoopty doo for you. I do."

My bandmates chuckle. I don't find anything amusing about this situation.

"Mike won't find out."

"Oh, now I'm your dirty little secret."

"How are you my dirty little secret? Mike knows you're pregnant with my baby."

"And he wants to fire me for breaking the 'no sex with the talent'-rule," she fires back at me.

"We're not going to let him fire you."

"Yeah, Aurora. We've got your back," Cash says and the rest of the band nods in agreement.

Aurora sighs. "And I appreciate it. I do. But you can't control Mike unless you're willing to fire him and firing him would be the end of your career. So, let's stop this useless discussion and have the driver drop me at the commercial terminal."

"I'm down with firing Mike," Gibson says. "Anyone who uses my addiction as an excuse to create a public relations spectacle doesn't deserve my loyalty."

Aurora grimaces. "I'm sorry. I did try to stop him."

He pats her arm. "I know you did."

She smiles at him and I grit my teeth to stop myself from growling. She shouldn't be smiling at him. All her smiles should be directed at me. I'm the one who should make her smile. Me and only me.

What am I thinking? I need to stop these possessive thoughts. They won't lead anywhere. I can't have Aurora for myself. It's unfair of me to act possessive toward her.

"But, you have to face it, almost any other manager in the music business would have done the same thing," Aurora says.

I frown. "Why? We're an established band. We don't need to drum up publicity the way we did in the beginning."

"Wrong. With the amount of competition out there and because of how social media works, you need to be in the spotlight all the time. Otherwise, you're forgotten for the next bright shiny thing."

"I hate social media," I mumble.

"And you don't even have to manage your own account."

It's true. In addition to everything else she does, Aurora handles our social media accounts. I don't know how she does all she does. I know she works long hours. Which I'm not happy about now she's pregnant.

"I can't fly on the jet with you without risking my job, so please drop me at the commercial terminal."

Aurora's voice is pleasant but there's a current of steel in her words. Too bad for her I'm as stubborn as she is.

"Not happening."

"You want to wake up with a fish in your bed?"

I shiver. I can't help it. Fish are slimy.

"You wouldn't."

"Watch me."

I grin. "I heard the smell of fish makes pregnant woman gag."

Her face pales and she swallows. "You're cruel."

"I don't want you and our baby flying commercial. How am I being cruel?"

"You really want to have another discussion about why Little Bean isn't yours?"

Gibson raises his hand. "I want to hear this discussion." The rest of the band nods their heads in agreement. Nosy fuckers.

"You are not placing bets on my relationship with Aurora," I order.

"What about on Little Bean?" Gibson asks. "Can we place bets on it?"

"Him," Aurora corrects.

"Yes!" Cash pumps his fist in the air. "I knew it."

Before I can explain how we don't know the sex of the baby yet, the car pulls up to the private terminal. The band piles out of the car, but Aurora doesn't move.

I hold my hand out to her. "Come on."

"No. I'll have the driver drop me off at the commercial terminal."

I nod toward the driver who steps out of the car.

Aurora glares at me. "I can call a taxi."

I thread my hands through my hair and pull on the ends. "Will you stop being stubborn? You know as well as I do it's better for you to fly with us. It makes no sense to have our assistant on another plane where we can't contact you because you refuse to pay extra for Wi-fi."

"The prices they want for an hour of Wi-fi on planes are ridiculous," she mumbles.

She's adorable with her bottom lip jutted out and her arms crossed over her chest. My feisty girl thinks she can out stubborn me. She's wrong. I'm not letting her and our baby fly commercial.

"I don't want to give Mike another reason to fire me."

"I promise he won't find out and if he does, he won't fire you. He'd be an idiot to fire you. You do the work of five women. You never complain when he phones you in the middle of the night."

She snorts. "I never said I don't complain."

"Come on." I wiggle my fingers. "We're holding up the departure. You don't want us to leave late, do you? Don't we have a schedule to maintain?"

"You know how to piss me off," she says but she does accept my hand and I help her out of the vehicle.

I escort her through the private terminal. There's no reason to stop since we don't have to check in or go through security. The workers are already carrying our bags toward the plane, and we follow them out of the building toward the waiting jet.

When we enter the aircraft, my bandmates clap.

"Well done, Jett!"

"We knew you could do it!"

I resist the temptation to flip them off.

"Show me the money!" Gibson shouts. Cash, Dylan, and Fender slap money into his hand.

"I had complete faith in you," Gibson says. "These yahoos did not."

Cash snorts. "I didn't not have faith in you. I just had more faith in Aurora."

Fender grunts in agreement.

Aurora winks at them. "Thanks."

"Wow." She surveys the interior. "This is swanky. The seats in economy are not leather and the width of half of the plane. No wonder Mike doesn't want me flying with you. He's afraid I'll get used to fancy stuff."

"Get used to it. You won't be flying commercial again."

She rolls her eyes at my statement. "Where can I set up to work?"

I want to tell her to get some rest. But I'm not stupid. I may have won the battle to get her on this jet, but I didn't win the war.

I lead her to a chair and table in the back of the plane away from my bandmates. It should be quiet here so she can work without interruption. "You can use this area. The band won't bother you."

She immediately pulls out her computer and starts tapping away.

"What do you want to drink?" I ask.

"A glass of water is fine."

"I have ginger ale, decaf coffee, and some of those herbal teas you like."

She glances up at me. "You planned for me to fly with you the entire time, didn't you?"

I shrug. "I told you I don't want you flying commercial."

"Whatever. I'll have a mint tea."

I tell the flight attendant what Aurora wants before I settle in a seat at the front of the plane with my bandmates.

"You have a struggle in front of you," Cash says.

"Aurora's stubborn but she won't do anything to harm the baby." It's true. Aurora will protect Little Bean with her life. She's going to be a wonderful mother.

"I meant with Aurora," Cash clarifies.

I frown at him.

Dylan chuckles. "He's cute. He thinks we don't know he wants her."

Of course, I want her. I got her pregnant, didn't I? I keep my thoughts to myself. My bandmates enjoy sticking their noses into my life. They can keep their noses to themselves. I'm not discussing my relationship with Aurora with them.

"Good thing I already broke our pact to not fall in love since you hate to lose," Gibson says.

"I'm not falling in love with Aurora."

"Sure, you aren't," Fender grumbles. Figures. The one time the grumpy bass player deigns to speak, he manages to piss me off.

"Look. I'm happy for all of you. I'm glad you found love but it's not for me. I don't do relationships."

"Correction. You used to not do relationships."

I flip Gibson off and he chuckles. "This is going to be fun."

I don't bother correcting him. He's not listening anyway.

What's gotten into him? He knows my history. He knows why I don't do relationships. Why I can't be a good partner.

Aurora moans and I glance back at her. Her eyes are closed as she sips on her mint tea.

I can't believe I'm jealous of a fucking cup of tea. But I want to be the one to make her moan. I want to be the one she's cradling with her hands. My cock twitches in my pants.

I need to stop thinking about making Aurora moan before I get hard in front of my bandmates. I'd never hear the end of it.

I turn around and catch Gibson watching me. He grins and mouths *fun.*

This time I flip him off with both hands.

Chapter 21

Defend – when you stick up for someone because her boss is an asshole

AURORA

I run through my to-do list checking items off as I go. "Done. Done. Done."

Today is the first concert of the week-long tour for *Cash & the Sinners* and there's still a ton of work to do. Especially since Mike wants everything done his way. And his way is a pain in my ass.

The members of the band tumble into the room. I check my watch before ticking sound check off of my list.

"The sound check is finished?"

Jett collapses on a sofa and taps his sticks on his thighs. "Yep. We're ready to rock."

"And roll," Gibson finishes.

Jett's body vibrates with excitement. He gets off on the adrenaline high of the concerts. He usually enjoys other adrenaline highs as well. But since suffering a concussion at the surfing competition, he hasn't been able to go on any adventures.

I frown. Is this why he's been so concerned with me and the baby? He's stuck at home with nothing to do. Will he abandon us the second he's medically cleared to go rock climbing or skydiving or whatever adventure catches his fancy?

Abandon us? I nearly snort. Jett isn't *with us.* Is he being sweet and considerate? Yes, he is. But he also hasn't claimed the baby as his. And he's made it perfectly clear he doesn't ever plan to.

I scowl. What is his problem? I know he doesn't want children. But this child is here whether he wants him to be or not.

I rub a hand over my stomach. *It's okay, Little Bean. I will never abandon you.*

"Are you okay?" Jett asks from in front of me. He must have snuck up on me while I was daydreaming.

"I'm fine."

"You're sure you're not feeling nauseous? It's common to feel nauseous in the second trimester."

"How do you know? Have you been reading a baby book?"

"Yeah, Jett. Have you been reading a baby book?" Gibson teases.

Jett scowls. "None of your damn business."

Dylan frowns. "You didn't buy the baby books I recommended?"

Jett's cheeks darken, and my mouth drops open.

"Have you seriously been reading baby books?"

Gibson waves Jett's phone in the air. "According to his kindle app, he's reading *What to Expect When You're Expecting.*"

Jett dives for Gibson. "Give me my phone."

They wrestle on the couch. I sigh before stomping over to them. I snatch the phone from Gibson and hand it to Jett.

"Stop fooling around before I decide to throw up on the two of you."

Jett jumps to his feet. "You are feeling nauseous. Why don't I grab some of the ginger tea you were drinking on the jet?"

"Drinking on the jet?" Mike asks as he walks into the room.

Jett and his stupid mouth. My boss isn't supposed to find out about me flying on the jet with the band. This is bad. He's going to fire me for sure.

"It isn—" I begin but I don't get to finish my sentence before Jett is there shoving me behind him.

"I insisted Aurora fly on the jet with us," he says.

Does he not realize he's making things worse? I'm not supposed to fraternize with the members of the band. Let alone have the baby of one of them. Jett sticking up for me is equivalent to him waving a big red sign with the words *Aurora broke ALL the rules* on it.

I try to move him out of the way. "It won't happen again."

"Damn right, it won't," Mike grumbles, "because you're fired."

I hang my head. I knew this would happen. It was only a matter of time.

"You are not firing Aurora," Jett declares.

Cash, Dylan, Fender, and Gibson come to stand behind him.

"Aurora is a damn fine assistant. You can't fire her for flying on the jet with us," Cash insists and Fender grunts in agreement.

"She's having Jett's baby," Gibson says and I groan. Don't remind him! "Of course, Jett insisted she fly on the jet instead of fucking economy class."

"For the amount of money you make off of us, you could at least fly her business class," Dylan adds.

Mike waves Dylan's concern away. "Aurora's fine in economy class." Said with the confidence of a man who hasn't flown economy class in two decades. Asshole.

Mike steps closer. "What is not fine is Aurora breaking all of my no fraternizing rules."

"You can't fire her for fraternizing with us," Jett claims.

Yes, he can. He's done it a million times before with other assistants. I've managed to last as long as I have at his management company because I didn't fraternize with the band I was assigned to.

Until I blew that rule out of the water after Jett got injured. Stupid sexy rockstar I couldn't resist.

"I can fire Aurora for any reason I want," Mike insists and visions of Jett and all the naked fun we had at my apartment disappear.

"Do you want me to finish out the tour? Or shall I pack my bags and leave now?" I ask since there's no sense in fighting the inevitable.

Jett growls. "You aren't going anywhere."

"Yes, I am, drummer boy. I just got fired."

"Mike is not firing you."

"Mike is right here and Mike is definitely firing Aurora," Mike insists.

Jett places a hand on my shoulder. "Do you like your job?" I nod. "Do you want to keep your job?" I nod again. "Then, you're keeping your job."

"You're not in charge of the world, Jett. You can't snap your fingers and make things happen. You're not a magician."

His eyes light with humor, and he snaps his fingers. "Watch me."

He starts to turn around to face Mike again but I grab his arm to stop him. "Stop it, Jett. I'm not worth all the trouble."

He kisses my forehead. "You're worth all the trouble in the world."

I nearly melt at those words. At the feeling of his soft lips on my skin.

"Fire her and we fire you," Jett says.

I gasp. "You can't fire him."

"Yes, we can," Cash says as he stands next to Jett. Fender grunts as he joins them. Dylan and Gibson step forward.

Mike grits his teeth. "I don't enjoy being blackmailed."

"This isn't blackmail," Gibson says. "Blackmail is when we stuff your ass into a speaker box and demand you pay us a ransom."

Cash smirks. "A speaker box is too big for him. We need to think smaller."

"Naked in a speaker box," Fender grumbles.

Dylan rubs his hands together. "Now we're talking."

Mike studies their faces. "When did you become this crazy?"

"After I went to rehab and you used my addiction for publicity for the band," Gibson says.

"You're serious? You'll fire me if I fire Aurora?" Mike asks.

Judging by the tone of his voice, he thinks they're bluffing. I don't know about the rest of the band, but Jett isn't bluffing.

"In a fucking heartbeat," Jett snarls.

"Fine. Aurora stays." He wags his finger at me. "But one more transgression and these assholes won't be able to save you."

He marches out of the room and slams the door behind him.

"I think I'm having hallucinations. What was it like when you took mushrooms?" I ask Jett. "Did everything turn purple?"

He shackles my wrists. "Are you seeing purple? Do we need to go to the hospital? Gibson, look up the nearest hospital."

My skin tingles where he touches me. Tingling skin is bad. No matter how much Jett just defended me. I can't afford to succumb to my hormones. I wrestle out of his hold.

"I'm fine. Well, not exactly fine. I'm in shock you defended me."

Jett's brow wrinkles. "Why wouldn't I defend you?"

"Maybe because you spent the last decade trying to get me fired."

"He tried to get you fired because he wanted you but didn't think he could have you," Gibson says and Jett hits him. "What? It's the truth."

"Maybe we should let these two discuss things in private," Dylan says as he herds the rest of the band toward the door.

Panic hits me. I can't be alone in a room with Jett after he defended me. I can't trust myself not to jump him and have my wicked way with him.

I clear my throat. "It's fine. I need to get back to work."

I whirl around and walk to the door as fast as I can without breaking into a sprint.

"We can talk about this when we're back home," Jett calls after me.

Back home? I gulp.

It's been hard enough resisting Jett before. Okay, fine. I didn't exactly resist him when he stuck his tongue down my throat and I melted into him. But I did stop things before clothes disappeared. I pat myself on the back for my restraint.

But how am I going to continue to resist the drummer when he's being all sweet and defending me? When he insists I travel in the jet with the band? When he stocks the plane with all of my favorite foods and drinks?

I groan. I am in so much trouble.

Chapter 22

Fuck up – what Jett's about to do

JETT

I enter the room backstage and spot Aurora chatting with some guy in the corner. As soon as she notices me, she rushes out of the room. The same way she's rushed out of every room I've walked into for the past six days. Ever since Mike tried to fire her, she's been hiding from me.

I'm done with this shit. I'm done with Aurora hiding from me. I want the friendship we were building in Winter Falls back. I want my Aurora back.

I hurry to follow her. I spot her scurrying down the hallway and speed up. She glances behind her and scowls at me. Her scowl is adorable. It makes me chase her faster.

But when she turns a corner and flashes me her baby bump, I skid to a halt at the reminder of why I can't have Aurora. Of why I need to leave her alone.

I can't be a father. I can't be in a relationship. I'm not good enough for her.

The door next to me bangs open and Mike steps out. Great. He's been a bear to work with this week.

"Jett. Just the guy I've been looking for."

Suspicious. He's never looking for me unless he wants something.

"What do you want?"

I don't wait for his answer and spin around to march back to the rest of the band. There's safety in numbers.

"The press are arriving for our after concert meet and greet."

He throws an arm over my shoulders but I shrug him off. I don't want the man who bullies Aurora to touch me. I draw a hand down my face. Why does every thought come back to her?

"What do you want?" I repeat my question.

"I need you to do your thing."

"My thing?"

"Charm the press. Charm the fans. Be your charming self."

"You have me confused with Gibson. He's the charming one."

He smirks at me. "Rumor has it the two of you are equally charming with the female fans. In fact, the last I heard you were winning the bet on who can sleep with the most women."

I was never winning the bet. I haven't slept with nearly the number of women Gibson has. Most of the time, I was faking it. The excitement of women throwing themselves at you didn't last long for me.

Unlike my excitement with Aurora. She never threw herself at me. She's prickly as a pear.

Enough! There's no sense obsessing over Aurora when I can't have her.

I need to get over her. I need to get her taste, her feel, out of my mind.

Mike steers me toward the press room. It's packed from wall to wall with female fans. They notice us and begin screaming. I smile. I know the perfect way to stop obsessing about Aurora.

"Jett! Jett!"

"Over here, Jett!"

"I can rock your world, Jett!"

I wink at the female fans screaming for me. "Later," I promise.

Gibson scowls at me when I take my place on the sofa next to him. "What the hell are you doing?"

"I'm meeting and greeting the fans."

"You can't flirt with the fans."

"Why not? Are you jealous?"

He glares at me. "I'm not jealous. But you are fucking stupid."

"I'm not stupid," I grit out.

He raises an eyebrow. "Oh really? You're not ruining the best thing in your life by flirting with fans who mean nothing to you?"

"I don't know what you're talking about." I focus my gaze forward. I'm not having this discussion with him. Not here. Not now. Not ever.

"You can pretend to ignore me all you want. You know I'm right."

"You don't know jack shit."

I start to stand. I'll find somewhere else to sit. But he stops me with a hand on my thigh.

"I do know jack shit. I know all about your past. I know why you're scared. You need to stop running from your past before you lose the chance of a beautiful future."

"My future is rock 'n roll and this band. There's no white picket fence in my future. I know better than to drink the Kool-Aid."

I pull away from him and find a spot next to Fender. At least grumpapottamus won't talk to me. He grunts at me and I hold up a hand.

"Not you, too. I don't need my bandmates to manage my life."

"You're making a mistake."

"I haven't done anything. I'm sitting here waiting for this meet and greet to begin."

He growls. "Don't let your past ruin your future."

I throw up my hands. "Is everyone going to tell me how to live my life?"

Cash and Dylan nod from where they're sitting across from us.

I cross my arms over my chest. My bandmates are my best friends, my family, but they don't know what's best for me. They don't know everything.

"Time for our group picture," Aurora announces.

The rest of the band joins me and Fender on the sofa and the fans gather behind us. The photographer quickly snaps a few shots. When he's finished, he nods to Aurora.

"You have thirty minutes to ask the band questions," she says before leaving the room.

I try to watch her leave but several female fans block my view.

"Hi, Jett." A woman draws a fingernail down my chest. Her touch feels wrong. But I allow it. I need to get over Aurora somehow.

Another woman licks her lips as her gaze rakes over my body. I lock my muscles before I retch at the predatory way she sizes me up. "I'm Shannon."

"And I'm Cherie," the first woman says.

"I'm willing to share if you are," Shannon offers.

Cherie bites her bottom lip. "There is a lot to share."

I wrap one arm around Cherie and one around Shannon. "I know just the place."

I lead them toward the door. I can practically feel the gazes of my bandmates on my back. But I ignore the burn. Despite what they think, they don't know what's best for me.

Cherie and Shannon drape themselves over me as we walk down the hallway. I open the second door we come to. It's a smaller version of the room we were just in.

"Now," I say as I nudge the women away from me. "Why don't the two of you give me a show to start with?"

And give me some time to warm up to the idea of touching a woman who isn't Aurora.

Cherie whips off her top to reveal a pink lace bra. It barely contains her breasts. Not to be outdone, Shannon removes her t-shirt and her skirt.

This show is going entirely too quickly for my liking. I dig out my phone and find some music. I hit play and motion for them to dance. Without missing a beat, the women begin grinding against each other.

Now we're talking. I lean back on the sofa and get comfortable.

I enjoy watching the women kiss and lick each other. Except neither one has long, curly blonde hair. Or light green eyes. Or a smile that can get her anything she wants.

I rub a hand down my face. I'm supposed to be getting Aurora out of my mind. Not fantasizing about her while watching two women go at it.

My cock doesn't care. It's not interested in either one of these women. It wants Aurora. If it could huff and glance away, it would.

Fuck. This isn't working. I stand with the intent to stop this charade.

The women think otherwise. They squeal and throw themselves at me. Their hands on me feel wrong. I bat them away.

This isn't what I want. Who I want.

Fucking hell. If I can't be with other women, there's only one thing to do. I need to take a chance on Aurora. The woman I do want. The one I long for. The one I can't live without.

The door opens and I glance over.

Shit. Aurora is here. Her eyes flash with pain before they harden. If she could spit swords at me with her eyes, I'd be holier than a block of Swiss cheese.

"I should have known," she grits out. "You're an asshole. I hope you get every STD in the book and your dick falls off."

"Wait!" I holler after her when she whirls around to leave.

She peeks at me over her shoulder. "Wait for what? You want to give me a show? I'll pass."

"This isn't what it appears to be."

She lifts an eyebrow. "Really? I'm hallucinating again? There aren't two half-naked women rubbing all over you as if they're convinced you're a magic lamp about to give them three wishes?"

She doesn't wait for me to explain and stomps out of the room.

"I know what my three wishes are," Cherie whispers.

The feel of her breath on my skin has me recoiling. I shove them away and rush after Aurora.

"Aurora!" I shout when I don't see her in the hallway.

I try every door I come upon, but I can't find her anywhere. She's disappeared.

Crap. I finally realized I can't live without Aurora and I screw everything up. She's never going to forgive me after today. She's never going to give me a chance.

I'm such an idiot. I should have never tried to get her out of my mind by using two fans. It was a stupid, desperate move made by a man who was denying what he wanted.

But I'm not that man anymore.

I will get Aurora to forgive me. I will get her to give me a chance. Because I'm not giving up on her and our baby.

Chapter 23

The past – doesn't have to rule the future

AURORA

The driver pulls to a stop in front of Jett's rental house in Winter Falls. I want to tell him to turn around. Take me back to Denver. To anywhere but here. But I am not a chicken.

Although, me ignoring Jett and scurrying from the room whenever he showed up makes me appear to be one. And then there's the whole grabbing a commercial flight to avoid sitting on a jet with him thing. Even I can admit that action spells chicken in big, fat capital letters.

Jett has messaged me about a million times since I pulled the flight stunt. My phone beeps in my pocket. I sigh before pulling it out. Speak of the devil.

> **Are you going to sit at the curb all night?**

> **I'm making certain the coast is clear.**

I know. I know. It's petty to remind him of the two women he was with when I walked in on him.

> **No one's here. You're safe.**

I'm safe? Maybe my body is safe but my heart? It's shattered into a million pieces.

Which is utterly ridiculous. Jett and I aren't together. But he was being sweet to me. Looking after me and Little Bean. I thought—

It doesn't matter what I thought. I was wrong.

My stomach rolls and tears threaten. I inhale a calming breath. I am not crying. I refuse to let Jett see how much he hurt me. Not when it's obvious how little I mean to him.

"You okay?" The driver asks and I realize I've been sitting in this taxi at the curb for a while. Time to pull on my big girl panties and get this over with.

"I'm fine." My voice almost sounds steady.

I open the door and climb out of the vehicle while the driver gets my bags out of the trunk. I follow him to the porch where he sets my things down.

I reach for the door but it opens before I get there.

"I just need to pick up my things and I'll be out of your way."

Jett crosses his arms over his chest. I keep my gaze pinned to his face. I will not look down at his arms. I will not notice how his muscles flex.

"Pick up your things? Where the hell do you think you're going?"

His angry voice has thoughts of how strong his arms are and how they can lift me up without straining flying out of my mind.

"Wherever I want. You're not the boss of me."

The driver backs away. "I'll just…," he says before fleeing.

Great. I was counting on him helping me move my stuff out of Jett's house.

"You're carrying my baby," Jett grumbles. "I have a right to know where you are."

I roll my eyes so hard I'm surprised I don't go blind. "*Your* baby? He isn't *your* baby. He's *my* baby. You don't want him, remember?"

I place a protective hand on my stomach. *I got you, Little Bean. Don't you worry.*

"We need to talk."

"I don't want to hear it. I saw enough."

He scowls. "I didn't fuck those women."

"I don't care." I lie. "It's none of my business. We're not together."

"We need to talk," he repeats.

"Yoo-hoo! Aurora!"

I glance over my shoulder. Feather waves from across the street where she's standing on her porch.

"How was your trip?" she asks and begins walking down her sidewalk toward us.

"It was good. But I'm tired. Exhausted."

If there's one thing I've learned about being pregnant, it's how the word exhausted can be used as a 'get out of jail free' card.

I wave to Feather before hurrying into the house. I trudge up the stairs toward my bedroom. No, not *my* bedroom. The guest bedroom. I don't live here anymore.

The sight of the comfortable bed has my resolve nearly crumbling. I can sleep here tonight and figure out a plan tomorrow. But then Jett enters the room and sets my bags down at the end of the bed.

Nope. No staying here. I need to leave before I decide I can survive a lifetime in jail for killing Jett. How bad can prison really be?

Contemplating prison? Yep. I need to go.

"Not that it's any of your business, but I reserved a room at the *Inn on Main.*"

Jett growls. "You're not staying at the Inn."

"How many times do I need to say this for you to get it through your thick skull? You are not the boss of me."

He snorts. "You made yourself perfectly obvious when you snuck off to the airport and left on a commercial flight."

"I didn't sneak off." I'm not a troubled teenager sneaking away from her parents. By the time I hit my troubled teen years, my parents were gone. I didn't need to sneak at anything. No one cared what I did.

"You did, but I don't want to argue about it."

"Good."

I glance around the room. I know the closet is full of clothes. As is the dresser. Plus, there are the bags of dirty clothes on the ground. I don't have the energy to deal with all of it.

"I'll be back tomorrow for my things."

I open a drawer and grab a pair of pajamas. Jett shackles my wrist before I can gather any more clothes.

"You are not leaving."

I shake off his hold. "You don't own me."

"I want you to be comfortable. You're carrying my baby."

Not this again. "Stop saying Little Bean is yours. You don't want to be the father of the baby."

"Wrong. I am the father of this baby."

A spark of hope flutters in my stomach but I ignore it. It's probably indigestion from those spicy nachos I ate at the airport. I'm not getting my hopes up again. I'm not letting him hurt me again.

"I told you, Jett. You're either all in or all out. I won't accept anything else."

He tucks a strand of hair behind my ear. "I know. I'm all in."

Butterflies explode in my stomach. "You are?" Dare I hope?

"I am." He kisses my forehead.

"You're sure? You're not going to back out when you get scared again?"

He sighs as he grasps my hand and leads me to the bed.

"I need to tell you about my past."

My eyes widen. "You're going to tell me about your past?"

Jett keeps his past hidden. Mike may be an asshole but he's helped Jett to hide his past from the media. I don't know what's a bigger miracle. Mike not jabbering to the press about Jett's past. Or Jett's past remaining a secret when he's famous and the paparazzi would pay big bucks for his story.

"I don't enjoy discussing my past. It isn't pretty."

I blow out a breath. "I want to say you don't need to tell me, but I need to know. I need to know why you wouldn't claim Little Bean as your own."

He swallows. "You have a right to know."

He stares off into the distance as he begins. "I don't know who my parents are. I never met them. I was abandoned as a baby."

I bite my tongue before I gasp. What kind of person abandons a baby?

"I grew up in care. No one adopted me as a baby since I was sickly."

I want to ask what was wrong with him but I'm not interrupting him now. I can't chance him stopping.

"By the time I was ten, I was perfectly healthy but the chance for adoption was gone. I moved from place to place. Never settling anywhere. Never finding a home."

He turns to me. "This is why I didn't want to be a father. I don't know how to be one. I never had one. The people who took me in as a foster child weren't my parents. Most of them were in it for the cash. You deserve better than the likes of me."

I frown. I hate when he puts himself down. "Not having a dad doesn't mean you won't be a great one. You're awesome with Isla."

He scowls. "She's an honorary niece, not my daughter."

"The principal is the same. You make sure she's safe, teach her about life, and don't let her eat too much chocolate."

"You make it sound easy."

I chuckle. "It's not easy, but it's not complicated either." I squeeze his hands. "You can do this, Jett."

He frowns. "There's more to my story."

Oh no. What I've already heard has been heartbreaking. I don't know if I can handle more. But I won't be a wimp. I need to be strong for him. I nod for him to continue.

"When I was thirteen, a girl came to live in the house where I was. She was nine but small for her age. Frail and frightened. She had been living with her aunt, but the aunt died and she had no other relatives. Cindy was adorable. She had the biggest smile. She latched onto me right away. She followed me wherever I went.

The house we were living in wasn't great. There were too many kids and not enough space or food. When I saw the other kids bullying her, I took her under my wing. I made sure she had enough food and helped her with her homework."

My heart warms at the image of a thirteen-year-old Jett looking out for an adorable little girl.

"One day I had to stay after school for detention. Cindy wanted to wait for me but hanging around school after hours was asking for trouble. I told her to go back to the house. It was the biggest mistake of my life. When I got there, she was dead."

My stomach hollows out and I place a protective hand over my bump. "What happened?"

"The other kids were fooling around on the stairs. They dared her to slide down the railing. She was probably afraid to say no. They'd tease her if she didn't join them. She fell. She hit her head and broke her neck."

I throw my arms around Jett and hold him close. "It wasn't your fault."

He pushes me away and jumps to his feet. "If I had been there, she never would have been fooling around on the stairs."

I stand and place my hand on his shoulder. "You can't blame yourself. You were a child yourself."

"I was thirteen. I was old enough to know better."

"Listen to yourself. You were thirteen."

He inhales a deep breath and turns to face me. "This is why I didn't want to take responsibility for Little Bean. I don't know how to be a father. I probably shouldn't be a father."

I scowl at him. "It wasn't your fault. I'll repeat myself until I'm blue in the face."

He kisses my nose. "Think of the baby."

"I am. I want Little Bean to have two parents."

"I said I'm all in and I mean it. I made mistakes in my past, but I don't want this baby to grow up without a father."

Warmth fills me. Jett is claiming Little Bean. I won't have to do this alone.

"Good. We can co-parent."

He growls. "We're not co-parenting."

I retreat a step. "You are not stealing this baby from me."

"Nope. But there's no need to co-parent when the parents are together."

My head rears back. "Together? You and I aren't together."

I quash the hope trying to escape. This can't be real. I must be dreaming.

"We are from now on."

"And you just decided this on my behalf?"

His smile is smug. "Yep."

He's offering me everything I've ever wanted, but I still can't believe it. "What if I don't want to be with you?"

"I'll change your mind since you're the only person I want to be with."

Tingles erupt throughout my body. Jett only wants me? I've been hoping to hear those words for years now. Maybe I'm not dreaming. Maybe this is real. "What?"

He cradles my face in his hands. "You, my feisty girl who drives me absolutely bananas with how stubborn you are, are the only person I want to be with."

"And what about the two women you were with last week?" I spit out the question. I don't want to be with a man who can't keep it in his pants.

"I told you. Nothing happened."

I narrow my eyes on him. "Nothing happened? They were naked and nothing happened?"

"I was trying to forget you. To get you out of my mind. It didn't work. The second one of them touched me, I wanted to hurl."

I snort. "I bet that went over well."

"They were pretty pissed when I stopped the party to chase after you."

"To chase after me?" He chased after me? He didn't stay with those women?

"I'll always chase after you, Aurora. You try to leave me and I'm chasing after you."

I chew on my bottom lip. "I don't know if this is a good idea."

I know how it feels to have your dream man and for him to then run away. I don't know if I can survive it again.

"You're right. It's not a good idea. It's an excellent idea."

"This is a huge change. A week ago, you didn't want to be a dad."

He removes my lip from my teeth. "Wrong. A week ago, I thought I couldn't be a dad. I'm still not sure I can be. I'll probably suck at it. But I can't let you go. I can't let our baby grow up without a father."

"You can be a dad without us being together."

"I can, but I won't be." His thumbs soothe over the lines in my forehead. "I've been trying to resist you since the moment we met and you told me I needed a haircut and then proceeded to make me an appointment before I had a chance to reply."

"You did need a haircut."

He chuckles. "What do you say, feisty girl? You ready to take a chance on us?"

Don't be a chicken, Aurora. He's offering you the world. Dare to reach for it.

"Okay. Let's give this a go."

His blue eyes light with happiness. "You won't regret this."

"I'll probably regret this on a daily basis, but I'll regret it more if we don't try."

"There's my girl."

His lips meld to mine and I forget all about how this is a bad idea. How he's probably going to break my heart.

All that exists now is Jett and his taste and his feel.

Chapter 24

First date – a cause of panic for a man no matter his age or rockstar status

*J*ETT

I pace the kitchen as I go over my plans for the day.

What was I thinking? Getting my first girlfriend and going on my first date since high school on Christmas Eve. No pressure then.

Maybe I'll skip this whole first date thing today. We can do it later. After the holidays. Today, I can go bungee jumping or rock climbing or …

No. I cut those thoughts off. I'm not running away. If I run away now, Aurora will never trust me. How can we create a family if she doesn't trust me?

The microwave beeps and I blow out a breath. Showtime.

I knock on Aurora's door but I don't wait for her reply before opening it and entering. She's lying curled on her side with her blonde hair spread over her pillow. She appears relaxed in her sleep. She's not trying to do a million things at once while ticking items off her to-do list. She needs to relax more and work less.

I set the tray on the dresser before kneeling at the side of the bed. I brush her hair off her face and she bats her hand at me.

"Go away," she mutters. I kiss her forehead and her eyes fly open. "Jett."

I waggle my eyebrows. "The one and only."

"I thought you were a fly."

"Sorry to disappoint. I don't buzz and I don't fly."

She snorts. "Except for when you decide to jump out of perfectly good airplanes."

"Don't be jealous of my adventurous spirit."

The happiness in her eyes dims. "What if we have a boy and he's as adventurous as you? We'll have to cover the entire house with padding."

I shrug. "No biggie. I'll teach him my best landing techniques."

"I've changed my mind. I want a girl."

I smile. "I want a girl anyway. A little girl with your blonde curls and green eyes."

"The boys would chase after her."

My smile falters. "Boys? She won't be involved with boys."

She raises an eyebrow. "You're going to stop her?"

"Hell yeah, I am."

"It's going to be fun to watch you try."

"And here I thought I needed to go bungee jumping for an adventure," I mutter.

She pats my hand. "Don't worry. Kids are an adventure in and of themselves."

I stand and grab the tray from the dresser. "Sit up. I have our breakfast."

"*Our* breakfast?" she asks but rearranges the pillows until she's leaning against the headrest.

I lay the tray over her lap before climbing into bed next to her.

"Yes, our breakfast. I know sex is off the table." Aurora surprised me with the no sex rule last night. I was not amused but I understand her trepidation. I deserve it. "But I wanted to have breakfast in bed with you."

"I should probably shower and get ready for work."

"It's Christmas Eve. You're not working. I cleared it with the guys – no special requests, no social media. They'll leave you alone today."

"And what about Mike?"

"The vulture can go fuck himself."

"As much as I'd enjoy watching him try to do that, he is my boss and expects me to work today."

"In which case, you are working today."

"I better eat this breakfast quick then."

She picks up a piece of toast but I grasp her wrist before she can begin to eat. "Slow down, Aurora."

"But I need to work."

"You'll be working for me today."

She narrows her eyes on me. "Working for you?"

"Yep. I realized it's Christmas Eve and I haven't decorated for the holidays. I need to pick out a tree and all the trimmings."

"And you want my help?"

"I *need* your help. I've never decorated for Christmas before."

She bites her bottom lip. "I haven't decorated for Christmas since my parents died."

I pull her teeth from her lip. "Are you okay with decorating today? Or does the idea bring back bad memories?"

She gets a faraway look in her eyes. "It brings back good memories. Mom would blare Christmas music while Dad cursed as he tried to unwind the strings of lights. We'd make popcorn and string it up on the tree. On Christmas day, Mom would wake me up with hot cocoa and she'd sit on my bed while we discussed all my dreams as we drank our cocoa."

I nudge her mug. "Maybe you should take a sip."

She lifts the mug to her nose and sniffs. "It's cocoa. You made me cocoa." Her bottom lip trembles and a tear escapes down her cheek. I wipe it away.

"Please don't cry. I didn't mean to make you cry."

"These are good tears, Jett. Good memories I didn't allow myself to think about before because they were too painful. But I want Little Bean to know about his grandparents. I want him to feel their love even if he will never meet them."

I kiss her forehead. "You're going to be a wonderful mom."

"Thank you. My mom was the best. She's a good example for me to follow."

The familiar emptiness when someone speaks about their parents hits my stomach but it's not as bad as it usually is. I don't feel hollow. For once, I don't want to run away.

"I'm sorry I don't have any good examples to follow."

"Yeah, you do."

"Aurora," I grumble. "I told you about my past."

She squeezes my hand. "I don't mean your past. There are examples all around you. Fender with Isla. Mercury with his niece Mercy. And I bet Dylan will be a wonderful father once Virginia has her baby."

"You're right."

She winks. "Of course, I am. Get used to it. It happens a lot."

"Now, eat your breakfast and drink your cocoa. We have a Christmas tree to buy."

She salutes. "Aye, aye, Captain."

It turns out selecting a tree is not as easy as those cheesy Christmas movies make it out to be.

"I want this tree." Aurora sticks out her bottom lip and pouts.

I run a hand through my hair and try not to pull on the ends. "This tree has all its roots attached. We'll need to water it and it's going to shed needles all over the house."

She snorts. "As if you do the cleaning."

She has a point but I can't tell her the real reason I don't want a live tree. I want her Christmas present to be a surprise.

"Besides," she continues. "We live in Winter Falls. If we return home with a cut tree, they'll probably banish us. Maybe chase us out of town with shovels."

Winter Falls and its crazy environmental rules strike again. I still don't know what the big deal is about driving a car with a combustion engine around. Especially if it's fuel efficient.

But I know better than to say anything to the town's inhabitants. They have PowerPoint presentations prepared for all your environmental questions. I wish I was kidding.

"Fine," I give in.

Aurora squeals and rushes to me. She throws her arms around me. When I feel all her curves against my body, I don't give a shit about how messy the house is about to be.

"Thank you." She pushes up on her toes to reach my lips.

The second her mouth touches mine, I forget all about the Christmas tree. All about us standing in the middle of a Christmas tree farm on Christmas Eve. All I can feel is her curves. All I can smell is her flowery scent. I want to drown in it.

"Ahem. AHEM!"

I force myself to break the kiss and meet the gaze of the throat clearer. "Cash or credit?" the attendant asks.

I pay for the tree and together we attach it to the top of Cash's car, which I borrowed for the day. When we arrive home, I ask Fender to help me set the tree up in the corner of the living room.

"What do you think?" I ask Aurora once Fender has left.

Her eyes are alight with happiness. "It's perfect."

"Do you want to pop some popcorn while I figure out the light situation?"

"Perfect."

Yip.

Aurora freezes on her way to the kitchen. "Did you hear something?"

I swallow my smile. "No."

She narrows her eyes. "You're lying."

"Me?" I grasp my chest. "I wouldn't lie to the mother of my child on Christmas Eve."

She snorts. "You are such a liar."

Yip.

"There! I heard it again." She rushes toward the den. She screeches to a halt in front of the giftwrapped box sitting on the table. The one Fender snuck into the house when he came to help with the tree.

"Can I open it?"

"How do you know it's for you?"

She rolls her eyes. "Of course, it's for me. Your presents are still…"

Her voice trails off when the lid of the box lifts. She doesn't hesitate to pull the lid the rest of the way off. She gasps before removing the puppy and cradling her to her chest.

"Is he mine?"

I scratch the puppy under its chin. "He's a she and yes, she's yours. Or, rather, ours."

"You weren't kidding about being all in."

"I want it all, Aurora. I was afraid to reach for it before. But I want it all. The kids, the puppy, the white picket fence."

Her eyes twinkle. "You realize you're not supposed to show your cards on the first date?"

"I don't give a fuck. This may be our first date but we've been dancing around each other for a decade and you're having my baby."

"*Our* baby," she corrects.

I place my hand over her stomach where our baby is growing. "Our baby."

"This is the best Christmas ever."

"This, my feisty girl, is merely the beginning."

I plan to give Aurora everything she ever wanted. Everything she's missed since she was fifteen. Everything I have to give. It's all hers for the taking.

Chapter 25

All in – includes doctor appointments

AURORA

My phone alarm beeps to remind me I need to get going. I finish the email I was writing as quick as I can before shutting down my laptop.

I stand and Bowie barks in her sleep. I cuddle the puppy to my chest as I search for Jett.

"Jett!"

"What is it?" he asks as he saunters down the stairs in an old pair of jeans and a threadbare t-shirt. The jeans hug his thighs and the t-shirt strains against his chest. I know exactly how sexy those muscles are without any clothes on them. I itch to touch them again.

Whose idea was the no sex rule again? Oh, right. Mine.

I clear my throat. "I have an appointment. Can you watch Bowie?"

I try to hand him the pup but he holds up his hands. "What kind of appointment?"

"Ob/gyn."

"Hold on. You're going to an appointment about the baby and you didn't tell me?"

I shrug. "I didn't realize you'd care."

Or, more accurately, I was afraid he wouldn't. My life is perfect at the moment. I don't want to push it and find out it was all a dream.

He palms my neck and squeezes. "I said I was all in. All in means I'm going to every doctor appointment with you."

Bowie licks my chin. She doesn't enjoy being forgotten.

"What about this fur ball?" I ask. "She can't come with us."

"Give me five minutes. I'll drop her off at Fender's and grab his car keys while I'm at it."

He's gone before I can tell him I already ordered a cab. It's probably better this way. He'll complain I should have never ordered a cab in the first place. Jett can be a Mr. Bossy Pants when he wants to be.

He returns less than two minutes later. "Let's go. You don't want to be late."

"Aren't you going to put on a coat?"

"I'll be fine."

I roll my eyes as I grab his coat and shove it into his hands. He'll give every woman at the doctor's office hot flashes if he doesn't cover up. Judging by the smirk on his face, he knows what I'm thinking.

We settle in the vehicle. It's a huge Hummer. It should be obnoxious, but it's not since Fender is six-foot-six and as wide as a football player. He needs his space.

Jett pairs his phone to the radio and switches on some music as we begin to drive.

"Who is this?" I ask after we've listened to two songs.

He shrugs. "I'm not sure. I'm always getting demo tapes to listen to."

"They're good. I wonder if they have a manager yet."

He glances over at me. "You want to recruit them?"

I grimace. "I wish. Mike isn't interested in the bands I want to recruit."

"So, start your own management firm."

I snort. "Yeah, sure. I'll get right on that."

"I'm serious. You have a ton of experience managing *Cash & the Sinners.* You can use me as a reference if you want. I'm sure the guys will agree."

"I don't manage *Cash & the Sinners.* I'm your PA."

Now, it's his turn to snort. "I'm a musician, but I'm not stupid. I know you do most of the work and Mike only shows up for photo ops. What's holding you back?"

"I wouldn't know where to begin. I'd have to start my own company. I have no idea about laws and financial requirements and … I don't even know what I don't know."

"Leia could help you. She has an MBA and basically manages Brody's business while he develops software."

It's a tempting idea. But it's all too much. "Did you forget I'm having a baby?"

He shrugs. "If you want to quit working to stay home with the baby, I'm fine with it. But I can't imagine you sitting at home for very long."

I can't deny it. "We'll see what happens when the baby comes."

He chuckles. "Learning how to say no already without actually using the word no. Your mom moves are coming along fine."

Warmth spreads through me. I can't wait to be a mom. I've always wanted a family. And this baby will want for nothing. He'll be surrounded by so much love, he won't notice he's missing grandparents.

"This is a different band," Jett says as he increases the volume. "What do you think of them?"

We listen to various bands as we drive to the next town for my doctor's appointment. The conversation is relaxed but lively. This is what I've always wanted with Jett. Not the animosity he threw around before.

But since I now know his back story, I can understand why he was afraid to start a serious relationship. Lord knows this relationship is going to be full of bumps. But I'm resilient. I can handle it. Anything for Little Bean.

"Wait there," Jett says after he parks in front of the doctor's office.

I debate whether I should listen to him or not for a few seconds. On the one hand, I love the idea of a man opening my door for me. On the other hand, I'm afraid to get used to it.

Before I can make up my mind, Jett's opening the door and offering me his hand. I take his hand and let him help me down from the vehicle.

"I don't know how Leia gets in and out of this monstrosity. She's even shorter than me."

Jett chuckles as he leads me into the building. I check in for my appointment and we find seats in the corner.

The other women stare at Jett but there are no signs of recognition. This crowd apparently doesn't know what the drummer of *Cash & the Sinners* looks like. Good. Because he's mine and I'm not sharing.

"Ow." Jett removes my nails from his thigh.

"Oops."

He leans close to whisper in my ear. "Don't be jealous. You're the only woman I want."

I ignore the shiver his breath on my skin causes. I refuse to get all hot and bothered before a doctor's appointment.

"Aurora Sharpe!" A woman calls and I stand.

To my surprise, Jett stands with me. "All in."

I nod. All in.

The nurse leaves us in the room after instructing me to strip and put on a gown.

"I didn't know I'd get a strip tease today."

I glare at Jett. "Turn around."

He chuckles but he does as he's told. Once I'm wearing the gown, he helps me onto the table. The doctor enters a few moments later.

"Good morning, I'm Dr. Edwards. And you must be Mr. and Mrs. Sharpe."

Jett growls but I slap him before he can respond. "I'm Ms. Sharpe and this is Mr. Peterson, but you can call us Aurora and Jett."

"Aurora and Jett." She smiles. "Are you ready for your first ultrasound?"

Jett's eyes light with excitement. "Yes."

"Do you want to know the sex of the baby?"

"I don't know." I bite my lip as I consider the question. "What do you think?"

Jett bobs his head. "Yes. I want to know."

I giggle. "You didn't hesitate."

"What?" He shrugs. "I'm excited."

"I love an excited Daddy," Dr. Edwards says as she preps the ultrasound machine. "What does Mom want?"

I love the sound of her calling me Mom. I can't wait for our child to say it.

Jett squeezes my hand. "If we know the sex, it'll help us figure out what clothes to buy and how to decorate the nursery."

"We're not doing pink for a girl and blue for a boy. We're sticking to gender neutral colors and clothes."

"I'll need a second to come up with another excuse why we need to know the sex of the child," Jett tells the doctor.

"How about names?" she suggests.

I groan. "You're not supposed to be helping him."

She snorts. "Can you blame me? I'm over sixty and I want to have his babies."

I roll my eyes. "Great. His ego can barely fit in the room with us as it is."

She lifts up my gown and smears gel on my stomach. "What'll it be? Yes or no."

My gaze meets Jett's. His eyes are pleading. Damn. I can't resist him. I blow out a breath. "Yes."

"Ready, Mom and Dad?"

Jett nods. "Ready."

She places the transducer on my stomach and moves it around until a whooshing sound fills the room.

"What you're hearing is your baby's heartbeat."

"It's really fast. Is that normal?" Jett asks.

Dr. Edwards nods. "It's normal." She points to the image on the display. "This is the baby's arms. Here are the legs."

"Are those fingers and toes?" I ask.

"Yes. Now if baby Sharpe will just rotate for us, we can confirm if baby is a boy or a girl."

She presses the transducer a bit harder against my stomach and moves it around. "This might help."

Jett squeezes my hand as we watch the screen and wait for *Little Bean* who isn't so little anymore to move. I'm about to give up when the baby rolls.

"And?" Jett asks.

"Sorry for him. When they were handing out patience, he was off causing trouble."

"No worries," Dr. Edwards murmurs as she studies the screen. She smiles. "I believe we have a girl on our hands."

"A girl?" Jett asks. He kisses my forehead. "We're having a girl. I hope she looks exactly like her momma."

"But with your blue eyes."

Dr. Edwards sighs. "I love new parents. Do you want a picture?"

"Yes!"

"Jett," I warn.

"Yes, please."

"If your little girl is anything like her momma, she's going to have the boys eating out of her hand," Dr. Edwards says.

"I think I need to buy a shotgun," Jett mutters.

The doctor barks out a laugh before handing me a picture and switching off the machine.

"Make an appointment at the front desk before you leave," she says before exiting the room.

Jett leans his forehead against mine and places a hand over my stomach. "I can't wait to meet her."

"Me too. I…"

I bite my tongue before I say I love you. I don't love Jett. I can't. It's too soon. We've been a couple for less than a week. And before we got together, he ran hot and cold ever since he found out about the pregnancy. And then there's the whole decade of animosity toward each other.

It's too soon for love. It must be the hormones speaking.

Chapter 26

Hunger – not always related to food

AURORA

"Are you hungry?" Jett asks as we drive out of the city toward Winter Falls.

My stomach growls in response and he chuckles.

I slap him. "No laughing at the pregnant lady. I'm growing a human being over here."

He immediately sobers. "Sorry. What do you want to eat? Fender told me about this great hamburger place."

I narrow my eyes on him. "When did Fender mention this great hamburger place to you?"

"I messaged him while you were in the restroom. You were in there a long time. I thought you drowned."

More like I was answering emails and messages from Mike. But I know better than to say Mike's name in front of Jett. Someone gets a bit snippy about how much I work.

"What did Mike want?"

I feign shock. "Mike? What?"

"I can always tell when you're lying."

"I'm not lying."

He pulls my hand away from my sweater. "You always pluck at your clothes when you lie."

"Do not." Great. I sound about the age of the baby I'm growing. Way to be a grown up.

"Hamburger place?" he prods.

"Sounds good." I speak in a loud voice to cover the sound of my stomach growling. Judging by the grin on Jett's face, he isn't fooled.

It isn't long before he pulls into a roadside diner.

"This place is cute. I didn't think roadside diners still existed," I say as we walk hand in hand into the restaurant.

"Go ahead and find yourself a seat," a waitress hollers as we enter.

We settle at a booth near the window. The booths are red leather, the tables are Formica, and the floor is squeaky vinyl. I feel as if we've traveled back in time.

"I love these kinds of places," I say as I scan the room. The walls are filled with pictures of 1950s movie stars and there's an old-fashioned jukebox in the corner. I point to it. "Do you think it still works?"

"It works," the waitress says as she slaps two laminated menus on the table. "I'm Lucy. What can I get you to drink?"

I gaze longingly at the coffee pot she's holding but I don't order any. I've had my one cup for the day. "Ginger ale, please."

Jett orders a coke and she leaves us to peruse the menu.

"I already know what you want. The biggest bacon cheese-burger they have."

He shrugs. "I enjoy a good burger."

I open my mouth to respond but then there's a thud on the window next to me. I nearly jump in my seat in surprise. I glance over to discover a teenager with her face pressed to the window.

"Crap." Jett groans when the girl points at him. "I think I've been spotted."

"Did you bring a hat? Sunglasses? Or some other kind of disguise?"

"I didn't think to. I'm so used to no one making a big deal out of the band when I walk around Winter Falls."

I can't complain. I've become complacent as well. Normally, I carry a large bag with everything I could possibly need to wrestle the band under control – disguises, hangover remedies, condoms, etc. – but I didn't bring my bag today.

"Do you want me to hide in the bathroom while you greet them?"

There's now a small group of girls gathered outside. They're squealing as they jump up and down while pointing at Jett. It won't be long until they invade the diner.

He growls. "You're not fucking hiding in the bathroom."

I point to my stomach. "I can't exactly keep my condition a secret."

"And?"

"What do you mean and?"

"And what's the big deal? The world is going to find out I have a baby on the way sooner or later."

"Later would be better. We'd have a chance to control the narrative."

And I could prepare myself for Mike losing his ever-loving mind.

Jett barks out a laugh. "As if there's any controlling the media."

He's not wrong but I'm not ready for the world to know I'm carrying the baby of the drummer of *Cash & the Sinners.* I'm not ready for the pure vitriol that will be thrown at me once the news is out. How I'm not pretty enough. Not skinny enough. How I used my position to catch a rockstar.

"Hey." He grasps my hands and squeezes. "What's wrong? Do you not want people to know you're carrying my baby?"

His eyes are full of hurt and, despite the situation, warmth flows through me. He doesn't care if people know I'm carrying his baby. He's claiming Little Bean as his own.

"No, no. I'm not embarrassed of you or us or Little Bean. It's just…" I wave a hand in front of me to indicate my body.

"I'm confused."

I blow out a breath and explain, "I'm not exactly what anyone would call skinny."

"Your body is sexy as hell."

My stomach dips as excitement flows through me. "You think I'm sexy?"

He chuckles. "Hell yeah. I—"

"As much as I'm enjoying this conversation," Lucy says and I notice she's standing in front of the door keeping the teenaged fans outside. "I don't think now is the time to have it."

My face warms. "Sorry."

"No need for you to be sorry." She points to the back hallway. "There's a back entrance. I figure if I let them in when you exit the backdoor you should have enough time to make it to your car."

Jett growls. "The woman carrying my baby is not fleeing a restaurant."

"It's fine. I can run. My legs work."

"No. I'm keeping you and Layla safe."

"Layla?"

He grins. "You gotta admit Layla is a kickass rocker name."

I groan. "You're going to buy her a drum set before she can walk, aren't you?"

"Or a guitar. I'm not picky."

An image of Jett teaching our baby to play the drums pops into my head. He'd be such a good teacher. Patient and supportive. Love for the two of them fills my heart with happiness.

Not this again. I don't love Jett. It's the hormones talking.

"Come on." Jett holds out his hand. When I grasp it, he pulls me out of the booth.

"Where are we going?" I ask when we start toward the door.

He squeezes my hand. "I got this."

Seriously? Jett has this? I'm the one who usually handles these types of situations. I'm the one who usually is the recipient of the rage from the fans who don't want me. They want the band. This'll be interesting.

Lucy frowns at us. "Are you sure? I can hold them off until you sneak out of the back. There's no reason to play the hero, Jett."

"Jett?" He raises an eyebrow. "You know who I am."

"Fender comes in here all the time. When you looked familiar, it wasn't hard to figure out who you are."

"Thanks for your help, Lucy."

"No need to thank me. This is the most excitement we've seen in ages."

"Nonetheless." He winks at her.

"You ready?" she asks and he nods. She opens the door and the teenagers scream.

It is him!

Oh my god!

I love you, Jett!

Will you sign my boob?

Jett ignores the shouts. He wraps a protective arm around me and begins to make his way through the crowd.

"Excuse me, darlings. I need to get my lady home."

Your lady?

Who's his lady?

Is this woman his lady?

I groan at the obvious disgust in their voices. I fist my hands to stop myself from cradling my belly. Better a fat girlfriend than a pregnant one.

Jett ignores their shouts and leads me to the passenger door. He opens it and helps me inside. Once I'm buckled up, he shuts the door.

I assume he's going to give his fans some attention now. After all, I'm safely burrowed away in the vehicle. I can wait a few minutes.

But he doesn't. He saunters around the car waving at the girls but doesn't stop until he's sliding into the seat next to me.

"Don't you want to spend some time with them?" I ask when he switches on the vehicle.

His brow wrinkles. "Why would I want to spend time with them when I have you? You're the one I want to spend all my time with."

My heart melts at his words. I'm the one he wants to spend time with. *Me.*

I reach across the console and squeeze his thigh. "Thank you."

He scowls at me. "No need to thank me." He waggles his eyebrows. "Unless you want to thank me naked."

There's the Jett I know and love.

Love? Welp. There's no more denying it. I love Jett Peterson, drummer for the world famous *Cash & the Sinners* band. The man who wouldn't even consider having a girlfriend a few months ago, let alone having a child.

This situation has disaster written all over it. But I'm all in.

Please don't break my heart, Jett.

Chapter 27

Lucky – how Jett feels

JETT

"I'm sorry." I apologize as I drive away from the restaurant.

"What are you sorry for?"

"Those fans."

Aurora snorts. "You're a rockstar. Female fans throwing themselves at you is hardly a new experience."

I don't want anyone throwing herself at me except Aurora. She's the only one I want.

She pats my thigh. "It's okay. It's not my first rodeo with a rock band. I know how things work."

I scowl. Does she honestly think things haven't changed? I'm not the man I used to be. I'm not letting women throw themselves at me when I have her.

She's the only one I want to throw herself at me. The only one I want to see naked. The only one I want in my bed.

My cock perks up at the idea. It remembers how it feels to be buried deep in Aurora. It's more than ready for a repeat.

"Things have changed," I growl.

"They have?"

I hate the uncertainty in her voice. I hate how she rubs her hand over her belly where our baby is growing as if to protect her from me. I hate the distance between us.

"I told you I'm all in."

She stares at me from underneath her lashes. "All in as in ready to have sex with me?"

My hands jerk and the car swerves to the side of the road. My brain manages to come online before we crash into a tree.

"You're a tease."

She points at her belly. "Little Bean is proof I'm not a tease. I put out."

My cock immediately lengthens and hardens at her words. "Do you want me to pull over to the side of the road and have my wicked way with you in the backseat of Fender's car?"

She bites her bottom lip. "Maybe."

I tighten my hands on the steering wheel as my blood heats at the idea of stripping Aurora down. Of tasting every inch of her skin. Of touching every curve. Of burying myself deep into her heat. Until I don't know where I end and where she begins.

I growl. "I am not fucking the mother of my child in the backseat of a car."

"I guess you better hurry home then."

Home. I've never had a home before. I have a house in San Diego but it's not a home. It's the place I sleep in when I'm in town.

But I want a home with Aurora. Somewhere filled with love and laughter. Somewhere for our children to grow up.

"When we get *home,* I'm going to lick every inch of you until you beg me to stop. Then, I'm going to bury myself deep in your pussy until you scream my name."

She shivers and her eyes flare. But then she sniffs and lifts her nose in the air. "You can try."

"Challenge accepted, feisty girl. Challenge accepted."

I want to speed down the road to get home as fast as I can, but I grit my teeth and force myself to drive the speed limit. I have precious cargo aboard this vehicle and I'm not allowing any harm to come to either one of them.

By the time I park in front of the house, my zipper is imprinted on my cock. I jump out and rush around the front to open Aurora's door.

I blow out a breath before I throw her over my shoulder. She's pregnant. No stupid stunts with this woman who's having my baby.

"Yoo-hoo, Aurora, Jett!" Feather shouts from across the street. "How did your appointment go?"

"I'm not telling you the sex of the baby so you can win the bet!" Aurora shouts back.

"But you do know the sex?"

Aurora groans.

I chuckle. "You walked right into that question."

I grasp her hand and begin tugging her up the sidewalk. We need to get inside the house before Feather reaches us. I have no interest in fending off a gossip gal when my cock is hard enough to pound nails.

Leia walks out of her house next door with Bowie on a leash. She starts across the lawn, intent on returning Aurora's puppy to her, but I motion for her to stop. She studies me for a moment before a grin overtakes her face.

"I'll bring Bowie over later. Much later." She winks.

"Don't you dare steal my puppy, Leia!" Aurora yells.

"No need to worry. I have my own puppy, a daughter, and a fiancé to worry about. I don't need another thing."

"Really?" Feather asks. "You don't need another child?"

Leia wags her finger at her. "Don't you start a bet about when I'm going to get pregnant."

"What if I didn't start the bet?"

I usher Aurora into the house. When I shut the door behind us, she pouts. "But I want to hear how Leia holds off Feather and the gossip gals."

I pin her against the door and press my hard length against her stomach. She gasps and her eyes flare. I lick a path from her neck to her ear before nibbling on the lobe.

"Do you want to listen to them, or do you want to finish what we started in the car?"

Goosebumps break out on her skin. "I want to finish what we started in the car," she breathes out.

"Correct answer," I murmur before picking her up.

She slaps my shoulder. "Set me down. I'm too heavy."

"You are not heavy. Don't you dare put yourself down."

She rolls her eyes. "I'm not putting myself down. I'm being realistic. I'm chubby *and* pregnant."

"You are not chubby. Do I need to spank you?"

Her eyes narrow but she can't hide the way her body shivers with excitement. "Jett Peterson, you will not spank me."

"You don't want to feel my hand on your naked ass? You don't want to feel the sting?"

"No fair. Your voice could make eating snakes sound appealing."

I grin. I know exactly how much Aurora enjoys dirty talk when we're in bed. And I plan to use the knowledge to my advantage. It's only fair since she holds all the cards.

I enter my bedroom and lay her down on my bed.

"From now on, you sleep in this bed. With me. No more separate bedrooms. No more separate beds."

Her eyes narrow. "You can't order me around, Jett Peterson."

I smirk. "Sure, I can."

"Don't be a pompous ass. We'll discuss when we move into one bedroom. You're not a caveman. You can't order—"

Her words cut off with a gasp when I pinch her nipple. She thrusts her chest into my hands.

I knead her breasts until she's writhing beneath me. Then, I stop to ask, "What were you saying?"

"Don't stop." She grabs my wrist and places my hand back on her breast.

I frown. "No, I don't think you were begging me to continue."

She growls. "I don't beg."

I raise an eyebrow. "You don't?" I glide my hand over her breast down her chest. I pause at her stomach where our child is growing. I cradle the area with both hands.

"Our baby is growing here," I murmur.

She places her hands over mine. "Yes, she is."

"We're having a girl. I hope she has your green eyes and blonde hair."

"I hope she has your blue eyes."

"If she's as gorgeous as her mother, I seriously need to buy a shotgun."

"There's no need to flatter me. I'm already in your bed. I'm a sure thing."

I tear my eyes away from where our baby is growing to meet her gaze. "I'm not flattering you. You are gorgeous."

She opens her mouth to respond but I place a finger on her lips. "No. I told you before I won't have you putting yourself down."

Her face softens. But then she bites my finger. There's my feisty girl.

"Did you forget what we're doing here in this bed?"

"I didn't forget." I squeeze my cock through my jeans. Her eyes flare and she licks her lips. I groan. This woman is going to be the death of me. But I wouldn't want it any other way.

She opens her mouth – probably to sass at me more – but I slam my mouth down on hers before she has a chance to speak. She sighs and I push my tongue inside. Her flower taste hits me. Damn, do I love flowers.

Her fingers dig into my shoulders and she pulls me closer, but I resist since I don't want to squash her or our baby. I will never let any harm come to the two of them. I will protect them from everything and everyone. Even if the person I need to protect them from is me.

She wraps her legs around my waist and begins to rub her core against my cock. My cock strains against my zipper. I'm going to have permanent zipper marks at this rate.

Hold on. I don't need to have zipper marks. Aurora is here. In my bed. Waiting for me to fuck her.

I slow the kiss and pull away. She mewls in protest. "Need to get you naked."

"I approve."

I chuckle as I remove her sweater and bra as quickly as possible. I throw the garments behind me before getting to my knees to work on her jeans. I frown when I notice they're held together with a rubber band.

"What's this?"

She rolls her eyes. "I haven't exactly had time to go shopping for maternity clothes."

The mother of my baby will not walk around with jeans held together by a rubber band. But I know better than to tell Aurora what I'm thinking. My feisty girl will argue with me and I'm done talking.

Once she's naked and laid out before me, I stand to undress. I throw my clothes off and climb back onto the bed.

Aurora widens her legs and I fit my hips in between her thighs.

"Are you wet for me?" I ask as I hitch my cock at her entrance.

"Why don't you find out?"

I inch inside and groan. "You're dripping wet for me."

"It's your fault for being so sexy."

I inch further inside. Her eyes fall closed and she wraps her legs around my hips.

I grit my teeth to stop myself from plunging fully into her. I don't want to rush this. I want to show Aurora how special she is. How much I want her. How much I want to keep her. And prove to her I'm all in.

"You feel like heaven. I want to bury myself inside your pussy and never leave." Crap. There's a reason she feels better than anyone before. I freeze. "Oh shit. Oh shit."

Her eyes fly open. "What's wrong?"

"I'm bare. No condom."

She rolls her eyes. "It's not as if you can get me more pregnant." She points to her belly. "Mission accomplished."

I push her hair off of her face. "But I should be tested. Make sure I'm clean. I don't want to risk you or the baby."

She glares at me. "You said you haven't had sex since we were together."

"I haven't. I promise. I wouldn't lie to you about that."

Her face softens. "Then, we're good."

"What?"

"When you were in the hospital in San Diego, I asked the doctor to run all the 'usual' tests."

I should probably be mad at her. But if this means I can enter her bare, I don't care.

"I'm clean?"

She smiles. "You're clean and free to proceed."

"I guess it's time to make you scream." I sink into her until my balls slap her ass.

She groans and her head falls back. "Yes."

Groaning is good but I want more. I want her gasping for breath. Begging me to let her come. Time to get to work.

I sneak a hand between us and rub her clit as I thrust in and out of her.

"Your pussy is my favorite place to be."

"My cock never wants to leave."

"He wants to be buried here every second of the day."

Her walls flutter around me each and every time I utter a dirty word.

"Do you want to come?"

She nods.

"I need to hear the words. Jett, owner of my orgasms, please let me come."

She opens her eyes to snarl at me. "You do not own my orgasms."

I get to my knees and throw her legs over my shoulders. "I can get deep this way. Has anyone else ever been this deep inside of you?"

She shakes her head.

"Has anyone ever made you feel this good?"

Another shake.

"Do you want me to rub your clit until you see stars?"

When I touch her clit, she gasps, and her walls tighten around me.

"Are you ready to come?"

"Yes."

"Who's making you come?"

"Drummer boy."

My feisty girl never gives in. But I don't push her anymore since my balls are heavy and tingling. I don't have long before I explode.

I pinch her clit. "Come, Aurora. Come all over my cock. Milk me. Make me see stars."

"Jett!" she shouts as her climax hits.

Her walls squeeze my cock until I have no choice but to come. I empty myself into her pussy. My thrusts are erratic as I come harder than I've ever come before.

"Aurora. Aurora. Aurora," I chant until I'm wrung dry.

Once my heart rate returns to normal, I withdraw. I lay her legs on the bed and stand to go to the bathroom. When I return to clean her, she's curled up on her side with a big smile on her face.

I use a warm washcloth to clean her before throwing it on the floor and climbing into bed. I wrap my arms around Aurora and pull her near.

"I love you," she murmurs.

I freeze. Aurora loves me?

Chapter 28

Run away – easier than playing the drums for a three-hour concert

AURORA

I snuggle into the warmth surrounding me. I haven't slept this well since before I got pregnant. Since the night I gave in and had sex with Jett.

The man I'd been obsessing about for a decade. The man I love. The man I told I love you to last night. The man who didn't respond.

Well, shit. I never should have told Jett I love him. The man can barely handle being in a relationship. The last thing he needed was for me to vomit love all over him.

He sighs in his sleep and his arm tightens around my waist. His hand is lying on my baby bump as if to protect it. My eyes water at the tenderness.

No. Stop it. I need to protect my heart from this man who doesn't love me the way I love him.

A dagger stabs my heart at the thought of Jett never loving me. My throat catches as the pain radiates from my chest throughout my body. This is why I should have kept my big mouth shut. I've had enough heartache in my life. I don't need more.

There's only one thing to do.

I lift Jett's hand and scoot out of the bed.

"Where are you going?" His voice is gravelly with sleep. It sounds the same as when he's buried deep inside me. My knees wobble and my breath catches.

No, Aurora. No! No going weak at the sound of a man's voice. Especially if the man froze you out after you said you love him.

"Gotta pee." It's not a lie. I always have to pee thanks to Little Bean.

I rush out of the room to the bathroom down the hall. I'm not using Jett's bathroom. I don't want to get comfortable with what I can never have.

After I take care of business, I get ready for the workday. As much as I'd love to spend the day lounging around, work is a surefire way to stop myself from obsessing about Jett and our 'relationship'.

I'm settled at the kitchen table going through emails when Jett saunters into the room. I keep my eyes focused on my computer.

"Hey." He kisses my hair. "I thought you'd come back to bed."

He thought wrong. Go back to bed and lay with the man I love who clearly doesn't love me? I am not a glutton for punishment.

"Nope. Work."

"I thought Mike gave you the week between Christmas and New Year's off."

"And I thought you wanted this charity concert to happen."

He frowns. "Maybe we should delay it. I don't want you working too hard."

"I always work hard."

"Maybe you should learn to relax a little. You won't be able to work this hard when Layla arrives."

I'm not arguing about how hard I work. It's a waste of breath. "I never agreed to the name Layla."

"You admitted it's a kickass name."

Whatever. I return my attention to my emails.

He squeezes my shoulder. "Hey. What's wrong?"

What's wrong? Is he serious right now? Or is he just a complete idiot with no social skills whatsoever? Time to find out.

"What's wrong?" I sneer. "You seriously have to ask me?" I shake my head. "Idiot."

He blows out a breath as he scratches his bare stomach. My gaze gets caught on those hard muscles. Muscles I know feel warm to the touch.

My hand reaches for him without my brain giving it permission. I fist my hand. No touching.

"Look. I—"

His words are cut off by a knock on the door. He rushes off to answer it. Of course, he does. It's what Jett does best. Run when things get tough. If it weren't for the gorgeous kitchen in front of me, I'd think I was having déjà vu from a few months ago when he fled after our first night together.

The door opens and I strain to hear who's here before nine o'clock in the morning.

"Good morning, Leia," Jett greets before a dog barks. I guess Leia brought Bowie home. "Hey, girl. Did you miss me?"

My stomach clenches. Dang it. Now I'm jealous of a puppy. *Get your shit together, Aurora.*

"Bowie!" I call.

The puppy bounds into the room seconds later. She bumps my hand with her snout, and I scratch her behind the ears.

"Did you have fun with Leia and Fender and Isla?"

Leia grunts. "If you consider dragging every single shoe in the house into the living room fun, then, yeah, she had fun."

I groan. "Please tell me she didn't pee on the pile."

"Princess arrived and the two of them got into a tug-of-war match with one of Fender's sneakers. I thought Fender was going to have an aneurysm when he caught them. He banished them outside to the little fenced in area he made for Princess and made them stay out there until Isla cried because Princess was whining. My girl has that man wrapped around his finger."

"Isla's awesome," Jett says.

Will he love our child the way he loves Isla? Or will he run away from her now? I bite my tongue before the questions tumble out of me.

I need to keep my mouth shut in front of Leia, who won't hesitate to tattle to our group of friends. Judging by the way she's glancing between me and Jett she already knows something's up. Great. Another interrogation. Just what I need.

Jett clears his throat. "I promised Gibson I'd help him with something today. Make sure you eat breakfast."

"Whatever," I mutter.

"We'll talk when I get home."

I snort. "Sure, we will."

He doesn't reassure me. He whirls around and practically runs out of the house. Is there a record for how fast a woman can chase a man away? If so, I'm winning. Can I get my prize in chocolate?

"Pancakes, dried toast, or eggs and bacon?" Leia asks the second the door closes behind Jett.

"You're not going to interrogate me?"

"Nope."

"You're not going to feed me copious amounts of food and then attack when I'm in a food coma?"

"Nope."

"Are you going to say more than nope for the rest of the morning?"

She smiles. "Yep."

I growl and she giggles.

"Sorry. Sometimes it's fun to be the grumpy person. Instead of the one dealing with the grump all the time."

"And yet you love Fender."

"And you love Jett."

I scowl at her. "I thought this wasn't going to be an interrogation."

She shrugs. "Just putting it out there in case you need to talk."

"I don't need to talk. I need to work."

She motions to my laptop. "You work while I prepare breakfast."

"You don't have to make me breakfast."

"Um, yeah, I do. The longer I stay in your home, the more I can tease the gossip gals about how I know everything going on while they know nothing."

I bark out a laugh. "You're evil."

"I prefer the word mischievous."

My phone rings and my mood immediately plummets. "Sorry, I need to get this."

"Pancakes it is." She whirls around and marches to the kitchen.

I answer the phone. "What do you want?"

Mike launches into a list of items I need to get done now. So much for my week off and getting caught up on work.

I hang up my phone and Leia slides a plate of pancakes in front of me. "Eat."

I'm not arguing with a plate of homemade pancakes. I dig in.

She sits across from me as I eat. "Have you considered quitting your job and starting your own management firm?"

"No." Thought about it? Nearly every damn day. Considered it? No way.

"You should consider it. I'm sure the band would hire you as their manager. Gibson wants to fire Mike anyway."

"Firing Mike would be career suicide," I say in between bites.

"Why? Don't bands switch record labels all the time?"

I finish chewing my bite and set my fork down. Leia nods to the glass of orange juice. "You need your vitamins."

I roll my eyes as I pick up the juice.

"Now explain to me why you're an 'assistant' when you're actually running the show," Leia continues her barrage of nosiness.

"I'm not running the show."

"And I don't have a plot picked out to bury my boss in."

I frown. "I thought you liked Brody."

"I like Brody the man fine. Brody the boss, on the other hand? Him, I don't like."

"I'm sorry."

"Don't be sorry. Start your own management firm and hire me as your right-hand woman."

I narrow my eyes on her. "Have you been talking to Jett?"

"No. Why?"

"He said the same thing about me quitting."

"Why don't you?"

"It's not that easy. I'd have to go out on the road and find a band to manage. A band no one else has heard of. A band willing to take a chance on a brand-new manager."

She rolls her eyes. "Don't be silly. *Cash & the Sinners* would be your first client. Bands would be lining up at your door to be associated with you."

"The band isn't firing Mike."

"It's cute you think you could stop them."

I grin. "It's not cute. I have dirt on every single one of them. They know not to piss me off."

"You have dirt on Fender? Please, please, tell me. I'll be your slave forever."

"I'm sure you could get Fender to reveal all his secrets to you."

She sighs. "Probably."

My phone beeps with a message. "I should get back to work."

Leia stands and gathers the dishes. "I'll get out of your hair."

"And go brag to the gossip gals that you know all of my secrets?"

"Nah. I avoid those ladies. But I did get your mind off whatever had you looking like someone killed your dog when I walked in the house."

"You're not mischievous. You're devious."

She winks. "You're welcome."

Chapter 29

Lightbulb moment – the moment you realize how badly you screwed up

JETT

As soon as I'm outside the house, I want to go back inside. I want to explain to Aurora why I didn't respond to her declaration of love.

But I can't go back.

I don't know how to explain. I don't know how to tell her I don't feel the same way without hurting her. Hurting Aurora is the last thing I want to do.

I walk around town until I find myself in front of Gibson and Mercy's house. I debate walking past it but I could use a friend.

"What are you doing here?" Gibson asks when he opens the door.

"Do I need a reason to visit my best friend?"

"Your best friend? You haven't been treating me like a best friend for a while now."

I scowl. "You weren't supposed to fall in love."

He claps me on the back and ushers me inside. "The same way you weren't supposed to fall in love?"

No way. There's no way I love Aurora. I can't love her. Hell, I'm not sure I know what love is.

"I haven't fallen for Aurora. We're dating and having a baby together but I'm not in love."

He barks out a laugh. "Really?"

"Yes, really."

"You didn't change your entire stand on relationships and children because of her?"

He doesn't give me a chance to respond before continuing.

"She isn't the only woman you've ever let sleep in the bed with you? You don't want to give her everything? Like a puppy for Christmas? You're not worried you're not good enough for her?"

"I'm not good enough for her."

He smiles. "What you're feeling is called love."

"I don't love her."

"Okay. Maybe you don't love her. But the seeds of love are there. Give them a bit of attention and soon enough – Bam! – love will be in your heart."

Is he right? Is this the start of love? I did change my entire stance on relationships and children for Aurora. And I do want to give her everything. I never want to hurt her or see her cry. I rub a hand over my chest where it aches from watching how hurt she was this morning.

"What did you do?"

I drop my hand. "What do you mean?"

"Come on." He motions me through the house and out the backyard to the tiny home they built for Mercy's great uncle.

"Mercury isn't living here yet," Gibson explains as he opens the door. "Mercy insists we add panic buttons and guardrails everywhere before she'll let him live here on his own."

He opens the refrigerator and pulls out two bottles. When he hands me one and I see it's water, I blow out a breath in relief.

"Don't worry," he says as he motions for me to take a seat on the sofa. "I'm still sober. It helps that my parents haven't contacted me since I filed a restraining order against them."

"I don't get it."

"Get what?"

"How could a dad ever treat his son the way yours treats you?"

His shoulders sag in relief. "You're not going to bug me anymore to give my parents another chance?"

Guilt swamps me at how relieved he is. Shit. I've been an asshole. I've been pushing him for the past decade to reconcile with his parents. I couldn't understand how he didn't want anything to do with them since I'd give anything to have parents in my life.

But now I'm going to be a father myself, my feelings have changed.

"Fuck no. They don't deserve you. I sure as hell won't treat my daughter the way your parents treat you."

He smiles. "A daughter? Aurora is having a girl?"

I nod.

He lifts his bottle and touches it to mine. "Congrats, bro."

"Thanks." I smile at the idea of a little girl who looks like Aurora. Assuming Aurora ever lets me see our child after last night.

"What did you do?"

I frown. "Why do you think I did anything?"

"Because you're at my house instead of hovering over your woman."

"I don't hover over Aurora."

He snorts. "And Dylan didn't try to get Virginia to quit her job because being a librarian is too strenuous a job for a pregnant woman."

"Dylan's an overprotective idiot. Virginia is going to stab him in the eye one of these days."

"Nah," Gibson disagrees. "She's gaga over his blue eyes. She's more likely to hide his guitars away."

"Glad I don't play guitar."

He cocks an eyebrow. "Because you think Aurora would hide your guitars?"

I blow out a breath. "You're like a dog with a bone."

"Woof. Woof."

"Fine. Aurora told me she loves me and I didn't respond."

He studies me. "Not at all?"

I shake my head.

"You didn't say, I don't know, thank you or I care for you, too?"

"Nothing at all."

"What did you do?"

"I may have run out of the house when Leia brought back the dog this morning."

He laughs. "You are in so much trouble."

I throw my water bottle at him. "Don't be an asshole. I seem to remember Mercy telling you she loves you and you not even remembering because you were drunk off your ass."

He sobers. "I fucked up. But I got my shit together now and I'm not doing anything to put my relationship with Mercy in jeopardy."

"Good. I like Mercy. I don't know what she sees in your ugly ass, but I don't want her hurt."

He picks my bottle up from the floor and hands it back to me. "What are you going to do about Aurora?"

I shrug. "Apologize?"

He groans. "Please don't tell me you're going to apologize for not loving her."

Even I know better than that. "What do you think? I'm an idiot?"

"Dude, I've been on tour with you. I've watched you run around the tour bus convinced there were snakes all over your body. I've rushed to the hospital because you fell while climbing Mount Etna and fractured your leg."

"What's your point?"

"I know you're an idiot."

This time I make sure the cap on the water is off before I throw the bottle at him. He laughs as water sprays his sweat-shirt.

"I haven't done any adventure sports for a while," I say in my defense. Once the words are out, I realize I haven't felt the need for an adrenaline rush in a while. Not since I let Aurora into my life.

I groan as I bury my face in my hands. Shit. I am falling in love. I'm falling for my feisty girl. It's not love yet but the seeds are there the way Gibson described it.

"What am I going to do?"

He digs his phone out of his pocket. "Let me call the guys. We'll figure out a plan."

I slap the phone out of his hands before he can dial. "I don't need the entire band to know what happened."

"Didn't you say Leia was at your house when you left?" I nod. "Dude, they already know."

I refuse to believe him. Aurora wouldn't betray me by telling everyone our business. She knows how private a person I am despite the entire band living and working together. Besides, I doubt she wants everyone knowing what happened.

"Hey. Hey." He squeezes my shoulder. "We can fix this. Does Aurora know about your past?"

"She knows everything."

"Everything? You told her about Cindy?"

"I did."

"If she knows about your past, she'll understand how hard love and relationships are for you. This is totally fixable. You'll win her back."

The fear threatening to overtake me eases a bit at his words. "But I can't tell her I love her."

"Maybe not. But you can show her." He grins.

"You have a plan?"

"Of course, I have a plan. I'll always have your back."

I hope so. Because if I irrevocably fucked things up with Aurora and lose her, I'll be the one living in this tiny house instead of Mercy's uncle Mercury.

Oh, who am I kidding? I'll fuck things up plenty. I should probably build a tiny home of my own.

But first, I need to win Aurora back. I can't lose her. I can't live without her.

Chapter 30

Tease – an action Aurora will never admit to enjoying no matter how much she secretly does

AURORA

I wake when arms wrap around me and lift me from my bed. I slap at them. "Need sleep."

"Shush, baby. Go back to sleep."

"Jett?" What is he doing here?

He kisses my forehead. "I'm here. Go back to sleep."

"You're the one who woke me," I grumble.

He lays me down and I force my eyes open. I scowl when I realize where I am. "What am I doing in your bedroom?"

"I told you. This is where you belong from now on. No more sleeping apart."

"I thought the agreement was null and void when you ran away this morning."

"Do you want to sleep, or do you want to talk?" he asks as he climbs into bed with me.

"What are you doing?"

"What does it look like? I'm taking a nap with you."

"You? Mr. Rockstar who spends all of his free time bungee jumping over rivers and hiking up volcanos wants to take a nap?"

He wraps his arm around my middle and snuggles into my back. "Yep."

"But—"

He places a finger over my mouth. "Shush, baby. Get some sleep. We can talk later but first you need your rest."

I debate arguing with him but then a yawn hits me. I do need sleep. Growing a baby is exhausting.

"Fine," I mutter. I'll sleep in his comfortable bed because I'm exhausted and I'm already here. But I'm not snuggling with him. I have some pride.

When I awake sometime later, the room is dark. Shit. How long did I sleep? I still have several items on my to-do list to finish. I better get back to work. I try to roll out of bed but an arm stops me.

"Where are you rushing off to?" Jett asks.

I tug on his arm. "I need to work."

"It's dinner time. The workday is over."

"Crap. Mike is going to kill me."

"Mike isn't going to kill you. You have the week off. You shouldn't be working this much."

I groan. Not this again. "I'm not arguing with you about this."

"Good. Because I have a trip planned for us."

"A trip planned for us? What makes you think I want to go anywhere with you?"

"Because you love me."

I growl. "And you made it perfectly clear how you feel about me when you fled the house this morning without responding."

He sighs before reaching over and flipping on the lamp on the nightstand. "I was hoping you'd accept my grand gesture without us having to rehash what happened."

I snort. "Have you met me?"

"I'm sorry."

"Sorry for what?"

"You're not going to make this easy for me, are you?"

"I repeat. Have you met me?"

He chuckles. "Yes, I have. You're my feisty girl."

"Wrong. I'm not *your* anything."

How dare he? How dare he claim I'm still his? Has he lost his mind? I start to climb out of bed, but he stops me again. My belly flips at how gently he places a hand around my waist to avoid injuring the baby.

No. Damn it. No! No belly flips. This is the man who didn't simply ignore me when I said I love you to him. He ran out of the house and didn't return until I was sleeping.

"Please let me explain."

A part of me I'm not proud of warms at the pleading in his voice.

"Explain how you're a coward?"

"Yes."

I motion to him. "Please proceed."

"No one's ever told me they love me before."

I rear back. This can't be true. I know he didn't grow up with parents or a family of any sort but his bandmates are his family. They love him. Surely, they've told him so.

"No one?"

He shakes his head.

"Gibson never said 'I love you, bro' to you?"

Another shake of his head.

"Cash? Dylan? Fender?"

He cocks an eyebrow. "Can you imagine Fender saying I love you?"

My nose wrinkles. "Not really. I figured the grumpy bass player would never fall in love. I have a folder prepared with the best places for rockstars to retire when they're too old to take care of themselves."

He chuckles. "Of course, you do."

"Don't laugh. Your name is on the folder, too."

He sighs. "I deserved that."

He deserves a hell of a lot worse but how can I kick him when he's down? No one's told him they love him before? He's thirty-one years old. No wonder he has issues with relationships.

Okay, fine. I'll put on my big girl panties and handle this the way an adult should.

"So, when I said I love you what happened? You panicked?"

He tucks a strand of hair behind my ear. Damn. How can I not love him when he looks at me with tenderness in those piercing blue eyes? I'm such a goner for this man.

"Not at first. First, excitement filled me at the idea of someone loving me. I couldn't believe it. This wonderful woman who's having my baby loves me. It was a dream come true."

"And then the panic came?"

He smiles at me. "You know me so well."

"I thought I did," I mutter. Stupid me. I thought he'd respond to my declaration. Not with words of love. But with some sign of happiness. I didn't think he'd run out of the house at the first opportunity.

He grasps my hands and pulls me near until I'm forced to straddle him. "You do know me." I open my mouth to respond but he continues. "You know me better than anyone. The only other person who knows about Cindy is Gibson. And I didn't tell him. He found out because I had a nightmare and was calling out her name."

The thought of him having nightmares about the death of the little girl has my heart breaking.

I place my hands on his cheeks. "Cindy's death is not your fault."

"If I agree, will you forgive me for running away from you?"

"I want you to agree because you believe it. Here." I tap his heart.

He captures my hand and lays it against his heart. "I'm working on it."

"Close enough. I forgive you."

His eyes light up. "You do?"

I shrug. "What can I say? I'm an idiot when it comes to you."

He palms my neck to bring me near before his mouth slams down on mine. I moan and he thrusts his tongue into my mouth. His taste is wild, the same way he is. I thread my fingers through his hair to keep him close.

I feel him harden and lengthen beneath me. I shuffle forward until his hardness hits my core where I need it.

"Yes," I hiss.

This is what I need. This is all I need.

Jett wrenches his lips from mine and lifts me before setting me next to him.

"What are you doing?" I gasp out.

"We have an appointment. I don't want to miss it."

"But." I motion toward his crotch.

"We'll handle this later."

"What appointment could be more important than this?"

He rolls off the bed. Once he's standing, he offers me his hand. "I wasn't going to tell you but I guess I have to."

"You're not telling me anything. You're teasing me."

He helps me off the bed and kisses my forehead. "You enjoy it when I tease you."

I stick my bottom lip out in a pout. "Not when my panties are damp and you're not removing them from my body."

His eyes close as he groans. "Don't make this hard."

"I'm pretty sure you're already hard."

He chuckles. "Now, who's the tease?"

I shrug. "If it gets me what I want."

"I thought you wanted some maternity clothes."

My brow wrinkles. "Maternity clothes?"

He cups my stomach. "For when little Crimson grows."

"Crimson?"

"Another kickass rockstar name."

I groan. "The next thing I know you'll want to have another baby and name her Clover."

He grins. "Not a bad idea."

I lift my eyebrows. "You're not running away to base jump in the Grand Canyon at the idea of having another baby?"

He shrugs. "I haven't felt much like base jumping lately."

I slap my palm on his forehead. "Are you feeling well? Do I need to make an appointment with the doctor?"

"Maybe having a family with you is enough adventure and I don't need anything more."

My heart melts. Those words are practically an I love you in Jett's world. But I know better than to point out the observation. The rockstar drummer is skittish. Witness the running away this morning.

"What's this about an appointment and maternity clothes?"

His eyes sparkle. "I knew you wanted some maternity clothes."

I'm not excited about buying clothes because I'm getting as big as a house, but I'll do pretty much anything to make Jett happy.

"Go on." He releases me and pushes me toward the bathroom. "Get ready to go. Our appointment is in an hour."

I refuse to budge. "We don't need an appointment to buy clothes."

"We do if we want privacy."

Ah, now I understand. "You're worried about being recognized."

He stalks toward me. "I don't give a shit about getting recognized. But my time with you and Elton is precious. I don't want anyone interrupting it."

I nearly swoon at his words. My knees go weak and I find it hard to catch my breath. But there's a reason Jett calls me his feisty girl.

"We are not naming our baby Elton."

"You don't like it? It's a good name."

"For a boy."

"Don't be judgmental."

"I'm vetoing the name. End of discussion."

"Fine. Elvis it is."

I growl. "You're going to drive me crazy before Little Bean is born."

"Then, we'll be even since you drive me crazy all the time, feisty girl."

I do the mature thing. I stick out my tongue before whirling around to march toward the bathroom.

"Be ready to leave in fifteen minutes," Jett hollers after me.

"Whatever," I mumble.

Once I'm behind a closed door, I slump against it and place a hand over my racing heart. I was pissed as hell at Jett for walking out on me this morning. But now I'm ready to be all in with him again.

This rockstar is not going to be easy to catch. But catch him, I will.

Or I'll break my heart.
It's a toss-up at this point.

Chapter 31

Belting – can be stopped by an inappropriate chocolate stain

AURORA

Jett snatches the phone from me. "You're done."

I hold out my hand. "Give it back to me. I was in the middle of an email. A very important email."

He shoves the phone into his pocket. "It's New Year's Eve. It can wait. You're not working anymore."

I roll my eyes. "It's six o'clock in the evening. It's not 'New Year's Eve' for hours."

"We're having dinner with the band at the brewery."

This is news to me. No one told me about a get together. Although, I haven't checked my private messages all day.

"At six?"

"Dylan wants Virginia to be home at a reasonable time."

Dylan the overprotector strikes again. "And you?" I raise my eyebrows. "You didn't jump on the bandwagon to make sure I wasn't out late partying on New Year's Eve."

Jett palms my neck. "You can party all you want, baby. But it'll be in our bed."

Heat rushes through my body and my panties dampen. "We can skip dinner."

"Tempting but no."

"Why not?" I pout.

He kisses my nose. "You've been cooped up in this house for days. If I don't force you outside, your ass will be glued to your chair. You need to get out."

"Have you seen outside? There's snow and it's cold."

I'm not exaggerating. The weather here is not anything like San Diego where the last snowfall happened more than a decade before my birth.

"Good thing someone has some warm clothes to wear."

Because our 'little trip' to pick up 'some' maternity clothes ended up with Jett buying me the entire store. I wish I was kidding. My bedroom, which I'm no longer allowed to sleep in, has become a closet for all my clothes.

"What about Bowie? We can't leave her alone."

"Nice try. She's staying with Fender and Leia's dog."

"Fine. I'll go change."

Jett helps me to stand and leads me to the stairs.

"I can climb the stairs on my own."

"I know. I'm being a gentleman is all."

I snort. "Jett Peterson is no gentleman."

"People can change."

I hope so since I'm banking on Jett changing into the type of man who can fall in love with a woman. This woman in particular. Otherwise, my heart is toast.

Thirty minutes later I've changed into a sweater dress and am ready to go. When I walk down the stairs, Jett whistles.

"Damn, baby. You clean up good."

I curtsey. "Thank you. You don't look so bad yourself."

Jett's wearing a pair of dark jeans and a button-down shirt. The sleeves are rolled up to reveal the tattoos on his forearms. There's something about a well-dressed man showing off hints of tattoos that revs my engine. Although, if I'm being honest, everything about this man revs my engines.

He kisses my cheek before tucking my hand into his elbow and opening the door. "Your chariot awaits."

I frown at the golf cart. "It's a five-minute walk. Why are we using the golf cart?"

"It's slippery. I don't want you to fall."

"You might as well give in," Leia hollers from next door where she's climbing into Fender's Hummer with her daughter Isla. "We'll never make our reservation otherwise."

"Fine. Whatever."

Jett leads me to the golf cart and off we go. We drive behind Fender and arrive at *Naked Falls Brewing* in less than five minutes where we park next to Cash's car.

Dylan climbs out of the car and helps Virginia out. I gasp when I see her.

"Don't start," Virginia groans. "I know I'm as big as a house."

Dylan growls. "You're not fat. You're growing our baby."

"I had to fall in love with a giant."

Leia joins us. "It'll all be worth it once the baby's here."

"Let's go inside before we freeze to death out here," Dylan says.

Virginia rolls her eyes. "It's not freezing out here but what do I know? I'm merely a vessel for this baby until it's born."

Dylan takes her arm and leads her to the door.

I glare up at Jett. He holds up his hands. "What did I do?"

"If you get as protective as Dylan, I'm killing you in your sleep."

"I wouldn't dare," he murmurs before kissing my forehead.

"I'd hide the kitchen knives anyway," Cash says.

Indigo slaps his stomach. "Do not encourage Jett."

Fender grunts and Leia rolls her eyes. "We need to go inside before Isla freezes to death."

"I'm not cold, Dad." Isla stomps to the door.

We gather inside in front of the hostess station. Miller and Elder, the owners of the brewery, are greeting guests this evening. When they spot us, Elder immediately steps forward and motions toward the stairs.

"Come on." He herds us up the stairs.

"What's going on?" I ask him once we're on the upper floor.

"The tourists are out in droves tonight. I didn't want anyone to catch sight of you."

Cash claps him on the back. "Thanks, bro. We appreciate it."

Cash isn't kidding with the 'bro' thing. They are actually brothers. Half-brothers to be accurate. It's a long story but basically, Cash found his birth father and the discovery led him to find six half-brothers. All of whom live in Winter Falls.

"I'll keep the out-of-towners downstairs, but you'll have to share this area with locals." Elder leans close. "And by locals, I mean the gossip gals." He nods to a table where the five elderly women are seated with two men who appear to be watching something on a phone.

We gather at a large table in the corner. Elder slaps some menus on the table before departing.

"Five, four, three," Indigo counts down.

"What are you counting down for?"

She points to the other side of the room where the gossip gals are making their way toward us. "They're here."

"Happy New Year," the gossip gals greet in unison when they arrive. They're wearing bright pink t-shirts with the words *Drop it like it's hot* printed on them above a picture of a disco ball.

"Happy New Year," Cash greets. He's the spokesperson for the band. There's a reason the band is named *Cash & the Sinners* after all.

Sage addresses Virginia. "Is there any chance we could measure your belly?"

Virginia's eyes widen as she slowly inches away from her. "Um…"

Dylan growls at the women while placing a protective arm around his pregnant fiancé. "You are not betting on the size of my woman's belly."

Geez. Jett wasn't kidding when he said these women will bet on anything. Baby names I get. The size of a pregnant woman's belly? No.

"Okay." Sage switches her attention to me. "What about you?"

I place a hand over Little Bean. "In your dreams."

"Come on, neighbor," Feather coaxes. "I'll make it worth your while."

I'll play. "How?" I ask.

"How what?"

"How will you make it worth my while? Are you going to drive to the next town to buy me pickles in the middle of the night? Or maybe answer the phone for me? How about doing my laundry for the next year?"

Petal giggles. "Feather doesn't do her own laundry."

Feather's lips purse. "I do too."

Cayenne leans close to the table. "Which is why she showed up to our coffee klatsch with a big ole chocolate stain on her pants," she whisper shouts.

"I can't help it if I sat on a piece of chocolate right before I left the house."

"Ah ha. Chocolate. Sure," Clove says.

Feather crosses her arms over her chest. "I did not lose control of my bowel movements." She glances around at her friends who are all avoiding her gaze. "I own an ice cream shop. I was experimenting with different types of chocolate in the ice cream."

"And the chocolate just happened to end up right where—"

Feather slashes her hand in the air to cut Sage off. "Enough. Since I'm not appreciated here, I'm leaving."

She storms off and the gossip gals rush after her.

The second they're out of view, I burst into laughter. "This town is a hoot."

Virginia laughs with me. "Did they honestly think Mr. Overprotective would allow them to measure my belly?"

I point to Jett. "This one isn't much better."

Virginia groans. "Oh no. I better go to the restroom before this little one makes me pee my pants."

"I'll go with you."

Jett and Dylan stand. I wag a finger at them. "No. You're not going with us. We're perfectly safe on our own. Besides, you'll get recognized downstairs and then I'll end up having to work to spin the whole PR thing."

They don't appear happy, but they sit back down. I grasp Virginia's hand and we hurry away before they change their minds.

"I think I really did pee my pants laughing," I admit once we're at the restrooms.

I enter the stall and work my leggings down my legs. I should have worn pants. It would have been quicker than trying to peel these leggings off.

I finally manage to sit down to pee. Phew. Made it. But when I finish and stand, I notice the toilet bowl water is red. I check the toilet paper. Blood. It's blood.

Panic slams into me with such force I have to grab hold of the toilet roll holder to stop myself from sliding to the floor.

"Virginia!" I shout.

She groans. "I'm hurrying as fast as I can."

"Hurry faster. I'm in trouble."

"What's wrong?"

"I think I'm losing the baby."

Oh god, no. I can't lose Little Bean. I love her already. She's my world.

Chapter 32

Fear – an emotion Jett thought he'd experienced before. He was wrong.

JETT

Virginia runs toward us and slams into the table. Dylan takes her hand. "Be careful, my love. You don't want to hurt the baby."

She wrests out of his hold. "Not me. Aurora. Baby," she gasps out.

My heart stops beating. "What's wrong with Aurora and the baby?"

"She's losing her."

I jump to my feet and shove everyone out of the way before running down the stairs to the restrooms. Cash yells at his brothers behind me but I ignore whatever commotion is happening. I have to get to Aurora.

I crash through the ladies' room door. "Aurora!" I bellow.

"In here." Her voice is small and wobbly. My fear ratches up another notch.

I open the stall door to find her sitting on the toilet crying. I drop to my knees and grasp her hands. "What happened? What's wrong?"

"It's Little Bean. I think I'm losing her," she wails.

"Not if I can help it." I pick her up and carry her into the hallway.

Cash is waiting for me. "This way."

I follow him out the back door where Fender is waiting for us with his car. Cash opens the rear door, and I climb in with Aurora in my arms.

"Drive," I order Fender. "Drive."

"Who's your doctor?" Leia asks from the front seat.

"Dr. Edwards."

"I'll call her and have her meet us at the hospital."

Once she finishes the call, she crawls between the seats to the back. Fender growls at her.

"Shut it, grumpy pants. We've got bigger issues than my not wearing a seatbelt."

"Put your seatbelt on now," he grumbles.

She buckles herself in before grasping Aurora's hand. "It's okay. You're going to be okay."

"Little Bean," Aurora whispers.

Leia smiles at her. "Little Bean will be okay, too. Both of you will be fine."

I want to believe her, but… "You can't know that."

"Be nice," Fender orders.

Leia continues to utter assurances to Aurora for the entire drive while my words are caught in my throat. I don't know what to say. I don't know how to reassure her. I don't know how to make this better.

My fear intensifies until I struggle to breathe. I've never been this afraid before. Not even when I graduated high school at seventeen and was kicked out of the foster home I was staying in with no job or place to go.

"We're here." Fender screeches to a halt in front of the emergency room.

I open the door but I can't climb out with Aurora in my arms. But I can't let her go either.

Fender stands at the door. "I've got her."

"Precious cargo," I remind him.

"The most precious," he says as he takes Aurora from my arms. I jump out of the car and he immediately places her back in my arms.

The doors open and Leia leads two nurses with a gurney outside. "She's pregnant and bleeding. Her doctor is on the way," she instructs as I lay Aurora down.

Aurora clutches my hand as they roll her into the hospital. "Don't leave me."

"Never, baby. Never."

I keep hold of her hand as we enter a room. The medical staff buzzes around us. Dr. Edwards arrives a moment later.

"I need the father out of here," she orders one of the nurses without addressing me. The nurse pulls me away from Aurora.

"No. Don't leave me," Aurora begs as she reaches for me.

"Can't I stay?"

Dr. Edwards glances my way. "I need to concentrate on my patients. I can't have you distracting me."

"I'll be quiet."

She nods to the nurse to take me away.

"It's better this way," the nurse says as she pushes me out of the room.

Fender and Leia are waiting for me in the hallway.

"You shouldn't be back here," another nurse complains as she rushes past us.

"Come on." Leia grasps my elbow and leads me to the waiting room where the rest of my bandmates and their partners are waiting for us.

"Any news?" Indigo asks.

Leia shakes her head. "The doctor just arrived."

I pace the floor. "How long will it take?"

Gibson steps in front of me. "What do you need?"

"Need?"

"We can go for a run or have a sparring match, or you can hit your drums and pretend to make music."

"I don't need any of that shit. I need Aurora and my baby girl to be okay. I need them. I can't live without them."

Mercy wraps her arms around me and sways me from side to side. "Hold on, Jett. Hold on. They're doing everything they can. You just hold on."

Indigo, Virginia, and Leia join in and I find myself being hugged by four women. But not by the one woman I need.

"Jett Peterson," a man announces and I untangle myself to rush to him.

"I'm Jett. What's going on? Is Aurora okay? What about the baby?"

He motions toward the hallway. "The doctor's ready to speak to you."

I hurry to the room and burst through the door. Aurora is laying on the bed with a machine attached to her belly. I come to a halt when I hear the whoosh-whoosh of the monitor.

"Is that our baby?"

Aurora holds out her hand and I grasp hold of it.

"It is." She smiles at me. "Little Bean is fine."

"You're certain?"

She nods toward Dr. Edwards. "The doctor is."

I feel as if I can breathe for the first time in days. "What happened? How can we prevent this from happening again? What can we do?"

Dr. Edwards smiles. "Slow down, Daddy. Vaginal bleeding is perfectly normal during pregnancy. Ms. Sharpe's bleeding was a bit heavier, but nothing to worry about. You can hear the baby's heartbeat. She's doing fine. As is Mom."

"But why did this happen? How do we prevent it?"

I don't think I can handle another mad dash to the emergency room. Maybe we should move to a town with a hospital. And I need to buy a car no matter what. I can't always rely on my bandmates.

"Make sure Mom gets as much rest as possible. Stress may be a factor."

"Stress? As in working too much?"

"It's possible."

The doctor's beeper goes off before I can ask her any further questions. "You're free to go home. The nurse will be in with your discharge papers soon."

"You should quit working," I tell Aurora once the doctor's gone.

Her brow wrinkles. "Quit working?"

"Yes." I nod. "The doctor said working isn't good for you."

"No, she didn't. She said stress *might* be a factor and working too much is a *possible* indicator."

"I knew you were working too hard. I've been telling you the entire pregnancy to slow down. And see what happened? You nearly lost the baby."

Aurora wrenches her hand from mine. "I didn't nearly lose Little Bean. I overreacted at a bit of bleeding. Dr. Edwards was being nice while you were here but before you arrived, she gave me a lecture about pregnancy and overreacting."

"I can't chance this happening again. You're quitting."

"Excuse me?"

"It's fine. I have enough money for the both of us. Once the baby is a bit older, you can go back to work."

"I can?"

I rub my hands together as I warm to the subject. "This is an excellent plan. I travel a lot when the band's touring. If you don't work, we can make sure there's always someone at home with the baby."

"Someone, being me?"

"Yes. It's easier this way."

"Easier this way?"

"Exactly. I'm glad you understand."

She points to the door. "Get out."

"You want to see your girls? They're all waiting for you."

"Yes, I want to see Indigo, Virginia, Leia, and Mercy. But more importantly, I want you to get the hell away from me."

I rear back. "Get the hell away from you? What's wrong?"

Her eyes widen. "What's wrong? You seriously have to ask me?"

"Yes."

"First, you accused me of working too hard which caused me to nearly lose the baby. Then, you basically ordered me to quit my job and become a stay-at-home mother because my job isn't as important as yours is."

"I thought we agreed you'd quit your job."

She points to the door. "Get out. I can't look at you right now."

"You begged me not to leave you before."

"I'm not discussing this. Get. Out." She reaches for the button to call the nurse.

I hold up my hands. "Fine. I'm leaving. But this discussion is not over."

"Wrong. This discussion is not only over, it's never happening again."

"Don't you want what's best for the baby?"

She reaches behind her and grabs her pillow. "Get out," she screeches as she throws the pillow. "Get out before the next thing I throw at you can hurt your big idiotic skull."

I rush out of the room before she follows through with her threat.

"What's wrong?" Gibson asks from where he's standing in the hallway waiting for me.

I shrug. "I don't know. I thought we were discussing the baby and raising our child but Aurora lost it."

He throws an arm around my shoulders and leads me away. "Let's discuss this back home."

I plant my feet and refuse to move. "But Aurora? How is she getting home?"

"We got her," Leia says as she walks past with Indigo, Virginia, and Mercy on her heels.

"I really don't know what I did wrong," I say as I allow Gibson to herd me away.

"I know." He slaps my back. "We'll figure this out."

Chapter 33

Idiot – the nicest word Aurora can think of to describe Jett

AURORA

"Jett is getting a ride home with Cash," Leia explains as she switches on the engine of Fender's Hummer.

"I really don't care," I mumble as I fasten my seatbelt.

As soon as I kicked Jett out of the room, Leia, Mercy, Virginia, and Indigo invaded. They helped me get dressed and ushered me to the car without any questions asked.

I have a feeling my time is limited, though. Indigo is practically bouncing in her seat. The questions will burst from her any second now.

"How are you feeling?" Leia asks as she begins the drive back to Winter Falls.

"Like a fool."

She pats my arm. "There's no need. Every pregnant woman has overreacted at some point. I was convinced I was in labor with Isla a month early. When I arrived at the hospital, they barely looked at me before announcing I wasn't in labor and ordering me home."

"I'll probably do that three times. At least," Virginia pipes in from the backseat.

"Thank you for the reassurances but I'm not feeling like a fool because I thought I was losing the baby."

Indigo peeks her head between the seats. "Why do you feel like a fool then?"

"I walked right into that, didn't I?"

"You did," Mercy says. "But if you don't want to answer any questions, let me know. I can hogtie Indigo to the backseat."

Indigo snorts. "I'd like to see you try. You don't have anything to hogtie me with."

Mercy chuckles. "The seatbelt will work just fine."

"Why are you being mean to me?" Indigo whines.

"Maybe because you're being super nosy," Virginia answers.

"I prefer the word inquisitive."

"Snoop," Virginia accuses.

"Meddlesome," Mercy corrects.

"Intrusive."

"Busybody."

Leia sighs. "They could continue for hours."

"Did they bring a dictionary with them?" I ask.

Mercy shakes her phone at me. "No need for a dictionary when I have this."

My phone beeps in my pocket but I ignore it. There are only two people who could be messaging on New Year's Eve – Jett and Mike. And I'm not talking to either one of them.

Leia nods toward my purse. "Don't you need to answer your phone?"

"Nope, I'm good."

"What if it's Jett?" Indigo asks.

Virginia smacks her. "Stop it. Aurora will tell us what happened when she's ready."

"Oh, come on. Don't lie and say you're not curious."

"I can be curious and keep my mouth shut. You should try it sometime," Virginia tells Indigo.

"Sounds boring."

I sigh. "How long is the drive home?"

Home? Shit. I can't go home. I'll probably stab Jett in the heart with a rusty knife if I see him now. Then he can experience how it feels to have your heart torn out of your body. Asshole.

"I hate to say this but you need to calm down," Leia says.

"I'm calm," I grit out.

"Which is why your hands are balled into fists and your jaw is clenched. I'm afraid a vein is going to pop in your forehead any second now. Should I turn around? Go back to the hospital?"

I glare at her. "Ha. Ha. You're funny."

She grins. "Thank you."

"I was being sarcastic."

She shrugs. "I don't care. I'll accept any compliment spoken in actual words to come my way."

"How do you put up with Fender and his propensity for grunting instead of speaking?"

Her smile is wicked. "Trust me. He makes it worth my while."

Virginia groans from the backseat. "No. No sex stories. I can't handle it."

"If anyone can complain about sex stories, it's me," I claim. "I'm the one who's known your men for over a decade. They were barely out of the pimple stage when I met them."

"Trust me. Pimples didn't stop Cash from being sexy." Indigo sighs.

"No! No! No!" Virginia shouts. "No sex stories."

"What's your problem?" Mercy asks. "Dylan not giving you the Big D lately?"

"Nope. All I get is soft lovemaking," Virginia complains. "He's afraid he'll hurt the baby if the sex is too wild."

"I'm speechless," Indigo says. "You would have given anything to have Dylan any way you could have him in high school and now you're complaining."

"For someone who's speechless, she sure has a lot to say," Mercy mutters.

We pass the sign for Winter Falls and my body tenses. Where am I going to go? What am I going to do?

"All right, Aurora," Leia begins. "We've given you thirty minutes to come to terms with whatever happened with Jett. It's time to spill the beans."

I should have known these ladies were up to no good when they didn't push me for answers sooner.

I cross my arms over my chest. "I don't want to."

"I guess I'll drop you off at Jett's house then."

My stomach dips and my jaw clenches as anger fights with heartbreak for supremacy. "No. I don't want to go there."

Virginia squeezes my shoulder. "Men do stupid stuff when they're worried about the person they love."

I snort. "Jett doesn't love me."

I thought he was on his way to loving me. I thought he cared about me. I was wrong. He doesn't care about me. He cares about this baby. But not me.

"What did he say?" Indigo pushes.

"In a nutshell, he blamed me for almost losing the baby because I work too hard. His solution was for me to quit my job since my work isn't important. I can stay home with the baby while he goes on tour all over the world."

Leia pulls to the side of the road to face me. "Does he not know today was a false alarm?"

"He wouldn't listen to me. He completely ignored me. Me! The woman in the hospital bed who thought she was losing her baby."

Tears escape my eyes and roll down my cheeks but I dash them away. I'm not having a breakdown. I refuse for Jett to find out how much he hurt me. As much as I love these women, they have big mouths and will blab everything I say to their partners who will blab to Jett. No one can keep a secret in this family.

Leia grasps my hand. "I'm sorry."

Mercy squeezes my shoulder. "I'm not excusing what Jett said. He was clearly an asshole. But maybe he was scared. Considering his past…"

I blow out a breath. "I know all about his past."

And, I hate to admit it, but she could be correct. Jett might have overreacted due to his past. But I can't have him become this gigantic asshole whenever he gets scared. We're having a child. There are going to be more scary times. Many, many more.

"I don't know. I love Jett, but I don't know if I can be with a man who runs every time he gets scared."

"Don't make any decisions tonight," Mercy suggests.

"Yeah." Leia nods. "Get some rest and recover from your scare."

"Tomorrow, your mind will be much clearer." Virginia sighs. "Or as clear as the mind of a pregnant lady can be. Pregnancy brain fog is real."

"Okay," I agree. "But I don't want to go home. Jett's house, I mean."

"You can stay with me," the four of them practically say in unison.

"Duh. She's staying with me," Indigo proclaims.

"Explain," Virginia orders.

"She can't stay with Leia because she's next door to Jett. Mercy's out because Gibson is Jett's best friend. And there's no way Dylan can handle two pregnant women in his house at the same time. My house."

"She can stay in the tiny home Gibson built for my uncle," Mercy says. "Uncle Mercury isn't staying there yet and there are panic buttons everywhere in the house."

"She's not staying alone tonight," Indigo says.

"Um, hello. She is right here." I point to myself. "And I can make decisions for myself."

"Well," Indigo prods. "Where do you want to go?"

I consider my options. I hate to admit it, but Indigo is right. Her house is the best option.

"I'll stay with you." She whoops and I wag a finger at her. "But I won't hesitate to shave your head in the middle of the night if you ask me any more questions."

She smirks. "You'd have to get past Cash first."

"Good thing I have a prescription for sleeping pills."

She glares. "You're mean."

I shrug. "You say mean. I say smart."

"I guess it's settled then." Leia switches on the vehicle and pulls back onto the road. "But for future reference, Fender would never let Jett into the house if you didn't want to see him."

I raise my eyebrows. "And Isla? Jett is her best friend."

She frowns. "Whatever."

"Gibson is Isla's best friend," Mercy claims.

Leia and Mercy begin to argue about who is her daughter's best friend. I ignore them.

The only thing I care about now is Little Bean. I love Jett more than life but Little Bean is my life. I can't allow Jett in her life if he's going to run away from her. I know how it feels to be abandoned by your parents. I won't let Jett abandon our child.

Chapter 34

Grovel – synonym for grand gesture time

JETT

My bandmates are quiet as we drive back to Winter Falls. I expect them to push me, ask me what happened, and judge me. But they don't.

When Cash parks in front of my house, I hop out. I turn to wave goodbye to them but everyone follows me.

"I don't need any company."

Gibson snorts. "You're getting company whether you want it or not."

Shit. I should have known the quiet was too good to be true.

"This is my house. You can't barge in without my permission."

He dangles a key in front of me. "My name is still on the lease."

Damnit.

"I don't know how Mercy puts up with you," I mutter as I open the door and walk inside with my bandmates on my heels.

I aim for the stairs and my bedroom but Fender blocks me. He crosses his arms over his chest and glares at me.

"It isn't fun when you're the one in trouble, is it?" Gibson mocks.

"I didn't get drunk and say nasty shit to the woman I love."

I'm probably an asshole for bringing up his drinking days when he's working his best on staying sober, but I don't want to have this conversation. I want everyone to leave so I can be alone.

He frowns. "No. You said nasty shit to the woman you love without the drunk part."

I narrow my eyes on him. "Were you eavesdropping on me and Aurora?"

"No need to eavesdrop when she was yelling at you to get out."

"I don't know why she was pissed."

"Seriously? You have no clue?" Dylan shakes his head. "I wouldn't let my woman get mad at me in the hospital."

I rear back. "Virginia is mad at you all the time. You're overprotective and driving her nuts."

"And she puts up with me because she loves me."

"Aurora loves me."

Dylan grins. "And do you love her?"

I rub a hand over my heart where it hurts from Aurora kicking me out of the hospital room. All I wanted was to make sure our baby is safe. But she got mad and threw a pillow at me.

"What did you say to her?" Gibson asks.

I collapse on the sofa as I think back to the hospital room. There was no relief when the doctor said the baby was fine. Terror had me in its tight grip.

"Dr. Edwards said the baby could be in danger from how much Aurora works."

"Beep!" Gibson shouts. "Try again."

"You were eavesdropping." I lunge at him but Dylan blocks me.

"No fighting," he orders.

I point to Gibson. "He offered to fight me earlier."

Gibson peers around Dylan's shoulder. "I offered to spar with you to stop you from spiraling into despair."

I fist my hands. "Spar? Fight? Same thing."

Dylan shoves me onto the sofa. "No, it's not. Stop being an asshole."

"Are you kidding me? I'm the asshole?" I pound my fist on my chest. "I wasn't the one who listened in at the door of a hospital room where I didn't belong."

Gibson crosses his arms over his chest and glares down at me. "And you weren't the one who listened in at the window when Mercy and I had our fight."

I shrug. "You were drunk. I knew you wouldn't remember what an idiot you were being."

"You're not drunk. What's your excuse for being an idiot?"

I fly at him but this time Fender steps in my way. "Sit down." I try to go around him but he picks me up by the back of my shirt and dumps me on the sofa. "I said sit down."

"Being half a foot taller than me does not give you permission to throw me around."

"Stop being an asshole and I'll stop throwing you around."

"I didn't throw you around when you were an idiot about Leia."

He grins. "Because you can't."

Cash pushes his way in front of Fender. "As much fun as it is to watch Fender use actual words instead of grunting, this isn't helping."

"Helping what?"

He frowns at me. "Helping you get Aurora back."

"She didn't break up with me. She's mad but she'll get over it. She'll realize I'm right."

My bandmates erupt into laughter.

"He's hilarious."

"Idiotically hilarious."

"He thinks he's right."

"Such an idiot."

"Hey!" I shout. "Stop talking about me as if I'm not here."

"Dude," Dylan starts but he doesn't continue.

I throw my hands in the air. "What?"

Gibson wipes tears of laughter from his eyes. "You think you're right. You told Aurora it was her fault she almost lost the baby. Then, you ordered her to quit her job. Told her that her job isn't as important as yours. And, to top it all off, you told her she could go back to work when the baby is older."

Dylan scratches his beard. "I don't know. Maybe Jett is a lost cause."

"Hold on. I didn't say any of those things."

Gibson grunts. "I was listening at the door and you definitely said all of those things."

"I…" I trail off as my mind rewinds to the scene in the hospital room. Did I say those things? Did I blame Aurora for nearly losing our baby? I wouldn't. I said she's been working too hard. And then I said she nearly lost the baby.

"I didn't mean it was Aurora's fault."

Gibson squeezes my shoulder. "I know you didn't, but she doesn't."

"She was lying in a hospital bed terrified about her baby. The last thing she needed was for you to start spouting bullshit about her job," Dylan says.

Cash shakes his head. "Aurora loves her job. She's the only thing keeping the band on track most of the time. Her quitting won't solve anyone's problems."

"But she works so damn hard. She gets calls from Mike all day and night. Not to mention the gazillion emails she has to answer. I hate seeing her stressed. I hate how she doesn't have time to care for herself. I want her to be happy, to have fun."

"Because you love her," Gibson pushes.

I open my mouth to yell at him. I'm more than fucking done with him telling me I love her. But there's no more denying it. I do love Aurora. She's my world. She's my everything.

Which is why I freaked out when she was lying in the hospital bed. All I could see was my world crashing down around me. My world ending when Aurora and Little Bean were no longer in it. I wouldn't want to walk this earth without them.

They're my family. My everything.

"Yeah, I love her and our little girl."

Fender groans. "A girl? You're fucked if she resembles Aurora."

"I know, man. I know."

"But first he needs to figure out how to get Aurora to forgive him," Dylan points out.

"Easy," Gibson says.

My brow wrinkles. "Easy?" Nothing about this situation is easy. "How is it easy?"

"You said it yourself. She works too hard."

"And she nearly decapitated me for it."

He grins. "But what if she didn't have to answer calls and emails from Mike? What if she was the boss?"

"I already tried to convince her to start her own management company. She wasn't interested."

"Because she's afraid we're committing career suicide by firing Mike," Cash says.

"I don't give a shit about Mike," Gibson grumbles.

Dylan nods. "None of us do. And we don't have anything to prove to anyone anymore. We've made our fortunes. As long as we can continue to make music and play in front of our fans, I don't care what number our song is at in the charts."

"Me either," Cash agrees.

The rest of my bandmates nod in agreement. Our days of chasing number one are apparently behind us.

"There are more important things in life than platinum records," Gibson says.

"And Leia said she'd love to work with Aurora and help her set up a company," Fender adds.

"Are we in agreement?" Cash asks. "We're going to fire Mike?"

"Hold on." I hold up a hand. "What if Aurora doesn't agree?"

Gibson smirks. "This is why we're firing Mike before you tell Aurora."

Cash digs his phone out of his pocket. "I'll handle it now."

"You're going to fire our manager of over a decade on New Year's Eve?" I ask.

He shrugs. "It's as good a time as any."

Gibson chuckles. "And here I was worried about my first New Year's Eve sober."

"You okay?"

He waves away my concern. "I'm fine. You're still a dead man."

"What do you mean? Isn't firing Mike enough of a gesture?"

"Dude," is all he says.

"What do you suggest?"

He smirks. "I have a few ideas."

Good. Because I'm all out of ideas. My mind is too busy coming to the realization that I love Aurora.

I shouldn't be surprised. The woman has tempted me since the first time she flashed me her smile. I've dreamed about having her in my arms and in my bed for a decade.

I finally have her right where I want her. I'm not letting her go. Ever.

If I have to grovel to get her to forgive me, I will. Aurora is worth everything. I won't lose her.

Chapter 35

AURORA

I lay in the bed in the guest room at Indigo's house and fantasize about staying here forever. Indigo may be the nosiest person I know and she thinks she's a spy, but she won't let Jett into the house without my permission.

I can hide away from him here until I can stop imagining the various ways to harm him. I'd start with breaking all of his drumsticks and go from there.

My stomach growls to remind me I haven't eaten since lunch yesterday. I roll out of bed and creep downstairs toward the kitchen. I listen for voices, but I don't hear anyone. Maybe I won't have to talk to anyone this morning.

I enter the kitchen and Indigo smiles at me. "Good morning."

So much for not having to talk to anyone today. "Good morning."

"Someone's grumpy in the morning."

"I can't drink coffee and I don't know where my phone is."

"I have decaf and your phone was dead. I plugged it in."

I glance around the room. "Where is it?"

"Charging."

I sigh. I know Indigo well enough by now to know the truth. "You're not going to give it to me, are you?"

"Not yet."

Fine. I don't want to talk to anyone anyway. Mike can survive for a day without me. It is New Year's Day and my day off. Not that a day off means anything to him.

"Where's Cash?" I ask when Indigo sets a cup of coffee in front of me.

She glances away. "He didn't come home last night."

I groan. "Please tell me the guys didn't get into any trouble. I have no interest in dealing with drama today."

"No trouble," she says but she won't look me in the eyes.

"You're lying."

"I'm not lying."

"Ha!" I point at her hands when she cracks her knuckles. "You're totally lying."

"I'm going to kill Virginia for snitching to everyone about my tell."

I sip on my coffee as I contemplate whether to push her. The band is obviously up to something. The question is – are they up to no good? And, if so, how much work is it going to be for me?

Assuming Jett doesn't try to get me fired again. Asshole. How dare he say I have to quit working? All he does is bang on the drums. I grant *Cash & the Sinners* all of their wishes.

Concert? Got it. Press release? Got that, too. You name it. I got it.

The door bangs open and Virginia rushes inside. "They did it!"

"Who did what?" I ask.

Indigo pulls out a chair. "You better sit down before Dylan has a heart attack because you've been running."

"Did you tell her yet?" Mercy asks as she runs into the kitchen.

Leia is hot on her heels. "How did you get here faster than me?"

Mercy winks. "I drove."

"Everyone needs to calm down and tell me what's going on," I order.

Leia jumps up and down. "Can I tell her? Can I?"

Mercy shoves her. "I get to tell her. Gibson has priority over Fender."

I slam my palm down on the table. "Will someone tell me already before my blood pressure shoots through the roof and Jett accuses me of trying to kill our baby again?"

Virginia frowns. "He didn't accuse you of trying to kill the baby."

I raise my eyebrows. "Were you there? Did you hear what he said?"

She glances away. "No."

"Have all of you been awake all night conspiring against me? What's going on? Don't make me ask again. I can make your lives miserable. And I'll enjoy it, too."

"You don't control us," Indigo says.

Leia grins. "But she does control the band."

Virginia nods. "Quite literally."

I'm about done with their avoidance. I stand. "Fine. I'll go ask Dylan. He can't resist a pregnant woman."

"He's not home," Virginia sings.

"Neither is Gibson before you ask."

"Or Fender."

I stare at the ceiling and pray for patience. "What is the band up to? I need to spin the story in the press before the band is cancelled."

"The band isn't cancelled."

"If anything, they're heroes."

I swipe my coffee from the table. "I'm going back to bed. I'm obviously having a fever dream of some sort. Can lack of sleep cause fever dreams? Probably."

"Here." Leia shoves her phone into my hand.

I blow out a breath and set my coffee back on the table before reading the article she open on her phone.

Cash & the Sinners fire long-time manager.

My knees wobble and I grab a chair before I fall to the floor. Leia helps me to sit.

"It's not bad. I promise."

Not bad? She doesn't understand. "They just committed career suicide."

"They didn't." She shrugs. "But, even if they did, they don't care."

"It's true." Virginia nods in agreement. "The entire band agreed."

"They don't want to chase number one anymore," Indigo adds.

"But they need a manager if they want to continue to make music. Unless they're going indie. Are they going indie?"

"If our new manager suggests we go indie, then we'll go indie," Jett says as he comes to stand in front of me.

I glare at him. "What are you doing here?"

"Having a meeting with our new manager," Cash answers as he stands next to Jett. Dylan, Fender, and Gibson join him.

I shake my head. "No. No. No. I told you firing Mike is career suicide. I can't resurrect dead bands."

Jett nods to the phone. "Finish reading the story."

Gibson smirks. "Yeah, Mike isn't feeling very powerful today."

I quickly skim the article. *Cash & the Sinners* isn't being cancelled, but Mike is. Turns out he's been skimming cash from every band he manages except *Cash & the Sinners.* The bands are also accusing him of bullying and forcing them to sell rights to their music they didn't want to.

"Holy crap," I murmur when I finish. "I knew Mike was an asshole but this is a whole new level."

"Total asshole," Cash mutters.

"I promise he never stole any of your money. I keep a tight watch over the finances. I would never let anyone steal."

"We know, baby," Jett says.

As much as I want to deny it, my body warms and tingles at his use of the endearment. I'm a goner for this man. I place a hand over my stomach. But I have to say goodbye to him anyway.

"It's why we're hiring you to be our manager," he continues.

"And I'm your new office manager/assistant/girl Friday." Leia beams at me.

I groan. "I don't want this."

Jett kneels in front of me. "Think about it. You can control your own schedule. You don't have to be at the beck and call of Mike anymore."

"I thought you wanted me to quit working. My job isn't important, remember?"

His cheeks darken. "I was wrong." He grasps my hands. "Can you forgive me?"

I don't know if I can forgive him. He said some awful things to me. But worse than those awful things was how he left me alone. Again.

"You ran away again."

"I didn't run away. You pushed me away."

"Because you were being a complete and utter asshole."

"He is an asshole," Gibson mutters and Jett flips him off.

"I'm sorry," Jett says. "The terror of possibly losing the woman I love and the baby I love was choking me."

"But then you— The woman you love?"

"I love you, feisty girl. And I love Little Bean. I can't live without the two of you."

Warmth fills me up until I'm bursting with happiness. Jett loves me. The man I've been obsessed with for over a decade loves me. And we're having a baby together. We're building a family. It's everything I've ever wanted.

A touch of fear worms its way through the happiness. What about the next time we disagree? Will he continue to run away from me? I need someone who can stand by me. Through all the bad shit. Through all the scary shit. Not someone who runs at the first sign of fear.

"How can I trust you to stay?"

He looks up at his friends. "Can you leave us alone?"

Gibson snorts. "No way. We're the ones who are going to have to pick your ass up when she beats it bloody the next time you're an idiot."

Jett frowns. "I guess this is how you know you can trust me. These assholes won't let me mess up."

"We won't," Cash agrees. "It's why we've been up all night."

"Dealing with the fallout of firing Mike? I'm sorry. Someone." I glare at Indigo. "Stole my phone."

Indigo raises her palms. "I had my orders."

"And we weren't dealing with the fallout of firing Mike," Jett adds.

Gibson sniggers. "Firing Mike took no time at all."

"Then why have you been out all night and why did Indigo steal my phone?"

"I can't tell you," Jett says. "I have to show you."

I frown at him.

"Trust me?"

I don't move. I don't know if I can trust him. Love him? Not a problem. Trust him? Hmm…

"I love you," he says. "I've never told anyone I've loved them before. You're it for me. I'm probably going to screw up a lot."

"Probably?" Gibson snorts but Jett ignores him.

"I will screw up a lot. I don't know how to be in a relationship. I've never been in one. I didn't grow up with loving parents. I didn't have a father. I don't know how to be a father. I need you to show me how. And be patient with me."

I practically melt into a puddle at his confession. I feel all warm and gooey inside. This is my man. I will never let him struggle alone. And, if I'm being honest with myself, I only hesitated on the trust part because I'm scared. Jett and I can be scared together.

"Okay. I trust you."

The happiness in his blue eyes is proof I'm right to give him a chance.

"Thank you, baby."

He stands and pulls me to my feet. "Now, let me show you what we spent all night doing."

Jett throws a blanket over my shoulders before leading me outside and into Fender's vehicle. We drive to the other side of town to Jett's rental.

"Welcome home."

I roll my eyes. "I was only gone one night."

"Do you know how hard it is to buy a house on New Year's Eve?"

I gasp. "What? Did you buy this house?"

"Do you love this house?"

I smile. "Yes."

"Then, I bought this house."

He rushes out the door to my side of the vehicle. "Come on." He tugs on my hands.

"Wasn't the house the surprise?"

"There's more." He leads me inside and up the stairs. "Now, be kind. We're not finished yet, but you can get an idea."

He opens the door to the bedroom next to ours. "Ta da!"

My jaw drops open as I glance around. "How did you do this in one night?"

The bedroom is no longer a bedroom. It's a nursery with a crib, changing table, and rocking chair. The walls are freshly painted a bright yellow and there's a cute rug with a sunflower on it on the floor.

"Most of the stuff is from Dylan but I already ordered replacements for their baby."

"We can't steal Virginia and Dylan's stuff," I insist.

"Yes, you can!" Virginia shouts from downstairs.

Jett pulls me into his arms. "You like it?"

I wrap my arms around him. "I love it."

He kisses my nose. "And I love you."

"I love you, too."

"No hanky panky!" Gibson shouts. "Unless you want us to delay our New Year's Day celebration while you get naked and sweaty."

I bury my face in Jett's shoulder. "Are they going to follow us around everywhere?"

He shrugs. "They're my family."

I lift my face to meet his gaze. "You're my family."

He places a hand over where Little Bean is growing. "Both of you are mine."

Chapter 36

It's time — what you say when the waiting's over

SEVERAL MONTHS LATER

Jett

I stand in front of Aurora. "It's time to go."

"Not yet."

"Baby, you've been in labor for hours."

She glares at me. "I am not going to the hospital too early and having Dr. Edwards yell at me again."

"She won't yell at you. I already phoned her and let her know we're on our way."

Her glare intensifies. "You did what?"

"You've been having contractions since this morning. I'm done waiting."

"You're done waiting?"

I blow out a breath and try to be patient. My girl is feisty. I need to tread carefully.

"I'm not delivering this baby in our house. I'm not pre-pared."

She snorts. "As if I don't know you have an industrial sized first aid kit. You drove three towns over to buy it."

"Nonetheless. I plan for Axl to be born in a hospital. Not on the kitchen table."

"We are not naming our baby girl Axl and I'm not having the baby on the kitchen table."

"I can deliver your baby," Feather shouts through the window.

I march to it. "Stop eavesdropping."

She shrugs. "I can't help it if I happen to pass by and hear you, can I?"

"You're literally standing in our yard a foot from the window. You weren't passing by. You've been standing there all morning sending the gossip gals updates with your walkie talkie."

She hides the walkie talkie behind her back as if I can't hear it squawking.

Aurora groans and I rush to her. She's hunched over in her chair. Her knuckles are white with how hard she's fisting the arms of the chair.

I rub her back. "Breathe, baby. Breathe."

She lifts her head to snarl at me. "I am breathing," she gasps out.

"How far apart are the contractions?" Feather asks from beside me.

I don't bother asking her how she got into the house. She probably had a key made.

I wait until the contraction wanes before checking my phone. "The contraction lasted 50 seconds and it's been five minutes since the previous one."

I hold out my hand to Aurora. "It's time to go, baby."

"Contractions should be three to four minutes apart. Not five."

Thanks to the scare in the hospital, Aurora has read up on everything pregnancy related. I even caught her and Dylan exchanging notes at some point. Considering Dylan believes himself a self-taught pregnancy guru, I pulled them apart and made sure they weren't alone together again.

"You've been having contractions every five minutes for three hours, we're going to the hospital," I insist.

I don't wait for her to take my hand. My feisty girl is the most stubborn person I know. She'd rather have the baby at home than suffer through the embarrassment of another false alarm. But I'm not letting her have this baby at home. I want her in the hospital in case anything goes wrong.

"Fine," she mutters as she swipes her phone from her desk.

I snatch it from her. "I think the world can survive without you answering your phone for a few hours."

"Don't you dare steal my phone from me, Jett Peterson. I control all the money."

I kiss her nose. "I don't care about money. I care about you and Jagger."

She groans. "I'm not naming this baby Jagger."

"You're not naming this baby? I thought we would name *our* baby."

"As soon as you push a watermelon through your penis, we'll talk about who's in charge of naming the baby."

"What name do you prefer?" Feather asks as she follows us to the door where the go bag is ready and waiting.

Aurora huffs. "I'm not giving you any clues so you can win the bet."

Feather bats her eyelashes. "What bet?"

"I'm pregnant. Not stupid. I know the whole town has a bet going about the name of our baby."

"Really?"

Aurora rolls her eyes. "The twenty baby naming books that magically appeared on our doorstep kind of gave it away."

I help her put on a pair of clogs before grabbing the go bag and leading her outside. She moans when she sees the car waiting on the street.

"I can't believe you bought this car."

"What's wrong with it?" I ask to distract her. I already know all of her issues with the car.

"It's way too expensive. We don't need a Mercedes."

I nod to next door. "Fender bought a Hummer."

"There's no—" She moans as another contraction hits her.

I dig out my phone to time her but she bats my phone away. "Stop timing me. I'm not a racehorse."

I pick my phone up from the ground but I don't respond since I can't win this argument.

Once Aurora's contraction has passed, I help her into the SUV. I kiss her nose. "It's time to meet Morrisey."

"What did you do? Buy a baby book with rocker names?"

I wink. "You'll never know."

I make sure she's buckled in and shut the door. Feather opens the back door but I stop her before she can climb in.

"No. You can ride with your gossip gals." I point to the car idling in the road behind us.

"But they won't give me any hints about the baby's name."

"Exactly."

I wait until she walks away to rush around to the driver's door and jump in. I switch on the car and peel away from the curb.

Aurora clutches the oh shit handle. "This isn't a drag race."

I grin. "But if it were, I'd win."

"Please be careful."

I sober. "With you and little Mercury in the car, I'm always careful."

Being careful doesn't mean I have to drive the speed limit. I race toward the hospital. I'm done with watching the woman I love be in pain. I make it to the hospital in record time and skid to a halt in front of the emergency room.

"You are not teaching our daughter how to drive," Aurora mutters as I help her out of the car.

I escort her inside and get her settled in a wheelchair. Before we can reach the reception desk, Dr. Edwards greets us with a smile. "I'm surprised it took you this long to make it here."

"No. False. Alarm," Aurora pants out.

The doctor's smile disappears. "How far apart are the contractions? How long are they? How long has she been in labor?"

I answer her questions as we make our way upstairs to a delivery room.

"It shouldn't be long before your baby is here," the doctor says after her initial examination.

"I can't wait to meet little Nirvana."

Aurora bats a hand at me. "No."

I smirk. "I have a ton of rocker names picked out. You're bound to agree with one of them."

"Um, doctor?" A nurse sticks her head in the room. "There are bunch of people wondering where Ms. Sharpe is. Can I tell them?"

"There's no need to tell us anything, young lady. We're here," Sage says as she pushes her way into the room.

"Out!" Aurora screams. "Out!"

I rush to Sage before my feisty girl screams the hospital down thereby alerting the press in three states of the impending arrival of a Sinner baby.

I herd Sage to the waiting area. When I open the door, the gossip gals cheer.

"I knew you wouldn't get away with it," Feather says.

"Everything going okay?" Cash asks.

"Yeah," I tell him and my other bandmates – except Dylan and Virginia who are at home with their baby. "Presley is ready to enter the world."

Leia snickers. "Aurora is going to get you back for all those rocker names someday."

I smirk. "I can't wait."

"Where is he?" Aurora shouts from down the hall.

"Duty calls." I rush out of the room and back to Aurora. I hold her hand. "How are you doing?"

"How am I doing? How am I doing?" she screeches. "How do you think I'm doing?"

I kiss her forehead. "I think you're doing awesome because you are wonderful."

Dr. Edwards giggles. "I love it when the baby daddies backpedal like their lives depend on it."

"I—"

My words are cut off when Aurora screams.

"There you go," Dr. Edwards coaxes. "We're nearly there."

Her definition of nearly there is clearly not the same as mine since it's another hour before she demands 'one last push' and our baby finally arrives.

"Congratulations, Mommy and Daddy. It's a girl."

I push the matted hair off of Aurora's face. "You did it, baby." I kiss her forehead. "I love you, my feisty girl."

Her green eyes light with love and happiness. "And I love you, drummer boy."

"Here she is," the nurse says as she places our baby into Aurora's arms.

Aurora kisses her nose. "She's perfect."

"Of course, she is. We made her."

"Hello, little one," she whispers to her. "I'm your mommy and I will always love and protect you. Welcome to the world, little Star."

"Star? You already picked out her name?"

She glances up at me. "It's the perfect name."

I grin. "Named after one of the best drummers to ever live."

"Since I fell in love with a drummer, I thought it was fitting."

"Thank you for loving me. Thank you for giving me this precious gift."

"I will always love you." She glances down at our baby. "And I will always love you, Star."

Chapter 37

Babymoon – an excuse for a vacation

AURORA

Jett shakes my shoulder to wake me and I growl. "Touch me again and I'm removing your finger."

"I guess you won't get your surprise then."

I roll away from him. "I'll get it when I wake up."

"Too bad. The plane will be gone by then."

I open one eye and glance at him over my shoulder. "Plane?"

He bounces on his toes. "Who's ready for a babymoon?"

I groan and cover my face with a pillow. "I don't have time for a babymoon. I have two new bands to manage. And a little baby who doesn't sleep."

Jett snatches the pillow. "Leia is perfectly capable of holding down the fort for a week. And I bet Star will sleep better after a full day of…"

I narrow my eyes on him. "A full day of what?"

He zips his lips. "Can't tell you. It's a surprise."

I moan. Jett loves to give me surprises. Anything from breakfast in bed to a brand new office.

"You don't have to spend money on me all the time. I love you, drummer boy, not your money."

"But it's fun."

I shouldn't complain. At least he doesn't feel the need to jump out of perfectly good airplanes anymore.

I throw my feet over the side of the bed. "Okay. How many days' worth of clothes should I pack? And what will the weather be like?"

"Nah-ah." He wags his finger at me. "No clues for you."

I fist my hands on my hips. "I need to know what to pack."

He tweaks my nose. "Good thing you're already packed."

"Please tell me you didn't pack for me. I'd like to have something besides sexy lingerie to wear."

Buying lingerie is one of Jett's favorite surprises for me. The surprise is really for him but I'm fine with it since I never end up unsatisfied. He knows how to take care of me.

He chuckles. "Leia packed your bags."

"Phew."

"Chop. Chop." He claps his hands. "We've got a plane waiting for us."

We land several hours later.

"Where are we?" I ask since the pilot didn't announce our location.

"It's a surprise," Jett sings as he gathers Star into his arms.

I sigh. There is nothing sexier than a rockstar covered in tattoos cradling a tiny baby girl to his chest. I'll give him a dozen children, if he lets me. Only to witness the soft look on his face as he trails his finger down Star's nose.

My stomach growls. "Fine. But this surprise better include food. I'm starving."

"Don't you worry. I've got you covered."

The baggage is loaded in an SUV and we're off. We drive an hour before we cross a bridge onto a small island.

"Smuggler's Hideaway," I read as we drive onto the island. "I've never heard of this place before."

"The island is known for hiding smugglers during prohibition. And now it's a vacation destination."

My stomach rumbles again. "As long as these smugglers have a restaurant, I'm happy."

We arrive in a small town. It's nearly as cute as Winter Falls with all the Mom and Pop stores lining the street. Except most of these stores are touristy. I spot a restaurant and point to it.

"There! *Smuggler's Cove.* They're really leaning into the smuggling angle."

Jett parks on the street in front of the restaurant, and I jump out. Shouting on the sidewalk stops me before I have a chance to get Star out of the backseat.

"What is your problem?" A woman screeches. "Why won't you leave me alone?"

A man steps closer to her. But she doesn't back up. She holds her ground.

"I don't have a problem. I want you."

She throws her arms in the air. "Tell it to someone who will believe it." She whirls around and marches away. The man can't drag his eyes away from her.

Jett comes to stand next to me. I smile up at him. "I changed my mind. This is going to be fun."

He wraps his arm around my shoulders. "Of course, it is. I'm here."

"You're annoying."

"You love me."

"I'm obviously crazy."

"Crazy about me."

I'm not arguing with him. I push up on my toes to reach his lips. The second his lips touch mine, I forget all about the couple arguing in the middle of the street and a baby who doesn't want to sleep and work that never ends.

All I can think about is Jett and how good it feels to be in his arms, surrounded by his scent and his warmth. I never want to leave.

It took me a while, but I finally caught my rockstar.

About the author

D.E. Haggerty is an American who has spent the majority of her adult life abroad. She has lived in Istanbul, various places throughout Germany, and currently finds herself in The Hague. She has been a military policewoman, a lawyer, a B&B owner/operator and now a writer.

Printed in Great Britain
by Amazon

55812062R10169

Ken
Lussey

BLOODY
ORKNEY

Other books by Ken Lussey

Thrillers featuring Bob Sutherland and Monique Dubois
and set in Scotland in World War Two:
Eyes Turned Skywards
The Danger of Life

For younger readers:
The House With 46 Chimneys

First published in Great Britain in 2021 by
Arachnid Press Ltd
91 Columbia Avenue
Livingston EH54 6PT
Scotland

www.arachnid.scot
www.kenlussey.com

ISBN: 978-1-8382530-3-5

Cover design by Carolyn Henry
Cover photography by Maureen Lussey
The front cover photograph is of the Ring of Brodgar in Orkney
Printed and bound in Great Britain by Inky Little Fingers Ltd,
Unit A3, Churcham Business Park, Churcham, Gloucester, GL2 8AX.

For my daughters Carolyn and Natalie

PROLOGUE

'There's nothing greets your bloody eye
But bloody sea and bloody sky,
"Roll on demob!" we bloody cry
In bloody Orkney.'

Attributed to Captain Hamish Blair, RN

*

The weather forecast had been good, but it had been wrong. Sally Fowler was more irritated than worried. She'd been told before leaving Lossiemouth that she'd have clear skies all the way. There was meant to be a front coming in from the south-west later, but it had clearly moved faster and turned up earlier than expected.

If she'd known in advance, Sally would have taken a route round the Aberdeenshire coast and set off earlier. She didn't want to be late, not today. She knew that Roger had taken off that morning from Filton near Bristol. He'd flown south the previous day to drop off three pilots due to collect Beaufighters and return them to Lossiemouth.

They'd agreed he would meet her when she arrived at RAF Errol and they would have an enjoyable flight back, just the two of them. Roger had booked a table at the Grand Hotel in Elgin for dinner and Sally wondered how things might progress from there. She'd known Roger for some weeks now, and while she found him very attractive, his approach to the world seemed rooted in a genteel, pre-war era. In her more insecure moments, Sally wondered whether Roger had real feelings for her, or whether being seen with her was simply a convenience for him, a way of fitting himself neatly into the sort of relationship that others expected of him. Sally was running out of patience. There were, as they said, many other fish in the sea, and she'd had offers. As far as she was concerned, tonight would be Roger's last chance.

Timing therefore mattered. It wasn't a long flight in a straight line, but the expected weather meant their trip back would need to take the indirect coastal route. If she took too long getting to Errol, then they'd never make it back in time to get themselves ready for dinner.

Sally knew this area well. She'd crossed the broad valley of the River Spey and the tighter, more upland course of the River Don before she'd realised that the deep bank of cloud ahead of her, which she'd been trying not to think about since first seeing it, was going to be a serious problem. Her route would take her over the large village of Ballater and the valley of the River Dee. Then she'd have to cross mountains that in places rose to over 3,000ft.

Sally considered her options. The safest course of action would be to head east along Deeside, as far as Aberdeen if necessary, staying above low ground and then following the coast south-west and then west as it passed Dundee. But that would nearly double the length of her remaining journey and the Avro Anson she was flying was not what anyone would ever call swift.

The next best option would be to take a more direct course, hoping that the cloud base remained above the height of the highest ground she needed to cross. But what if it didn't? In that case, she decided, she would climb through the cloud to medium altitude. When she was further south, she'd be able to descend through a gap in the cloud or, if necessary, get a triangulation on her radio transmissions from ground stations. That would give her position accurately enough to allow her to let down through the cloud. Air Transport Auxiliary pilots weren't meant to use their radios on delivery flights, but exceptions could be made in circumstances like this.

With her mind made up, Sally continued over Ballater, losing height as she did so. Her aim was to fly along Glen Muick to the south-west and over the short stretch of high ground at its head, before dropping into Glen Clova and following it south-east then south to the lower and much safer ground beyond.

It didn't take long for Sally to realise that, even in the glen, the gap between the base of the cloud and the ground was shrinking quickly. As the near end of Loch Muick passed beneath her, she applied full throttle, aiming to climb through the cloud as rapidly as possible. Three things worked against her. The first was that most of her recent flying had been done in the high-performance Bristol Beaufighter fighter-bomber, a type of aircraft that she'd often flown from the factory at Filton to Lossiemouth and then from Lossiemouth to operational units in various parts of Britain. Like the Beaufighter, the Avro Anson she was flying today had two engines, one on each wing, but there the similarities ended. While the Beaufighter would have soared gleefully upwards, the Anson climbed sluggishly and reluctantly.

The second thing working against Sally was the way Loch Muick curved round to the west ahead of her, with steeply rising ground on its south-eastern side.

Then there was her knowledge that once she was high enough, clear of the glen and the surrounding mountains, she needed to turn a little to the left, to head due south. Somehow this knowledge found its way from the back of her mind to her hands and feet before it was wanted or needed and without her noticing. As the Anson entered the cloud in Glen Muick it started a gentle turn to the left.

Sally first knew there was a problem when she caught a brief glimpse through the windscreen of the hazy outlines of trees. She had no time to react before the Anson smashed into them, and a split second later into the mountainside that rose steeply above and behind them.

There was no fire or explosion, but the impact was catastrophic. The aircraft was smashed into fragments by the force of it. Most of the wreckage came to rest at the foot of a rock face, screened from view by the trees below it. If anyone looked carefully, the damage to the trees would be evident, but no-one was likely to come close enough to look that carefully. The track along this side of the loch was at a lower level and some distance away. The Anson's passage had been noticed over Ballater, but no-one had seen or heard the crash.

The only witnesses to Sally's death were the sheep that grazed the rough pasture below the trees, and even they were only very briefly distracted from their main role in life, of turning grass into sheep.

Roger was going to have a long wait at RAF Errol.

*

The men always took a lot more pushing to get going on a Monday morning. Peter McInnes had some sympathy, though he tried not to show it. After a Sunday off, the idea of another six days of muscle-sapping toil weighed heavily on everyone. And that was before you added in the demotivating effects of

Orkney's short winter days. It didn't even begin to get light until well after eight, and sunrise at this time of year wasn't until a little after nine.

If there was a sun to rise, of course. Today was the sort of wet and miserable day that Peter knew from experience would never allow anything resembling proper daylight to puncture the gloom. At least he spent part of his working day in the end of a Nissen hut that passed for a site office, which benefitted from a stove for heating. And at least he knew that at night he could retreat to a comfortable bed in a requisitioned stone cottage on the edge of Kirkwall. Many of his men were not so fortunate, spending their days outside in all weathers, and their nights in poorly insulated temporary buildings like this one.

On the other hand, if the rate of work fell behind schedule, it was Peter who got the blame. He'd decided there was time for a first cup of tea before venturing outside when the door was flung open and one of the foremen, Andrew Christie, burst into the room.

'Peter, there's something you need to see. Come quickly.'

McInnes stood up and reached for his coat. 'What's wrong?'

'You need to see for yourself,' said Christie. 'Though I hope you've not had a big breakfast because it's not very pleasant.'

Peter McInnes followed the other man out into a scene that offered few concessions to the human scale of the men who worked here. Huge piles of freshly excavated rock filling one side of the area could be glimpsed through the pre-dawn gloom and the light provided by generator-powered floodlights. Large pieces of machinery could be seen at the far end of the site. The group of men standing silently next to a crane showed where Christie wanted to take him.

Some of the men turned to look at him as Peter approached.

'What's going on?' he asked.

'Look sir.' It was an Irish machine operator called Michael O'Sullivan who replied.

The man was standing beside a rock-filled steel mesh container measuring some 6ft long by 4ft by 4ft. Peter knew it was one of the many thousands of gabions they had prepared, and would continue to prepare, to form the base of a series of causeways between Mainland Orkney, on which he was standing, and the string of islands to the south.

Peter looked at the gabion. At first, he could see nothing wrong, but in response to a gesture from O'Sullivan he focused on an area towards one end of the side nearest him. He realised he was looking at a bloody human forearm and hand, pressed hard against the inside of the steel mesh container. He suspected from its position that there was every chance the rest of the body was attached, buried amongst the rocks inside the gabion.

Peter sent Christie to telephone the police from the office and turned to face O'Sullivan. 'What can you tell me?'

'I'm fairly sure that when we finished on Saturday, we'd formed the next gabion from the mesh, removed the former, and placed it in the skip to be loaded. But I don't think we'd started to fill it. I suppose that didn't cross my mind when we arrived this morning and found the gabion full of rocks inside the skip. We folded over the top wings to close it and inserted the rod to lock them together. Then we hooked it up to the crane to be lifted over to join the others waiting to be dropped into the sound. As it came out of the skip, I thought something just looked odd. We lowered it to the ground and found that.' He indicated the arm.

'Thank you, Michael. The police will want to talk to you.'

Peter found himself privately wishing that Michael O'Sullivan had been just a little less awake and aware of his surroundings

6

that morning. If the gabion had been sunk in the sound with the others, no-one would have ever been any the wiser, whoever the arm belonged to. As things were, he could see the week's production schedule being derailed before it had even begun. It took no great leap of imagination to see that the arm hadn't got into the gabion by accident. Even with a war on, the police would want to investigate. He returned to the office to make that cup of tea and telephone his boss to pass on the bad news.

CHAPTER ONE

'Christ, this place is well named!' Lieutenant Commander Michael Dixon had cleared a hole in the condensation on the inside of the cabin window and was peering out into the rain. His voice seemed loud in the silence that had suddenly replaced the roar from the engines.

It was certainly loud enough for the pilot to hear, despite his leather flying helmet. He turned round in his seat to look back into the cabin and grinned at Dixon. 'You're right there, sir. Welcome to RAF Grimsetter!'

There was more banter as Petty Officer Andrew MacDonald, sitting next to Dixon, unclipped his seat belt and shuffled round to make sure he'd got his bag and coat.

Bob Sutherland wasn't really listening from his seat in the row behind. He was a poor passenger and the latter half of their flight had been bumpy and unpleasant in the fully loaded aircraft. Things had been fine as far as Inverness. But then the weather had steadily deteriorated. As they'd flown over RAF Wick, the pilot had told his passengers that although he was prepared to press on in the hope they'd be able to land in Orkney, there was every chance he'd have to turn back to Wick or Skitten or Castletown and they'd have to find another way of finishing their journey. In the event, the visibility in the worsening gloom of a winter's afternoon was just about good enough for him to find the airfield and put their de Havilland Dominie biplane down on a runway.

'Are you all right, Bob?' He glanced to his right to see

Monique looking at him. 'I never thought people actually turned green, but you're proving me wrong.'

Bob smiled back, not trusting himself to speak. He knew that if he succumbed now, especially after their aircraft had landed and parked, he'd never live it down within his team. And he knew, too, that the pilot would ensure the story of a group captain and one-time fighter ace being airsick would spread far and wide. Bob would prefer that not becoming common knowledge at RAF Turnhouse. At least the four men in the back two rows of seats were now clambering out of the aircraft and he could make a move.

Out on the tarmac Bob paused, pretending to check his bag was closed, while the others hurried towards the Royal Navy bus that had pulled up nearby. His peaked cap and the upturned collar of his greatcoat kept the rain at bay, and he needed a moment to catch a few breaths of fresh air. Military aircraft had a characteristic smell: a combination of leather, rubber, oil, fuel and vomit. After breathing in the aromas of the Dominie for far too long, Bob desperately needed to clear his lungs and his nose. It never bothered him when he was sitting in the pilot's seat and doing the flying. It had certainly bothered him today.

Bob realised that the weather seemed to be worsening and the light was fading even more quickly. He reminded himself that it got dark twenty minutes sooner here than in Edinburgh at this time of year. The pilot might have been able to see sufficiently well to land with the airfield lights on, but right now all Bob could see were the vague shapes of a control tower and the sorts of buildings you expected to find gathered round an airfield. As far as aircraft were concerned, there were a few Spitfires and a Wellington bomber visible, lined up further along the area of concrete he was standing on, but there was no sense that anyone was interested in flying any of them in the immediate future. He assumed that in this weather as many aircraft as possible would be sheltering in RAF Grimsetter's available hangar space.

The thought struck him that this could be almost anywhere. Anything that helped set it apart from all the other airfields that had been built across the UK over the past few years was lost in the mist and rain and gathering gloom. He turned and walked over to the bus.

Bob knew that it was only a matter of a few miles from the airfield into Kirkwall, but he got little sense of the place during the journey. He was seated near the front, just behind the door. Although the windscreen wipers coped well enough and gave a view directly ahead, the window beside Bob steamed up completely, and repeated wiping with the sleeve of his greatcoat did little to improve matters.

He'd never been to Orkney before and by the time the bus pulled up outside what the driver said was the St Magnus Hotel, he felt he had very little more sense of the place than he had before they set off from Edinburgh. He'd glimpsed a huge church on the right as they drove through Kirkwall, and he could see that their hotel faced across a road to the harbour, but that was about it. Despite the weather, there had still been people on the streets, mainly in uniform. Bob hadn't felt up to asking the driver for a guided tour on the way but did remember to thank him before getting out. The look of surprise on the sailor's face suggested it wasn't the norm here for officers with gold braid on their caps to thank mere mortals.

*

It was Robert Burns who wrote: 'The best-laid schemes o' mice an' men gang aft agley'. His poem was meant as an apology after he'd ploughed up a mouse nest. It only took a couple of minutes in the St Magnus Hotel for Bob to realise that his own best-laid plans also seemed to be going astray.

There were a few people, mainly men in various uniforms or in civilian clothes, passing through the hotel lobby, either heading out into the rain or towards what Bob assumed was the bar, off to one side. A few more were sitting at tables in a lounge area, smoking and reading newspapers or chatting. The check-in process went smoothly enough. Although they'd been advised that accommodation was very scarce anywhere in Orkney, Bob and Monique had each been given a double room on the top floor of the hotel, looking out over the harbour. The others occupied three twin rooms, one with a harbour view and the other two at the back of the hotel. Bob found it interesting to see how three officers and three non-commissioned officers from three different services worked this out between them. In the event they stayed in their service teams, with Lieutenant Commander Dixon exercising his newly gained promotion to ensure he and Petty Officer MacDonald were given the remaining front-facing room.

'There's a message for you, Group Captain Sutherland. It was delivered a little while ago.' The receptionist was in her early twenties and spoke with a beautiful accent that had a sing-song quality and a noticeable Nordic influence. She retreated to a rack on the back wall and shuffled through some envelopes. 'Here you are, sir.'

Bob tore open the envelope and read the handwritten note it contained. He looked up at the others, then handed the note to Lieutenant Commander Dixon. 'What do you make of that, Michael?'

Dixon looked round to see if they could be overheard; and

11

decided they could. He turned to the receptionist. 'Is there anywhere a little quieter where we could talk?'

'I'm afraid we're pretty busy, sir. We're about the only major hotel in Kirkwall that's not been requisitioned by the navy.' She smiled. 'Whenever I complain about it, my dad – he's the owner - tells me there's a war on.'

The lieutenant commander smiled back. Bob got the sense of a mutual attraction at work.

'That's understandable,' said Michael. 'Which of us has the largest room?'

'That would be the group captain, sir.'

Michael looked at Bob. 'Do you mind, sir?'

They reassembled ten minutes later in Bob's room, the others having offloaded their travel bags and coats in their own rooms. Bob had enough time to confirm that he did indeed have a view out over the harbour through a large bay window. Then he realised that he was going to have to close the blackout curtains before much longer. He was struck by how busy the place was, both on the harbourside and on the water. There was a knock on the door as Monique arrived. She was carrying a chair.

'It seems my room is next door to yours, Bob.'

'That could prove very convenient.'

'That's something we need to talk about,' said Monique, smiling. 'Though it will keep until later,' she added, as there was another knock on the now half-open door.

With eight people in the room, it didn't seem as large as it had initially. Especially as there were only three chairs, and no-one seemed to want to sit in a damp uniform on their boss's bed.

Bob looked round. 'The note I got when we arrived was from a Commander Prendergast, who is on the staff of Rear Admiral Hugh Kinnaird. The admiral oversees the naval side of things in

Orkney. As you all know, I was supposed to have dinner with him this evening in the Kirkwall Hotel next door, which serves as a naval headquarters here in Kirkwall, along with Lieutenant Commander Dixon, Flight Lieutenant Buchan, Captain Darlington and Madame Dubois. It seems that some undisclosed panic has blown up which is going to keep the admiral and his staff at their desks at the main naval base at Lyness over on the island of Hoy this evening. Dinner is therefore cancelled.'

Flight Lieutenant Buchan was the first to speak. 'If the purpose of tonight's dinner was to sign-off the terms of reference for our trip here, sir, does that mean we're going to be twiddling our thumbs tomorrow?'

Lieutenant Commander Dixon held up the note. 'It seems the idea is we meet Orkney's senior RAF and army commanders at 6 p.m. to cover their side of things. They were also meant to be at the dinner tonight. That should allow us to begin work on their aspects of what we want to look at tomorrow. Those of us who would have been at the dinner will be picked up at the front door of the hotel at a quarter to six. Apparently, we're now meeting in the Kirkwall Sector Operations Room, which is on the outskirts of the town.'

Flight Lieutenant Buchan looked at Dixon. 'That's one of the places on my hit-list. It's on a hill between here and RAF Grimsetter.'

The lieutenant commander continued. 'We can fill in the blanks on the naval side of things tomorrow morning at a meeting now planned with Rear Admiral Kinnaird at his HQ in Lyness on Hoy.'

Sergeant Peter Bennett, the junior member of the RAF team, half raised his hand. 'The three of us not scheduled to eat for our country tonight were planning to find out what Kirkwall had to offer in the way of pubs. Do you want us to change that, sir?'

'Perhaps we can kill two birds with one stone,' said Bob. 'Let's all eat together in the hotel. We should be back from this meeting by 8 p.m. at the latest. Could you book a table, Peter? Anyone wanting to paint the town red afterwards can do so, subject of course to the need to be ready to do our jobs nice and early in the morning.'

The sergeant grinned. 'I'm not sure Kirkwall has a lot in common with Melton Mowbray, sir, but we'll do our best.'

Bob decided to take the bait. 'You're going to have to explain that one to me.'

'Painting the town red, sir. The phrase was first used after the Marquis of Waterford, or the Mad Marquis as he was often known, went on an alcohol-fuelled rampage with a bunch of friends through Melton Mowbray one night in the 1830s. It seems they literally painted the town's toll-bar and assorted other buildings red.'

'The joys of a privileged upbringing,' said Bob.

*

They could see little of their destination as they were flagged down by a pair of RAF policeman at a security gate. When their two staff cars then came to a halt in the open area beyond, what Bob could see of the Kirkwall Sector Operations Room gave no clue as to its purpose. It did, however, give the impression of being slab-sided and large. Although it was difficult to tell in the blackout, it also seemed entirely without windows.

Beyond the bomb-proof security doors were two more RAF policemen, armed with Sten submachine guns, who asked to see their passes again. The policemen then stood back, and Bob was greetcd by a RAF air commodore who seemed to be in his late forties. Although he sported pilot's wings, his medal ribbons confirmed Bob's impression that his flying days had been in the last war, and in the various lesser conflicts that had followed. 'You'll be Group Captain Sutherland. Welcome to Orkney. I'm Howard Chilton.'

'Thank you, sir. This is…'

'Perhaps we should hold the introductions for the moment. No point you having to repeat everything. Follow me and we can get started.' Air Commodore Chilton led the way along the corridor before turning through a doorway into a large, high-ceilinged room.

Bob found himself in a corner of the room, standing on a raised platform that wrapped round three sides of the space. This formed a balcony that looked down onto the main body of the room from a height of perhaps half a dozen feet. At the near end of the room, to Bob's right as he had entered, was a further balcony raised above the first. The central, sunken, area was home to a large octagonal table on which a map of Orkney was laid out, surrounded by a depiction of sea on three sides, with the Scottish mainland to the south. The wall at the far end, to Bob's left, was covered in blackboards.

Bob had been in rooms like this before, during the Battle of Britain. It was in places like this that he'd had the chance to meet those who were making life and death decisions about the deployment of fighter squadrons, including his own, in the face of overwhelming Luftwaffe attacks. The role of the staff in the Sector Operations Rooms was to take in information from radar and the Royal Observer Corps about enemy attacks and represent what they had been told using markers placed on the map. It was then the responsibility of officers at desks on the surrounding raised balcony to decide what response to make, and then contact those who needed to act. In Bob's time that had usually meant deciding which fighter squadrons to launch from which airfields to intercept the German attackers.

A larger-than-life man in an army officer's uniform was standing on the near side of the map table talking to another army officer. He was tall and heavily built; and turned as Bob climbed down the short flight of steps from the balcony.

'Hello group captain. I'm Stuart Blanch.' Bob saw from the red patches, braid and insignia on the man's uniform that he was a major general. 'For my sins I am the commander of the Orkney & Shetland Defences, or "OSDef" as it tends to be called round here. Air Commodore Chilton, who you've met, commands the RAF units we have on the islands and on the north coast of Caithness. Meanwhile Rear Admiral Kinnaird, who it seems has found a reason not to give us all dinner tonight, is the Admiral Commanding, Orkneys and Shetlands, and as such he commands, inter alia, the naval forces stationed in Orkney. By that I mean the naval forces defending Scapa Flow, the main base at Lyness on Hoy, two naval air stations, the base in Kirkwall and assorted other units, either on land or afloat. There's a certain irony in that the admiral can sometimes have more aircraft operating from his airfields than the air commodore has from his, though not at present.'

Bob found the general hard to read, but a glance at Air Commodore Chilton showed he'd taken this in good humour.

The air commodore picked up the conversation, apparently by prior agreement. 'We thought it would be helpful to give you an overview of what we are doing here, and this map seems the best way to give some life to that. I've asked this evening's duty shift to take an extended tea break in the canteen while we talk. I gather you'd prefer it if the purpose of your presence on the archipelago isn't broadcast too widely. If the phones do start ringing it could get very busy in here very quickly, but I don't think that's likely. Would you mind kicking off with the introductions I stopped you making a short time ago?'

'Not at all, sir. As you've deduced, I'm Bob Sutherland. I'm the deputy head of MI11, based in Edinburgh. We have a responsibility for military security and seek to work alongside other agencies both in the military and in the intelligence community.

'We're a fairly small unit, and operationally we're divided into three teams, each comprising an officer and a senior non-commissioned officer. Lieutenant Commander Michael Dixon here is my deputy and currently heads up the naval team; Flight Lieutenant George Buchan heads up my RAF team; and Captain Anthony Darlington here heads up the army team, having recently joined us from the Commando Basic Training Centre.'

Bob turned to face Monique. 'And this is Madame Monique Dubois, who is seconded to the unit from MI5, or the Security Service if you prefer. We have other roles, but our bread and butter work involves visiting military units and bases and checking their security. It helps if the units involved aren't expecting us, which is why I requested that our presence shouldn't be broadcast too widely.'

Major General Blanch coughed, pointedly, Bob thought. 'I'm sure you'll forgive me airing the personal view, as we're all friends here, that we've plenty of resources available to look after security on the islands. But I'm aware that your activities have the backing of my boss in Scottish Command in Edinburgh and the support of our collective superiors in Whitehall. I am therefore happy to offer you every cooperation. Your day-to-day point of contact should be Major Arthur Gilligan here.'

The army officer standing beside the general, who looked as if he'd have preferred to be somewhere else, looked at Bob and nodded.

'On the RAF side I'll be your contact, Bob,' said Chilton. 'Anything you need, talk to someone on my staff and I'll get back to you. On the naval side, I gather you've been invited to travel over to Lyness tomorrow morning to talk to Rear Admiral Kinnaird. He tends to like to run things his own way and will appreciate you making the effort to go and see him on his own ground. He's got a base here in Kirkwall, HMS *Pyramus,* which is what they call the operations run from the Kirkwall Hotel, but his headquarters are on Hoy.'

Major General Blanch turned to the map on the table. 'We thought it might help if we set our operations in Orkney in a little context. You may have seen the figures, group captain, but the first thing to keep in mind is that the pre-war population of Orkney was not all that much over 20,000 people. The influx of men, and some women, from the armed forces and support organisations has roughly trebled that figure. To put that another way, at any given time, there can be up to around 40,000 soldiers, sailors or airmen in Orkney. That figure is made up of around 12,000 men from army units under my command, around the same number of naval personnel permanently based on the islands, and perhaps a little under half that number under the air commodore's command. The overall total depends heavily on how many Royal Navy ships are anchored in Scapa Flow at any given time. We've also got over a thousand Italian prisoners of war working on a project I will describe in a moment, plus a variable but often large population of civilian contractors building roads, runways, barriers, gun emplacements, piers and harbours, underground fuel tanks on Hoy, a new water supply for Kirkwall, and all the other infrastructure Orkney needs to fulfil its wartime role and support its vastly expanded population.'

The major general waved a hand at the extensive blue area, largely surrounded by islands, at the heart of the map on the table. 'Scapa Flow is why we are all here. This was an important naval anchorage during the last war, and it's become one again. At the risk of tempting fate, I'd like to think that Scapa Flow as we see it today is the most heavily defended and most secure naval base anywhere in the world. It's not always been that way, as you may know. A U-boat found a chink in the armour in October 1939 and made its way into the anchorage. The result was the sinking of HMS *Royal Oak,* with huge loss of life and even greater loss of morale. We also had several air raids that same month, and again in March and April 1940. The Luftwaffe hasn't been back in strength in the two-and-a-half years since, but they do make fairly regular small raids and individual incursions that are a continuing threat.'

'There was a single raider in September who successfully penetrated the defences, wasn't there?' asked Bob.

'True. If a brave pilot wants to take his chances with an approach that skims the waves from a considerable distance out, it can be possible to fly under the radar coverage. The aircraft you are referring to came in from the north-west at extreme low level, made one quick pass over the anchorage without running into any barrage balloons, then headed south. We think he was checking on what was anchored in Scapa Flow. While we were surprised by his arrival, we did get him before he was able to get home.'

There was a laugh from Air Commodore Chilton. 'Actually, sir, I think you'll find that it was Group Captain Sutherland who got him. That's right, isn't it, Bob?'

'Yes, it is, sir. I was flying from Oban to Wick in a Hurricane, minding my own business. I pretty much bumped into him, coming down the coast. I didn't know that two Spitfires from RAF Castletown were in pursuit, so I shot him down.'

'Yes, you had a spot of radio trouble when the control tower at RAF Wick told you to get out of the area, didn't you?'

Bob tried not to blush. 'Something like that, sir.'

The air commodore smiled, and Bob wondered if he'd stumbled upon a kindred spirit. 'As I heard it, you got quite a few kills back in the Battle of Britain as well, didn't you, Bob?'

'Counting the Ju 88 south of Wick in September the official tally is 22. By my count it's 24.' Bob saw a couple of his team look at him in surprise and realised the details of his career as a fighter pilot were probably news to them. 'Anyway, my apologies, I interrupted what you were saying, sir.'

Major General Blanch took only a moment to collect his thoughts. 'In terms of military defence, and I do understand that your role is to look at other aspects of security, Orkney is about as well-defended as it is possible to make it. Access to the anchorage is protected by anti-shipping booms and anti-submarine nets, backed up by induction loops that can detect ships and submarines electrically, and minefields that can be controlled remotely. The passages between the islands on the eastern side were protected – incompletely as it turned out – by sunken block ships. Over the past couple of years, we've been building a series of solid barriers between the islands that will eventually form causeways linking them together. These have progressed to the point where it is now impossible for anything much larger than a rowing boat to gain access to Scapa Flow from the east. That's where the Italian prisoners and a lot of the civilian contractors are involved.

'Meanwhile, every approach to Scapa Flow and to Kirkwall Bay is also covered by coastal batteries, over 20 of them, with more planned. In terms of anti-aircraft defences, the islands now have excellent radar coverage, subject to the limitations I described a short time ago. We also have 88 heavy anti-aircraft guns and perhaps half that number of light anti-aircraft guns, plus the guns of any ships that are in the anchorage. If the Luftwaffe were to turn up in serious numbers, the gunners wouldn't aim for specific targets. Instead, they'd put up a curtain of fire that the attacking aircraft simply couldn't find their way through. We call this the Scapa Barrage. It's only been used in anger once, on the 10th of April 1940, when 60 aircraft tried to mount an attack. The barrage deterred two thirds of the attackers from getting anywhere near Scapa Flow. Of the 20 or so that did press home their attacks, five were confirmed destroyed by the guns or by RAF fighters operating further out. Intelligence suggests that a significant number of other attackers were so severely damaged that they never made it back to their bases. This seems to be confirmed by the absence of large-scale raids since then, which to my mind tells us all we need to know about the Luftwaffe's opinion of our anti-aircraft defences. We test the Scapa Barrage every month, just to help keep everyone on their toes, not to mention awake.

'I'm actually quite grateful for the pinprick attacks the Luftwaffe does make. Without the reminder they provide of why we are here, it would be far more difficult to keep our anti-aircraft defences ready for the next big raid, if one were ever to happen.

'The lack of large-scale action does mean that making sure my men don't go round the twist with boredom in what many of them call "Bloody Orkney" is an important part of my job. My infantry units within OSDef take it in turns to "attack" gun batteries and remote units periodically, often at night, just to test their defences and watchfulness. The infantry's main role is to counter beach landings, so these exercises add a little interest to their life too. I should perhaps conclude by saying that my headquarters is in Mackay's Hotel in the centre of Stromness.'

The general looked across at Air Commodore Chilton, who took up the story. 'I've got three fighter airfields under my command. RAF Grimsetter is a little to the east of Kirkwall, and RAF Skeabrae is over in the heart of West Mainland.' He used a pointer to draw their attention to the relevant parts of the map on the table as he listed each location. 'My third fighter airfield is at RAF Castletown close to the north coast of mainland Scotland. The fighters tend to form an outer ring of defence around Orkney in order to avoid falling victim to the Scapa Barrage. In addition, there are several radar stations, plus the Sector Operations Room we're standing in.

'Meanwhile, as the general mentioned, the navy also has two airfields on Orkney. HMS *Sparrowhawk* is at Hatston, north-west of Kirkwall, while HMS *Tern* is at Twatt, over near RAF Skeabrae on West Mainland. Their role tends to be one of housing aircraft normally embarked on aircraft carriers that are at anchor in Scapa Flow; and training their crews. HMS *Tern* has been extremely busy of late as the home to several Fleet Air Arm squadrons preparing for Operation Torch, the landings in North Africa that have been under way for over a week now. For obvious reasons they are no longer there, but others will take their place before long.

'I should add that we have several dummy airfields scattered about the place to confuse any attackers who survive the barrage, and I also have two squadrons of barrage balloons under my command. I'll leave it to Rear Admiral Kinnaird to talk you through the rest of the naval presence in more detail tomorrow.'

The general had been looking at the map, but now turned back to face Bob. 'Against that background, can I ask what you hope to achieve in Orkney, group captain?'

'The plan is to be here for three full days before we head back to Edinburgh on Friday,' said Bob. 'During that time, I expect the team led by Flight Lieutenant Buchan to visit all four airfields on the islands, the naval ones as well as the two under Air Commodore Chilton's command in Orkney, plus some of the radar facilities. The aim isn't to try to catch people out. Rather it's to see how security is being maintained, and whether there are lessons that can be learned from what others are doing elsewhere on our patch, which covers Scotland and northern England. If we do identify major shortcomings, then we report back to senior officers. Meanwhile, Captain Darlington will be visiting as large a sample as we can manage of your units, general, making sure we look at a selection of coastal defence, anti-aircraft batteries and other units. Lieutenant Commander Dixon, Madame Dubois and I will look at the naval side of things, subject to the discussion we will have tomorrow with the admiral.'

'That does sound as if you are trying to cover an awful lot of ground in a very short time, group captain,' said the general. 'Isn't there a danger of your findings being very superficial?'

'There is a danger of that,' Bob agreed, 'but to an extent we are constrained by the resources available and the huge amount of ground we have to cover. I'm quite new to this myself, but the impression I'm getting is that it's possible to work out fairly quickly if those looking after security in a particular unit are doing a good job or not. Our role is to take a broad view and, as I said, flag up problems we encounter to senior officers.'

Major General Blanch looked at his watch. 'Fair enough. I think that's about all we can usefully do for now. You'd better let your people know their extra tea break's finished, Howard, and that they can have their Sector Operations Room back.'

CHAPTER TWO

Bob thought that the dinner had gone well. They were seated at two tables pushed together at one end of the hotel's busy and increasingly smoky dining room, under a row of framed prints of what he presumed were Orcadian landscapes on the wall. None of the MI11 group were smoking. Since his arrival in MI11, Bob's colleagues had realised that he simply didn't smoke and had stopped doing so around him.

Bob had caught the occasional quizzical glance from other diners and realised that they must have looked an odd group. Officers and non-commissioned ranks tended not to mix socially in any of the services, and the class system seemed particularly alive and well in Orkney. Bob thought this must be because the islands, though vital to the war effort, were very self-contained. Perhaps because the military presence was so overwhelming, there wasn't much of an outside world to relate to. Despite what the general had said about pinprick attacks and keeping his men on their toes, Bob wondered whether the lack of any serious enemy attacks on Scapa Flow in well over two years meant that complacency had set in and ingrained pre-war attitudes had been allowed to flourish.

It was no surprise that Petty Officer Andrew MacDonald and Sergeants Peter Bennett and Gilbert Potter were the only non-commissioned diners in Kirkwall's largest available hotel. What Bob found slightly more surprising was that his was, with one exception, the only group that included officers from more than one of the services. Over the course of the time they had been in the dining room, there had been a significant turnover of diners. Other than a few men in civilian suits, dining singly or in pairs, the clientele was made up entirely of military officers, who kept, it seemed, almost exclusively the company of other officers of the same service. The navy seemed best represented but there was no shortage of army or RAF officers happy to spend time in nice surroundings while eating very acceptable food and drinking beer or, in a few cases, wine.

Amongst the diners was the occasional couple. A Fleet Air Arm commander with pilot's wings on his uniform was accompanying a Women's Royal Naval Service officer, and later a RAF squadron leader came in with an Auxiliary Territorial Service officer. The combination of a man in RAF uniform and a woman in army uniform attracted obvious attention, which Bob assumed was because they formed the only mixed service group other than his own.

The MI11 party, not the description used when the booking had been made with the hotel, also differed in one other respect. It was the only group that crossed the apparently rigid boundary between military personnel and civilians.

Bob looked across at Monique Dubois. She was, as usual, dressed smartly but plainly. He knew that her grey jacket and skirt were intended to help her blend into the background in any setting. But she had a compelling presence that tended to work against her efforts to remain anonymous. Her dark hair framed a face that was classically beautiful, but oddly flawed in a way that to his mind made her even more attractive. She had on her happy, convivial face tonight. Bob knew that there were moments when, especially if she was caught unawares, her face could cloud over and her eyes take on a faraway, haunted look. He knew Monique well enough to understand there were good reasons for that. She was a few weeks short of turning 30, some seven months younger than him. She'd packed a lot of living into that time, not all of it pleasant. She had told him her dark and complex story while they'd been locked up together in the cellar of a shooting lodge in Caithness and Bob knew she carried with her more than her fair share of ghosts.

Her background also left her with an odd identity issue. Monique Dubois was the name she'd used when working in Scotland previously, and it had been agreed she would continue to use the name as cover while working with MI11. Her colleagues in London knew her as Vera Duval but Bob was aware that name, too, was only one of many that Monique had used over the years.

Not for the first time, Bob wondered if Monique's reasons for accepting a secondment with MI11 in Edinburgh were in any way compatible with his own reasons for accepting her as MI5's liaison officer. Some of those reasons were open and above board. Monique had shown herself to be highly effective and resourceful. He had to be able to trust anyone who joined his team. Monique was the only person he'd worked with from MI5 and he trusted her. Personally, if not always in the past professionally.

But Bob also had other reasons for welcoming Monique's move north, and this was where his uncertainty lay. The secondment had been agreed a fortnight earlier, and Monique had arrived in Edinburgh a little after 9 p.m. the previous night. She'd been booked into a guest house on the western side of the city, not far from where Bob's parents lived, and said she wanted the chance to rest after her ten-hour train journey from Kings Cross. As a result, the first he'd seen of her had been when she arrived at the MI11 offices on the first floor of the large old house on the army base at Craigiehall earlier that morning. She knew some of his MI11 team already, but what was left of the morning had been lost in a flurry of introductions and preparations, then the eight of them had set off on the short drive to RAF Turnhouse to catch their flight north.

There was plenty of background noise in the dining room, and in the adjacent hotel bar someone was playing a piano. Nonetheless, everyone at the table was very aware of the need to avoid being overheard discussing the reasons for their visit to Orkney. This had the welcome effect of ensuring that the talk stayed at a social level.

Sergeant Peter Bennett, who had studied to be an architect before the war, was persuaded to tell them a little about the architecture of the Orkney Islands. It turned out that the large church Bob had glimpsed earlier was St Magnus Cathedral. Peter also talked about the wealth of prehistoric remains that apparently littered the islands, something he was clearly passionate about, though he said he'd never visited Orkney before.

Monique was content to listen rather than talk, as was Bob himself, though he had to gently fend off a suggestion by Flight Lieutenant Buchan that he elaborate on what he'd said earlier about his exploits as a Battle of Britain fighter pilot. It wasn't that Bob was particularly sensitive about the subject. He just knew that with a large table in a busy dining room he'd have to speak up to make himself heard and he really didn't want to seem to be bragging or broadcasting.

Everyone else chipped in. The other new arrival on Bob's team, Captain Anthony Darlington, had been in post for only a week and was initially rather quiet, as if forming assessments of his new colleagues. Bob knew he was 25 years old, and that he had impressed while serving as a junior officer in an infantry unit in France in 1940 in the chaos leading up to Dunkirk. He'd then been very highly rated at the Commando Basic Training Centre at Achnacarry, where he'd been sent as an instructor after the discovery of his talent for unarmed combat and knife fighting. The captain was sitting next to Monique and spent some time talking quietly to her as the wider conversation went on around them. After a beer or two he did begin to contribute, telling a couple of highly amusing stories of things he'd seen at Achnacarry. These would have sounded far-fetched to anyone who'd never visited the place but to Bob they had the ring of truth.

Once what passed for coffee had been drunk, it was Peter Bennett who pointed out that if they were going to be able to visit any of Kirkwall's pubs before closing time, then they needed to leave quickly. The three non-commissioned officers departed, in the company of Captain Darlington and Flight Lieutenant Buchan. Bob found himself wondering how such a mixed group would fare in less refined surroundings than the hotel's dining room. Then he realised that no-one in their right mind would pick a fight with a group that included Sergeant Gilbert Potter, a giant of a man whose looks belied a gentle nature and a highly intelligent mind. And if they did, then they'd have Anthony Darlington to deal with.

Lieutenant Commander Dixon pushed back his chair and stood up.

Bob thought the promotion suited him. He knew that Dixon was still only in his mid-twenties, but in war those who were good, and survived, tended to be promoted quickly. Bob's own career was ample evidence of that. 'Are you going to catch up with the others?' he asked.

'No, I don't think so, sir. If you'll excuse me, I fancy a walk. I heard someone say a little while ago that the weather's cleared and the moon is visible. That should ensure I don't fall into the harbour in the dark.'

'Can you check that the dinner's been put on our bill on your way out. Michael?'

'Yes, of course sir. Goodnight to both of you.'

Bob watched the lieutenant commander walk out of the dining room. Turning back to the table, he realised that Monique was watching him from her seat on the opposite side, with an amused expression on her face. He also realised that a waiter was loitering nearby, obviously wanting to clear the table.

'What now, Monique?'

'That's a good question. Perhaps we should go for a walk too?'

They agreed to meet, with coats and gloves, a few minutes later in the lobby. Bob arrived first and realised that Lieutenant Commander Dixon still seemed to be sorting out the billing of their dinner with the receptionist. He was about to intervene when he saw Monique coming down the stairs.

When Bob had been shot down over Kent in November 1940, he'd suffered an injury to the left side of his head that damaged the optic nerve and left him functionally blind in his left eye. As a result, he didn't see the man in his fifties and dressed in civilian clothes who'd just come through the front door of the hotel and was walking towards the bar from Bob's blind side, looking down at a folded newspaper he was holding in his hand. The two collided.

Bob smiled and apologised.

The man looked at him angrily and grunted, 'Watch where you're going!' in a distinctly Glaswegian accent. He then bent down to pick up the newspaper he'd dropped and carried on into the bar.

Bob watched the retreating coat and trilby hat, wondering why the man seemed familiar.

'Hello Bob,' said Monique. 'Are you ready for that walk?'

'Of course.' Bob returned Monique's smile and walked over to pull back the blackout curtain and open the door for her.

*

Michael had been right, there was enough light from the moon to see Kirkwall's harbour on the far side of the road. Monique tucked her arm in his and after checking there were no unlit vehicles coming along the street, he led her across to the harbourside, their breath slightly steaming in the cold night air.

'Do you fancy a walk along the pier?' asked Bob.

'Yes, once we've convinced these nice young men to let us through.'

Bob was shocked that he'd not noticed the barbed wire fence separating the road from the harbourside or the two sentries standing at a barrier controlling access through a gap in the fence.

It took only brief flashes of torchlight on their passes for the sentries to be convinced to let them onto the pier. Monique took his arm again.

'How do you feel about me being here, Bob? By "here" I mean seconded to your unit.'

'The idea was suggested to me by Sir Peter Maitland, the Director of Military Intelligence, at a meeting in London with my immediate boss, Commodore Maurice Cunningham, the head of MI11. As you know, Sir Peter is responsible for the entire rats' nest of military intelligence sections, including MI11 and MI5. I frankly thought it was too good to be true. I said yes to the proposal there and then and before anyone had a chance for second thoughts. Subject to your being happy to be seconded, of course. They said you were.'

There was enough light for Bob to see Monique smile. 'Perhaps the part you don't know, Bob, is that the idea for a secondment was first floated in the report I wrote as soon as I got back from my last trip to Scotland. It obviously struck a chord, because by the end of the day my department head, Matthew Sloan, was taking credit for the idea. When they then approached me, I agreed that I'd be the right person for the job. The whole thing was put forward as a proposal from MI5 to Sir Peter Maitland and to MI11 very quickly indeed.'

'I'm really pleased you did make the suggestion, Monique.' Bob looked round. Despite the lack of light there were still a few people going about their business around the harbour.

'There is a "but" coming,' said Monique. 'It's perhaps as well I committed myself at the time, because I've been suffering from fairly severe second thoughts over the past few days.'

'Why?'

'This is ground we've covered before, Bob, but please bear with me. I told you once that I have a disastrous effect on the men I've cared for. I was widowed at the age of 24 when Count Sergei Ignatieff was shot in Russia as a spy in 1937. I was widowed for a second time at the age of 27 when Hans Friedrich von Wedel was killed in a car crash in Berlin in 1940. My taste in husbands was abysmal and I didn't mourn either of them after they were dead, but that's not the point. There have been other men who I've cared for, sometimes deeply, who've also ended up dead for one reason or another. Never by my hand, I hasten to add, but that's not really the point either. As I've told you before,

I've had a policy for some time of not getting close to anyone. That way I can't feel responsible if they end up dead.'

'That explains the second thoughts,' said Bob. 'What was the reason for you suggesting the secondment in the first place?'

There was a long pause. They continued to walk along the pier in the moonlight, but Bob could feel himself holding his breath.

Monique stopped and Bob turned to face her. 'I don't know, Bob. No, that's a lie, I do know. Call it a moment of weakness if you like. When I got back from Scotland after that last trip, I wondered whether there might be a chance to put the past behind me and find some of the happiness that everyone's apparently meant to feel but which has always eluded me.'

They turned and started walking back towards the landward end of the pier and the hotel beyond it, still arm-in-arm. The moon was climbing towards its highest point in the southern sky.

'We can't predict the future, Monique, but I'm happy to try to make things work between us.'

'You do know, of course, that MI5's reasons for wanting to have someone inside MI11 are not completely altruistic?'

'Yes, I do. More importantly, so do Commodore Cunningham and Sir Peter Maitland. What matters is that I trust you, both personally and professionally.'

'Are you sure you do, Bob? You've had doubts in the past.'

'I'm sure, Monique.'

'It's going to be rather awkward, managing a relationship in a small office.'

'Not if we're sensible about it. When Sir Peter mentioned your name, I did tell him there was a potential complication, but he already knew about our relationship and was unconcerned. Meanwhile, I'm sure your new colleagues in MI11 all know the score. You'll remember that it was Michael Dixon who came hammering on our bedroom door – your bedroom door, if you prefer - at the North British Hotel to tell me that Captain Bell had been killed at Achnacarry.'

'What's your idea of "sensible" Bob? No, let me tell you my idea of "sensible" first. I think the most important thing is to avoid being too brazen about our relationship in a work setting. That means we keep things at a wholly professional level in the office.'

'Agreed.'

'And by "work setting" I include trips like this, when we are with other MI11 colleagues. I don't want anyone thinking they need to knock on my bedroom door if they are looking for you and I'd prefer not to be found in your room in the middle of the night if you get any callers.'

'I'm less enthusiastic about that, for obvious reasons,' said Bob. 'But I can see the sense in it. Separate bedrooms tonight, then? What about once we get back to Edinburgh? You've got a room in a guest house, even if you're not using it this week, and I'm living in the officers' mess at RAF Turnhouse. It might be nice to find something a little homelier we could rent together.'

Monique laughed. 'Isn't Edinburgh meant to be rather prim and proper? How do you think our "living in sin" together would go down with the fine citizens of the city? Remember your parents live there, and gossip spreads. It's not just your reputation at stake.'

'I could rent somewhere myself and offer you your own room, which you'd not need, of course. If I'm honest, I don't really care what people think. There's a war on and prehistoric attitudes need to change.'

'Perhaps we might be getting a little ahead of ourselves. Should we discuss it when we get back to Edinburgh?'

'Fair enough. Look, would one kiss count as unprofessional in your book? It's dark enough to be sure that no-one will see.'

Monique smiled. 'I think we could manage that.'

A little later, as they walked slowly back towards the security barrier at the head of the harbour, Monique said, 'You'll be suggested we go and visit your parents in Cramond next.'

'I was going to, Monique.'

She laughed. 'Could I remind you of something I said to you at Dunrobin Castle, Bob? How do you think any man's parents would react to the idea that their son had fallen for a recovered cocaine addict who had slept her way round Europe by the time she was eighteen and could speak the languages of all of the security services that actively wanted her dead?'

Bob smiled. 'Yes, you did say something like that. I might need to ease them gently into the idea.' Perhaps it was the thought of his mother's reaction to Monique that caused his memory to lurch suddenly into action. 'Dammit!'

'What's wrong, Bob?'

'Did you see me bump into a man in the hotel lobby as you were coming down the stairs?'

'Yes, a civilian in a fawn gabardine-type coat and a hat. I didn't see his features as he turned towards you and away from me.'

'I knew I'd seen him somewhere before. He's my uncle. His name is Frank Gordon and he's my mother's younger brother and the black sheep of the family. I've not seen him since before I left school. I went with my parents to the wedding over in Glasgow of some relative of my mother's and he was there. That's why I didn't recognise him sooner. Last time I heard his name mentioned, he was in Barlinnie Prison. He'd got mixed up in some sort of gang war in Glasgow, fighting over the territorial rights to charge protection money. He'd cut someone up badly, nearly killed them, and was in for a long stretch. I had no idea he was out.'

'Are you sure it was him?'

'I only saw him briefly but I'm fairly certain. I wonder what he's doing in Orkney?'

'Well, you can be sure he's not here on holiday. Look, I'm getting cold, should we go back to the hotel?'

CHAPTER THREE

It was still dark when Bob awoke next morning. He'd had a disturbed night. He'd been running through the conversation with Monique in his mind, thinking about the possible implications, balancing hopes for one possible future against fears about others. He'd also found himself worrying about the presence in Orkney of Frank Gordon. Would Frank have recognised Bob? Bob doubted it. The schoolboy he'd been when they'd last met had become just another military officer, with his features obscured by a peaked cap and the upturned collar of his greatcoat. Would it matter anyway if Frank had recognised him? Bob wasn't sure, but for some reason he didn't feel comfortable about the idea. Bob was still very new in his post, and he really didn't want family complications arising that could compromise his position.

After getting back from the bathroom across the corridor, he switched off his room light and pulled back the curtains. It was obvious from the pre-dawn stars that the improvement in the weather had lasted overnight. He got the sense there might have been a frost but could see little more now than he could the previous night of the harbour below him, the bay beyond and the low-lying northern islands of the archipelago that he knew would soon appear in the middle distance.

Breakfast was served in the dining room. Bob didn't knock on Monique's door on the way down. Turning up together for breakfast was just the sort of thing they needed to avoid. In the event she was already there, sitting at a table with Petty Officer

Andrew MacDonald. They were each drinking a cup of something brown and steaming and apparently waiting for their food to be served.

MacDonald looked up. 'Morning, sir.'

'Morning. Is Lieutenant Commander Dixon joining us?'

'Your guess is as good as mine, sir. I've not seen him since I left with the others to find a pub at the end of dinner last night.'

Bob felt a sense of shock. In the short time he'd been in the job, one of his team leaders had already been killed. He really didn't want to lose another. 'But aren't you sharing a room with him?'

'That was the idea, sir. But as it turned out I was spared his snoring.'

Bob could feel real anger building at MacDonald's incredibly relaxed attitude. Didn't the man realise the implications? Then he saw that both Macdonald and Monique were smiling.

Monique put her cup back in its saucer. 'It's all right, Bob. Can you remember when you last saw Michael?'

'He was sorting out the billing for dinner when we went out for our walk.'

'And who was he sorting it out with?'

'The receptionist. The attractive blonde girl who gave us our keys when we checked in. Ah… Do you think…?'

MacDonald's smile became a grin. 'Last night wasn't the first time I've been expecting to share a room with the lieutenant commander and ended up on my own, sir. He's very choosy, but he seems to have a pretty high success rate with the young ladies he takes a fancy to.'

'Didn't she say she was the hotel owner's daughter? I hope they're discreet.'

At that moment Lieutenant Commander Dixon came into the

dining room. He'd clearly been back to his own room, because he seemed to be freshly shaved and was wearing a clean shirt.

It was Monique who spoke first. 'Good morning Michael. Did you sleep well?'

Dixon paused and looked at each of them, then smiled. 'Very well, thank you Monique. What's for breakfast?'

*

After breakfast they went to get their coats and then met again in the lobby. There was an older woman on duty behind the reception desk who paid them no attention as they waited. Bob looked at his watch. They were a couple of minutes early. The plan was for them to be picked up and taken to board a boat that would then carry them over to the island of Hoy.

He looked at this watch again. 'I take it the others got off as planned?'

'Yes, sir,' said MacDonald. 'Bright-eyed and bushy-tailed. They were finishing their breakfasts as I arrived for mine and the last I saw of them was when they headed out to pick up the cars that had been allocated to them.'

At that moment Bob saw a woman come in through the front door and look briefly round. She was wearing the uniform of a Women's Royal Naval Service lieutenant. Bob reminded himself that in the WRNS the rank had a different title, though he couldn't remember what it was.

The woman, in her late twenties, walked over to Bob. 'Group Captain Sutherland?' He nodded. 'Hello, sir, I'm Second Officer Sarah Jennings. I'm based at HMS *Pyramus*, in the hotel next door, and I've been asked to escort you and your party over to Lyness. I've got a car waiting outside. May I see your

39

identification, please?'

As they walked out into the street, Bob saw that it was finally getting light. There was more traffic than there had been the previous night, and the harbour seemed busy once more. Second Officer Jennings sat in the front of the car with the driver, leaving Bob and his three colleagues to sit in the back, two on a broad seat at the rear of the car and two on drop-down rear-facing seats behind the driver and front seat passenger.

'It's not the most comfortable of cars, I'm afraid,' said Second Officer Jennings, 'but we don't have far to go.'

'Where are we going?' asked Michael Dixon.

'Just a couple of miles down to a pier on Scapa Bay, sir. Orkney's Mainland is almost cut in two at this point, by Kirkwall Bay to the north and Scapa Bay to the south. That also means we'll be crossing the widest part of Scapa Flow, from north to south, but we'll be using a motor gun boat that will get us over to Lyness quite quickly.'

*

As they walked past armed naval guards and onto the stone pier, Bob reflected on his first view of Scapa Flow. Their plane had flown to the east to avoid it the previous day. From this angle it was impossible to make out much beyond what seemed to be numerous grey ships at anchor and lots of smaller boats moving backwards and forwards between them. A striking feature was the number of barrage balloons that were visible. Some were floating limply over land, and Bob knew these were attached by wires to winches on the backs of lorries. Others were stationed out over Scapa Flow itself and Bob saw that these seemed to be attached to anchored trawlers.

As a pilot, Bob had never liked barrage balloons. They were indiscriminate: their wires could just as easily shear the wing off a defending Spitfire or Hurricane as a Luftwaffe bomber. He thought back to the aircraft he'd shot down in September. What he was seeing now suggested that the pilot had been a brave man, or a reckless one, to fly at low level across Scapa Flow. Bob thought about the length of time the aircraft would have spent over the anchorage, given its size. Even at full speed, the aircraft would have been completely exposed to fire from the defenders' guns for several minutes in the middle of a bright day with excellent visibility. Yet there had apparently been no defensive fire.

After they'd boarded the motor gun boat, Second Officer Jennings told them that it was about 12 miles across the anchorage to the naval base at Lyness.

Bob, who was standing on the boat's open bridge, realised that the day was turning out to be a glorious one. With the November sun still very low in the south-east, visibility in that direction was limited, even using his hand to supplement the peak of his cap in shielding his right eye. Michael Dixon had joined him, and Second Officer Jennings stood a little further away near the vessel's captain, just out of earshot of them given the roar that came from a combination of the engines, the wind and the passage of the boat through the water. Bob had seen Monique and Andrew MacDonald heading down into the small cabin below the bridge.

Dixon leaned over towards him. 'Sorry if I worried you earlier, sir.'

Bob smiled. 'Let's just say that I was a bit slow on the uptake, Michael. But as her father owns the hotel, could I ask that you avoid upsetting her, or her father, enough to have us kicked out before the week's finished?'

'I don't think there's any fear of that, sir.'

'What's her name?'

'Betty Swanson. As you might have gathered from her accent, she's from Orkney.'

Second Officer Jennings moved closer to them and Bob decided it was time to change the subject. He raised his voice and waved his arm to take in some of the warships that were at anchor around them amid the huge expanse of Scapa Flow. 'It's an impressive sight, second officer.'

'Yes, sir, it is. Believe it or not, the anchorage is far from full right now. But yes, there can be few sights like it anywhere in the world.'

As they neared the southern side of Scapa Flow, Monique joined them on the bridge. She pointed to their left. 'Is that a separate island over there, rather than part of Hoy?'

Jennings replied. 'Yes, it is. That's Flotta. They say that the name comes from the Norse for "Flat Island", and you can see why. It sits in the middle of the southern approaches to Scapa Flow, so is home to a lot of the defences at this end of the anchorage. Many of the nets and booms start or end on Flotta and as you'd expect it's heavily defended with anti-shipping and anti-aircraft guns. It also serves as the social heart of the fleet when ships are anchored in Scapa Flow. There's a huge canteen there that sounds like it's Orkney's answer to the wild west. Ships' crews are brought ashore to eat, drink and be merry. Until the time comes to return to their hammocks back on board their ships and nurse their hangovers.'

'Sounds like? You've not been?'

'Not a chance. Kirkwall can have its moments, especially after closing time in the pubs, but it's a beacon of polite gentility

42

compared with the southern islands and with Flotta in particular. In any case, there are no women stationed on Hoy or Flotta other than the nurses in the hospital at North Ness. I'm told that the WRNS will arrive in force when a new headquarters and communications centre has been finished but right now these islands are mainly men only.'

'You've got to be heavily outnumbered, even on Orkney's Mainland?'

Jennings smiled at Monique. 'I did hear it said that at one time there were 600 men stationed in Orkney for every woman and that it was the best place on Earth to catch your man. There are a few more of us here now, but it's still a happy hunting ground.'

As their motor gun boat passed between Flotta on the left and a smaller island on the right, Bob saw what he knew must be the island of Hoy come into view in front of him. 'I take it that's Lyness?'

'Yes, sir,' said Jennings. 'It's the navy's largest base in Orkney, by an awfully long way.'

Bob looked at Lyness with a feeling that teetered between awe and horror. Part of the shoreline was taken up by a series of piers projecting out from the land, each the focus of a bustle of small boats. In the foreground was an assortment of larger vessels, moored or on the move. A little further along the shore was a long waterfront along which two large ships were moored. Inland from the piers and waterfront were extensive areas of what might have been workshops or warehouses and administrative buildings, plus a series of large oil tanks. In the middle distance, where the land began to climb towards the hill that stood behind the base, were more buildings, including multiple rows of huts, and this pattern was repeated out on the flanks of the harbour frontage. The whole area seemed scarred by the effects of recent and continuing construction work that extended a considerable distance up the hillside. The scene was topped off by more barrage balloons.

Bob turned to Second Officer Jennings. 'I'm a fighter pilot rather than a bomber pilot, but even to me those oil tanks look like very tempting targets.'

'That's part of the reason for all the defences against air attack, sir. The ships in Scapa Flow are obviously another. Four of those oil tanks were built in the last war, and a further twelve in the years before this one. More recently they've been building a series of huge underground oil tanks that are rather less vulnerable to attack, beneath the hillside up there. The first one was finished a couple of months ago. Others are still being excavated by miners brought in for the purpose.'

Perhaps the others on the bridge were also reflecting on the rather shocking appearance of the place they had come to visit, because very little more was said before their vessel found its way through a flotilla of small boats to moor at one of the piers.

*

This time it took two smaller staff cars to transport them a short distance parallel with the waterfront to a long single-storey wooden building standing not far from the shore, apparently located to make the most of the views south over Scapa Flow.

'Is this where we're meeting Rear Admiral Kinnaird?' asked Bob.

Jennings half turned in her seat. 'Yes, sir. As I said to your colleague, they're building a new headquarters and communications centre further up the Wee Fea, that's the hill to the west, but I gather that's not likely to be finished for a few months yet. This has been the headquarters of the Admiral Commanding, Orkneys and Shetlands, or ACOS, since early in 1940.'

Bob got the sense that someone had tipped off the guards that security was being checked. Either that or they really were on the ball.

After the visitors' passes had been scrutinised and a clipboard consulted, one of the guards went to use a telephone at a desk parked in a side corridor. Perhaps ten minutes later a naval officer came through a dark blue double door at the rear of the reception area.

'Group Captain Sutherland?' Bob turned to face the newcomer. 'Hello, sir. I'm Commander Prendergast. Welcome to Lyness. Rear Admiral Kinnaird will see you in the main meeting room, though he's got someone with him in his office at present. He'll join you as soon as he can. Could I suggest that the petty officer and the lady wait in the headquarters canteen at the rear of the building until the meeting's finished? I'll have someone show them where it is.'

Bob saw Petty Officer Andrew MacDonald smile knowingly. He'd clearly been given the run-around by senior officers in the past. Monique, on the other hand, seemed to be taking the idea less well.

It was Lieutenant Commander Dixon who broke the awkward silence that followed. 'Petty Officer MacDonald will be more than happy to wait in the canteen.' He turned to look at MacDonald. Bob saw the slight wink Dixon gave MacDonald but knew that from his position Commander Prendergast couldn't have done.

Bob spoke up before anyone else had a chance to say anything. 'Madame Dubois, on the other hand, will be taking part in the meeting.'

'I'm afraid that's not in line with the admiral's orders, sir.'

'That's something we can discuss with the admiral. Perhaps you'd better lead on, commander.'

Bob, Monique and Michael followed the commander along a busy corridor that led through the building. Behind them, with an unhappy expression on her face, came Second Officer Jennings.

Bob and his two colleagues were deposited in a large room with windows along one side. These offered views out over a busy wharf area and past moored ships to Scapa Flow. On the end wall of the room was a large map of Orkney, very similar to the one they'd seen on the table in the Kirkwall Sector Operations Room. There was a chill in the air and the place smelled of fresh paint, of stale cigarette smoke, and of damp. The centre of the room was taken up by a meeting table apparently formed from several smaller folding tables. The commander left the room with the WRNS officer.

Bob could see that Monique was seething. To lighten the mood he said, 'You'd think they'd at least have laid on a cup of tea and a biscuit.'

'If they had, they'd probably expect "the lady" to pour it for them,' said Monique. 'Who does this bloody admiral think he is?'

Dixon smiled. 'On behalf of the Royal Navy, I apologise, Monique. As we keep telling everyone, we're the "senior service". I'm afraid that can mean that we're sometimes a touch inflexible and backward-looking. We have some outstanding senior officers, don't get me wrong. But we've also got some who think they're still fighting the last war.'

Bob looked at his watch. 'And now we're being made to wait. What was that with Andrew, anyway? You both seemed happy he'd been kept out of the meeting.'

'You might be able to argue with orders from an admiral, sir, but I'm in no position to. Besides, a canteen in a building like this will be a great place to find out what's really going on at Lyness. The navy's an awfully big service these days, but there's always a chance that Andrew will bump into someone he knows. Even if he doesn't, he's developed a few helpful strategies that tend to get people to confide in him.'

Bob grinned. Then frowned as he looked at his watch again. 'That's fifteen minutes we've been waiting. I'm prepared to wait for half-an-hour for a rear admiral, then we walk out and find a way of getting back across Scapa Flow under our own steam.'

They'd been waiting for twenty-five minutes when the door opened and a small and wiry man who looked to be about 60 walked into the room, wearing the uniform and insignia of a rear admiral. He was followed by Commander Prendergast and Second Officer Jennings. Bob and Andrew stood, in deference. Monique stood a moment after them.

'Sit down, please. I take it you are Group Captain Sutherland?'

'Yes, sir. I'll do the introductions. This is Lieutenant Commander Dixon, who is my second-in-command in the northern section of MI11. And this is Madame Monique Dubois, who is on secondment to MI11 from MI5 and forms an integral part of my team.'

'You are aware that I objected to Madame Dubois' presence at this meeting.' It wasn't a question.

'Yes sir, I am. But I felt that when you were aware of the full picture, you'd wish to revise your view.'

'It wasn't a view, group captain, it was a bloody order, which you have chosen to defy.'

'My presence here, admiral, and Madame Dubois' presence here, is sanctioned at the highest levels in Whitehall. You might outrank me, sir, but one phone call will put me through to people who outrank you.'

'We're an exceedingly long way from Whitehall, group captain. What happens in Orkney, and in this part of Orkney in particular, is my responsibility. So long as I'm in this post, the way I choose to discharge that responsibility is up to me.'

Monique sat back in her chair and smiled at the admiral. 'Might I ask whether it's me or MI5 that you object to so strongly, admiral? And if it's me, is it because I'm a woman or because I'm French?'

'Give me strength! Let's be clear, I have nothing against the Security Service, and I am aware that the Free French are our allies. Let me also be clear that I have nothing against women. I'm married to one. I'm the father of two more. I've a granddaughter who, God willing, will grow up to become one. But war is a nasty, brutal, thing. I simply don't believe that it's right for women to be exposed to its nastiness and brutality. I know that I'm swimming against the tide. The second officer's presence here today is ample evidence of that, and more Wrens are arriving in Orkney all the time, alongside women in the other services. But for the moment I can still say what goes, at least as far as the southern islands in the archipelago are concerned. Despite our best efforts, conditions here remain primitive. Hoy is no place for women who weren't born and brought up on the island.'

'That's two slightly different reasons, admiral, neither of which is entirely convincing. But let's take your concern about the nastiness and brutality of war which, believe me, I entirely share. I see you have many medal ribbons. Does that mean you have been in battle yourself?'

It was clear to Bob that the admiral was having to make a real effort to keep his anger under control.

'Yes. In the last war I had two ships destroyed under me and lost many friends and shipmates. During my time in command here I have lost more friends and colleagues, on ships that haven't returned from patrol.'

'I understand that must be traumatic. But nastiness and brutality can take many forms. Have you ever actually met your enemy face to face? Have you ever actually shot another human being yourself?'

'No, of course not. That's not the way naval battles work.'

'I have, admiral. I shot a Soviet spy in Leith only a couple of weeks ago, to save the life of a member of the group captain's team. I only wounded him because that was what I was intending to do. Before that, back in September, I shot and killed a member of the crew of a Luftwaffe flying boat that had landed on a loch in Caithness. He was trying to kill me, so I killed him first. There have been others over the years.'

The admiral sat back in his chair. 'Are you threatening me, Madame Dubois?'

Monique's voice hardened. 'Of course I'm not threatening you, you stupid man! I'm trying to show you that if you want to get into a discussion about who's been exposed to more of the nastiness and brutality of war, then I've seen at least as much as you.'

In the absolute silence that followed, Bob had to fight back the urge to laugh out loud. Then he found himself wondering what the navy cells in Lyness were like. They were sure to have some and he had a feeling that was where this conversation was destined to end for him and for Monique.

After what seemed like an age, the admiral leaned forward. 'To business, then. Could you please explain to me what you hope to achieve here, group captain, and what you want of me?'

Bob tried to conceal a sigh of relief before launching into his introductory comments.

When Bob had finished, Rear Admiral Kinnaird pushed back his chair, stood up, and walked over to the map at the end of the room. He then gave an account of the development of Scapa Flow as a naval anchorage, briefly touching on its role in the Great War, the scuttling of the German fleet afterwards, and the run down that followed.

'Despite all the warnings, we were as unprepared at the start of this war with Germany as we had been at the start of the last one. Lessons that ought to have been learned were ignored or forgotten. Scapa Flow was so ill-defended in 1939 that there were doubts in the Admiralty about whether it should be used at all.

'In the event it was used. Then, because of a gap in the eastern defences, HMS *Royal Oak* was sunk by a U-boat on the 14th of October 1939 with the loss of over 800 men. Three days later a modest Luftwaffe air raid all but sank the battleship HMS *Iron Duke,* the flagship of the fleet, in Scapa Flow. She was only saved by being beached. She remains beached today, as a depot ship. Faith in the defences of Scapa Flow diminished to the point where it was felt better to keep the fleet at sea than at anchor here. It was only Churchill's personal intervention as First Lord of the Admiralty that changed things. Defences were strengthened dramatically in the six months that followed, and the success of the anti-aircraft defences in fighting off the last serious air attack in April 1940 restored the fleet's faith in the anchorage. I'm sure my colleagues will have talked about coastal and anti-aircraft defences when you saw them yesterday evening?'

'Yes, sir,' said Dixon, 'and about your two naval air stations and the booms, nets and minefields and the barriers being built on the eastern side of the anchorage.'

'Well, that saves us some time. My main naval base here at Lyness is known as HMS *Proserpine*. As you'll have seen it's an impressively extensive if rather unlovely place. It's worth bearing in mind that as many people currently live in Lyness as live in Kirkwall. I've also got smaller bases at Longhope, along the coast, and on Flotta, plus many smaller outposts elsewhere. The fleet takes a huge amount of servicing, and this requires many small craft of various types, and their support services.

'Last but not least, I am also in command of HMS *Pyramus*, based in the Kirkwall Hotel in Kirkwall. I understand you are staying in the St Magnus Hotel next door?'

Bob nodded.

'Our rapid expansion meant that accommodation was very scarce, so we requisitioned most of the large buildings in and around Kirkwall, including the larger hotels. I'm not sure why the St Magnus Hotel slipped through the net. I did hear something about the owner serving with Winston Churchill in the Royal Scots Fusiliers on the Western Front in early 1916, but don't know if it's true or not. It might help explain how he kept his hotel when others didn't.'

The admiral looked at his watch. 'But I'm digressing. HMS *Pyramus* is a slight oddity as it has nothing to do with Scapa Flow or the defence of Orkney itself. It houses the headquarters of the Northern Patrol, the ever-changing but sometimes large fleet of warships responsible for maintaining an economic and military blockade of Germany and her conquered territories, including Norway. In practice this means covering an area which extends from beyond Iceland in the north-west to the North Sea in the south-east. Enemy ships are attacked, and neutral ships stopped and searched.

'I should perhaps conclude by saying that although the naval facilities in Orkney are under my command, I do not command the ships of the fleet that anchor in Scapa Flow, and neither do I command the ships of the Northern Patrol.'

'Thank you, sir,' said Bob.

The admiral looked at his watch again. 'Now we've got that out of the way, can I ask how you propose to proceed?'

It was Lieutenant Commander Dixon who answered. 'We'd like to make a start immediately, sir, by looking at security here in Lyness and perhaps on Hoy more widely.'

'That's agreeable to me. Commander Prendergast will assign you someone who knows their way around, and a car. I'm right in thinking that's all you want from us today?'

'Yes, sir, that would be ideal. I'll discuss arrangements for tomorrow with Commander Prendergast later, depending on how much progress we make. There is one final thing, sir, I had a Commander Napier listed as your naval provost marshal and assumed I'd be dealing directly with him. Do I need to update my contact list?'

Bob saw the admiral turn and look at Prendergast with an odd expression on his face. 'Yes, that is correct. I'm afraid Commander Napier isn't available at present. I'm sure that Commander Prendergast will let you have everything you need. Now, if you'll excuse me, I have somewhere else to be. The second officer here will see you and Madame Dubois back over to Kirkwall, group captain.' With that he stood up and walked out of the room.

The commander and the second officer followed him; Bob presumed to organise transport.

Monique turned to Bob. 'I'm sorry, Bob, it was totally

unprofessional to lose my temper with that… with that…'

'Maybe "misogynistic buffoon" is the phrase you are looking for, Monique?' suggested Michael Dixon, grinning. 'Please don't quote me on this, but I get the impression that someone should have put that man in his place years ago. Now you've done it, brilliantly, in front of members of his staff, and I sense nothing's ever going to be quite the same again around here.'

'Surely no-one's going to talk about what happened?'

'Don't you bet on it, Monique. With more than one witness, word is bound to get out, and you can bet the story will grow in the telling. Kinnaird isn't much liked by those under his command, and the idea that a woman has got the better of him will appeal to many of them.'

'Oh no,' said Monique. 'That makes it even worse. I still don't understand why he tried to keep me out of the meeting. It was obvious at the time that he was spouting nonsense. Why try to exclude me and not the WRNS officer?'

'Maybe he does have something against MI5 and threw in the stuff about women as a smokescreen,' said Michael. 'Or maybe it was your French name that raised his hackles. Perhaps he thinks he's Nelson and the enemy is Napoleon's navy? Who knows?'

'I'm wondering whether it was simply the fact that I'm not in uniform and don't have a clearly defined rank. Perhaps the admiral simply doesn't like the idea of dealing with women he can't order about.'

'You might be right,' said Bob. 'And he'll like the idea even less now. But while that was the most obvious oddity about his behaviour, I find myself more intrigued by what happened at the end.'

'You mean the absence from the meeting of the officer responsible for security?' asked Michael. 'My question did seem unwelcome. I'll see what I can find out.'

Bob smiled. 'Anyway, Monique, forget about Kinnaird and focus on what we're here to do. Look, how would you feel about joining forces with Michael and Andrew for the rest of the day? Lyness is by far the biggest single unit we need to look at in Orkney, and an extra pair of eyes and ears could do no harm.'

'That would certainly suit me,' said Michael.

'What are you going to do Bob?' asked Monique.

'There's someone I need to talk to in Kirkwall. I'll tell you how it goes later.'

CHAPTER FOUR

In the bright sunlight, Bob could see that the Kirkwall Sector Operations Room was a large concrete block, with smaller subsidiary blocks attached to it. The site offered excellent views over Kirkwall, but the absence of windows deprived the building's occupants of the benefit of those views. Though an attempt had been made to camouflage the building, it stood out starkly in its location and Bob suspected that its designers had decided to place more reliance for its protection in the thickness of its walls than in concealment.

Bob had asked Second Officer Jennings to drop him off at the gate leading to the Sector Operations Room en route back from Scapa Bay to her office in the Kirkwall Hotel. He'd thought about asking if he could use a phone there but decided he would feel more comfortable making this call in an environment in which others were wearing the same colour uniform as him.

It took him a little while to talk his way through the security at the gate and more to persuade the RAF policemen at the entrance to allow him in. The shift commander was a squadron leader who was more than happy to give Bob access to an office and a telephone.

It didn't take long to put the call through to Edinburgh.

'Hello, can I speak to Superintendent Sutherland, please.'

'Who's calling?'

'It's his son, I'm calling from Orkney.'

'Is it urgent? The superintendent is in a meeting.'

'Yes, I'm afraid it is urgent.'

There was a long pause.

'Hello Bob, what's up? They said it was urgent.'

'If I'm honest, Dad, I'm not sure if it is or not. Look, I'm with my team up in Orkney.'

'That must be lovely for you at this time of the year. I'd guess the weather's even worse than it is here.'

'Well, the sun's shining today but I suspect that's out of character. Anyway, last night, I bumped into a man in the lobby of the hotel we're staying in, literally bumped into him. It was only later that I realised it was Frank Gordon.'

There was a pause at the other end of the line. 'Right. How sure are you it was him?'

'Pretty sure. I last saw him at a wedding I went to in Glasgow with you and Mum before I left school. But the more I think about it, the surer I am. I must admit that I'd thought he was still in Barlinnie for attempted murder.'

'No, he was released a year or two back. I do keep informal feelers out with colleagues over on that side of the country. After he was released, he went to Dublin. Apparently, there were lots of business opportunities over there for someone with his range of skills and his particular moral outlook.'

'If I'm right, he's not in Dublin anymore.'

'Clearly. Look, Bob, I'll see if I can find anything out. I'm sure you can look after yourself, but my advice to you would be to steer clear of him if you see him again.'

'Do you have a particular reason for saying that, Dad?'

'Is this a secure line?'

'Relatively. I'm calling from the RAF Sector Operations Room in Kirkwall, so there's no public switchboard involved.'

'Good. There's never been any love lost between Frank Gordon and I, going all the way back. When your mother became engaged to a policeman, her evil younger brother took it into his head to change her mind and gave her a black eye at their parent's home in Glasgow. When I heard what he'd done I went and found him and put him in hospital for two weeks. The row with your mother that followed nearly ended our engagement, though as you'll have worked out, we got over it in time for our wedding. Frank wasn't invited, by the way.'

'This is all news to me.'

'It's not the sort of thing you broadcast. But I'm sure that Frank Gordon would welcome the chance to get even with me through you. At that wedding you remember seeing him at, I simply made a point of avoiding him and I think he reciprocated. I'm surprised you didn't come across him during your time with City of Glasgow Police, come to think of it.'

'I think I joined not long after he was put away, so our paths never crossed.'

'Where can I contact you if I find anything?'

'Just leave a message at the St Magnus Hotel in Kirkwall and I can phone you from here.'

'I'll do that Bob. Look, as we're talking, can I change the subject?'

'What to?'

'You mother's not happy that we've barely seen you since you moved up to Edinburgh.'

Bob's felt a pang of guilt. 'Pass on my apologies, Dad, and my promise I'll visit when I'm back from Orkney.'

*

The afternoon was still bright, but cold. Bob accepted the offer of a lift in a RAF Police Jeep to Kirkwall police station, which the corporal driving told him was in Junction Road. It turned out to be next door to the livestock auction market.

The constable behind the reception desk looked up from his newspaper. 'Can I help you, sir?'

'I'm Group Captain Sutherland and I'm with Military Intelligence 11 based in Edinburgh. Here's my security pass. I was wondering if it's possible to have a word with whoever's in charge?'

'That would be Inspector Flett, sir. I believe he's due to go over to Stromness shortly, but I'll tell him you're here. Would you mind waiting in our interview room? I'll make sure I leave the door unlocked.'

The constable was back a few minutes later with a cup of tea and the promise that the inspector was on his way.

Inspector Flett turned out to be trim man of above average height in his late thirties. Bob could see that he took pride in his job from his spotless uniform and his immaculately pressed trousers and polished shoes. The inspector held out a hand. 'Hello group captain, to what do I own the pleasure of a visit from military intelligence?'

Bob shook his hand. 'Military Intelligence 11 is a section of the military intelligence empire that looks after military security. You could say that we're run in parallel with MI5 and MI6, and assorted other sections, but we're a great deal smaller. I'm based at Craigiehall, just west of Edinburgh. We are in Orkney to review the security of the main military bases on the islands. I'm here now because I hope to be able to pick your brains about something that's come up that isn't directly connected with our central role.'

'I'd certainly like to be able to help you, group captain. But you need to know that we have almost nothing to do with the military side of things in Orkney. The military outnumber the civilian population by anything up to two-to-one and each of the services has what amounts to its own police force.'

'I understand that,' said Bob. 'I'd imagine you must be pretty stretched, even so.'

'Very true. The Orkney Constabulary isn't the largest in Scotland by a long way. We only have about thirty men on our strength in total, and nearly half of them are Police War Reserve constables. We also have one sergeant. I double as the deputy chief constable, and my immediate boss is the chief constable.'

'It's actually a civilian matter I want to talk to you about.' Bob had given some thought about how to approach this without telling direct lies. 'Before the war I was a detective sergeant with the City of Glasgow Police. I was also in the Auxiliary Air Force, and when war came, I chose to mobilise with my squadron.'

'It's a big leap from detective sergeant to group captain in three years, if you don't mind my saying so.'

'I suppose you could say I was lucky. Mainly because I survived when other more senior or more able men didn't. But now, in a strange sort of way, I've come full circle and am a policeman of sorts once more. Anyway, quite some time back I crossed paths with a Glasgow gangster called Frank Gordon. He spent a long time in prison for attempted murder, and I'm told that when he got out, he went to Dublin. Last night I'm fairly sure I saw him walking across the lobby of the St Magnus Hotel, here in Kirkwall. He's a nasty piece of work and my purpose in coming to see you is to ask if he's known to you, and if so whether you know what he's doing here.'

'I'm sorry, group captain, the simple answers are "no" and "no". It is of course possible that he's using a different name, but if there was a Glasgow gangster behaving like a Glasgow gangster on my patch, I think I'd know about him. You must take that in context of course. A good part of the economic activity in Orkney revolves round the military, and if your Mr Gordon was involved in something crooked there, then there's every chance I'd not get to hear about it directly, or perhaps even at all.'

'What sort of thing do you have in mind?' asked Bob.

'I'm sure there's criminal activity going on in or around some of the military units here. I have no direct evidence, and if I did, I'd just have to pass it on. But you don't need much imagination to realise that there are mountains of equipment and literally trainloads of supplies just begging to be redirected into the black market down south and I'd be surprised if there wasn't a healthy trade going on in illicit alcohol behind the scenes.

'Meanwhile, we've occasionally had cases of what you might call casual prostitution on the islands, usually girls who've come here from Aberdeen, Edinburgh or Glasgow. I suspect we'd have more if it weren't for the islands being a "Protected Area" under the 1939 Defence Regulations. Any civilian wanting to get to Orkney must apply for a permit to be allowed to enter, which cuts down on visitors.'

'Yes, I can see that helps, though it does suggest that Mr Gordon has found a way of getting a permit. Oh well, it was worth asking. What sort of thing tends to cross your desk on a day-to-day basis on the civilian side?'

'A large part of it is maintaining a presence that gives permanent residents some assurance that one day everything's going to return to normal. With the influx of a huge temporary population there's inevitably been an increase in petty crime, minor thefts of livestock for example. Most of those cases get passed on to the military, because most of the missing chickens or pigs tend to go missing in the company of men in uniform. We also get involved in occasional public order incidents. Fights outside pubs after closing time, that sort of thing. Back in the summer of 1940 this was bad enough for us to restrict pub opening hours in the evening to just two hours from 6 p.m. to 8 p.m. for a while. We also brought in a curfew that meant no-one could be on the streets between 11 p.m. and 5 a.m. without good reason. Neither measure helped. Indeed, one response to the curfew was a series of parties that started late in the evening and ran until the curfew ended.

'Wartime regulations do mean that we have a lot more to do in the way of checking on traders and on rationing. There is an active black market involving the civilian population in Orkney, as I imagine there is everywhere else, but it's small-scale and probably not likely to attract the interest of a professional villain from Glasgow. If I'm honest, it's almost a relief when some real police work comes along. We actually had a report of a murder yesterday.'

'Really?'

'Yes, a body was found yesterday morning at one of the quarries being used to extract stone for the barriers linking together the eastern islands. The circumstances suggest it had been put there deliberately, with a view to concealing it forever. It was only by chance that someone noticed part of an arm before the gabion it was in was dropped into the sea. The problem was that while there was an intact lower right arm, sufficiently hairy to be sure it was male, the rest of the body was so badly crushed by the rocks that had been placed on top of it that it was utterly unrecognisable. And no clothing or other effects were found. If the man was a member of the armed forces, then his identity discs had been removed along with his uniform. The RAF kindly flew the body to Aberdeen yesterday so the forensic people there can look at it. At least we'll get a right-hand set of fingerprints, to go with a tattoo showing the points of the compass on the inside of the right forearm.'

'Does that help?'

'We'll get the fingerprints back later in the week. If we can narrow down who the body might be, then they could provide confirmation, especially if their owner was in the military or had a police record. The problem with the tattoo is that it's a fairly common one amongst seamen. That includes many thousands of men stationed here with the Royal Navy or visiting on naval or merchant ships, but it also includes just about every native Orcadian adult male. These islands were built on the seafaring exploits of its menfolk, long before the navy thought of building a naval base here. I'd hoped we might tie the tattoo to someone who's been reported missing but that's not helped.

'We've naturally passed a photograph of the tattoo to the navy, but it's rung no bells there either. I think our best hope of an identification will come from the forensic people and our best hope of catching the murderer will be to identify the body. We've done the obvious things like take statements from everyone at the quarry and as far as we can we've checked their backgrounds. But the body seems to have been left there on Sunday, when no-one was around. Look, I'm sorry, group captain, but I need to get over to Stromness to interview two men who've applied to be Police War Reserve constables and I don't want to be late.'

*

Betty Swanson was on duty again when Bob returned to the St Magnus Hotel. 'Yes, group captain, there is a message for you.' She handed the envelope over with a broad smile, which Bob returned.

The smile disappeared from his face when Bob read the contents. It was an instruction sent on behalf of Air Commodore Chilton to call his office at RAF Grimsetter as soon as possible on a matter of urgency.

Bob thought of asking to use a phone at the naval HQ next door but decided a public phone would do, given the tone of the message. When he asked, Betty Swanson directed him to a phone booth at the back of the hotel lobby.

'Hello, Flight Lieutenant Munro speaking.'

'It's Group Captain Sutherland. I've had a message to call Air Commodore Chilton's office.'

'Ah, yes. Hang on a minute, sir.' There was a short pause. 'Where are you, group captain?'

'I'm in the St Magnus Hotel.'

There was another pause, then: 'Air Commodore Chilton has asked me to pick you up outside the hotel in ten minutes, sir.'

'Where are we going?'

'I'll explain when I see you, sir.'

Bob went back outside the hotel to wait.

The RAF staff car pulled up in less than the predicted ten minutes. Bob got in the front, next to the flight lieutenant.

'What's the problem?' asked Bob. He began to wonder if word of Monique's argument with Rear Admiral Kinnaird had reached the air commodore's ears.

'We are on our way to the army headquarters at Mackay's Hotel in Stromness, sir. Apparently two of your people are being held in custody there for sabotaging a military exercise.'

'My army team? There must be some misunderstanding.'

'No, sir. As I understand it from the member of the general's staff who phoned, the two men under arrest are RAF personnel, which is why they decided to involve the air commodore. I'm afraid I don't know any details, sir.'

Bob knew that Flight Lieutenant Buchan and Sergeant Bennett were due to be visiting RAF Skaebrae and the nearby naval air station, HMS *Tern* on West Mainland. He couldn't see how either visit could have resulted in their encountering the army, still less sabotaging one of their exercises.

*

Mackay's Hotel lay in the heart of Stromness. It stood a little back from a square that extended to the landward end of a pier on the waterfront. The hotel itself seemed taller than it was wide. It had four main storeys, with the lower three comprising a large bay window flanking a third window or, at ground level, an ornately pedimented doorway. Bob realised as the flight lieutenant manoeuvred the car that the hotel's narrowness when viewed directly front-on belied a considerable depth.

The flight lieutenant parked the car a short distance away and the two men made their way through the security barriers and sentries in front of the hotel itself. Bob briefly admired the tessellated design of the porch floor as he walked across it to reach the main entrance, beyond which was a darkly decorated corridor leading to a rotating door. Their approach had clearly been observed, because beyond the rotating door they were greeted by an army captain coming down the main stairs.

'Thank you for coming sir. The general has said that you can talk to your men in the small bar next to the reception desk on the first floor. They are no longer under arrest, by the way. I'll show you where it is.'

Bob thought that was the best news he'd heard since leaving

his hotel. He noted that there was still an armed sentry on the first floor landing, but then thought that might be the norm in the Orkney & Shetland Defences' headquarters.

Bob went into the room without knocking, followed by Flight Lieutenant Munro. Sergeant Bennett was seated at a table next to a fireplace, facing the door. He was just about to take a drink from a cup but stopped when Bob entered, replaced it on the saucer and stood.

Flight Lieutenant Buchan had been standing looking out of a window at, Bob imagined, whatever lay to the side of the hotel. He turned at the sound of Bob's entry and smiled. 'Hello sir. I'm glad to see you.'

'What the hell happened?'

It was Bennett who replied. 'I stopped the army destroying an ancient monument that's been standing for thousands of years, sir. They weren't too happy about it at the time.'

'That's putting it mildly,' said Buchan. 'I thought they were going to shoot you, Peter.'

'Hang on a minute,' said Bob. 'Can we take this from the start? You were meant to be visiting two airfields on West Mainland today. That's right, isn't it?'

Flight Lieutenant Buchan nodded. 'Yes, sir. And that's what we did. We'd finished by early afternoon, so I decided to head back to drop in on the naval air station at Hatston, just this side of Kirkwall. The most direct route follows a road that comes down between two large lochs before picking up the main road from Stromness to Kirkwall. The idea was to catch a glimpse of some standing stones beside the road there after visiting a famous stone circle.

'You get a good view of the stone circle, as you approach along the road. As we drove towards it, we could see there were maybe half a dozen tracked Bren carriers moving amongst the stones of the circle. Peter was driving the car. He stopped and ran off up a path towards the stone circle, which isn't far from the road. I followed.'

Sergeant Bennett picked up the story. 'You're not going to believe what we found, sir. A platoon of Gordon Highlanders, part of the garrison here on Orkney, was performing for the benefit of an army photographer who was taking some publicity shots. He was standing just outside the ancient ditch that surrounds the ring with his camera on a tripod and the Bren gun carriers were driving backwards and forwards through the Ring of Brodgar under his direction, so he could get pictures that showed them in an Orkney setting.

'That circle has been there for four thousand years or more and it would have taken just one slight misjudgement on the part of any of the drivers to destroy one or more of the stones. As it was, even though they are quite light, their tracks were gouging up the ground between the stones and in the ditch. I ran over to the photographer and tried to get him to stop. I was then approach by a lieutenant from one of the Bren gun carriers. When I told him that he was committing a crime against history that would leave a Waffen SS panzer commander ashamed, he took out his revolver and said I was under arrest. Then they arrested Flight Lieutenant Buchan as well.'

'I tried to reason with the lieutenant,' said Buchan, 'and showed him my security pass. But it did no good. I had the sense that the lieutenant's conscience had been pricked by what Peter had said, and that he felt the best way to respond was by raising the stakes and accusing us of sabotaging a military exercise. That's what they radioed back to their HQ, anyway, along with our names. They then drove us here under armed guard in our own car and locked us in a storeroom down on the ground floor. Things were looking a bit grim at first. But a short time ago the general returned to Stromness. I understand that he'd been away when we were arrested. When he got back, something about what they told him piqued his interest enough for him to come and see us personally. After Peter explained what had happened, the general ordered that we be brought up here and then stormed off. I'm not sure where things stand now.'

'Neither am I,' said Bob, 'though I have been told you are no longer under arrest.'

Two of the essential requirements his teams needed to do their work effectively were to blend into the background as far as possible, and to maintain the cooperation of those they were dealing with. Bob thought that Peter Bennett might well have been right and justified in what he did, just as Monique had been right and justified in her confrontation with the admiral that morning, but neither incident sat well with their need to be inconspicuous.

At that moment the door opened and Major General Blanch entered, followed by the captain who had met them on arrival. The general stopped and looked at Bob. 'I've just telephoned Air Commodore Chilton to apologise for involving him in this. My staff should have waited for my approval before trying to dump this problem on him. I'm something of an antiquarian myself and I'd like to apologise to your men, group captain, and to thank Sergeant Bennett for what he did. It would indeed have been tragic if we'd vandalised the Ring of Brodgar with our Bren gun carriers. It's a hugely important part of Orkney's heritage. Damaging it, especially in those circumstances, would have been dreadful for morale in the islands once word had got out, which it inevitably would.

'I intend to have words with the lieutenant concerned and ensure he gets to repent at leisure, from the distant perspective of the most unpleasant posting I can find for him. I will also ensure that orders are issued that all units should respect and avoid ancient monuments in anything short of an actual German attack. I'd rather assumed that would be obvious to everyone anyway, but clearly it's not.'

With that, the general turned and walked out. He was followed by the captain who, from the expression on his face, Bob thought was probably the one who'd decided it would be a good idea to contact Air Commodore Chilton's office about the arrests.

Bob looked round. 'Let's get out of here, before they change their minds.' He turned to Flight Lieutenant Munro. 'It sounds like he already knows, but could you update the air commodore when you get back to Grimsetter? I'll travel back to Kirkwall with Flight Lieutenant Buchan and Sergeant Bennett in their car.'

CHAPTER FIVE

Bob sat in the back of the car, while Flight Lieutenant Buchan and Sergeant Bennett were in the front, with the latter driving.

'Look, we've got time before it gets dark,' Bob said. 'You told me this stone circle wasn't far from the main Kirkwall road. If it was important enough to risk getting shot for, maybe I'd better see it for myself.'

Bob saw Bennett smile in the mirror. 'I'd be happy to give you a quick Cook's tour, sir. You should know that although I've read about it, I'd never been myself until earlier this afternoon. It would be nice to get a chance to see it in a slightly more relaxed and peaceful atmosphere.'

After running parallel with the southern shore of a large loch, the car turned left at a crossroads and travelled a short distance before pulling off on the right-hand side of the road.

'Is this it?' asked Bob.

'It's not, sir. If you'll indulge me, I wanted to give you a sense of why what the army were doing with those Bren gun carriers was quite so appalling.'

Bob and Flight Lieutenant Buchan followed Bennett across a field to a group of standing stones. They then walked beyond the stones before they all turned to look back.

'These are the Stones of Stenness, sir,' said Bennett. 'They are thousands of years old, and experts think that the stones we can see today were once part of a larger ring of perhaps a dozen tall stones.'

Bob thought the setting was glorious in the late afternoon sun.

One of the stones was taller than the others, and beyond it he could see the loch they'd driven round. In the distance, high ground was catching the light. 'I take it that's the island of Hoy we can see over there. Look, Peter, this is very impressive, but what was it you wanted to show me here?'

'I actually wanted to show you something that wasn't here, sir.'

Bob saw George Buchan smile and said, 'I'm afraid you're going to have to explain what you mean.'

'As I said, sir, there used to be more stones. They were already popular with visitors by the early part of the last century and Sir Walter Scott visited in the summer of 1814. At that time, the local farmer was a man called Captain W. Mackay. He lost patience with the numbers of visitors tramping across his land to see the stones. To stop the visitors, he decided to remove the stones. On Christmas Day in 1814 he toppled one of the stones in the ring and he destroyed another nearby stone. He was only prevented from doing more damage by the intervention of other local people. The stone he toppled was re-erected earlier this century, but the stone he destroyed was lost forever. It was called the Stone of Odin and was an especially sad loss. It had a circular hole, through which local lovers plighted their troth by holding hands.'

'And your point is?' asked Bob.

'My point, sir, is that Captain W. Mackay has secured himself lasting infamy in Orkney's history because of what he did that day. No-one would ever have heard of him otherwise, but now he will always be the man who tried to destroy the Stenness Stones, and partly succeeded. Can I just ask you to bear that in mind when we visit the Ring of Brodgar, which is only a short distance away? Look, you can see it over there, on the rising ground beyond the edge of the loch.'

Not far along the road, Sergeant Bennett pulled the car to one side once more. Bob had noticed on the short journey that they were now driving along a narrow spit of land between two lochs.

Once again, Bennett led the way. The ring turned out to be made up of several dozen standing stones arranged in a circular shape. Surrounding the circle was a ditch, and the whole thing was set on a raised area of moorland that offered excellent views over the surrounding landscape. Track marks, some of them extremely close to individual stones, were ample evidence of the activities of the Gordon Highlanders earlier that afternoon.

Bob's respect for his sergeant went up several notches. 'It is a wonderful place,' he said.

'Yes, it is, sir. When it was originally constructed, they think there were 60 stones here, set out in a perfect circle. There are fewer than two-thirds of that number still standing today. If the photographer and that lieutenant had carried on as they were, there might be even fewer left standing now. Frankly, sir, if they had shot me for sabotaging their exercise, it would have been worth it.'

Bob could see that he meant it. 'And the reason you showed us the other stones was to demonstrate just how badly it's taken if anyone tries to harm Orkney's heritage?'

'That's right, sir. The lieutenant who arrested us today might now be looking forward to a posting to Iceland or Burma but at least he's just "the lieutenant". The churned-up heather will heal in time but if he'd damaged the stones here, he'd have got his name in the Orkney history books for all the wrong reasons.'

'I take the point. More importantly, the general also took the point. Look, let's get back to Kirkwall while it's still light. We need to get the team together to discuss progress.'

As they walked back towards the car, a familiar noise made Bob stop and turn round. Military aircraft were so common in Britain's skies that normally he barely noticed them. This was as true over Orkney as anywhere else. But the sound of a Merlin engine still had the power to attract him. As he watched, a lone Spitfire performed a series of tight turns over the loch beyond the Ring of Brodgar. Part of him wanted to be there, in the cockpit of that aircraft. Rather more of him was grateful that his days as a fighter pilot were behind him.

He turned to follow the others, who'd not realised that he'd stopped.

*

'Can you thank Betty for getting her father to make this room available, Michael?' Bob looked round. The hotel's staff dining room wasn't large, but it was larger than his bedroom and there were more seats and a table. The walls were home to numerous public information posters. Bob suspected the impact of their messages had faded for the regular users of the room, but they did help brighten the place up.

On the far wall from where he sat, 'Save kitchen scraps to feed the hens!' was positioned next to 'Women of Britain, come into the factories'. Another poster nearly in his eyeline called on its readers to 'Keep a pig' and 'Join or start a pig club'.

Lieutenant Commander Dixon was sitting on the opposite side of the table and saw Bob looking. 'There's one about you on the wall behind you, sir.'

Bob turned round and saw a poster featuring a photograph of five RAF pilots beneath a blue sky, on which were printed the words, 'Never was so much owed by so many to so few', with the quote attributed to 'The Prime Minister'.

Monique, sitting next to Dixon, had caught the exchange and smiled.

Bob rapped the table. 'Right, the sooner we get this done, the sooner we can get some dinner and the sooner we can give this room back to those who I am sure will also want their dinner. I had thought of asking our navy friends next door for the loan of a meeting room but as I suspect we're going to be talking about them, it seemed better to find an alternative.'

Bob looked over at Captain Darlington. 'Anthony, can you kick off with a brief outline of what you've been doing today and any important points that have emerged?'

Darlington unfolded a map and laid it out on the table in front of them. 'This is the pre-war Bartholomew's half-inch map of Orkney. It's obviously not very detailed, but it does give a sense of location that will help you understand where we've been.

'Our focus today has been on East Mainland. We visited the coastal batteries at Carness, on the east side of Kirkwall Bay north of here; at Rerwick Head, which covers the approach into Shapinsay Sound; at Deerness, guarding Deer Sound; and at Holm, overlooking Holm Sound, on the south side of the island.' Darlington pointed at the relevant places on the map as he spoke. He went on to identify the two anti-aircraft batteries they'd visited and two searchlight units.

'As you all know, I'm very new to this, but Sergeant Potter kept me on the straight and narrow.'

'Did anything significant emerge?' asked Bob.

'A few minor issues, sir. And a searchlight unit that seemed to have taken the morning off, leaving just two men on guard who were playing cards in their accommodation when we walked in completely unchallenged. I'll obviously produce a full report on all our visits. Tomorrow we'll find our way to the island of South Ronaldsay and if time and transport permits, perhaps look at the defences on Flotta. Thursday will be spent either on West Mainland or on Hoy. We're not going to cover everything this week, but I think we knew that before we started.'

'Thank you, Anthony. Would you mind leaving the map laid out on the table? Others might also find it useful.' Bob turned to Flight Lieutenant Buchan. 'George, could you fill our colleagues in on your eventful day?'

Buchan did so, to expressions first of concern and then of amusement from others in the room as he detailed their encounter with the Bren gun carriers at the Ring of Brodgar and the events that followed. 'I intend to look at the naval air station at Hatston and at RAF Grimsetter tomorrow and to make a start on a couple of radar stations.'

'Thank you. Now I'll ask Lieutenant Commander Dixon to fill us in on his day. I accompanied him for the first part of it, and Madame Dubois was present throughout. I think we can safely say that our morning was almost as eventful as George and Peter's afternoon.'

Michael talked the team through the trip over to Lyness and their encounter with the admiral. 'The highlight was when Monique called the admiral a stupid man and completely destroyed his reasons for excluding her from the meeting.'

There was a collective sharp intake of breath from those who'd not been present, then laughter.

Monique held up a hand. 'As we will all be working together, I should say that I deeply regret losing my temper with the admiral. I consider what I said to be totally unprofessional.'

'Just so everyone is clear, I view what Madame Dubois said to the admiral to have been entirely justified,' said Bob. 'It certainly stopped him excluding her, when my own offers to go over his head had little effect. What happened during the rest of the day, Michael?'

'We were talked through security arrangements at Lyness and then given a tour of the place. Everyone was on best behaviour and we didn't really pick up anything of any significance. We also visited Longhope on the island of South Walls, which is connected to Hoy by a recently built causeway. I suppose that what makes Orkney different to anywhere else we've been is that it's so big that you never really see the outside edges, where security would normally be most important. I'm beginning to think that we need to treat the entire archipelago as a single military base and focus on things like the points of entry for the steamers from Scrabster, in Stromness and Lyness, and the handling of other shipping here in Kirkwall. There's a Security Unit mainly based in Stromness and Lyness that issues Protected Area permits for anything up to 200 civilians each day who are seeking access to Orkney under the Defence Regulations. I think the other place we need to look at, and this should be our priority for tomorrow, is the island of Flotta. People talk about it as if it's another world operating to a different set of rules, and it's certainly the place that is most often visited by the crews of the anchored warships.' Michael looked to the end of the table where Petty Officer MacDonald sat. 'Andrew has a couple of things he wants to add.'

MacDonald smiled. 'Yes, sir. You'll remember that while Madame Dubois was putting the admiral straight this morning, I was consigned to the canteen in the admiral's headquarters building at Lyness. I didn't see anyone I knew, but I did get a strong sense of a panic going on behind the scenes. There was an undercurrent that it was difficult to pin down, but which was causing people to feel uncomfortable. And I'm sure it wasn't down to my presence. At one point a rating who had just sat down to his morning tea was fetched by a senior officer and left without drinking it. In my experience, senior officers tend not to do their own fetching unless it's something really urgent.'

Bob sat back. 'Thank you, Andrew. I'd call that reasonable progress, subject to a couple of fallings-out. Perhaps we should adjourn and reconvene for dinner in, say, half an hour?'

'Don't you have anything to report, group captain?' asked Monique.

Bob was surprised by her intervention, then realised that he should bring his team up to date on what he'd been doing. Up to a point, anyway. 'Yes, of course. As Monique knows, last night I bumped into a man in the hotel lobby who I later realised was a Glasgow gangster called Frank Gordon. I found myself wondering what he was doing here. When I returned from Lyness I rang my father, who as most of you know is a superintendent in the Edinburgh City Police. He told me that Frank Gordon had been released from a long stretch in prison a year or two back and was last heard of in Dublin.

'I also called in this afternoon on an inspector in the Orkney Constabulary, to ask whether he had come across Frank Gordon in Orkney. He hadn't, but said that if a Glasgow gangster, whatever name he was working under, was active on his patch, then he'd know about it. He did raise the major caveat that "his patch" excluded anything to do with the military. He said he thought it quite likely that the huge presence of military personnel and military equipment and supplies in Orkney had opened a variety of opportunities for criminals. But if it's happening, then it's happening out of his sight.

'The main thing I took away from my visit to the police office was that on the civilian side, the local police force in Orkney has only some 30 men, nearly half of whom are Police War Reserve constables. It says a lot that the inspector I spoke to also serves as the deputy chief constable.

'He did say one thing I found particularly interesting. Apparently, there's been a murder. A man's body was found in a quarry yesterday morning in circumstances that suggest his death was neither accidental nor natural. The body was a mess, but the lower part of one arm was intact, including the fingerprints and a tattoo of the points of the compass on the inside of the forearm. The body's been flown to Aberdeen for forensic analysis, but the police don't currently have anything to go on. I did wonder whether our missing Commander Napier, who was unable to meet us with the admiral today, has or had a tattoo like that.'

'The naval provost marshal?' asked Petty Officer MacDonald.

'Yes, why do you ask?' said Bob.

'I know him. I came across him in Rosyth right at the beginning of the war. He was a lieutenant commander looking after security at the dockyard there. He's not my favourite officer, I must admit. The thing is, sir, he was the senior officer who fetched the rating from the canteen. I'd have said who it was if I'd realised it was relevant.'

'Well, that proves Commander Napier's not our dead man,' said Bob. 'It would have been very neat, though admittedly not for him, if he had been. It would certainly have explained why the admiral responded the way he did when you asked about Napier's absence from the meeting. And perhaps the unspecified panic that prevented the navy giving us dinner last night. It still doesn't explain what was going on behind the scenes that prevented their head of security attending the meeting this morning. Anyway, let's break for dinner.'

*

After dinner in the hotel, Bob and his colleagues moved through to the hotel bar. There'd been a debate about whether any of them would explore the local pubs again. But Flight Lieutenant Buchan had overheard two army officers complaining that it was now raining and that the rain was being driven horizontally along Harbour Street by a gale that had blown up out of nowhere. When he reported this, everyone decided that the hotel bar was the better bet.

They managed to push two tables together in a corner, which made a reasonably defensible space. The piano player was active again. The officers contributed to a kitty and drinks service was provided by the non-commissioned officers. Bob reflected that the class system was still at work, even in parts of the system that he liked to think of as enlightened. He had asked for a tonic and had decided to nurse it. Monique took a sip of her drink, also a tonic, before turning to talk to Sergeant Bennett, who was sitting next to her.

The conversation round the table was pleasant enough, but, as over dinner on both nights, steered clear of their reasons for being in Orkney.

When Peter, Andrew and Gilbert returned from the bar with the second round of drinks, they put the money they'd taken with them back on the table. 'There was no charge that time,' said Gilbert Potter.

'Why not?' asked Michael Dixon.

'It seems there was a party of WRNS officers in. I did notice them over the other side of the bar, and again when they left a short time ago. According to the barman they left money behind the bar to buy a round of drinks for "the civilian lady and her party". It seems we have you to thank for this drink, Madame Dubois.'

Michael laughed. 'I did warn you that word of your encounter with the admiral would get round, Monique!'

Bob was pleased to see that Monique smiled, apparently taking her new-found and highly unwanted fame in her stride.

When the others were well into their second drinks, Bob decided he could decently leave. He wanted to write a report on their first day's activities for Commodore Cunningham in London, which he would send by secure military mail the next morning. He'd not normally do so at this stage, but given that intelligence was his boss's stock-in-trade, it was always possible he'd pick up odd stories arising from the team's activities today. Bob wanted to be sure his side of the story was on his boss's desk before any questions were asked in Whitehall.

He was about to get up when Andrew MacDonald, who was sitting next to him, put his nearly empty pint glass down on the table. 'Did anyone else encounter Orkneyitis today?'

Anthony Darlington looked up. 'I did hear the word mentioned at one of the coastal batteries but didn't really understand what lay behind it, beyond extreme boredom. The men had planted a kitchen garden – there wasn't much growing in it at this time of year – and when I asked why, the officer in command told me it was an antidote to Orkneyitis. There wasn't a chance to pursue what he meant by it at the time.'

'I had a petty officer sit at my table in the canteen at Lyness this morning who told me exactly what it is,' said Andrew. 'When I said I was new to Orkney, he told me I'd have to watch out for Orkneyitis. When I asked what he meant, he told me it covered a range of odd behaviours that people had adopted to beat off boredom and make their lives here more bearable. It happens more widely but, according to him, it's common for men permanently stationed on Flotta to have imaginary pets. Invisible cats and dogs that they talk to and play with and groom and feed, sometimes with scraps from the cookhouse. Some of the men apparently keep imaginary lions or tigers or snakes instead of the more usual pets. According to him, these imaginary creatures are simply accepted as real, even by men who don't have one themselves.'

'Are you sure he wasn't pulling your leg?' asked Michael.

'You'd think so, sir, but he did sound horribly convincing. According to him there's a depot ship permanently moored at Longhope which has an imaginary garden set up on the deck at the rear of the ship. The whole crew share in the fantasy, asking one another about what they are growing and discussing the best varieties of potatoes to plant. It helps the crew pass the time and gives them something to think about other than the sheer tedium of their day-to-day lives. That's Orkneyitis.'

Bob made his apologies and left. As he crossed the lobby heading for the stairs, he became aware of a man standing at the reception desk, looking at him.

'It's Group Captain Sutherland isn't it? Congratulations on your promotion!'

It took Bob a moment to recognise the man. 'Captain Matheson, thank you. I was about to ask what brings you to Orkney, but that would be a rather stupid question.' Bob had met the captain a couple of months earlier and walked over to shake his hand. Captain Matheson made his living running the air mail service between Inverness and Orkney in a bright red de Havilland Dragon Rapide biplane that was very like the aircraft that had brought Bob and the team to Orkney, except for its colour. Matheson seemed to be about 50 and was dressed, as when Bob had first met him, in tweed plus fours, jacket and waistcoat.

Matheson lowered his voice. 'Did you ever find out what caused the Duke of Kent's Sunderland to crash?'

Bob smiled, apologetically. 'I can't really say any more than was in the official account given to parliament early last month.'

'But that was complete garbage, wasn't it? Sorry, I know you can't say, group captain. Anyway, I'm due to be meeting an old pal here shortly so I won't detain you. I'd suggest a drink tomorrow night, but I'm heading back down to Inverness in the morning.'

'It was good to meet you again. Have a good flight.'

Bob turned back towards the stairs. As he did so he saw a man in the phone booth at the back of the lobby look away, as if he'd been watching but didn't want Bob to know. The trilby was nowhere in sight, but Frank Gordon still had his gabardine raincoat on, now unbuttoned to reveal the dark suit he was wearing beneath it. Bob found himself wondering just how loudly Captain Matheson had called out the name 'Sutherland'. For a spilt-second he wondered if it was best simply to feign ignorance and innocence and go over and greet his uncle. Then he decided that if Frank Gordon had recognised him, it might be better to leave his uncle unsure about whether the recognition was mutual.

As he climbed the stairs, Bob regretted not being able to spend more time with Captain Matheson. It had been men like him who had sparked Bob's interest in flying a decade earlier and helped nurture it into a passion. The problem was that Bob couldn't tell Matheson what he knew about the Duke of Kent's death. Not just because the real story had officially been swept under the carpet, but also because Matheson had himself, entirely unwittingly and innocently, played a small part in the crash that killed the duke. Bob really didn't want to be the one to tell him.

CHAPTER SIX

When Bob came down for breakfast, his RAF and army teams had again made early starts, setting off before dawn. He realised that at this time of year in Orkney, that didn't make their starts especially early. Lieutenant Commander Dixon and Petty Officer MacDonald were tucking into large plates of fried food, while Monique looked as if she was waiting for hers to arrive. 'Did you sleep well?' Bob asked the table generally.

'Very well, thank you sir,' said MacDonald, with a broad grin. Bob deduced that he'd been spared the Lieutenant Commander's snoring again.

Bob turned to Dixon and smiled. 'I hope that when the admiral was talking yesterday morning, you understood the implications of Betty's father being an old war comrade of Winston Churchill's? You seem to be playing for high stakes, Michael.'

'Funny you should say that, sir. I mentioned it to her last night. It was news to her. She'd thought her father had been unable to join up in the last war because of his flat feet.'

Monique looked over Bob's shoulder, towards the door of the dining room. 'I think we may have a visitor, Bob.'

Bob turned round to see a naval rating in a greatcoat walking towards them.

'Are you Group Captain Sutherland, sir?'

'Yes, that's me.'

'No offence, sir, but I've been told to ask to see your identification.'

Bob complied.

'Thank you, sir. We've had a telephone call in the operations room next door, asking for you. The caller said his name was Commodore Cunningham and he said he needed to speak to you straight away.'

'You'd better lead on,' Bob said to the rating as he stood up. 'Am I going to need a coat?'

'It's pretty wild outside, sir, and wet, but we're only next door so you should be OK.'

As they entered the Kirkwall Hotel, Bob reflected that 'OK' was a relative term. His peaked cap should have helped keep his head dry on the rather undignified dash between the two hotels, but he'd had to take it off to stop it blowing away in the strong wind.

'The operations room is in what used to be the hotel's function rooms, sir, up on the first floor. I'll lead the way.' The rating led Bob up the main stairs and into an anteroom housing busy clerks and typists. Beyond it was a large room whose rear walls were adorned with a series of maps which, it seemed to Bob, between them covered a large part of the North Atlantic. There were also other maps, at different scales, depicting Orkney and Scotland. The front of the room was dominated by large windows offering views out over Kirkwall harbour. Bob imagined that on a nice day the views, despite the intrusion of the anti-blast tape that criss-crossed the glass, would make this a very pleasant place to work.

'Hello again, sir.' It was Second Officer Jennings. 'If you pick up the phone numbered "three" on the desk over there, you'll be connected to Commodore Cunningham.'

Bob did as he'd been instructed, wondering whether his report was simply going to be too late to head off the repercussions from yesterday. For all he knew, Commodore Cunningham and

Rear Admiral Kinnaird could be old shipmates.

'Group Captain Sutherland speaking.'

'Hello, Bob. How's it going in Orkney?'

'Fairly well sir. We're making good progress, though we might have ruffled a few feathers yesterday. I've written a report that I'll ask the operations room here to forward to you.'

'Ruffling feathers is part of your job. That's not why I'm ringing though.' Bob felt his spirits rise. The commodore continued. 'We've got a bit of a panic on at RAF Lossiemouth. It's all exceptionally sensitive, so I'll not give you any details over the phone.'

'Do you want me to send down Flight Lieutenant Buchan and Sergeant Bennett? They usually deal with the RAF side of things.'

'No Bob, this is one I'd like you to take on yourself, and I think you'll need to take Madame er... Dubois with you.' Bob realised his boss had stumbled over Monique's cover name. Cunningham continued, 'It's a one-off situation and military security is certainly involved. I'm sure you can leave the rest of the team to carry on with your reviews of security on the bases in Orkney. I'd like the two of you to get yourselves down to Lossiemouth as quickly as possible. By that, I mean as early as possible this morning. The station commander there, Group Captain Roebuck, will be expecting you.'

'The weather is extremely bad here, sir. How urgent is this?'

'It's literally a matter of life and death, group captain. Do your best.'

Bob put the phone down, then looked across to where Second Officer Jennings was seated at a desk. He walked over to her. 'Is it possible for me to call Air Commodore Chilton from here?'

Before leaving, Bob passed Jennings the envelope containing

the report he'd written for Commodore Cunningham the previous night and asked her to ensure it got into the secure mail. She assured him it would.

*

Bob found Monique finishing off breakfast in the dining room of the St Magnus Hotel, while Dixon and MacDonald kept her company with a cup of tea.

'Eat up, Monique, we need to be somewhere else.'

Lieutenant Commander Dixon looked at him. 'What's up, sir?'

'I've no idea, I'm afraid, but something certainly is.' Bob looked round to satisfy himself they couldn't be overheard by others eating breakfast. He didn't think they could, but he lowered his voice and leaned forwards anyway. 'It seems Madame Dubois and I are required at RAF Lossiemouth as early as possible this morning.'

'Are you going to have some breakfast, first, Bob?' asked Monique.

'Perhaps I'd better not. The weather's foul. We've got an Avro Anson waiting for us at RAF Grimsetter and it's going to be a very bumpy ride.'

'I assume you want the rest of us to carry on as planned here, sir?' asked Dixon.

'Yes, please. I have no idea how long we're going to be in Lossiemouth. For all I know we might be back later today, though I have a feeling that's unlikely. We'll keep our rooms in the hotel here until Friday, just in case, but take our belongings. You take command in my absence, Michael and if we're not back by Friday you should return to Edinburgh as planned. George and Anthony both know what their teams need to do. On your side of things, I would be grateful if you could see if you can find anything out about what's going on behind the scenes with the admiral and his head of security, as well as the more routine stuff. Right, I think you and I need to pack, Monique.'

Bob had an odd feeling as he entered his room. Housekeeping had clearly not yet been in to make his bed, but it felt as if someone had been in the room since he went down to breakfast. Bob didn't have much with him, but he did get the sense that someone had, very carefully, gone through his bag and the few clothes he'd put in a drawer, as if looking for something.

He went out into the corridor and knocked on Monique's door.

'Almost ready, Bob.' She pulled open her door, with her travel bag in her hand.

'Could you just come and look at my room for a moment, Monique?'

She smiled. 'I really don't think this is the time or the place, Bob.' She looked at him and the smile disappeared. 'You're serious, aren't you? What's happened?'

'I think my room's been searched.' She followed him into his room. 'Last night, when I left the bar, I met Captain Matheson, the pilot with the red biplane who you and I interviewed in Inverness. I talked with him for a couple of minutes, but as he was waiting to meet someone, I said my farewells and came up to my room. Then I realised that Frank Gordon had been in the phone booth at the back of the lobby and probably heard Matheson call out my name. I'm fairly sure he recognised me.'

'And you think he's responded by searching your room? Did you leave anything valuable, or personal or sensitive here?'

'No, thankfully. I had the report I wrote for Commodore Cunningham with me and posted it via the naval people next door while I was taking his phone call. But a few things aren't quite where I left them. A shirt in the top draw has been moved, just slightly. And my bag was closed when I'm sure I'd left it open.'

'The important thing is that nothing was taken. But I agree it does seem very odd.'

Bob thought so too. Then he realised that wasn't his immediate priority. 'Hell. I need to pack. Our car will be waiting outside by now.'

*

The flight to Lossiemouth had been every bit as bumpy as Bob had feared, though he found that sitting in the co-pilot's seat helped his stomach cope. Not quite as good as flying himself, but nearly. Monique, sitting in the main cabin, as usual had no problem.

The pilot, a flying officer, had greeted them in the briefing room under the control tower at Grimsetter. 'I've just spoken to the meteorologist, sir. He thinks that if we can take off, then conditions will steadily improve as we head south.'

'And do you think we can take off?'

'It's really marginal. It depends how badly you need to be there.'

'I'm told we need to be there quite badly. But you're the aircraft captain, so it has to be your decision.'

'In that case the weather's good enough to take off, sir.'

Things had improved considerably by the time they had reached Tarbat Ness, on the southern side of the Dornoch Firth. The pilot had said that if visibility was poor, he'd have been prepared to follow the north-western shore of the Moray Firth before turning east along its southern shore once it was clearly in sight. But with good visibility under high clouds, he simply set out in a south-easterly direction across the Moray Firth, making landfall on the southern shore just to the east of Lossiemouth.

As Bob looked down, it seemed to him that there were aircraft parked, sometimes very closely together, in many of the fields surrounding the airfield. A dozen identical aircraft in one place; a couple of dozen of a different type in a corner of the next field; more lined up facing inwards towards a curving track a little distance away; and so on. Many were Bristol Beaufighters, but there were also groups of Vickers Wellington and Avro Lancaster bombers visible, plus a bewildering array of other types. Most of the aircraft he could see near the hangars on the airfield itself were Wellingtons. He realised that in total he must be looking at hundreds of aircraft.

The pilot saw Bob looking. 'Those fields are storage areas for the maintenance unit that's based here, sir. The Air Transport Auxiliary fly in aircraft from the factories and 46 Maintenance Unit add weapons and various bits of equipment. Then the ATA fly the finished aircraft to units all over the country, usually as replacements for aircraft lost in training or on operations.'

'It's a hell of a target for any stray Luftwaffe bomber pilot,' said Bob.

'True, sir. It's just as well they tend not to stray this far west or south any longer.'

'And what's happening on the airfield itself? It looks like a construction site.'

'That's what it is, sir. Until now they've had to use grass runways. But now there's a United States Army Air Force construction unit here, building concrete runways. As you can imagine, using the place while work's been under way has been a bit of a challenge, but they've managed to keep it open. Last time

I heard, they were hoping to have the first concrete runway in use by the end of the month, with the other two ready next month. They're doing the same at Kinloss, just along the coast.'

There were two Wellingtons in the circuit at Lossiemouth so it took a little longer to land than it might have done. As the Anson came to a halt on a concrete area not far from the control tower, a RAF staff car pulled up beside it. Bob thanked the pilot before following Monique down the cabin and out of the door, which was being held open from the outside.

Bob climbed out to see Monique shaking hands with a group captain who was standing a few yards away, over towards the car. It seemed the aircraft door was being held open by the group captain's driver, who saluted as Bob stepped out. He returned the salute, then walked over towards the group captain, who had turned to face him. The group captain looked to be in his late forties and had pilot's wings and a line of medal ribbons on his tunic. He didn't look as if he had slept the previous night.

The man extended a hand. 'Group Captain Sutherland I presume? I'm Alexander Roebuck. I answer to "Sandy".'

'Good to meet you, Sandy. I'm Bob. I see you've already met Madame Dubois. I understand you have a problem.'

'Let's head over to the station headquarters building. We can talk in my office.'

Bob got in the back of the car with Monique, while Group Captain Roebuck sat in the front with the driver. As they drove past the control tower Bob leaned forward in his seat. 'You seem to have the builders in. I understand you've had a set of concrete runways built.'

'Yes, and only just in time. Last winter the surface of the grass runways got so bad that 20 Operational Training Unit, who fly most of the Wellingtons you can see around the place, had to move down to Lakenheath in Suffolk for a while, just to give the surfaces here a chance to recover. The first concrete runway is nearly finished, and we should be relatively weather-proof during the rest of this winter. Relatively rain-proof anyway.'

Bob looked at the aircraft they were passing. 'I commanded an Operational Training Unit, Number 55, down at RAF Annan, before I had this job bestowed on me. We were training fighter pilots rather than bomber crews though.'

'I bet you had many of the same problems we see here. Though we have a few additional ones you probably didn't have to tackle. Four times this year we've been called on to contribute crews made up of staff and trainees from 20 OTU to take part in some of the large bombing raids on Germany. We lost two aircraft as a result. That's small beer compared with our training losses, though that won't be any surprise to you.'

'How many aircraft have you lost in training?'

'So far this year, 20 OTU has lost over twenty aircraft in training accidents. With an average crew of six, an awful lot of young men have been killed as a result.'

'Good God,' said Bob. 'As least with fighters you tend not to lose more than one young man per crashed aircraft. And though I've never tried to get out of a bomber in a hurry, I suspect it's easier to accomplish in a fighter, both in the air and on the ground.'

The car pulled up outside a brick two-storey building that had a similar counterpart on just about every other RAF station Bob had ever visited.

Group Captain Roebuck asked his secretary to organise tea as he led Bob and Monique into his office. He gestured to two seats on the near side of his desk, while he went round the far side. 'It's just me, for the moment at least. I'll brief you on what's happened, and then we can discuss what you want to do about it.'

Bob nodded his assent, so the group captain continued. 'We talked about 20 OTU. We have another permanent unit stationed here at Lossiemouth, 46 Maintenance Unit.'

'I got a sense of what they do from the Anson pilot as we arrived,' said Bob.

'Good, I'll keep it brief then. Aircraft are flown here from the manufacturers. 46 MU prepare them for squadron service, adding radios, weapons and other specialist kit, and then they are flown out to squadrons up and down the country as they are needed. The actual flying is undertaken by No.10 Ferry Pilot Pool of the Air Transport Auxiliary. They're all civilians and they relieve RAF pilots of the need to make delivery flights. You'll have encountered the ATA yourself and know that there are some exceptional pilots amongst them.

'Anyway, back on the 1st of October, an Avro Anson was due to be delivered from here to RAF Errol, between Perth and Dundee.'

'I've been there, quite recently,' said Bob.

'The pilot was a First Officer Sally Fowler. She was young, but she was an experienced and very capable pilot. From what we've been able to establish, it seems she chose to fly a direct course, which ran her into poor weather in the mountains beyond Ballater. An Anson was seen flying south over Ballater at low level at about the right time but then she simply disappeared. We conducted aerial searches as soon as the weather cleared and asked the local police to keep a lookout, but it was as if the ground had simply opened up and swallowed both her and the Anson.

'Now let's wind things forward to late on the afternoon of last Saturday, the 14th of November. A farmer looking for missing sheep in Glen Muick, which runs south from Ballater, came across some of them in a field high on the south-eastern side of the glen, above Loch Muick. They were dead and had been dead for quite some time. Then he saw some aircraft wreckage at the foot of a rock face screened by trees just above the field. He didn't know it at the time, but it was our missing Anson. As far as we can tell, First Officer Fowler flew along Glen Muick at low level, perhaps hoping to stay below the cloud, and somehow flew into the mountainside. There had been no fire at the time, but the wreckage was highly fragmented because of the impact.'

'What about First Officer Fowler?' asked Monique.

'Her, too, I'm afraid. The farmer reported what he'd found to the local police, who remembered that we had a missing aircraft in the area. We had a recovery team of half a dozen men under a flight sergeant out at the site of the crash by mid-morning on the following day, Sunday the 15th of November. They had the highly unpleasant task of recovering the remains of the pilot and pretty much left it at that. With crashes quite so frequent in the mountains we tend to focus on recovery of the bodies of the crews and ensuring that any weapons and ordnance are made safe. There was no record of any weaponry being on board the Anson, so they left the wreckage where it was.

'Move forward to yesterday morning, Tuesday the 17th of November, and three of the recovery crew had fallen seriously ill overnight. Then we were contacted by the police in Ballater to say that the farmer who had found the crash site died in the early hours of yesterday morning. He'd been seen by a doctor after falling ill with a chest infection on Monday, but his condition had rapidly deteriorated overnight. The station medical officer here thinks that what my men are suffering from could well be anthrax and that the chance of any of the three surviving is very slight.

We've put them in isolation and isolated the other men who were at the crash site. But this was long after they could have infected other people if their condition is contagious. If there's any good news here, it's that if this is anthrax, then it's not contagious. It's caught through open wounds or by breathing in spores.'

'I understand the situation,' said Bob, 'but what led you to think that MI11 might be able to help? Our remit is military security rather than medicine.'

'Yes, I know, but when I discussed how to proceed with my boss, and he with his, it was suggested that MI11 might be able to assist, especially as its northern arm is now led by someone with a RAF background.' Group Captain Roebuck paused, as if to gather his thoughts. 'To understand the implications, you need to wind the clock back to early September. We received a request to help with some experiments the scientists from the government's research station at Porton Down in Wiltshire are running over on the west coast, at a place called Gruinard Bay in Wester Ross. They've set up a base over there, on the mainland, that they call "X Base".

'We were asked if we could provide a crew and an aircraft capable of dropping an adapted 25lb incendiary bomb at a specified location on Gruinard Island, which is in the bay. 20 OTU was happy to oblige, so on the 25th of September, the week before the Anson crash, a team of two men and a woman from X Base arrived at Lossiemouth. We loaned them a couple of our armourers and donated an incendiary bomb of the type they had specified to adapt. The following day, on the 26th of September, a Wellington dropped it on Gruinard Island. I've spoken to the aircraft's bomb-aimer, who tells me that the bomb was dropped within ten yards of the target. As soon as the bomb was loaded into the Wellington, the scientists got back in their car and headed back over to Wester Ross. The aircraft took off several hours later, to give the Porton Down people a chance to get back to Gruinard Bay to observe the drop.'

'What's the connection?' asked Bob.

'The connection is that the bomb was adapted to carry three litres of anthrax spores in three sealed cylindrical containers. Reading between the lines, I gather that X Base is all about testing the effects of anthrax as a biological weapon. I was told the bare outlines of this, in the strictest confidence, before I agreed that Lossiemouth should be involved. When the medical officer came to see me yesterday to tell me that he thought the three ill men had anthrax, I made the obvious connection.

'Late yesterday I spoke to the two armourers who helped the people from Porton Down adapt the bomb on the 25th of September. They said that the three sealed containers of anthrax – one of the scientists had let slip what was in them - were put in the space created by removing the fire-pots, the incendiary elements, from the bomb. My armourers got the sense the cylinders had been designed specifically to fit this type of bomb. The thermite charges in the nose and rear body of the bomb were left in place. It seems the idea was that these would detonate on impact and turn the canisters of anthrax spores into a cloud. When they'd finished fitting the canisters, the bomb was locked in a workshop, which was placed under armed guard. The next morning the bomb was loaded into the Wellington's bomb bay, and the aircraft was then left under armed guard until it took off.'

'And there's no indication of how anthrax contaminated the Avro Anson, nor any explanation of the gap of nearly a week between the Wellington bombing Gruinard Island and the Anson crashing?'

'That's correct, Bob.'

'Why was the Anson going to RAF Errol?'

'It was a new aircraft being delivered to No. 9 Advanced Flying Unit, which is based there.'

'What about the scientists over at X Base?' asked Monique. 'What have they got to say about what's happened?'

'Not very much, I'm afraid. I've been in touch with the lead scientist over there, a Professor Malone, several times by telephone, both yesterday evening and again this morning. He was able to confirm that there is no effective cure for anthrax, and that the mortality rate is extremely high, but he did also confirm that it's not contagious. He also agreed to let us have protective clothing and decontamination equipment, together with some men who can teach us how to use it. They are on their way over by road as I speak. That will at least allow us to take a closer look at the Anson to see if we can determine how it came to be contaminated and then try to tackle the contamination. I've not been prepared to send my people in using just gas respirators, so for now we are simply maintaining a wide cordon around the crash site. The professor wasn't able to come up with any ideas about how his anthrax, and I'm convinced it must be his anthrax, got into my Avro Anson.'

'It sounds like our starting point should be at Porton Down's "X Base" at Gruinard Bay,' said Bob. 'Madame Dubois and I will go and see what they've got to say for themselves. Can we borrow a car?'

CHAPTER SEVEN

It wasn't much more than a hundred miles from Lossiemouth to Gruinard Bay, but the roads were increasingly narrow and poorly-maintained the further west they went.

'It's a shame you couldn't arrange a flying boat,' said Monique. She was looking at a road map they'd been given. 'Where we want to be isn't far from Loch Ewe. Our flying boat trip over there was much quicker and more comfortable.'

'The thought had crossed my mind,' said Bob, 'but I've no idea how long we're going to be there, and a car seemed to offer more flexibility. Besides, a flying boat has a large crew and we probably don't want to broadcast our interest too widely.'

'You might at least have asked for a driver.'

'Again, it's less flexible. And it occurred to me a driver might constrain discussion. If you don't like my driving, you're welcome to take a turn yourself.'

Monique laughed. 'Your driving's fine, Bob, and I'm enjoying the navigating. It's quite satisfying when there are no signs to tell you where you are or where you are going, and you get it right anyway. That last village was called Garve, by the way. The level crossing was a dead giveaway. Now we're looking out for a junction. That looks like it up ahead.'

'Which way do we go?'

'Either left or straight on would get us where we want to be, but I think straight on looks like the shorter route, by a fair distance. The other road loops round through places called Gairloch and Poolewe.'

'I think we want the shorter road.'

A few miles further on, Bob said, 'You didn't say much in the meeting with the group captain.'

'There didn't seem to be much to say. We need to find out how a biological warfare experiment has gone so badly wrong it's caused at least four people on the other side of the country to fall ill, and one of them, so far, to die.'

'My war's been a fairly clinical affair,' said Bob. 'I've killed quite a few men, but with one exception all I ever saw were the aeroplanes I was shooting down. It helped not to think of their crews as real people, as young men just like those I was flying alongside who just happened to be born in a different place and who spoke a different language. That may have given me a very sheltered outlook. I must admit that I find the idea of using an animal disease, or any disease for that matter, as a weapon horrifies me. Your war's been very different, Monique. How did you feel about the idea when the group captain talked about it?'

Monique took a while to speak. 'Much the same as you, I think. You once told me that when you were walking through Germany in 1931 you found the Germans generous and welcoming. Remember that I've spent a lot longer in the company of Germans than you have. I was even married to one for a while. Certainly, the Nazis are a waste of other people's oxygen and I'd shed no tears if it were possible to call down a plague that killed each and every one of them. But you'd not be able to do that without killing many others too, people just trying to survive the war and praying that their loved ones survive it too. Ah, I don't know. On the whole it seems better not to think about it too much.'

It was a while later when Monique told Bob to look out for a turning off to the left from the Ullapool road. Immediately after they turned, they found the road was blocked by a barrier manned by three infantrymen wearing greatcoats and holding rifles. Bob doubted that the men had seen security passes quite like those he and Monique carried but they seemed satisfied and raised the barrier to let the car through.

The road beyond the barrier climbed through a glen, then crossed a broad upland area that offered distant views, especially of a distinctive mountain ahead of them. Not for the first time on the trip, Bob was happy that the morning's storm hadn't come any further south, leaving them with a pleasant drive under a layer of high cloud.

The road followed a river valley down to the head of a sea loch. 'How are we doing?' asked Bob.

Monique smiled. 'It isn't far, now. The road runs parallel with the south side of this loch until it opens out into the sea, and we then cross a shoulder of higher ground before descending to Gruinard Bay.'

As they descended, they could clearly see part of Gruinard Bay ahead of them, complete with a large island that seemed closer to their side of the bay. Bob assumed that was Gruinard Island, where the bomb had been dropped.

They encountered a second security barrier across the road at a farmstead on the descent to the shore. Again, it was manned by infantrymen and again Bob and Monique were asked the purpose of their journey and for their passes.

'We're visiting Professor Malone at X Base. Do you know where I might find the base?' asked Bob.

'Is he expecting you, sir?'

'Yes, he is.' Bob had phoned the professor from the station commander's office at RAF Lossiemouth. He didn't want to spend hours driving across the country only to find that the man he wanted to see wasn't there when he arrived.

'Very good, sir. Look out for a collection of Nissen huts and other buildings and animal pens on the right-hand side, a few hundred yards after the road stops running alongside the shore. They'll direct you from there.'

Bob thanked the man and drove under the raised barrier.

'What a beautiful place,' said Monique.

'Well, it was, until the war turned up on its doorstep,' said Bob. It didn't take them long to reach X Base. The guard at the gate barring access to the ramshackle collection of structures checked their passes, then asked Bob to wait while he made a telephone call. He went into a nearby hut, emerging a short time later.

'You'll find the professor at Gruinard House, sir. It's on the shore below the camp.' He pointed. 'You can just about see the top of the roof from here. There's a footpath and steps from the camp, but as you're driving, you'll need to go back the way you came for a couple of hundred yards and then take a sharp left along the drive leading to the house.'

Bob followed the instructions and they found themselves driving alongside the shore to a large house finished in light grey beneath a strong growth of ivy on the side nearest them.

'That's quite a contrast,' he said. 'It's not a castle, but someone's architect wanted to make people think it might be.'

The main three-storey house stood on a piece of land that seemed to jut out into the nearby bay. Joined to the far side of it was a two-storey range that would have appeared substantial except when set against its immediate neighbour.

Bob reversed the car into a gap in a row of several vehicles on the far side of a gravelled courtyard from the rear of the house. He then led Monique over to a large wooden door reached via an arch set in a single-storey lobby that looked to have been added on to the house. Bob used the door knocker provided. There was no response, so he tried the door, which opened. They entered and found themselves in a corridor that led through to a wood-panelled hallway at the front of the house. This had stairs doglegging up to a landing at first floor level.

'Hello!' he called.

There was the sound of movement from along a passage that led off from one side of the hall. A dark-haired man in corduroy trousers and a striped cardigan over a shirt and tie appeared. He looked at Bob through the circular lenses of his glasses. 'Can I help you?'

'We're here to see Professor Malone.'

'I think the professor is in his office, upstairs.' Then, as an afterthought, 'Is he expecting you?

'Yes, I spoke to him on the phone earlier today and I think your gate guard has told him we've arrived.'

'Follow me, then.'

The man led them up to the first floor, where there was more wood panelling on display, and knocked on a door. He pushed it open without waiting for a response, and went in. Bob and Monique followed.

Their guide stopped, and stood slightly to one side, halfway between the door and a large desk. Bob saw that they were in what must have been the house's library before the war. Now the shelves were largely empty, save for a few of those beyond the desk, which were home to untidy piles of books and papers. Bob found himself wondering how the owners of the property had managed to rehouse their books from such a remote location.

The man behind the desk stood up, breaking into Bob's thoughts. He was a rather rotund gentleman in his sixties with a trim grey beard and dressed in a well-worn but smart tweed suit over a mustard-coloured cardigan with leather buttons. The man placed a pipe in an ashtray on the desk and extended a hand. 'Hello. I'm Christopher Malone. You must be my visitors from military intelligence.'

As Bob reached across the desk to shake Malone's hand, he was struck by the remarkable blueness of the man's eyes, looking at him over the top of half-moon spectacles. 'Yes, I'm Group Captain Sutherland and this is my colleague Madame Dubois. I'm the deputy head of Military Intelligence 11, based in Edinburgh, and we have a responsibility for military security.'

'Please, take a seat. You've had a long drive from Lossiemouth. You've met Dr Martyn Taylor, who is on the scientific staff here. Martyn, could you see if you can get someone to rustle up three cups of tea, please? Look, let's sit over here.' He walked over towards a green leather sofa and two matching chairs on one side of the room.

The professor looked round. 'I often find myself wondering what became of the books that must once have filled these shelves.'

Bob smiled. 'That was my first thought on coming into the room.'

An army private brought in a tray. On it was a pot of tea and three cups and saucers, which he placed on the table in front of the sofa, along with a tea-strainer, a jug of milk, a sugar bowl and three teaspoons. Bob offered thanks and noticed that the professor didn't seem to acknowledge the man.

After the private had left, the professor poured tea into the three cups, and picked one of them up. 'I take it you are here because RAF personnel at Lossiemouth have contracted anthrax?'

'And a farmer near Ballater has died of it. Yes, professor. We'd like to understand a little more clearly what happened when your people went over to Lossiemouth and find out whether they are able to shed any light on how an aircraft there became contaminated with anthrax.'

'The man you need to talk to is my deputy here, Dr John Rawlins. He tends to run the actual trials. He also led the team that went over to RAF Lossiemouth in late September. Look, the best thing is for him to talk you through what happened himself. He's over on the island at the moment. He should be back in an hour or so, before it gets dark, and will be happy to talk to you then. Can I suggest you plan to stay here tonight? I'd not recommend driving back in the dark. We can allocate you a couple of rooms here in the house, and you are welcome to join my scientific staff for dinner in the dining room at 7 p.m. It's pretty utilitarian, but rather better than we manage for the platoon of troops who support us here and who have to reside in Nissen huts at the operational base.'

'That seems reasonable,' said Bob.

'I don't know how much you know about the background to what we're doing here.'

'If I'm honest, I didn't know you existed until Group Captain Roebuck told me earlier today. Madame Dubois and I visited the naval base beside Loch Ewe a couple of months ago, which can only be a few miles away, but I had no idea X Base was here.'

'That's how we try to keep it,' said the professor. 'It might help set what Dr Rawlins will tell you in context if I explain a little of the background. As you are probably aware, the Great War saw the advent of large-scale use of chemical weapons, of poison gas, if you prefer, for the first time. The impact was horrendous on both sides. So horrendous, in fact, that the possession of large stocks of poison gas by both sides in this war is probably what has prevented either side using it. There is of course also the Geneva Protocol, signed in 1925. Its purpose is explained by its rather awkward full title, which is the "Protocol for the Prohibition of the Use in War of Asphyxiating, Poisonous or other Gases, and of Bacteriological Methods of Warfare." Many of the signatories, including Britain, consider this to apply only to a ban on the first use of such weapons, which argues strongly in favour of making sure we can retaliate in kind if we must.

'A lot of the work in the UK has been done at what is now known as the Chemical Defence Experimental Station at Porton Down in Wiltshire, which originally opened under a different name in the Great War. In 1940 CDES established a Biology Department, and what we do here is part of that. As the full title of the Geneva Protocol implies, it has long been clear that biological agents such as anthrax might be developed for use as practical weapons. We are most certainly not the only nation to consider the possibility. There are strong indications, for example, that the Japanese tested the large-scale use of anthrax on prisoners in Manchuria in the early 1930s. Some reports talked of many thousands being killed. Going further back, the Germans had some success infecting Russian army horses and mules with glanders during the Great War, and so reducing the mobility of the entire army. They also tried, less successfully, to use agents to infect animals in the United States with the same disease.'

'I had no idea that biological warfare went back so far,' said Monique.

'Oh, it goes back much further than that,' said the professor. 'Back in the mists of time the Assyrians had a habit of poisoning enemy wells with a rather nasty fungus that incapacitated anyone consuming the water. In 1346, the Mongols threw bodies of warriors who had died of the plague over the walls of the city of Kaffa in Crimea, which they were besieging at the time. We British don't have entirely clean hands in all of this. At the siege of Fort Pitt in the summer of 1763, in what is now Pittsburgh, our troops gave clothes and other belongings of individuals who had died of smallpox to native Indians who they were negotiating with, in the hope it would result in the spread of the disease amongst local tribes.

'While the idea is an old one, it has always proved very difficult to turn biological agents into practical weapons. However, we know that the Germans have made considerable progress in this area. As with chemical weapons, the best form of defence is to ensure that we can retaliate in kind and, once we have a practical capability, to ensure our enemies know that we have it. That is where Porton Down's Biology Department comes in.'

'And your work here is to test how practical anthrax would be as a weapon?' asked Monique.

'Exactly. We needed somewhere remote but still accessible. A Scottish island seemed ideal. Gruinard Island has turned out to be far from perfect as the prevailing wind here is from the west. For obvious reasons we can only conduct tests when there is an offshore wind blowing, ideally from the south, though a south-easterly will do. The island was used for grazing sheep until it was requisitioned last year. We then set up X Base, a term that covers Gruinard Island itself, our operational site just inland from here, and Gruinard House.'

'And how is the work going?' asked Bob.

The professor took a sip of his tea. 'Sometimes, in science, a negative result can be considered a success. Proving something can't be done, or can't be done effectively, can help force you to develop better alternative approaches. It is early days yet and we have more testing to do. But the indications so far are that while a cloud of anthrax spores generated by an explosion can be effective in killing sheep, the problems involved in handling it and delivering it and controlling it could well outweigh its benefits.

'I perhaps shouldn't tell you this, but it will help you understanding the position if I do. Another team at Porton Down is developing an alternative approach that places a lethal dose of anthrax spores into cattle feed in a form that can be distributed widely over Germany by air. They've already established that cattle cakes that are randomly scattered from high altitude can easily be found by grazing cattle. They also know that once the anthrax is in the feed it is relatively stable and long-lived, so contaminated cattle cakes can be stockpiled easily. As the aim is simply to ensure we have a credible threat of retaliation if the Germans use biological weapons first, then that might be a better approach than what we are doing here.'

'But the trials are continuing anyway?' asked Bob.

'Of course. We've certainly not exhausted the possibilities here and I think there's enough work left to do to mean that trials will resume next summer.'

'Have you been able to keep your people safe?' asked Monique.

'Touch wood, yes, we have. Our systems have improved as the tests have gone on and we think we now have procedures in place that safeguard our people and the wider area.'

'You say that as if it's not always been the case, professor,' said Bob.

'Again, in the interest of complete openness, that's true. One of the things we've tightened up on is the disposing of sheep carcasses. They are now incinerated. After the first trial they were simply dumped on the shoreline of the island and covered in rocks. That seemed safe enough as Gruinard Island is three-quarters of a mile away from the mainland at its closest approach, on the eastern side of the bay, and much further away on its southern and western sides. Then we found that several dead sheep had floated away and reached the mainland, on the west shore of the loch, unfortunately, where there are a couple of small villages and some scattered farms and other habitation. The result was the deaths of seven cattle, two horses, three cats and around 50 sheep. But thankfully no people. Look, let's get you settled in and we can reconvene when Dr Rawlins is back.'

CHAPTER EIGHT

The rooms that Bob and Monique had been allocated were in the two-storey range at the side of the main building. On a brief first sight of his, Bob thought it seemed comfortable enough, if small.

After dropping off their travel bags, they donned their coats and walked out to the shoreline in front of the house. The sun had set in the south-west, beyond the bumpy profile of the mainland on the south side of Gruinard Bay.

Bob realised that the house was close to the point at which a river flowed into the sea. He also saw that if Gruinard House's architect had been trying to give the impression of a castle, it was undermined on the seaward side by the way the roof had been brought down, pitched very steeply, to turn the upper floor into a row of three dormer windows. He turned back to look across the bay. 'You could almost call this place idyllic, couldn't you?' he said.

'Except for one thing.'

'Yes, it's difficult to overlook the island, out there in the bay, and ignore what's happening on it.'

When they returned to the main house, they were met in the hallway beyond the front door by a civilian they'd not seen before.

'Hello, I saw you coming across the garden. I'm John Rawlins. I understand from Professor Malone that you want to talk to me. He's suggested we get together in the meeting room next door to his office if that suits you. I hope you don't mind, but I've suggested that the two colleagues who came over to

Lossiemouth with me are present.'

There was no tea this time. Bob found it difficult to guess at the original purpose of the room. It had a fireplace and there were indications from patches on the visible walls that several paintings had once hung here. The upper part of one entire wall, opposite the fireplace, was covered in blackboards, which seemed to have been used to aid discussion of some complex mathematical concept. The room was large enough to accommodate a folding meeting table that at least ten people could sit round. Professor Malone sat near the middle of one side, with Dr Rawlins beside him. The remaining two seats on their side of the table were taken by Dr Taylor, smoking a cigarette, and by a woman Bob hadn't seen before. Bob and Monique sat opposite Malone and Rawlins.

The professor looked across at Bob. 'You've met Dr Rawlins and Dr Taylor. I don't think you've met Dr Margaret Young, who looks after meteorology, air movement and dispersal modelling.' The woman smiled briefly.

Bob took the lead. 'Could you run me through what happened on your trip to Lossiemouth in late September, Dr Rawlins?'

'I set off from here early in the morning of the 25th of September with Dr Taylor and Dr Young and we got to Lossiemouth a little before lunchtime. We took with us three smallish wooden boxes, each containing a sealed and carefully packed one litre metal cylinder containing anthrax spores in a liquid suspension.'

'Just as background, Dr Rawlings, how does the anthrax reach here? I'm assuming it's not produced on site?'

'No, that's a fairly complex process that's carried out at Porton Down. The sealed containers of anthrax spores for this test, and for the other tests we've undertaken here, are flown to RAF

Stornoway in the Outer Hebrides, then brought here by RAF launch. On this occasion the containers had been designed to fit in the casing of a standard 25lb incendiary bomb, which it had been agreed would be made available to us by the people at RAF Lossiemouth. As you are probably aware, the aim of the test was to drop the bomb from a Vickers Wellington aircraft based at Lossiemouth at a particular location on Gruinard Island.'

'We're getting ahead of ourselves,' said Bob, 'but was the test a success?'

'Far from it, I'm afraid. The crew of the aircraft did very well. They dropped the bomb from 7,000ft as intended and it landed close to the centre of the target area. It detonated as it should have done and our sampling devices downwind of the target area, where the trial sheep are penned, showed that a cloud of anthrax spores had been created. It was much less concentrated than the clouds created in the two trials we conducted earlier in the summer, and we suspect that the problem was that despite the small parachute attached to it, the bomb buried itself in soft ground before exploding. No sheep died in the trial as none were exposed to enough anthrax to be affected.'

'Thank you,' said Bob. 'Now can we go back to the trip to Lossiemouth?'

'Yes. After we arrived, we took delivery of the incendiary bomb, and two armourers based at the station helped us remove the containers of incendiary elements and replace them with the three cylinders containing the anthrax spores. There was no problem with the fit and the job only took a few hours, far less time than we'd allowed. The casing of the bomb was then reassembled, and it was locked away in a secure workshop which had armed guards posted outside. The next morning, we were present when the two armourers transported the bomb to where the Wellington was parked and loaded it into the bomb bay. The aircraft was then placed under armed guard. We had a meeting with the pilot, navigator and bomb-aimer of the aircraft to confirm radio frequencies, timings, approach path, height, and the identification of the target. I then drove back here with my colleagues. Later that day the trial took place, with the result I've described to you.'

'What I need to work out,' said Bob, 'is how an aircraft on the base came to be contaminated with anthrax when it crashed on the 1st of October, on a flight from RAF Lossiemouth to an airfield in Perthshire. I hasten to add that it was not the Wellington that carried your bomb. It was a light transport aircraft on a delivery flight. Is there any way that any of your anthrax could have gone astray between your taking it to RAF Lossiemouth and the bomb being dropped on the island here?'

'I don't see how that's possible,' said Dr Rawlins. 'We know the three cylinders were successfully placed in the bomb and that the casing was reassembled.'

'As a matter of interest, what did these cylinders look like. How large were they?'

'Think of the sort of tin you get soup in, only rather larger. Each cylinder was a little over 4.5 inches in diameter, to fit snugly within the bomb casing, and about 4 inches in height. The cylinders themselves were plain aluminium, unmarked apart from a series of code letters on the lid. The outer wooden box that each came packed in, which is a couple of inches longer in each dimension and roughly cubic in shape, had a label with contact information on it for Porton Down.'

'Do you have one I could see?'

'No, we had no use for them once the bomb was prepared so left them at Lossiemouth.'

'Could one of the cylinders have leaked into its box?'

'No, we checked them as they were put into the bomb.'

'Could anyone not on the team have been left alone with the cylinders at any time?'

'I honestly don't think so. Besides, no-one at Lossiemouth other than the station commander had any idea what we were putting in the bomb. Yes, it would have been obvious that something rather unusual was going on, but I don't see anyone trying to steal them on the off-chance this wasn't just another mustard gas trial or something like that.'

'I don't think that's quite correct,' said Bob. 'The station commander at Lossiemouth spoke late yesterday to the two armourers who assisted with the bomb and they said that, and I quote, "one of the scientists" had let slip that the cylinders contained anthrax.'

Professor Malone cleared his throat and leaned forward in his seat to give himself a better view of his colleagues. 'Does anyone care to comment?'

Dr Taylor had gone bright red. 'I'm sorry. It was a slip of the tongue when the armourers were putting the bomb back together. One of them dropped a screwdriver on the table next to the bomb and I said something like, "whatever you do, don't puncture the anthrax cylinders." Neither of them made any response, and I'd hoped they'd not noticed what I'd said.'

'You bloody idiot,' said the professor.

'If they knew, then who else knew?' asked Bob. 'You were at RAF Lossiemouth long enough to spend a night in the officers' mess bar. Are you sure you told no-one else, perhaps after a drink or two?'

Dr Taylor was looking fixedly at his cigarette, burning down between the forefinger and thumb of his right hand. 'I'm absolutely certain. I'm sorry.'

'Let's put that to one side,' said Bob. 'Do any of you remember whether at any time the two Lossiemouth armourers, or one of them, had access to the bomb after the cylinders had been fitted and when none of you were present?'

It was Dr Rawlins who replied. 'No, I can be confident of that. At least one of us was always present until the workshop was locked and placed under armed guard. The only way I can see of anyone taking any of the cylinders would have been for them to evade the armed guards and break into the workshop during the night.'

'Wouldn't it have been obvious that the bomb was too light if one of the cylinders had been removed?' asked Monique.

'Probably not,' said Rawlins. 'A couple of pounds difference in weight for an object weighing 25 pounds might not be noticed.'

Bob could see the logic of this. 'You said that the trial had failed to kill any sheep because the bomb had landed in boggy ground. Is it possible that the trial was partly a failure because it didn't release as much anthrax as you expected?'

'Yes, that is possible.'

'You also said that you had detected some anthrax released by the bomb, so at least one of the cylinders was still on board. Is there any way of establishing from the drop site whether it was missing one cylinder or two? What's happened so far is bad enough. I dread to think that there might be another cylinder full of anthrax spores out there, still unaccounted for.'

'I'm sorry, group captain, the thermite charges ensured that very little that was identifiably part of the bomb remained after the explosion. We did dig up the impact site, in full protective gear of course, because we wanted to try to understand what difference the boggy ground had made to the results. All we found were a few bits of the bomb, notably parts of the tail fins. There's no way of knowing how many cylinders were in the bomb when it was dropped.'

*

Dinner was a subdued affair attended by perhaps a dozen scientists and support staff, plus an army captain old enough to have Great War medal ribbons on his uniform and a rather younger sergeant. Before they sat down, Captain Harris introduced himself to Bob as the commander of the infantry platoon that provided physical security for X Base and helped with the manual labour involved in handling sheep used in trials. Bob found himself sitting between the captain and Professor Malone and noticed that Monique had sat at the far end of the table with Margaret Young, who appeared to be the only woman at X Base.

The captain's comments had chimed with something Bob had been curious about. 'Professor, how do the trials actually work in practice?'

'I can show you if you like.'

'What do you mean?'

'We've got some film of the second trial we did in the summer. It's been cut together to give a sense of the process to help train any newcomers to X Base. I can show it to you in my office after dinner.'

*

True to his word, the professor had a projector and screen set up in his office and invited Bob and Monique to sit on the sofa. The professor sat in one of the armchairs puffing on his pipe, while Dr Rawlins stood by the projector.

With the lights off, the screen began to flicker and the projector began to make its distinctive whirring sound. The light from the projector could be seen illuminating the professor's pipe smoke.

The first few seconds of the film were taken up with a 'Secret' warning and then the action began.

Dr Rawlins embarked on what amounted to a commentary. 'We intend to have this worked up into something rather more professional in time. For the moment it's little more than a set of home movies, though you'll see it's shot in colour rather than black and white. It also has no sound. This first scene shows fifteen sheep being carried down the pier and into rowing boats. These are then towed over to the island by a requisitioned trawler we have allocated to us. Once on the island, the sheep are herded to the packing area.'

'You use a shepherd and a sheepdog,' said Monique.

'Yes, we have a clear division between clean areas of the island and what we call dirty areas, which have been contaminated during previous trials. It's safe to use a sheepdog where you are seeing it here. The sheep are then placed in individual crates that restrict their movement and just leave their heads exposed. These crates are carried to the trials area on trucks and manhandled into position in an arc 100 yards downwind of the detonation point. Now you can see the bomb being set up. It looks a very Heath Robinson affair, but it does work. That odd-looking scaffold suspends an inverted mortar, that fires the bomb directly at the ground beneath it.'

'I see the men are wearing protective equipment now,' said Bob. 'What does that comprise of?'

'The brown overalls are cloth. They also wear rubber boots and gloves, a respirator with an additional cloth pre-filter attached to the left shoulder, and the white hoods are also fabric. They are intended to ensure that nothing gets in round the edges of the respirator. As you can see, the mortar is triggered remotely from a safe distance upwind. It doesn't show up well in the film, but when you are there it's possible to see the cloud of spores as it drifts towards the arc of sheep. After the cloud has gone, the crates carrying the sheep are moved to a holding area where the sheep are released from the crates and individually tethered to see how they respond over a period of several days. The second test shown here killed all the sheep in the centre of the arc and infected the others, which were later shot.'

'What are the gas canisters positioned by each of the sheep in the arc?' asked Bob.

'They sample the air during the trial. It's possible to tell from them how much anthrax each sheep has been exposed to, which can then be cross-referenced against how the animals responded to the test.

'These next scenes show how the men are decontaminated, first being sprayed with hand-pumped sea water, and then having their protective outer layer of clothing removed by a colleague. Here you can see how the protective equipment is cleaned in containers that steam them in boiling water and formaldehyde for an hour. The sheep crates used in the trials are cleaned in the tanks you see here, which contain sea water, bleach and acid. This next scene is a bit grisly. It shows the dead sheep undergoing open-air autopsies. After cause of death is confirmed, they are incinerated in the structure you can see in use here. And that's about it.'

After the film came to an end, Dr Rawlins switched the lights on.

Monique stood up. 'I can see why you serve pork rather than lamb in your dining room, professor.'

'Indeed, Madame Dubois,' said the professor.

Bob also stood up, then looked at his watch. 'I know it's still early, but it seems to have been an awfully long day. I think I'm going to turn in. We're going to be setting off to drive back to Lossiemouth as soon as it's light. If I don't see you in the morning, thank you for meeting us at such short notice, professor, and thanks for the dinner and accommodation.'

'You are very welcome, both of you. Please make sure you have breakfast before you go. I can promise there are no lamb chops on the menu there, either.'

*

'How's your room, Bob?' asked Monique as the made their way along a corridor in what seemed to be the accommodation wing.

'It's not bad. The bed's a bit small and there's no obvious means of heating, but I'm sure I'll manage.'

'They gave me a room with a double bed and a paraffin heater.'

Bob stopped and looked at Monique. 'Is that an invitation?'

'It might be. I have missed you, Bob.'

'I've missed you too. What happened to "sensible"?'

'To hell with "sensible", Bob. Besides, there's no-one else from the team here.'

In the middle of the night, Bob felt Monique move and realised she was awake. 'It's cold, isn't it?' he asked.

'We could light the paraffin heater if you like. It's fairly cosy under the bedding, though.'

'Can we leave the heater? I always find the smell unpleasant.'

A little later Monique asked, 'What's the priority for tomorrow, Bob?'

He laughed. 'Ah, just like old times. Strategy meetings in bed.'

'No, seriously, what do you want to do when we get back to Lossiemouth?'

'I want to talk to the two armourers who helped put the cylinders in the bomb. I think I missed a trick by not doing so before coming over here but at the time it seemed more urgent to talk to the people here. The anthrax on board the Anson must be connected to the anthrax in the three cylinders. It would be far too much of a coincidence if it weren't. I just can't make the link.'

'It might help if you know that the supervision by the scientists in Lossiemouth wasn't quite as intensive as Dr Rawlins suggested. I was talking to Margaret Young at dinner tonight. She feels bad about what's happened and thinks we've not been given the whole truth. Apparently, she and Dr Rawlins are in a relationship. After the work on the bomb was finished, the two of them went into Elgin to do some shopping and then for dinner. They left Dr Taylor supervising the securing of the workshop. She didn't say as much but I get the feeling that he may not be the most reliable of men.'

'That makes it doubly important that we speak to the armourers. We need to hear their side of what happened in detail. Look, my arm's been out from under the covers and it's freezing. Do you think it's worth lighting the heater and putting up with the smell?'

'Probably not, Bob, but there is another way we could warm ourselves up.'

CHAPTER NINE

The journey back across the country had taken longer than the outbound trip. They'd awoken before dawn to find that fog and rain had set in. It had got light, or perhaps more accurately it had stopped being completely dark, as they ate breakfast in the company of bleary-eyed scientists and support staff.

When they did eventually get back to Lossiemouth, Group Captain Roebuck met them in his office. 'Were you able to make any progress?'

Bob sipped a very welcome cup of tea. 'The key question revolves round whether anyone other than the three scientists from X Base could get to the bomb after it was reassembled with the cylinders of anthrax inside. They claim that no-one could have had access before the workshop was locked and armed guards put in place. That raises questions like whether there could have been a break-in and whether your guards are entirely reliable. We also need to talk to the two armourers who helped with the bomb to see if their account of what happened matches the one the scientists gave us.'

I've nothing more important on my plate right now,' said Roebuck. 'Two of the three men who fell ill have died, and two more of those who were originally at the crash site, including the flight sergeant leading the team, are now ill. I don't know if whoever was in charge of the RAF Police detachment guarding the workshop that night is on duty at the moment. If you give me five minutes, I'll get him tracked down and have him meet us at the workshop where the work was done and the bomb was stored overnight.'

The station commander's car took Bob, Monique and Roebuck round the western side of the airfield to a small brownish concrete building close to a circular aircraft dispersal. There were a few small windows at just below the level of the asbestos roof. Bob didn't think anyone over the age of eight would be small enough to be able to gain access using them.

A RAF Police sergeant was standing by the blue-painted wooden door, looking nervous in his RAF battledress and white-topped cap with matching white Sam Browne belt and holster. He saluted as Bob, Monique and Roebuck got out of the car.

Bob took the lead. 'At ease, sergeant. I understand that you commanded the guard detail assigned to this building on the night of the 25th of September. Can you describe to me what happened?'

'Well, nothing happened sir. I'd initially been told we'd be needed that evening but that was brought forward, and two corporals and I arrived here mid-afternoon to find one of the civilians outside, smoking. I'd been told there would be three, but the other two civilians weren't present.'

'And what about the two armourers?' asked Bob.

'The civilian said that the corporal was round the back of the workshop, sir, relieving himself. When I went inside, the other armourer was sitting at the table reading a newspaper. He said he was pleased to see me. They'd finished work on the bomb more quickly than expected and he wanted to get a late lunch.'

'You are saying that the other armourer was on his own inside the workshop?'

'Yes, sir.'

'Did you see the bomb?'

'Yes, sir, it was sitting on some supports on the table.'

'Did you notice anything odd about it?'

'No, sir. I'm no expert, but it looked much like any small bomb. It was a sort of faded dark red colour, with two bright red bands round the nose separated by a black band.'

'There was no sign that anyone had been working on the bomb just before you went in?'

'As I said, the man inside was reading the newspaper. There was a canvas tool bag on the table, but it didn't seem out of place.'

'Was there anything at all that seemed odd when you went in?'

'I had no reason to look, sir, I'm sorry.'

'Did you see the armourer leave?'

'Yes, I did. I made sure the workshop was locked. The civilian and two armourers walked over to a Jeep that was parked close to where your car is now.'

'Was either of the armourers carrying anything?'

'One of them, the one who'd been inside, was carrying the tool bag that had been on the table, sir. Nothing more.'

'How large was it?' asked Monique.

'It wasn't large. It was the kind that rolls open, giving access to tools stored in pockets. Rolled up it was a few inches in diameter.'

'Possibly not large enough to carry what we are interested in then,' said Bob. 'Can we go inside?'

Bob saw the sergeant glance at Group Captain Roebuck, who nodded.

The building wasn't a large one, and much of the interior space was taken up by workbenches lining the inside walls, with racks and shelves above and a table in the centre of the room, plus three hard-looking chairs. There a telephone on the workbench in the corner furthest from the door. The place had an unused feel to it, though there was a rack of screwdrivers attached to a wall above one of the workbenches.

'Look,' said Bob, 'before we leap to any conclusions, is there any chance this building was broken into on the night in question?'

'There were no signs of a break in,' said the sergeant. 'And we would have seen or heard anyone approaching, even in the dark. You can see how small the windows are, sir. And anyone trying to enter via the door, with a key or without one, would have had to come past me.'

Bob pulled out a large metal bin from beneath a workbench and shook it from side to side, then took one of the screwdrivers from the rack and used it to explore the contents. 'Ah, this is interesting.' He lifted out a wooden box exactly like the ones described to him at Gruinard House. 'And here's another one.' He continued to rummage through the bin. 'Otherwise, it's mainly cardboard packaging and a couple of old newspapers. But the third box is missing. Sandy, have your people at the crash site found anything of note, yet?'

'They started work at the crash site late yesterday and resumed this morning. I'd expect to have a report by the end of the day.'

'I rather suspect that what they need to be looking for is any indication that there was a box like this one on board,' he held it up again, 'only the one on the Anson wouldn't have been empty. If there's any good news, it's that the presence of two empty boxes here makes it likely that only one of the cylinders was removed from the bomb. If a second had also gone missing, then one of these boxes would have been needed to transport it. Sergeant, would it have been possible to get a box like this into the canvas tool bag you saw?'

'No sir, I'm fairly sure of that.'

Isn't it a bit odd that the bin's not been emptied in nearly two months?' asked Monique.

'I don't know, and will check,' said Roebuck. 'But if the building isn't used much, then it's possible they'd only empty the bin when it became full.' He turned towards the sergeant. 'Thank you, that will be all.' He then looked at Bob. 'This is your investigation, not mine, but I'm guessing we need to talk to my two armourers. I'll get them brought to my office.'

*

Bob wasn't entirely surprised to hear that one of the armourers, Leading Aircraftman Michael Murray, was nowhere to be found. The man should have been on duty. Instead, he seemed to have disappeared into thin air. He'd been seen in his billet the previous morning, but no-one had seen him since. The timing seemed right. The station commander had spoken to both the armourers late on Tuesday. Word of illness amongst the men who had visited the Anson crash site would have quickly got round, even if the cause should have been kept secret.

It had been Murray who had been left on his own with the bomb and his disappearance seemed to Bob to suggest he had been involved in the theft of the cylinder of anthrax. If so, then he would have known full well that the trail would come straight back to him. Now he had more than a full day's lead on them.

Bob kicked himself. If he'd tried to speak to the armourers when he'd first arrived at Lossiemouth, Murray's absence would have been spotted much sooner, and it might have been a great deal easier to find him.

Bob assumed that the second armourer, Corporal Alan Deere, would also have heard about the illnesses and deaths. Yet the young man seemed confident when he was shown into the group captain's office.

Bob, Monique and Roebuck were sitting on the side of the group captain's desk furthest from the door, and the group captain waved towards a seat placed a little distance from the other side of the desk. 'Hello corporal, sit down, please. You know who I am. These people are Group Captain Sutherland and Madame Dubois from military security. They'd like to talk to you about the work you and LAC Murray did converting a bomb for some scientists back in September. You will recall I spoke to you about it on Tuesday. I'd like as much detail as you can remember.'

'It was much as I told you then, sir. We met the scientists at the workshop where we were due to do the work, having collected the bomb from the bomb dump.'

'What's a bomb dump?' asked Monique.

'It's where bombs are stored on the station, ma'am. It's heavily protected and in a remote part of the site. We wrapped the bomb in a blanket and put it in the back of the Jeep we were using and took it to the workshop.'

'Wasn't that rather dangerous?'

'Not really, ma'am. That type of bomb is armed by the action of a small parachute that opens after it's released from the aircraft dropping it. Until then it's quite safe. And it wasn't a large bomb, under three feet long, so that was the simplest way to transport it. It was clear that the scientists thought that converting the bomb would be a bigger job than it turned out to be, because they'd allowed the whole of the rest of the day for the work. As it was, the job was done by mid-afternoon. As soon as it was done, two of the scientists, the man in charge and the woman, left in the car they'd all arrived in. The third one didn't seem happy about that.

I got the sense the two of them had more than just a works outing planned. The one who'd been left behind to make sure the place was secure gave the impression he thought he ought to have got the girl.' He glanced at Monique. 'Sorry, ma'am.'

'You told the group captain that they'd let slip that it was anthrax in the cylinders?' said Bob.

'Yes, sir. That was the miserable one, a little earlier in the day. LAC Murray dropped a screwdriver and the scientist said something about being careful not to puncture the anthrax containers. The other two scientists weren't there at the time. I think they'd gone to their car to fetch some notes or something. It was clear we weren't meant to know so I didn't respond to what he said. I was shocked, to tell you the truth. You can bet that both Michael and I were even more careful than normal from then on.'

'How well do you know Murray?' asked Bob.

'I've worked with him quite a bit, sir, though I'd not consider him a friend. He's from Glasgow and is very able. I'm surprised that he's not been posted to a front-line station where they could make better use of his skills.'

'Can you tell me what happened in the half hour or so before you left the workshop?'

'Not a lot, really, sir. The scientist was on the phone several times asking for the RAF Police guard to start early. Then I nipped out to answer the call of nature, which I did behind the workshop.'

'Were you away long?'

'While I was there, I had a fag, sir. There was nothing left to do on the bomb, so I thought I might as well spend the time outside as anywhere else. When I came back to the front of the workshop, the RAF Police detachment had arrived and were talking to the third scientist, who was having a cigarette outside the front door. The police sergeant went inside, then came back out to say I should get my coat, so he could lock up. I got it and we left. Michael and I had driven over in a Jeep and we offered the scientist a lift back to the officers' mess, which he accepted.'

'Was LAC Murray carrying anything?'

'Yes, sir. He was carrying his roll-up tool bag. I'd asked him to bring his tools because we only needed one set.'

'Is there any chance he could have carried anything out in the tool bag? I'm thinking of one of the cylinders of anthrax spores, either in its box or just the cylinder by itself.'

'No, sir, not a chance. There's not much spare room in those bags. Besides, Michael was driving, and he gave me the bag to hold when we got into the Jeep. I'm sure it was just the canvas and the normal tools.'

'What about the third scientist, Dr Taylor?' asked Monique. 'Did you notice if he was carrying anything when you left?'

'He had a leather briefcase, not a large one. I'd seen him put some diagrams back in it a little earlier, when we'd worked out that the cylinders fitted correctly.'

'How large is "not large"?'

'I don't know, ma'am.' The corporal held out his hands to demonstrate. 'Normal briefcase size, I suppose you'd say. And maybe two or three inches deep.'

'Not large enough to hold one of the boxes the cylinders had been in? Or the cylinder itself?'

'No, ma'am. I'm sure of that.'

'Thank you. I just wanted to be certain. Back to you, Bob.'

'Thanks, Monique. You've already said that fitting the cylinders into the bomb wasn't as big a job as the scientists expected, corporal. How long would it have taken for someone to remove one of the cylinders once the bomb had been put back together?'

'I don't know, sir. The body of the bomb is a steel tube, covered in a cardboard fairing intended to streamline it. To get at the contents you'd need to unscrew the tail unit and slide out the innards. If you just wanted to remove one of the cylinders we'd fitted, you could probably do it quite quickly.'

'Could you do it in the time it took someone to smoke a cigarette?'

'Possibly, sir. You'd probably have to jam some cardboard or something into the space you'd created to stop the remaining contents clattering round, but it could be a fairly quick job if you were skilled enough.'

'As skilled as Murray?'

'It would have been a hell of a risk, sir. If I'd have come straight back, I'd have caught him in the middle of it. But perhaps he knows me well enough to know I'd take the opportunity for a fag while I was outside. The scientist really didn't want to be there, so I guess it was a reasonable bet that he'd not hurry to finish his smoke.'

'Thank you, that's very helpful. Can I ask what happened to the wooden boxes the cylinders came in once they'd been put in the bomb?'

'I think they were simply discarded, sir. It wasn't me who took them out of their boxes, but I think the empty boxes were simply put in a bin.'

'Which means that it would have been easy enough for Murray to retrieve one of the boxes, put the cylinder in it, and then hide the box somewhere in the workshop, for later collection?'

'Yes, sir, though it might have taken time to find a suitable hiding place, out of sight.'

'If it had been me,' said Monique, 'I'd have simply put the full box back in the bin with the two empty boxes. No-one would think of looking there and so long as I could get back into the building before the bin was emptied, which we know was very rarely, I'd have what I wanted.'

Bob smiled. 'Thank you, Monique. I'm quite sure that's what happened.' He turned back to Corporal Deere. 'What about the next morning, when the bomb was loaded into the aircraft? Could it have been interfered with then?'

'I can't see how, sir. LAC Murray and I arrived at the time we'd been told to. The scientists arrived at the same time. Their car pulled up behind us as we were getting out of the Jeep. The police were still there, and the building was locked. The aircraft was parked close by and loading one small bomb into the empty bomb bay only took a short time. Everyone was standing around and no-one would have had the opportunity to do anything to the bomb without it being obvious. When we left, the aircraft was being guarded by a replacement RAF Police detachment. One thing you should know is that LAC Murray returned to the workshop later in the day, after the aircraft had taken off and the RAF Police guard removed.'

'How do you know?' asked Bob.

'I asked him to. We needed to return the fire-pots we'd removed from the bomb to the bomb-dump. They are cylinders containing magnesium, a bit less than half the length of the cylinders the anthrax was in. There were seven of them which we'd left on the side in the workshop after doing the work. It was safe to leave them there temporarily, but I wanted to get them to a proper home as soon as it was quieter at the workshop.'

'Which means he'd have had the perfect opportunity to collect the stolen cylinder of anthrax,' said Bob. 'Thank you, that's helpful. When did you last see Leading Aircraftman Murray?'

'When the group captain talked to the two of us, sir, on Tuesday evening.'

Bob looked at Roebuck, sitting beside him, and nodded. The group captain stood up. 'Thank you, corporal, you may leave. I'd be grateful if you could keep everything that's been said here completely to yourself.'

'Of course, sir.'

As the door closed, the group captain sat back down. 'What now?'

'Well, we're a bit late, but I think we need to get everyone we can think of looking for Murray. Perhaps we should put out the story that he's a suspect in a murder case, which isn't all that far from the truth. We need to get the civilian police on the job, both here and in Glasgow as that's where he's from. It is also now particularly important that we know whether what's left of the Avro Anson has anything resembling one of those small packing boxes in it, though I'm virtually certain it will. Is there any way of checking whether the aircraft ought to have been carrying anything other than the pilot?'

'We do sometimes use delivery flights to carry urgent spare parts. I'll ask 46 Maintenance Unit.'

'Thanks, Sandy. If you don't mind, the two of us will go and find the officers' mess. It seems an awfully long time since breakfast.'

*

The food was pleasant but unremarkable. It was far too late for lunch but too early for dinner. Despite that, there was still a reasonable choice on offer. Bob was hungry but found it hard to focus on eating when he had so many thoughts buzzing round in his head.

He gave up on his apple crumble and custard and put his spoon down on the table, looking around to see if anyone was close. 'It seems that our Dr Taylor lied to his colleagues about never leaving the armourers alone with the bomb.'

'Yes, it does look that way and that puts Murray firmly in the spotlight. On the other hand, don't you think that this is all slotting into place a little too easily, Bob?'

'What do you mean?'

'I'm getting the sense that someone might actually want us to think Murray took the cylinder. I've been trying to work out if it was possible for Dr Taylor to have done it.'

'Yes, it pays to have an open mind,' said Bob. 'The thing is that Dr Taylor returned to X Base on the 26th of September. I can't see any way he could have been responsible for the anthrax being on the Avro Anson on the 1st of October. On the other hand, Murray was at Lossiemouth at the right time.'

'Should we at least check whether there was any chance Dr Taylor returned to Lossiemouth? He could have got here and returned in a day, even if it would have been a long drive.'

'Yes, you're right, we do need to see if he left X Base at all during that time.'

'There's another thing, Bob, and perhaps this time it's me who's leaping to obvious conclusions. I've been thinking about the Avro Anson's destination, RAF Errol.'

Bob smiled. 'Great minds think alike, Monique. It's a relief to hear you say that, because I'd begun to think I was being too single-minded in my approach. Let me guess, you are thinking that although the aircraft was being delivered to the RAF pilot training unit based at RAF Errol, we know that's not the only unit operating there.'

'Exactly, Bob. It's also the base of that Soviet Air Force ferry unit.'

'No. 305 Ferry Training Unit, commanded by my particularly good friend Colonel Irakli Kuznetsov.'

Something in Bob's tone caused Monique to stop what she was about to say and look at him. 'What are you implying, Bob? Just how good a friend is Colonel Kuznetsov? I read the report you wrote after your visit to RAF Errol last month. In that you gave the sense of a cordial but guarded discussion with him.'

Bob looked round again and lowered his voice. 'I gave an extra, verbal, report to Commodore Cunningham and Sir Peter Maitland afterwards. While I was there, Kuznetsov made a joke about my getting a medal if I stole a de Havilland Mosquito and defected to Russia with it. After we'd been for a flight together in one of his unit's aircraft, we were best pals. I ran the idea of defection back at him. We reached a gentleman's agreement that he would pass any useful information he encountered to me and in return Britain would provide him with a new identity and a permanent home when he wanted or needed them at some point in the future.'

'That's brilliant, Bob.' Monique beamed. 'We'll make a great intelligence officer of you yet!'

'Thanks, Monique. Sir Peter Maitland said much the same thing at the time. The thing is, if this container of anthrax was intended to go to my chum Irakli Kuznetsov's No. 305 Ferry Training Unit, it begs the question of why he didn't tell me.'

'Let's think about the timing, Bob. The Avro Anson crash took place on the 1st of October. Your visit to RAF Errol was much later last month, wasn't it? It was the same day I shot Sergei Avdonin and ended his NKVD operation in Leith, which would make it the 29th of October. As the Anson had disappeared nearly a month earlier and the anthrax with it, perhaps Colonel Kuznetsov didn't think it worth mentioning. Presumably, the idea was to have the unit fly the anthrax back to the Soviet Union in one of the aircraft they were going to deliver.'

'I don't think they are due to fly any of them over until after the winter,' said Bob. 'I suppose it's possible they were hoping to get the cylinder to the USSR when they tried to steal that Mosquito from RAF Leuchars the week before I met Kuznetsov. If so, I'm surprised he didn't mention it.'

'Alternatively,' said Monique, 'having the cylinder flown to Errol might just have been the first link in a chain. Maybe they intended to have Sergei Avdonin pick it up and transfer it to a Soviet ship due to take part in one of the Arctic convoys.'

'Either way,' said Bob, 'I think I need to have another chat with my friend Irakli.'

'Look, Bob, do we actually know that the Soviets would be interested in acquiring anthrax produced at Porton Down? From what Professor Malone told us, everyone's making progress in the area. Isn't anthrax just anthrax? Producing the stuff is the easy part, it's turning it into practical weapons that is hard. Simply acquiring someone else's anthrax wouldn't help with that.'

'Let's see if there's a secure way of asking the professor. It could certainly help to know.'

CHAPTER TEN

The miserable day was getting steadily gloomier by the time Bob and Monique arrived at Group Captain Roebuck's office. The group captain wasn't there, but his secretary was happy to let Bob use his phone while Monique stood close by, so she could hear what was being said at the other end of the conversation.

It took a while to make a connection to Gruinard House and then for Professor Malone to be tracked down. Bob was relieved that the professor hadn't been on the island or otherwise out of touch. Then he remembered it would be getting dark there too.

'Hello group captain. What can I do for you?'

'Are we able to talk securely on this line?'

'We're as secure as we're ever going to be at this end, but no system is ever foolproof.'

'In a way that's part of what I want to talk to you about, professor. I'm at RAF Lossiemouth. I've talked to the RAF Police sergeant who commanded the overnight guard on the workshop used to adapt and store the bomb and I've also talked to one of the armourers who did the work. It has emerged that things didn't work out the way your team told us they did when I spoke to them yesterday.'

'In what way?'

'The work didn't take nearly as long as expected. It seems that when it was finished, Dr Rawlins and Dr Young went into Elgin to do some shopping and have dinner.'

'Ah, yes. I am aware they have formed a close attachment. I don't think that based on what you've told me, Dr Rawlins actually lied when answering your questions.'

'No, but his absence from the workshop did mean that he unwittingly misled me. I understand that Dr Taylor was left in charge. He spent his time trying to get the RAF Police guard on the building put in place earlier than originally planned. He did so, but when the RAF Police arrived, they found Dr Taylor outside the building smoking a cigarette.'

'Which means that he left the two armourers in the building with the bomb containing the cylinders?'

'Worse than that, one of the armourers had already gone round to the rear of the building to answer a call of nature and then had a cigarette of his own. When Dr Taylor went outside for a smoke, he left just one of the armourers alone with the bomb.'

'For how long?'

'According to the other armourer, for long enough to have removed one of the cylinders and hidden it in the workshop. I can't ask the armourer who remained in the building about it, because he has since disappeared.'

'Damn! Dr Taylor is the best in his field when it comes to animal diseases but there are times when I question his commitment to what we are doing here. I'll talk to him.'

'No, please don't professor, not yet. I'm right in thinking there are no trials in the offing, are there?'

'No, the weather's too unpredictable and, frankly, too unpleasant. We're still fully occupied analysing all the data we collected from the trials in the summer and the aircraft trial in September.'

'In that case would you mind keeping what we've discussed about Dr Taylor to yourself for the moment? You can help to put my mind at rest on one point, though. After your team returned to X Base, is there any chance that Dr Taylor could have made another visit to RAF Lossiemouth during the following week?'

'No, absolutely none. Remember that we had the aircraft test on the 26th of September, the day the team arrived back from Lossiemouth. Dr Taylor was fully stretched during the week that followed. We were constantly checking the sheep involved in the trial for effects and, when we found none, trying to work out what had gone wrong. I can say with complete confidence that if he'd driven across the country and back, even if he'd not stayed long at Lossiemouth, then his absence would have been obvious.'

'Thank you, professor. Could you answer another question that's been puzzling us?'

'Of course.'

'How much value would the cylinder full of spores have been to a foreign power? You told Madame Dubois and I that a number of nations were working in this area, but it sounded as if the challenging part of the process was the development of practical weapons, not the production of the spores themselves.'

'That's true, but if you offered my colleagues at Porton Down the chance to examine samples of anthrax produced by the Germans or the Japanese they'd jump at it. There are different strains of anthrax and they vary in virulence and in their responses to different factors such as temperature and decontaminants. Seeing how others are getting on in developing their preferred strains would be helpful. Not as helpful, of course, as detailed information about how far they've got in developing practical weapons to deliver the anthrax, but we'd certainly welcome samples of spores that had been developed elsewhere.'

*

Bob had just put the phone down when Group Captain Roebuck

entered the office, as if he'd been waiting with his secretary for the call to end. 'I'm sorry, Sandy, we didn't mean to evict you from your own office.'

'Don't worry about it, Bob. I've got a piece of information that might be of interest to you. 46 Maintenance Unit's records suggest that five items of freight were being carried in the Anson that crashed on the 1st of October. They were all small and light, so wouldn't have influenced the aircraft's handling. They also assure me that they would have been properly secured, so wouldn't have moved round in flight.'

'Do we know what they were?'

'We do. Four of the items were urgent spares for Avro Ansons being provided by the maintenance unit at the request of No. 9 Advanced Flying Unit. The fifth was being carried at the request of Leading Aircraftman Murray and was described in the paperwork as an artificial horizon for an Armstrong Whitworth Albemarle. It was addressed to the adjutant at No. 305 Ferry Training Unit at RAF Errol. It seems no-one thought to query why an armourer at RAF Lossiemouth would be involved in the supply of spares to the ferry training unit. The weight was recorded as a little over three pounds, which sounds about right for the cylinder in its box.'

'That is helpful. Do I take it that there's no confirmation from the crash site?'

'Not so far, and maybe not at all. I'm told the area is a real mess and, except for the engines, there is not much that is recognisable as the remains of an Anson, even though there was no fire. I must take a decision tonight about whether it's worth continuing to pick over the wreckage. The alternative is to have my people dig a large hole in the field in the morning and bulldoze everything into it, including a lot of dead sheep, and then fill the hole in. The people over from X Base are advising that if the wreckage and the dead sheep are sprayed with a solution of formaldehyde, and then we spray the entire place including the crash site with more formaldehyde after everything's been buried, then the area will be made safe. We will also have to cut down and burn the trees in the vicinity. I'm tending to the view that we should call it a day on the aircraft and get on with the decontamination. It's your investigation Bob. What do you think?'

Bob looked at Monique, then turned back to Roebuck. 'I agree with you. We're as certain as we need to be of the chain of connections between the adapted bomb and the Soviet unit at RAF Errol. A broken box and an anthrax cylinder casing from the crash site would give us the last percent or two of provability, but this isn't a case of what we can prove, it's a case of what we know. We may have pursued this as far as we can. I think that means there's nothing we can now usefully do until the morning.'

'You're obviously both welcome to stay in the officers' mess here,' said Roebuck. 'I think the officers of 20 OTU are planning a party in the mess this evening. It's the end of a course. There will be another, probably more restrained and mature, celebration by the non-commissioned aircrew in the sergeants' mess. Perhaps I'm getting too old, but I can't see this sort of thing as anything other than their graduation from being killed by flying into Scottish mountains to their being killed by being shot down over the Ruhr or over Berlin. I'll turn up and smile as usual but, again as usual, I'll look at them and wonder how many will still be alive in three months' time.'

'You're really making this sound like an enjoyable event, group captain,' said Monique.

'Sorry. You'll both be very welcome, though.'

'There is one other thing you could do for us, Sandy,' said Bob.

'What's that.'

'We need to get back to Edinburgh tomorrow, I don't suppose there's any chance that 46 Maintenance Unit has a Mosquito I can borrow, is there? One that could be ready to fly in the morning? And preferably a bomber or reconnaissance variant rather than a fighter?'

'I'll call the duty officer there and find out. That's not a type that the unit normally deals with, so it's a bit of a long shot. You do know they are tricky aircraft to fly, don't you Bob? Have you ever flown one?'

'I do, Sandy, and I have, though only once. How do the ATA delivery pilots cope with all the different types that they have to fly?'

'If it's a new type to the individual pilot then in an ideal world we do give them some training. Sometimes, though, that's not possible, and we simply give them the pilot's notes for the type to read.'

'Fair enough, I'll need an aircraft and a set of pilot's notes then. Come to think of it, while I can fly a Mosquito, I'm not confident I can remember exactly how to start one, so the notes could really come in handy.'

'This seems an oddly specific request if you simply want to get back to Edinburgh. Can I ask why you want it?'

'You can ask, Sandy, but you'll have to trust me when I say that you'd prefer not to know the answer.'

*

'It seems we're back with "sensible" then,' said Monique. They were sitting in a relatively quiet corner of the noisy and smoky bar, sipping gins and tonics.

'Sorry Monique, but in this environment these four rings on my sleeve make me stand out like a Belisha beacon and I have to really watch my step.'

'You are saying that it was "rooms" not "room" because you didn't want your air force comrades to know that the respectable group captain is sleeping with a mysterious French spy?'

'I think the rooms are all singles, anyway…' Bob stopped when he saw the smile on Monique's face.

'I'm sorry Bob. You are far too easy to tease sometimes. I'm only joking.'

Bob smiled, but then he caught the eye of Group Captain Roebuck on the far side of the room and his smile faded. 'I know how Sandy feels, you know. This is a horrible business sometimes. Look at those men over there. Some of them are no more than boys. He's right. For many of them the posting to their first operational bomber squadron that they'll already have in their pockets will be a death sentence.'

'Well, they're certainly following biblical guidance.'

'What do you mean?'

'Somewhere in Corinthians, I think. "Let us eat and drink; for tomorrow we die." It was a popular expression amongst Abwehr agents about to head off on a mission. It's just as appropriate here.'

'Hello,' said Bob. 'I don't think that's in the plan.' He watched as a flight lieutenant made his way across the bar to where Group Captain Roebuck stood. They spoke together for a few moments and then Roebuck followed the flight lieutenant out of the room.

Bob and Monique watched the party, now in full swing.

'This place will need a new set of fire extinguishers by

morning, said Bob. And the piano in the corner looks like a wreck. They'll have used it to replace their normal piano, which they'll have locked away in a storeroom somewhere.'

'Why?'

'By midnight they'll have pulled that one out through the French windows and set fire to it on the grass outside. It's a sort of tradition.'

'You make it sound like you've burned a few pianos in your time.'

'Oh, I have, believe me. There comes a point, if you survive long enough, when it begins to seem a little silly. But those men over there are going to enjoy tonight, even if they don't remember all of it in the morning. They certainly deserve to.' Bob saw Roebuck return to the room and wave to catch his attention. 'Finish your drink, Monique, it looks like we're wanted.'

The group captain waited until they'd emerged from the bar. 'I'm sorry to break into your evening but there's someone here I think you'll want to talk to. You know about our pool of Air Transport Auxiliary pilots. One of them, a Second Officer Robert Day, has asked the duty officer if he can speak to me. Given what he wants to talk to me about, I think you should be there too. All I know about him, after a very quick telephone call to his commanding officer, is that he's a reliable and highly experienced pilot who flew in combat over the Western Front in the Great War but was too old to sign up for active service this time round. He says he wants to see me about Leading Aircraftman Murray, whose name is now on just about everyone's lips. He's waiting in the mess manager's office.'

The four of them sat round the desk that occupied much of the small office. Bob thought Second Officer Day looked to be in his fifties. He was wearing his ATA uniform, similar in style to an RAF officer's uniform but whose dark blue colour always made Bob think of civilian airline pilots. Which was probably the idea, he reminded himself.

Bob introduced himself and Monique. 'Group Captain Roebuck tells us that you want to talk to us about Leading Aircraftman Murray.'

'Yes, sir. Michael is a nephew on my wife's side, maybe once removed. It's a bit unclear to be honest but we met at a funeral in Glasgow at the beginning of the war.'

'You're not from Glasgow yourself?'

'No, sir, Oxford. But my wife's Glaswegian and proud of it.'

'When did your paths cross again?'

'It was here in Lossiemouth, back in the summer. I was looking for a driver and car to take me out to where the aircraft I was due to fly was parked, and Michael was in the motor transport flight for some other reason. He recognised me and we briefly exchanged greetings and agreed to get together to catch up properly. After that we had the occasional drink together in Elgin.'

'What is it you want to tell us?' asked Bob.

'He came to see me, sir, late on Tuesday evening. He said that he'd heard that his sister was dangerously ill in Glasgow. He'd been given compassionate leave and a rail warrant but thought that by the time the first train next morning from Lossiemouth got him to Glasgow, and then he got out to Govan, he might be too late. He asked if I knew whether anyone was flying south the next morning and could drop him off at RAF Renfrew.

'As it happened, I could help him myself. I was scheduled to deliver a Bristol Beaufighter to 254 Squadron, who have just taken up residence at RAF North Coates in Lincolnshire. At first light yesterday morning, I put him in the navigator's station, which on a Beaufighter is a little way back down the fuselage, and took off. I got him to RAF Renfrew far sooner than a train could have got anywhere near Glasgow. At Renfrew he thanked me and headed off, I assume to Govan, where his mother and sisters live. When I got back to Lossiemouth this evening I found that everyone was talking about him being wanted in connection with a serious crime. I realised he'd duped me.'

'Do you know where his family live?' asked Bob.

'Yes, sir, I can give you the address.'

'Thank you. Can you tell me anything about them?'

'Not much, sir. I know his father worked in the shipyards in Govan but was killed in an accident at work when Michael was still a boy. I think the whole family were heavily involved in the Red Clydeside movement for a while but, according to my wife, everyone who didn't wear a tie to work at the time supported the movement. That's about it.'

'Is it a regular thing, for delivery flights to carry passengers on an ad hoc basis?' Group Captain Roebuck asked.

'It certainly happens, sir, but probably no more than on every other RAF station up and down the country. Though there, of course, it would be "training" flights on a Friday afternoon that happen to carry a planeload of Liverpudlian aircrew and ground crew to RAF Speke where, for unspecified reasons, they find they can't continue the flight back to their home base until the Monday morning. In this case there did seem to be an urgent and legitimate need to get Michael to Glasgow.'

Bob tried to hide a smile as he nodded in agreement. 'I think that will be all, Second Officer Day, thank you.'

'There is one more thing, sir.'

'What's that?'

'It may not be connected, but it's not the first time recently that I've helped Michael. I've checked my logbook and I can tell you that I took him to RAF Northolt on the 28th of September. Again, he'd sought me out to ask if I knew if anyone was taking an aircraft to London. I was due to fly a Beaufighter to RAF St Eval in Cornwall and Northolt wasn't all that far out of my way.'

Bob thought that it would have added considerably to the journey but didn't say so. 'Why did he want to go to London?'

'He said he'd been going out with a WAAF who he'd met here, but she'd been posted to somewhere down south. I can't remember if he said where. He'd arranged a couple of days' leave and they'd agreed to meet in London. The problem was, if he went by train, he'd spend most of his leave travelling and not much of it with his girlfriend.'

'How did he get back?' asked Monique.

'I'm sorry, ma'am, I've no idea.'

After Second Officer Day left there was a brief silence. It was Group Captain Roebuck who broke it. 'I'll get the officer commanding the RAF Police detachment here to shake up the civvy police down on Clydeside. Now we know for sure that Murray is there, we need to get them actively looking for him. And I need to do something about the fact that we seem to be running a bus service around the country for all and sundry.'

'Don't go too hard, Sandy. We've all done it. I did once ground a Hurricane pilot who'd taken his fiancée for a spin, literally, as it turned out, as her sitting on his lap interfered with his control of the aircraft. But that was an exception. I grounded him, and she broke off the engagement, on the very reasonable grounds that his stupidity had nearly killed her. But which of us hasn't done it ourselves, or turned a blind eye to others doing it?' Bob laughed, self-consciously, as he realised what he'd said.

'I've always found that morale can be boosted by the odd treat in the way of an air-mail visit home.'

'You're right, of course, Bob. It's the sort of thing it's better not to know about. Or at least to be able to deny you know about.'

'We need to know why Murray went to London just two days after he'd stolen the cylinder of anthrax,' said Monique. 'He clearly didn't have it with him, or it wouldn't have been in the Anson. But I can't believe it's not connected.'

'Maybe he really was going to see a girlfriend,' said Bob, 'though we won't know until we catch Murray and ask him.'

'I know some people who might be able to help,' said Monique. She turned to the group captain. 'Would it be possible to get hold of a photograph of Murray that I can send down to my colleagues in MI5?'

'Yes, of course, I'll get someone to see what we can let you have straight away. You can get it in the post in the morning.'

'It may be more urgent that that,' said Monique. 'Is there any way you can have someone fly it to London first thing in the morning? You've got people flying from here to all parts of the country.'

'Is it really that important?'

'The honest answer? I'm not certain, but I think it might be.'

'I'll see what I can do, Madame Dubois. Incidentally, Bob, you'll be pleased to hear I've found you a Mosquito.'

CHAPTER ELEVEN

'Of all the stupid things I've ever heard of, Bob, this really has to be the most ridiculous and infantile yet!'

Bob grinned at Monique, sitting on his right-hand side and slightly behind him, in the navigator's seat of the de Havilland Mosquito B Mk IV he'd been loaned. 'Are you worried about my flying, Monique?'

'It's not that, Bob. It's just that the group captain said this was a very tricky aircraft to fly and you've only ever flown one once, and never on your own.'

'I'm not on my own now.'

'You know what I mean.'

Bob looked at Monique and could see that her face, framed as it was in a leather flying helmet, showed real signs of concern. 'It will be all right, honestly.' She didn't look convinced. 'Look, I'm not about to kill the woman I love for the sake of playing the showman. It took me thirty years to find you. I'm not going to lose you now.' Bob saw Monique's concern turn to surprise and then she looked away as her eyes welled up. 'Right, he said. Remember that you are wearing two harnesses over that leather jacket and life vest. If we need to get out in a hurry, you release the outer harness, which attaches you to your seat, but not the inner harness. If necessary, you use that to attach your parachute, in the way we demonstrated before you got on board. The parachutes are just down there, as we discussed. Try to ensure you attach a parachute and not one of our travel bags, which are in the compartment just in front of them. We'll be flying at low level, so it's unlikely that the parachutes will be relevant anyway. If we were to crash land, then there's an escape hatch in the cockpit roof, which is released with this handle. Don't expect me to say, "Ladies first" if we do have to get out in a hurry.'

Monique smiled.

Bob had read the pilot's notes that morning and found he could start the engines without having to refer to them again.

'At least the weather's improved,' he said. 'It looks like a magnificent day for flying.'

Monique didn't reply and Bob realised that he was talking mainly to calm his own nerves. This wasn't the most mature or deeply considered thing he'd ever done, and the Mosquito could be a real handful, especially on takeoff. It was probably best not to tell Monique that if an engine failed in the first few moments of flight, before the speed had built up, then a crash was inevitable. It was probably also best not to tell her that the only Mosquito that Lossiemouth could come up with was an aircraft that had made an emergency landing there two months earlier after an engine failure and had suffered undercarriage damage during the landing. After being, he had been assured, returned to 'as good as new' condition complete with two new Rolls-Royce Merlin engines, the aircraft appeared to have been forgotten or abandoned by the Norfolk-based squadron it was allocated to. Bob found this surprising as the type had only been in service for a year and still had a 'new toy' feel. He wasn't about to complain, though.

Bob got the aircraft safely off the ground and retracted the undercarriage, then began to breathe again. 'Right, you're the navigator, Monique. We want to fly on a heading of 170 degrees, which is a bit east of south. That's the compass there. I'll be watching it too. Can you also tell me if you see any other aircraft?'

The trip south over Speyside was exhilarating and Bob could tell that Monique was beginning to enjoy herself. At low level, the sense of speed was incredible as the ground whipped past beneath them.

'Right, tell me one more time,' said Monique. 'You know that Colonel Kuznetsov will be there because you've set him up with a fake meeting?'

'Yes, a Flying Officer Frost is responsible for security on the station and at my request he contacted Colonel Kuznetsov and asked to meet him later this morning to discuss the need to change the security passes for the colonel's unit. That means we know the colonel will be there when we arrive.'

'And what do you want me to do while you're giving the colonel his heart's desire?'

'Simply wait in whatever passes for a canteen or crew-room at No. 305 Ferry Training Unit and look decorous. And ideally see if you can find out anything about the unit's adjutant. I'm afraid I don't even know his name. I ought to have asked Frost.'

'You are saying that you want me to play the dumb brunette?'

'Sorry, but yes. And a dumb brunette who doesn't speak Russian.'

'You know Bob, I'd never have thought of that if you'd not mentioned it.'

Bob could no longer see the lower part of Monique's face under her mask, but he could tell from her eyes that she was smiling. He pushed the throttles forwards to increase the speed, then pulled a hard turn to the left to follow a valley, and another to the right.

Monique screamed, then laughed. 'You know what, Bob, I think this is even better than sex!'

'Why do you think I ignored the doctors when they told me I couldn't fly again?' Bob pulled back on the throttles and let the speed slowly reduce. 'That's Ballater we can see ahead of us. We're looking for a glen that heads roughly south-west from the village. That's it.' Bob kept the aircraft low, within the confines of the glen. 'Look ahead, on the left-hand side of the glen, above the loch.' He could see activity high in a field. There were men, and a mechanical digger, and lorries parked lower down on a track running above the side of the loch. 'I'm afraid that's where First Officer Sally Fowler died.'

Bob dipped his left wing in salute as they flew past, then climbed out of the glen. 'Now we need to be heading pretty much due south, over the mountains first, and then over lower ground. RAF Errol is just this side of the River Tay.'

*

Bob's plan included a flamboyant arrival. There was no other traffic in the circuit and the control tower cleared him to do a run in and break. Bob made sure that his approach was both exceptionally low and off the line of the runway, closer to the main hangers, one of which was home to No. 305 Ferry Training Unit. This also brought him much closer to the control tower and Bob had a sense of startled faces looking down on him as he flew past. He then broke hard to the left and climbed, then circled back, slowing down enough to lower the undercarriage and flaps as he came round to approach the runway once more.

'Jesus, Bob! Is this how you normally land?'

'No, it's not, Monique. That was more what you'd call "beating up" the airfield. The aim is to spill as many cups of tea as you can in the control tower as you pass. I warned Flying

Officer Frost I'd make sure I got noticed when I arrived. I've grounded pilots for much more conservative efforts than that one but, as they say, rank has its privileges.'

Bob chose to come to a stop alongside two Armstrong Whitworth Albemarle aircraft parked on the concrete hardstanding in front of the hangar used by the Soviets.

Once the engines had stopped, the access hatch was opened from the outside by an airman who had first put chocks under the wheels.

'You go first,' said Bob. 'Getting the telescoping ladder out is simply the reverse of what we did to stow it away at Lossiemouth. That's it. When you're standing on the concrete, take off your helmet and shake your hair loose. If our Soviet friends aren't thoroughly intrigued by the Mosquito, they are bound to be entranced by the idea of a woman flying one.'

Monique looked at him. 'Are you being serious, Bob?'

'Completely. Trust me.'

Bob took his own leather helmet off after he'd climbed out of the aircraft and looked round to see Colonel Kuznetsov striding over towards him, followed by three other men also in Soviet uniform.

As Kuznetsov came closer, a broad grin broke out on his face. 'Group Captain Sutherland! Bob! And you've brought a Mosquito and a beautiful woman. My world is suddenly complete! Seriously, my friend, to what do I owe the pleasure?'

'Last time I visited we talked about the de Havilland Mosquito. I thought you might like a trip in one. Just a short trip over Scotland, mind. We're not going to Moscow in her, however much you might like to. Have you got a flying jacket handy?'

The Colonel turned to a man who, going by the quality of his uniform and the number of his medal ribbons, was the most junior of the three who had followed the colonel over to the aircraft. After a brief exchange in Russian, the man ran off towards the hangar.

'I would love to join you, group captain. But what about your beautiful companion? The Mosquito only has two seats does she not?'

'I'll wait on the ground,' said Monique. 'Do you have somewhere I could get a hot drink?'

'Of course. Let me introduce you to my second-in-command, Major Nikolay Malinovsky. He will be happy to break out our best coffee for an occasion like this.'

Malinovsky was a man of about average height and in his thirties. He was unremarkable apart from eyes that had an unsettling sense of hardness.

He smiled at Monique. 'I would be delighted. Please follow me.'

Monique shot Bob a glance that he found hard to interpret and then set off after the major. The other man, who had not been introduced, followed them. They crossed with the man bringing out the colonel's leather flying jacket, still at a run.

Bob handed Kuznetsov the spare flying helmet he'd brought with them and the Mae West life jacket Monique had taken off. 'Right, Irakli, I need to get in first, then you follow.'

After takeoff, Bob put the aircraft through its paces, frightening himself at one point as he flew lower than he'd intended through one of the Angus glens. Then he climbed to a few thousand feet and turned the nose of the aircraft back towards RAF Errol.

'Thank you, Bob. I thoroughly enjoyed that. But perhaps you should now tell me why you are really here.'

'I wanted a private conversation with you, Irakli, and I

couldn't be sure we'd not be overheard in your office.'

'True. What do you want to talk about?'

'When you and I met at the end of last month, I'd thought we'd reached an understanding.'

'We did, Bob.'

'Very well. Let me ask you what you know about an Avro Anson that went missing while on its way to RAF Errol from RAF Lossiemouth on the 1st of October?'

'Nothing at all, why?'

'The aircraft was carrying a box that was meant to be delivered to the adjutant of No. 305 Ferry Training Unit.'

'We don't really have an adjutant, but I suppose that Major Malinovsky is doing the job until we can get a more junior officer in post.'

'The box had in it a cylinder of anthrax spores, stolen from field tests being undertaken in Scotland. Were you aware that this box was being delivered to your unit?'

'Absolutely not, but then that's no surprise to me. Malinovsky is NKVD through and through. He's also a good pilot, mind, and he does his job well. I just need to accept that he serves other masters as well as me. And, of course, he reports to them about me, so he will have plenty to say about today.'

'I'd wondered whether it was the plan to have the anthrax taken back to the motherland in the Mosquito that you tried to steal from RAF Leuchars?'

'I'm sorry, Bob. If there was a plan to have anything taken back in the Mosquito, I didn't know about it. You have my word that I knew nothing at all about the anthrax or what was planned for it.'

'Fair enough, thanks anyway, Irakli.'

'Is it "fair enough", Bob? Is our arrangement still going to be honoured?'

'Of course. It's been agreed at the highest levels. You need have no concerns there. What about Malinovsky? Is the way I've played this going to cause you problems with the NKVD?'

'No, of course not. He thinks I'm a brainless fool who cares about nothing except flying. He'll just conclude that you're another. He knows from your last visit that you are in military intelligence, but he's arrogant enough to underestimate you, as he does me.'

*

'Did you enjoy your little trip with Irakli, Bob?'

They had taken off from RAF Errol and set a course for RAF Turnhouse, west of Edinburgh.

'Up to a point. But it was a complete waste of time. I believed the colonel when he said he knew nothing about the anthrax. We might as well not have bothered with this charade. Did you enjoy the coffee?'

'The coffee was the best I've tasted in some time. The company, on the other hand, made my flesh crawl.'

'Kuznetsov told me that Malinovsky's first loyalty is to the NKVD. He also said that anything arriving at the unit addressed to the adjutant would find its way to Malinovsky.'

'Neither of those things surprise me.' said Monique. 'He smelled of the NKVD. He spent much of the time trying to undress me with his eyes and clearly sees himself as a cut above everyone else. When it became clear I wasn't about to swoon into his arms he left me to my own devices, though I couldn't stray from the crew-room without arousing suspicion. I'll ask my colleagues back in MI5 if they have anything on Malinovsky.

They really ought to be aware of his presence at least, yet I don't recall his name being mentioned as a possible threat when we were discussing your visit to Errol and mine to Leith last month. He made some comments to another officer in Russian that suggested more than a little contempt for his boss, by the way.'

'Yes,' said Bob, 'I think Kuznetsov goes out of his way to let Malinovsky think he's a fool. Ah well, it was worth a try.'

'Changing the subject, are you sure that the station commander at RAF Lossiemouth isn't going to mind you leaving his Mosquito so far from home?'

'He said he'd get someone to pick it up, but it's not really his Mosquito anyway. It was sort of abandoned on his doorstep a while back after an emergency landing. It's become a bit of a waif as a result. If it's not collected, then I might just carry on using it. It will be like having my own Hurricane again, only faster and with twice as many seats. The only drawback is the lack of guns in the bomber version, though perhaps that's no bad thing either. I'll make sure they keep it in a hangar at Turnhouse, though. God knows what Edinburgh's winter weather would do to an unprotected wooden airframe.'

'This thing's made of wood? Seriously?'

'Almost entirely. That's what makes it perform so well. The crews call it the "wooden wonder".'

'Just promise me you'll land more sensibly this time, Bob.'

Bob called the control tower at RAF Turnhouse and then performed what felt like a near-perfect approach and landing from the north-west, coming in with the Forth Bridge on their left after passing almost directly over Hopetoun House.

After he stopped the engines, Bob took off his mask and turned to face Monique. 'We put off having that discussion about our living arrangements here in Edinburgh. Would now be a good moment?'

'You can take me somewhere expensive for dinner tonight, Bob, and perhaps we'll talk about it then. Don't we have other things to discuss first?'

Bob looked at his watch. 'Very true, Monique. Michael and the rest of the team ought to be back from Orkney before long. I think that's our car waiting over there. Let's head back to Craigiehall and see how the last couple of days have gone for them.'

CHAPTER TWELVE

Bob and Monique were met by his secretary, Joyce Stuart, as they walked into MI11's first floor offices in the main house at Craigiehall.

'Welcome back, sir. Welcome, ma'am, nice to see you again.' Joyce was a stereotypically Edinburgh lady in her fifties and in Bob's brief experience of her, she had seemed a model of efficiency.

'I'd feel a lot more comfortable with "Monique" you know. May I call you Joyce?'

'Of course. I'll get some tea on for both of you. I know Lieutenant Commander Dixon suggested you use Major Miller's old office, Monique. We've sent the last of his things on to him. Sir, a Group Captain Roebuck tried to reach you on the telephone a short time ago. He asked that you call him back as soon as you can.'

Bob went through to his office. He knew that Joyce would have cleared as much as possible during his absence but noted that the pile of files and papers waiting for him in his in-tray was still depressingly large.

It didn't take him long to get through to RAF Lossiemouth on the phone.

'Hello, Bob. Thanks for calling back.'

'What can I do for you, Sandy?'

'I've got some bad news, I'm afraid. The police in Glasgow have been in touch with us. It seems that Leading Aircraftman Murray has disappeared.'

'Did they give any details?'

'As you know, they've been looking for him. They received a report this morning from a woman he'd been staying with in a place called Springburn, which I'm told is on the opposite side of the city to where they'd been focusing their search. Apparently, she's an old girlfriend who had no idea the police were after him. The story is that he didn't return from a visit to a nearby pub last night. By this morning she was worried enough to go and see the police. They've confirmed he left the pub at closing time after drinking heavily. He then seems to have disappeared into thin air. They are continuing to look for him, now in Springburn as well as in Govan.'

'I suppose we can hope he'll turn up somewhere after sleeping it off. He remains our best chance of tying the loose ends together.'

After he finished the call, Bob went through to see Monique to let her know. 'I hope they can locate him. I was counting on getting Murray to tell us exactly what the Soviets were planning to do with the cylinder of anthrax, assuming he knew, and why he went to London.'

'He's not our only hope, Bob. Until they do find him there are a couple of threads that can still usefully be pursued. As you know, I had Murray's photo sent down to MI5. I spoke to my ex-colleagues there on the phone from Lossiemouth earlier this morning and asked them to look at another possibility, too.'

Bob smiled. 'That sounds slightly mysterious.'

'It was meant to, Bob. If my idea comes to nothing, then we can forget it. If it helps, then so much the better.'

'Right,' said Bob. 'There's another call I want to make before the others get back to the office.'

The meeting table in Bob's office wasn't large enough to comfortably seat eight, but with a couple of extra chairs carried across from what was now Monique's office, they managed without it seeming too cramped.

Bob looked around, noticing again the unfaded patches of wallpaper where his predecessor had hung paintings. Bob had been told these had depicted scenes of historic battles. He made a mental note to find something with a more aeronautical theme to bring the place back to life.

'Welcome back, everyone,' he said. 'At least we all had good weather for our flights back to Edinburgh. Now we've had a chance to grab a quick lunch, it would be helpful if we could discuss what we've achieved this week.

'I'll begin. As you know, Madame Dubois and I flew down to RAF Lossiemouth on Wednesday.' He paused. 'Only two days? It seems much longer. To cut a long story short, there had been a major breach of security there leading to the theft of a cylinder of anthrax spores. Several men are dead as a result, and more are likely to die. Monique and I were able to establish the sequence of events leading to the theft but there are still loose ends because the man who stole the cylinder escaped to Glasgow and has since disappeared. The thing of particular significance is a link with our Soviet friends at RAF Errol, who it would appear were due to take delivery of the anthrax and ensure its onward carriage to Moscow. Quite how they would have done that is one of the outstanding loose ends, despite a flying visit Monique and I made to Errol earlier today. Right, can I ask Flight Lieutenant Buchan and Captain Darlington for brief verbal reports on your activities over the past couple of days?'

Both men gave accounts that showed they'd been fully occupied, that the reports they'd write would show up several minor issues, but that nothing major had emerged.

'Was there any further interaction with Air Commodore Chilton or Major General Blanch or their staffs?'

'No sir,' said Buchan. 'We were as discreet as you'd have preferred us to be earlier in the week.'

Bob turned to Lieutenant Commander Dixon. 'Your turn, Michael. What about the naval side of things?'

'There are two different answers there, sir. On the one hand, our visits to review security went much as they usually would. I particularly tried to look at the bigger picture, following our last discussion, and focus on entry and exit points. While we were able to offer some suggestions at the time, and will make some recommendations in our report, it's all fairly low-key stuff.'

'What's the other answer?' asked Bob.

'The morning that you left, you asked me to try to find out what was going on behind the scenes, to try to make sense of the oddities we'd identified with the admiral and his elusive head of security. We weren't able to reach any firm conclusions, but both Andrew and I got the sense more than once of something odd not far beneath the surface.'

Petty Officer MacDonald nodded his agreement.

'What sort of things do you mean, Michael?'

'We never did get to see Commander Napier, or his deputy, a man called Lieutenant Rose, despite raising a couple of specific issues that they should have responded to us about. Instead, we got responses from Commander Prendergast, who seems to be the admiral's senior staff officer. On one occasion we got the information we asked for. On the other we got some unconvincing garbage he seemed to have thought up on the spot, just to fob us off.

'And then there's the sense that odd things are happening in ways you don't expect them to happen. It seems that until this spring, it was the norm for ships of the Northern Patrol to detain neutral ships they suspected of dealing with the enemy and bring them to Kirkwall to be searched by a unit called Contraband Control, who were based in the Kirkwall Hotel. I was told that early in the war there could be large numbers of ships waiting to be processed in Kirkwall Bay. Over time the need for this diminished, especially after Norway, the Faroe Islands and Iceland ceased to be neutral for different reasons. But the process went on, as I said, until earlier this year. What's a little odd is that Kirkwall seems to have continued to be a regular stopping-off point for a small number of neutral ships, even though the requirement is no longer there. When we tried to probe more deeply, the shutters came down and all we got was "you'd better ask Commander Prendergast". We did, of course, which was the occasion I've just referred to when he was totally unhelpful.'

'Perhaps the ships' captains have all found the loves of their lives on the islands,' said Monique.

'Perhaps,' said Michael, 'who knows? Anyway, that wasn't really our biggest concern. That revolves round what happens on the island of Flotta. What worried us there was the sheer amount of money in circulation, and a real lack of clarity about whose pockets it ends up in.'

'Can you talk me through that in more detail?' asked Bob.

Petty Officer MacDonald shifted his chair back a little. 'I think everyone already knows that the island of Flotta serves as the main social centre for the ships of the fleet that are at anchor in Scapa Flow. At the discretion of individual ship's captains, members of their crews are permitted to go to Flotta periodically.

There they try to forget that they are living in a tiny space under strict discipline and risking their lives every time they put to sea.

'Plenty of hearty food plays a part in that process, and beer plays another important part. But the navy doesn't want its sailors getting too drunk, so each man going ashore is given tickets for three pints of beer. They must pay for their beer as well, mind you, but the tickets are meant to serve as a rationing mechanism. The problem comes because of the existence of a market for beer tickets amongst those visiting Flotta. Some men may not want their three pints, or any beer at all, though they seem to be in the minority. They can sell their tickets to others who want to buy more than three pints of beer. That's probably reasonable as far as it goes, but when I visited, I got the strong impression that some of those present were acting as dealers in beer tickets. They'd buy from men who didn't want to use their tickets and sell to those who wanted extra. It's only a small step from there to the suspicion that they might actually be selling more than they buy, having secured stocks of unissued tickets by the back door.'

'Is there much money to be made that way?' asked Bob.

'Plenty, but that's small beer, if you'll excuse the pun, when compared with the money that's being made from the Crown and Anchor games.'

'The what?'

'It's a traditional navy game, sir.' MacDonald unfolded a felt cloth that he had taken out of his uniform jacket pocket and laid it on Bob's meeting table. It was green and perhaps three feet long by two feet wide. The top surface was divided by white lines into six boxes, each a little less than a foot square. Four of the squares, the corner squares, carried the symbols of the suits in a pack of cards: a heart, a diamond, a spade and a club in the appropriate colours. As Bob looked at the cloth, the far centre square, between the heart and diamond, had a crown symbol in red, while the near centre square, between the spade and club, had an anchor symbol in black.

'I'm guessing there's more to it,' said Bob.

Petty Officer MacDonald put his hand in his other jacket pocket and took something out. Then, with a flourish that would have done credit to a stage magician, he threw three dice across the table in Bob's direction.

Bob picked one of them up and looked at it. 'It's got six symbols, matching the six symbols on the cloth.'

'Correct sir. All three dice are the same. Right, I'm the banker. I'd like you to place a bet on one of the squares. A penny will do.'

Bob found some change in his pocket and placed a penny in the square with the club symbol.

'Thank you, sir. Now throw the three dice.'

Bob did so. When they came to rest, the three uppermost faces of the dice showed a crown, a diamond and a club.

'You've won, sir. There was one club, so you get your penny back and you get another penny from me.'

'Is that all there is to it?'

'If two clubs had been showing on the three dice, you'd have got your penny stake back plus two pennies from me, and if all three dice had come up with clubs uppermost, you'd have got your penny stake back plus three pennies from me. And that really is all there is to it.'

'That sounds like a good deal from my perspective,' said Bob.

'That's what you're meant to think, sir. But if you run through all the probabilities it's possible to show that for every hundred pennies bet on the table, the players get a little over ninety-two pennies back, counting both original stakes and winnings. That of course means that for every hundred pennies played, the dealer is guaranteed to win a little under eightpence.'

Bob sat and looked at the cloth and the dice. 'All those eightpences will soon mount up if there are lots of players.'

'Exactly, sir. It's effectively a tax of 8% on everything gambled on the table, and over time that will turn into serious money. Especially as not every player plays for pennies.'

'Doesn't the navy try to control what's going on?'

'You'd expect them to, wouldn't you sir? The Ship's Police, that's what we in the navy call our equivalent to the RAF Police, are very visible on Flotta. Most of the entertainment takes place in a vast canteen. There are Ship's Police on entrances and watching the bar, and just wandering around. I saw one fight break out between two drunk seamen and the police were on it in no time at all. Yet even to a newcomer like me, the trade in beer tickets was obvious, and there were four Crown and Anchor games going when I was there, which apparently wasn't a particularly busy time. The authorities weren't interfering at all. It had a really uncomfortable feel about it.'

'You think that those who should be enforcing the rules and protecting the seamen from being fleeced are taking a cut of the profits in return for turning a blind eye?'

It was Lieutenant Commander Dixon who answered. 'That's exactly what we think, sir. But it's clear that the blind eyes are being turned quite some way up the chain of command for it to be happening on this scale. It really stinks but I'm not sure what we can do about it. You heard the admiral say, in effect, that his word was law on Hoy and Flotta. I'm not alleging that he knows what's going on in the canteen on Flotta, but he must have an idea that something isn't right. I think that if you wanted to investigate our suspicions, you'd need to take on the admiral, and for that you'd need some friends in extremely high places.'

'Thanks, Michael. That's food for thought. Do I assume that none of this will find its way into your written report of the visit?'

'Of course not, sir. I have a career in the navy to consider.'

'For my part, I'll think about this over the weekend before deciding whether to draw what we've found to the attention of Commodore Cunningham. He's better placed than any of us to understand the politics in the upper echelons of the navy and decide whether this is something we could and should take on.' He looked at his watch. 'Right, I'm sure I'm not the only one with an in-tray to tackle before we can call it the weekend. I know it's become the norm here to regard weekends as just a means of catching all those bases out there unawares, but I'd like us to treat this one as genuine time off. Everyone, and I mean everyone, should be out of the building before it gets dark, and no-one should return before it gets light on Monday morning. Contact information for the three team leaders and myself are on the cards we each hold, and that information is also available to the MI11 duty officer in London, should the Germans invade Scotland before Monday. Just so everyone is aware, I will be staying at the North British Hotel over the weekend, that's all three nights, and can be contacted there rather than at the officers' mess at RAF Turnhouse. Right, meeting closed.'

The army and RAF teams stood up and left. Petty Officer MacDonald folded his Crown and Anchor cloth and picked up the three dice. 'Have a good weekend, sir,' he said as he walked towards the office door.

Monique and Lieutenant Commander Dixon stayed seated.

'What is it Michael?' asked Bob.

'You do know we'd be poking a stick into a hornets' nest if we tried to prove corruption amongst Royal Navy personnel based in Orkney, don't you sir?'

'Yes, I do, Michael. But that's not going to stop me if I think it's the right thing to do and if I think we can succeed.'

Dixon grinned. 'I was rather hoping you'd say that sir.'

'That's because you want an excuse to go back to the arms of the beautiful Betty Swanson, isn't it?'

'The thought had never crossed my mind, sir.' Dixon stood, still grinning, and followed the others out.

'Which leaves just you and me, Monique.'

'Do you have anything to tell me about your change of contact information for the weekend?'

'You said earlier that you wanted me to take you somewhere expensive for dinner tonight. I took that idea and built on it a little. I'd very much like it if you'd join me for a weekend in Edinburgh. We know how wonderful the North British Hotel is. I rather liked the idea of a proper weekend there with you, away from the war and all of this.'

'I'd love to, Bob, but I've only got the travel bag I took to Orkney with me. I left everything else, such as it is, at the guest house.'

'That's not a problem. Get the duty driver to run you to the guest house now, so you can repack, and then come back here. Then you and I can take a taxi into Edinburgh as soon as it gets dark. That way no-one under my command works after nightfall. The two drivers have hardly been overworked this last week, but I don't want to be seen to make a proclamation from on high and then breach it for my own convenience.'

'I'll do that, Bob. But first I need to contact the duty officer at MI5 to let them have my contact information for the weekend. As you said, just in case Scotland is invaded.'

CHAPTER THIRTEEN

'I'm sorry, Bob, but he insisted. When I told Private Jenkins that you and I were planning to go into Edinburgh, he took the idea we might go by taxi as a personal affront. He said, and I quote, that he'd been sitting on his arse watching the world go by all week and he needed to feel useful and valued too. He also pointed out that you'd need to go to the officers' mess at RAF Turnhouse to repack your bag before we could go into Edinburgh. He's right, of course.'

'Yes, he is. That had passed me by. I've made all the inroads I'm going to make today into this in-tray. Let's call it a day.'

'Taffy, as he likes to be called, is also adamant that he should pick us up on Monday morning and drive us back to Craigiehall. And before you ask, no, I didn't tell him we were spending the weekend together. It just seems to be assumed by everyone in the team, which I don't find a problem if you don't.'

'No, it makes life easier, really.' Bob smiled. 'And nicer.'

*

Later, much later, they were sitting together on a sofa Bob had pulled in front of their bedroom window. Bob sat at one end, while Monique lay against him. The room lights were out, and Bob had opened their blackout curtains, so they could look out across an unlit Edinburgh. Both were drinking champagne.

'I could get used to this,' said Bob.

'A life of decadence and champagne?'

'Yes.'

'No, you couldn't. You'd be bored after a week. So would I. But the idea of three nights of it is lovely.'

Bob gestured with his champagne glass. 'It's nearly a full moon. You can see parts of the city beautifully, all the way from Calton Hill to Salisbury Crags. I'm so pleased that the sky's stayed clear. It's quite something to think that this is the first time in centuries that anyone's been able to see this view with no man-made lights in it. And while the moonlight overpowers the stars a little, I bet we can still see more of them than anyone's been able to see over Edinburgh in at least two hundred years.'

'You know what you said earlier, Bob, when we were getting ready to take off from Lossiemouth?'

Bob feigned ignorance. 'No, what did I say?'

'Come on, Bob, be serious. This is important. And it's really difficult for me.'

'You mean the bit where I said I wasn't about to kill the woman I loved?'

'Yes, that bit. Did you mean it?'

'If I'm honest, that first takeoff was a bit hairier than I'd expected.'

'Please, Bob.'

'Sorry. Of course I meant it, Monique. I mean it now as well. It does feel like I've been waiting all my life for you to come along, and though I don't know when I first realised it, I do love you. It might have been when you commandeered that Luftwaffe flying boat, come to think of it.'

She laughed with him. There was a long, comfortable silence as they looked out over the moonlit city beyond their window.

'Thanks, Bob.'

'What, for telling you that I love you?'

'Partly for that. Mostly for not making me feel that I have to tell you how I feel about you.'

'I thought you'd get round to that in the time that seemed right to you.'

'Perhaps I will, Bob, though perhaps not. I've only ever told one man I loved him. I was very young, and Sergei Ignatieff was a bastard who got me hooked on cocaine and involved in espionage. Maybe that last bit I should thank him for. I was good at it and it's provided me with a reliable living long after I ceased to get by as a dancer. I have loved others – my second husband wasn't one of them – but I never told any of them that I loved them. It felt like I'd be placing a curse on them. I still feel like that. I just know that if I tell you I love you, the next time you take off in that bloody Mosquito you've acquired, something will go wrong and you'll be killed in a burning wreck.'

'Is that the only reason you won't tell me you love me?'

'Yes.'

'I can live with that, Monique.' Bob took another sip of his champagne. 'Look, this is the first time we've had a room with its own bathroom since we last stayed here. No more skittering along the corridor wearing only a bath-towel or accidentally locking yourself out of your room when you go to the toilet. How do you feel about a nice soak in that large bath in there, and then going to bed?'

'That sounds extremely nice. Can we keep the curtains open and the light off?'

'Yes, and I'll do my best to prove to you that flying at 100ft in a Mosquito isn't better than sex.'

'The really great thing is that we can do both, Bob.'

*

167

Bob wasn't sure what time it was when he awoke next morning. It was well before dawn. Then he realised he had nowhere else he needed to be. The sense of relief that swept over him was tinged with an anxiety he couldn't quite put his finger on.

'Are you awake, Bob?' whispered Monique.

'Yes, I was just wondering what time it was.'

'I was laying here thinking that someone's certain to come and knock on the door and break the spell. In our short time together, we've had more than our share of early morning door knocks.'

Bob realised that his own edge of anxiety had the same cause. 'You know, each time that's happened, I've meant to ask you afterwards if you actually keep your gun under your pillow. It always seems ready to hand when needed.'

'A gentleman should never ask where a lady keeps her gun; and a lady would never tell.'

Bob laughed. 'Mine's in the shoulder holster on the back of the chair by the window, under my uniform jacket.'

'I know, Bob. You've had the good fortune to live a life in which people can knock on your door early in the morning without necessarily wanting to kill you. There have been times when I've not been so lucky.'

There was enough pre-dawn light coming in through the window for Bob to see Monique smile. 'What do you want to do today?' he asked.

'This is your city, Bob. I want you to show me the best of it. But first I think we need either more sleep or more sex, and then we should go down and have a really large breakfast.'

*

The knock on the door they both feared never came.

168

In later years, Bob always thought back on that weekend as the happiest time he'd known in the first three decades of his life. The weather was cold but magnificent, without a cloud in the sky. Even Edinburgh's notoriously penetrating wind stilled itself for the occasion.

That first morning Bob took Monique to see the city from its best viewpoints. They walked along Waterloo Place, passing the oddly painted pillbox outside the General Post Office before climbing Calton Hill to drink in the city below and around them. That done, they walked past Holyrood Palace and the nearby brewery into Holyrood Park. Monique was fascinated by the hillside ruins of St Anthony's Chapel and even more so by the views from the path along the top of Salisbury Crags. They decided against a scramble up Arthur's Seat, then Bob led Monique up the Royal Mile to the Castle Esplanade at its upper end, dominated by Edinburgh Castle beyond it. Although an active army headquarters, some parts of the castle were still open to tourists, so they went in to enjoy the views over the city from its upper reaches. Then they retired to a nearby pub.

The two days passed all too quickly. As they did, Bob could feel cares he was never normally aware of falling away. The early part of his war had been intense, culminating in the air battles of the summer and autumn of 1940. He knew the faint scar on the side of his head was minor compared with the inner scars he carried. Scars caused by having so many friends killed, by killing so many enemies who were just like his friends, and by so nearly being killed himself. The two years since had largely been years of frustration as he tried to recover from his injury and then come to terms with his partial blindness. Only in the last two months had he really found his place in the world again and Monique was a central part of that. That he had both killed and almost been killed in his brief career in intelligence would doubtless leave further scars, but right now he could forget about everything but the moment and the woman beside him.

The weekend also seemed to do Monique good. It was as if the darkness that Bob had sometimes seen just behind her eyes had retreated. He knew it might never leave her entirely, but the weekend was enough to give him hope that one day they might both be able to put their experiences of war behind them.

CHAPTER FOURTEEN

Private Owen Jenkins was, as arranged, waiting in the car outside the North British Hotel at 8.30 a.m. on Monday morning. It was starting to get light, but Bob knew that sunrise wouldn't be for another half hour.

Breakfast had been enjoyable, but Bob realised that both he and Monique were steeling themselves to face real life again. They'd talked a little while getting ready, but Bob could feel himself rebuilding defences he'd let drop over the weekend. Part of him just wanted to stay at the hotel with Monique forever. Another, larger, part of him knew that she was right. It had been a lovely break, but it could only ever be a break. He wasn't meant for a life of decadence and champagne.

They were both lost in their thoughts in the car and, after initial greetings, Taffy Jenkins drove in silence.

Back in his office, Bob sat and looked glumly at his still large in-tray. Despite what he'd said at the meeting on Friday, he'd tried to avoid thinking about the situation in Orkney over the weekend. He really did need to seek guidance from Commodore Cunningham. He wondered whether he should fly down to London and see his boss face to face, then realised that was simply an attempt to avoid doing all the other things he needed to do. A phone call would be more than sufficient. He looked at his watch and decided to give the commodore another thirty minutes before making the call.

Bob heard a phone ring in the outer office, then Joyce Stuart put her head round his open door. 'Do you want to talk to an

Inspector Flett from the Orkney Constabulary? He says it's important.'

'Put him through, Joyce.' Bob waited until his phone rang, then picked it up. 'Hello, Group Captain Sutherland here.'

'Hello group captain. I hope you don't mind me calling you. Something's come up which I think may be of interest. I've talked it through with the chief constable here and, frankly, we're out of our depth. When I told him that you'd called in last week, we both thought I should make a formal approach to you.'

This seemed a very uncertain opening from a man who Bob had thought had been very assured in the way he approached his duties. 'I'm intrigued, inspector, tell me more.'

'When we spoke, I told you about the body that had been found in a quarry last Monday morning.'

'The apparent murder victim. Yes, I remember.'

'He's no longer an "apparent" murder victim. The forensics people in Aberdeen were able to tell us on Wednesday that the body belonged to a male of average height with dark hair, probably aged in his thirties. More importantly, they were able to tell us that the cause of death was two shots in the chest from a weapon firing .455 calibre ammunition, probably a Webley revolver.'

'Are you any further with an identification?'

'That's the thing, group captain. I told you when we spoke that we'd passed a photograph of the tattoo on the man's forearm to the naval provost marshal's office at Lyness. That was on Monday, the same day that the body was found. We took the photo before the body was flown to Aberdeen and got it developed and copies printed immediately.'

'As I recall, it rang no bells with them.'

'That's right. And when we got a photograph of the

fingerprints taken from the man's right hand back from Aberdeen on Thursday, we passed a copy over to the navy on the same day. Records of fingerprints of navy personnel are kept as part of their files. If they had turned up anyone missing, then this would allow them to check, even if the tattoo wasn't mentioned in the records.'

'That's not what you rang to tell me, is it, inspector?'

'No, it isn't, group captain. On Saturday morning a letter was delivered to Kirkwall police station, addressed to me personally. I was off duty over the weekend and opened it this morning. It was unsigned and I've established there are no fingerprints on it other than mine. It was postmarked as having been posted in Kirkwall on Friday afternoon.'

'Now I'm really intrigued,' said Bob.

'Both the envelope and letter were typed. Let me read the letter to you. It says: "Dear Inspector Flett. The tattoo in the photograph you passed to the navy this week belonged to Lieutenant Malcolm Rose, who was the deputy to the naval provost marshal, Commander William Napier. The clue is in the symbol, a compass rose. Malcolm was proud of his tattoo and showed if off widely after he had it done this summer. I last saw Malcom Rose last Saturday morning in his office. Then he disappeared. Officially no-one is saying anything. I am sure that Commander Napier recognised the tattoo when he saw the photograph you sent over. I also know they have told you that they do not know who the tattoo belonged to. That is clearly wrong. Malcolm deserves better. That is why I am writing to you." And that's it. There's no signature, as I said.'

'Thank, you, inspector. It's expressed in an odd way, almost as if written by a child, but I have to say that the claim made in that letter rings true given our own dealings with the navy last week.

It certainly seems to have been written by someone who knew Rose and who knows what's going on within the naval provost marshal's office. What do you propose to do now?'

'I've already done it, group captain. In normal circumstances, I'd pass something like this to the naval provost marshal's office, but for obvious reasons I can't on this occasion. As I've told you, the military in Orkney inhabit a separate world, and one that's largely outside my jurisdiction. You, on the other hand, work for the section of military intelligence that looks after military security. I need formally to turn this over to you. The Orkney Constabulary, and this is the official line from the chief constable, can offer MI11 assistance, but we are in no position to take the lead ourselves. Do you want me to send you the letter?'

'There's no need, inspector. I've spent the weekend wondering whether I need to return to Orkney anyway.' Bob forgave himself the lie. 'You've made my mind up for me. I need to talk this through with those I report to, but I'm sure they'll agree. I'll see you tomorrow at the latest. In the meantime, who knows about the letter?'

'Only the chief constable and I know about the contents. The constable who handled the post and put it in my tray on Saturday left it unopened because it was marked personal.'

'Good, thank you, inspector. There is one other thing, though.'

'What's that, group captain?'

'I came to see you on Tuesday because I thought I'd recognised Frank Gordon, a Glasgow gangster. That evening I saw him again, and again it was in the lobby of the St Magnus Hotel. This time I'm sure he recognised me.'

'Yes, you said you'd crossed paths with him in your time in the City of Glasgow Police.'

'I need to be completely honest with you inspector. He's my

uncle, my mother's younger brother. My father is a superintendent in the Edinburgh City Police and the two of them have been enemies since my parents got engaged. I only ever saw Frank Gordon at a family wedding when I was still at school and thought it unlikely that he'd recognised me when I bumped into him in the hotel lobby. But as I said, I'm sure he did the second time we met. The next morning, while I was at breakfast, my hotel room was searched.'

'Was anything taken?'

'No, I suspect that my uncle, assuming it was him, was trying to find out what I was doing in Kirkwall. There was nothing in my room to enlighten him.'

'And the reason you've brought this up now, group captain, is that you want me to see if I can find out what Frank Gordon is doing in Kirkwall in return for your taking Lieutenant Rose off my hands?'

'I'd not have put it as bluntly as that, inspector, but I'm sure he's not on your patch for a holiday, and he is a civilian.'

'Fair enough. Can you describe him to me and tell me anything I might need to know about him?'

*

Bob replaced the phone and sat back in his chair. Suddenly his day was looking much more interesting.

He was distracted by the sound of a knock on his open office door, and smiled as Monique entered, then closed the door behind her.

'What's up?' he asked, 'you look like you've just won the Christmas raffle.'

'Better than that, Bob. I've caught a Soviet spy!'

It took Bob a moment to collect his thoughts. 'You're going to have to explain that to me. I know that Sandy had a photo of Murray flown down to MI5 in London on Friday. You did hint at something else but were a little vague.'

'Let me tell you what's happened. I got Sandy to fly Michael Murray's photo down to MI5 as you said.' Monique sat down in the chair on the opposite side of Bob's desk. 'What you need to know, Bob, is that MI5 routinely photograph all visitors to the Soviet embassy in Kensington Palace Gardens in London. Certainly, all those who visit in daylight when decent shots can be taken. I know the Soviet Union is formally our ally but we both know what that means in practice.'

Bob saw where Monique was going. 'You're going to tell me that Michael Murray visited the Soviet embassy when he was in London on the 28th of September?'

'Got it in one, Bob.'

'I'm sorry, Monique, but I'm not really sure how that takes us forward. We could have guessed that something like that happened.'

Monique's smile broadened. 'But that's not the best bit, Bob. The best bit is that I suggested that my MI5 colleagues get hold of a photograph of Dr Martyn Taylor direct from Porton Down and cross-check him against their rogues' gallery.'

'Are you telling me that he was also photographed visiting the Soviet embassy?'

'No, even better than that. The NKVD agents who work at the embassy are routinely followed and their contacts photographed. One of the agents is a first secretary who is believed to be quite senior in the NKVD's British operation, a woman called Helena Berdyaev. The Soviets of course know they are followed and are good at shaking off tails when they need to. Sometimes our people are even better. Back on Wednesday the 2nd of September, Helena Berdyaev was photographed feeding ducks in St James Park. Standing next to her, also feeding the ducks, was a man who was not identified at the time. They talked for ten minutes before the unknown man left. As it was a routine surveillance focusing on Berdyaev, the man was not followed. After he left, Berdyaev picked up the paper bag he'd been feeding the ducks from, which he'd discarded, and she returned to the Soviet embassy with it.

'By comparing photographs, MI5 established yesterday evening that the unknown man was Dr Martyn Taylor. I found out when I rang them just now. A team from MI5 is on its way to Wester Ross to arrest him as I speak and should be at X Base by the end of the day.'

'Congratulations, Monique. That's a real feather on your cap! I'd not liked the man, but I'd never for a moment suspected anything more than demotivation and frustration. Does this mean that Taylor and Murray were working together?'

'I don't know. It seems to me that what Murray did compromised Taylor's position. We'd never have stumbled over him otherwise. Hopefully, Taylor can be persuaded to give us the full picture when he's taken back to London. That now seems the best chance of getting the loose ends tidied up.'

'Well, that's added to a Monday morning that was already looking much brighter than seemed likely,' said Bob. 'I need to tell you about a phone call I received just before you came in.'

'What was that about?'

'Can we see if Lieutenant Commander Dixon and Petty Officer MacDonald are about? I'll tell the three of you together.'

After Bob had recounted his conversation with Inspector Flett to his colleagues, Michael Dixon sat back in his chair and whistled. 'Suddenly everything seems much more in focus. What do you want us to do about it, sir?'

'Pack our bags and get an aeroplane organised. The four of us need to head back to Orkney. This is going to be like fishing with hand grenades and it has the potential to upset some important people. I want to talk to Commodore Cunningham before we leave. We will need his support if we're going to land any worthwhile fish. Look, why don't the three of you sit there while I get Joyce to put the call through?'

*

Bob felt deeply frustrated. The commodore was in a meeting somewhere in Whitehall that was expected to last until after lunch. Bob had asked the others to pack and provisionally arrange for a plane to take them to Orkney that afternoon. He'd suggested that an Avro Anson would be better than the biplane they had used on the previous trip and was large enough to take the four of them in relative comfort. He'd asked Michael to contact Betty Swanson to see if accommodation could be organised at the St Magnus Hotel. When Michael had asked how many rooms they'd need, Monique had replied that a double and two singles would be fine. When Michael asked whose names the rooms should be in, Monique said that they should use 'Mr and Mrs Smith' for the double, then simply suggested Michael was open with Betty, and leave it to her to sort out the niceties of the details to be entered in the hotel's registration book.

Bob had also spoken to Flight Lieutenant Buchan to let him know that he was likely to be left in charge.

He then had Taffy Jenkins take him to the officers' mess at RAF Turnhouse, so he could repack his travel bag. As he walked back out to the car, he realised that he still had too much time to kill before he could talk to Commodore Cunningham. The right thing to do would be to return to the office and attack his in-tray while he had the chance.

But the weather was still excellent, especially for November, and he really couldn't face the office. 'Do you fancy going for a flight, Taffy?'

'Pardon, sir?'

'I need to get used to the handling of that Mosquito you saw me arrive in on Friday. I thought I'd do a few circuits and wondered if you wanted to come along.'

'Just point me at it, sir.'

With Private Jenkins in the navigator's seat, Bob took off from RAF Turnhouse. He did half-a-dozen circuits, each time approaching from the south-east before touching down and then throttling up to take off, out towards the River Forth, then coming round again. There were a few other aircraft taking off and landing, but Bob didn't have the sense his own informal training was getting in anyone's way.

'Let's try a full stop landing at RAF Kirknewton before taxying round and taking off to come back here. It's only a few miles to the south.'

'Whatever you say, sir. I'm loving this.'

Bob landed as planned at Kirknewton and then taxied round to the south-east end of the active runway. He had to wait for a few moments to allow a Hawker Hurricane fighter to take off ahead of him, then he lined the Mosquito up on the runway and brought it to a halt. As he pushed forward the throttles, with an asymmetric action that by now felt quite natural, he remembered the unhappy consequences of an engine failing in the first moments after takeoff. He was suddenly deeply grateful that

Monique had chosen not to tell him that she loved him.

*

Monique, Michael and Andrew again gathered in Bob's office for his call to Commodore Cunningham. Bob talked his boss through what they'd found and what they suspected. He finished by recounting the conversation he'd had with Inspector Flett that morning. Cunningham initially sounded surprised by what Bob told him, then cautiously positive about what Bob proposed to do.

When Bob put the phone down, the others looked at him. It was Michael who spoke. 'I wasn't sure how that ended, sir. Good news or not?'

'I think it's good news. The commodore wants to talk to his boss, Major General Sir Peter Maitland, and has promised to ring back within half an hour.'

Joyce Stuart served tea while the four of them waited. It took twenty minutes before Bob heard the phone ring in the outside office, with his own ringing shortly afterwards. The conversation was short, and he replaced his phone with a broad smile on his face.

'It looks like we're off to Orkney. Taffy Jenkins is primed to get the car to take us to Turnhouse. I've two more calls to make before we go. I shouldn't be more than about fifteen minutes.'

CHAPTER FIFTEEN

They arrived at RAF Grimsetter as it was getting dark. The flight had been bumpy in the strengthening westerly winds, though by no means as bad as on their first trip to Orkney. At least this time the cloud base had been generally high enough to give them good visibility and, other than some scattered showers south of Inverness, they avoided rain.

Bob had resisted the temptation to sit in the co-pilot's seat. The idea of helping the pilot fly the aircraft was appealing, but he'd realised that the diminishing light of the late afternoon would steadily erode his sense of depth perception. He knew that his 'acquired monocular vision' meant he'd never again be able to benefit from proper stereoscopic three-dimensional sight. In the two years since his injury, he'd found that he was increasingly able to unconsciously recognise a wide range of depth cues that meant he could operate nearly as effectively as he could before he'd been shot down, but only in daylight. At night it was quite different, and Bob made sure he never flew in the dark or in anything approaching it.

Instead, Bob had sat with the other three in the passenger cabin, which allowed them to swap ideas and discuss how they should approach their investigation. As they'd flown over Wick, two Spitfires had briefly formated on their Avro Anson before banking away and heading north-west, Bob had assumed towards RAF Castletown.

Two staff cars drove up to meet the aircraft as its engines stopped on the concrete area in front of the hangars at RAF

Grimsetter. As agreed, Monique, Michael and Andrew left in one, driven by an airman, to book into the St Magnus Hotel. When the registration debate had taken place, Bob had briefly wondered about the desirability of having Michael book all three rooms in his own name, and so keeping Bob's and Monique's quiet, before deciding that there was no point seeking to conceal their return. Anyone who might be interested would be fully aware they were back as soon as they walked into the hotel dining room for dinner.

The second car took Bob to the station headquarters building at RAF Grimsetter. Air Commodore Chilton met him in what Bob took to be the station commander's office.

'I understand that you helped clear up that mess at Lossiemouth, Bob.'

Bob must have looked surprised. Chilton continued, 'Yes, I'm aware that no-one's supposed to know anything about it, but this can be a small world at times. It sounds like you did a good job, so on behalf of my opposite number who looks after stations on the south side of the Moray Firth, thank you.'

The conversation paused while an airman brought in and served tea.

'You sounded rather veiled on the phone, Bob. I take it you want to tell me what's brought you back to Orkney?'

'Yes, sir. Do you mind my asking how well you know Rear Admiral Kinnaird?'

'The short answer is not very well. We've been colleagues of sorts since he took up post as Admiral Commanding, Orkneys and Shetlands late last year. We obviously need to work together in the interests of safeguarding Scapa Flow but, as you'll realise, he's one rank senior to me and it seems that in the Royal Navy they take rank very seriously. I get the impression that he feels he's more on a par with Major General Blanch because they are of equivalent rank. It must be a very lonely life if, on an archipelago of 20,000 civilians and 40,000 military personnel, there is only one other person you feel is your equal. I don't think it helps him keep a grip on the detail of what's going on that he can spend days at a time away from the islands.'

'Why's that, sir?'

'As far as I can tell, it seems the rear admiral takes a broad view of his responsibilities and prefers to be afloat rather than ashore. From what I hear, he resents having been given a land-based posting and spends time out with the ships of the Northern Patrol. They aren't actually part of his command but that slight technicality doesn't seem to stop him.'

'You're saying that the rear admiral is a bit of an absentee landlord, sir?'

'That's about the size of it. Anyway, I think this is the moment when I ask you why you want to know more about Rear Admiral Kinnaird than you seemed to need to know last week?'

'I'm back in Orkney for two related reasons, sir. Partly it's in response to some concerns that arose last week about what we saw on the naval side of things here. And partly it's because we've received a formal request from the Orkney Constabulary to take over the investigation of the murder of a naval lieutenant.'

'I'm intrigued. How much can you tell me?'

Bob briefly ran the air commodore through the issues that had arisen during his team's visit, before going on to talk about the navy's apparent efforts to conceal knowledge of the identity of the body that had been found from the police. Having weighed up the pros and cons of doing so, he then told Chilton about the anonymous letter and the reasons why the police felt unable to act, and why they had sought MI11's help.

Air Commodore Chilton sat back and sipped his tea, which Bob thought must by now be cold. 'Aren't you taking a bit of a risk telling me all this? If there's something rotten extending up to senior ranks in the naval command in Orkney, then who's to say that the other services aren't involved?'

'I am, sir. But I've a strong instinct it's not much of a risk. You don't strike me as the kind of man who'd get involved in something crooked.'

'And Rear Admiral Kinnaird does?'

'No, sir, actually he doesn't. But he does strike me as someone who wants to live in a world that's long gone and I'm wondering if that's blinded him to what's happening around him.'

'Does the fact that I wear the same uniform as you, and the rear admiral doesn't, have any bearing on your approach?'

Bob smiled. 'It would be easy to say "yes" to that, sir, but it wouldn't be true. I think that the moment I decided I could trust you was in our meeting with Major General Blanch in the Sector Operations Room, when you mentioned the "radio trouble" I'd had before shooting down that Ju 88 off Caithness.'

Chilton laughed. 'I had to fend off the commander of 167 Squadron at RAF Castletown over that. He wanted me to make a formal complaint about your "stealing" a kill that he felt rightly belonged to one of his pilots. I sent him away with a flea in his ear. I told him to tell the pilot concerned that if he let a Hurricane flown by a non-operational pilot "steal" his kill, then he needed to learn to fly his Spitfire better.'

'Thank you for that, sir. There is another reason I've decided to brief you on why we're back in Orkney. I have cleared what we are doing at the highest levels in military intelligence in Whitehall but I'm aware that it's another world when you get this far away from London. Our investigation has the potential to upset some important people, and, if the lieutenant's murder is anything to go by, perhaps some dangerous people. It seems prudent to have someone in Orkney who knows what's going on.'

'Yes, I can see why that might be desirable. Look, I imagine you'll be wanting to get to your hotel. We loaned you a couple of cars last week. Do you want us to do so again?'

'That's very kind, sir. One ought to be sufficient. There are only four of us and we can always call on other transport if we split up.'

'Yes, that's no problem. I'll get someone to sort something out now.' As Bob started to stand, the air commodore continued. 'There is one thing I would say to you, Bob.'

'What's that, sir?'

'We've just talked about a rear admiral who is so reluctant to let his seafaring days slip away from him that he may have taken his eye off the ball and neglected his duties here in Orkney. In the same conversation we've talked about a young RAF wing commander, now a group captain, who is so reluctant to let his flying days slip away from him that he was prepared to ignore instructions he should have obeyed in order to get a shot at an enemy aircraft, nearly colliding with one of my Spitfires as a result.' Bob looked at the air commodore awkwardly in the short silence that preceded the inevitable follow-up. 'Do you see any similarities there, Bob?'

'I take your point, sir.'

'Good. Just so long as we understand one another. I'll get someone to organise that car for you.'

*

It wasn't just flying that Bob found difficult in the dark. Driving at night in the blackout was a nightmare for everyone. Painting alternate kerbstones white, whether in Kirkwall or in London, could only go a small way to make up for the simple lack of light to drive by.

Until September the previous year, vehicles had only been allowed to use a single masked headlight at night, and Bob had avoided driving in the dark, much as he still avoided flying in it. Since then, two masked headlights had been allowed on vehicles and Bob had found that at a push he was able to judge positions and speeds – always very slow speeds – sufficiently well to get from A to B without incident, so long as A and B weren't far apart. His drive to Kirkwall police station from RAF Grimsetter was, he knew, only some three miles, but it seemed to take him forever. Bob saw that blue and red oil lamps had been positioned at certain junctions and corners in Kirkwall but felt they did little to help.

The constable at the front desk had clearly been told that Bob was expected. 'Inspector Flett asked me to send you along to his office, sir. It's at the far end of the corridor over there, on the right. I'm afraid I can't leave the desk unmanned and there's no-one else to stand in for me at present.'

As Bob made his way along the corridor, he wondered how the constable coped if nature called.

'In here, group captain!'

Bob followed the sound of the inspector's voice. As he pushed open the door and walked into the dimly lit office, the inspector stood. 'Thank you for calling earlier to confirm you were coming, sir. Help yourself to a seat.'

Bob thought that might have been the first time that the inspector had recognised his senior rank. 'I just hope I've not delayed the end of your shift, inspector. I had to talk to Air

Commodore Chilton at RAF Grimsetter before driving into Kirkwall.'

'Not at all, I'm just grateful you can take Lieutenant Rose, assuming the body is his, off our hands. Now you're here, is there anything I can do to help, bearing in mind my remit and limited resources?'

'We are going to need premises to operate from. Do you have any scope here? We don't need much. Just an office space large enough for four of us to squeeze into, the use of a phone and an interview room, and somewhere secure we can leave notes and papers. I'm very aware my hotel room was searched last week.'

'I can offer you two options. We have plenty of space in Kirkwall's old police office, which forms part of the sheriff court building in Watergate. That's not far from here, close to the cathedral. The problem is that's not manned outside office hours, so there would be no overnight security and access might be awkward. The second option would be for you and your colleagues to shoehorn yourselves into this office. I will use my boss's office. Chief Constable Menzies has asked me to apologise for not meeting you himself. His brother-in-law in Birmingham has suffered a serious heart attack and the chief constable caught the boat for Scrabster this afternoon with his wife. I'm not sure he believed they would get there in time, so we can only pray. If you worked from here, you'd also have use of the interview room where we met last time you called, and of the cells if you needed them. The benefit is that this building is open and manned, if rather thinly manned, 24 hours per day and seven days per week. I can also let you have use of a secure filing cabinet.'

'Thank you, inspector. We'll go for your second option and will start tomorrow.'

'If you could give me until around 9.30 a.m. I'll make sure

'we're ready for you.'

'There's no rush, inspector. We will be going over to Lyness tomorrow morning. I wouldn't expect to be back before lunch at the earliest.'

'Fair enough, that gives me a little more time to get things organised.'

'While I'm here, would it be possible to have a look at that letter you read to me earlier?'

'Of course.' The inspector walked over to a filing cabinet and pulled a folder out of the second drawer. He laid it on the desk between them. 'I'm no expert, but it seems to me that there is one very distinctive feature about the typewriter the author used.'

Bob studied the letter. 'You mean that the lower case "m" has almost no middle leg each time it appears?'

'I thought that might help track down the author. I assume you'll want to leave the letter itself here?'

Bob nodded and slid the folder back towards Flett's side of the desk. 'I would appreciate a photograph of the tattoo if you have one to spare? There's no sensitivity about my having that with me.'

This time Flett found what he wanted in one of the drawers in his desk and passed it over. 'There is one other thing, sir.'

Bob had a flash of déjà vu as he was taken back to the close of his conversation with Air Commodore Chilton. 'What's that, inspector?'

'It's Frank Gordon, your uncle. The City of Glasgow Police are sending up some photographs of him which I hope to receive by Wednesday at the latest. In the meantime, and based on what you told me this morning, I've provisionally identified him as a man who's staying in a boarding house on the edge of Kirkwall under the name of Peter Mcilvenny. He apparently has valid identity documents in that name and the appropriate permit to be in Orkney, though for obvious reasons we've not checked his documents today to avoid warning him we are interested. I'm told that he's been in Orkney for the last three months and that he's meant to be an antiques dealer based in Glasgow. I know you can identify him anyway, but getting the photographs seems a reasonable fall-back.'

'That's very quick work. "Antiques dealer" seems an odd cover. I can't imagine that buying or selling antiques is anyone's top priority when there's a war on.'

'I thought so, too, until I realised that there might be good deals to be had for someone interested in buying cheap and storing until there is an upturn in the market. It also seems to me that it might not be a bad cover for someone involved in handling stolen or black-market goods. As for our speed in tracking him down, I simply asked my men if anyone had heard of a smartly dressed Glaswegian civilian hanging round the St Magnus Hotel. It seems that he's a regular visitor there. It's been suggested to me that he acts as if he's in business with the owner, Edward Swanson, or Teddy to his friends. Quite how that bears on the antiques trade is also a mystery to me. I've sometimes had my doubts about Mr Swanson, but if he's doing anything illegal, we've never heard about it.'

'I was told by Rear Admiral Kinnaird last week that he'd heard that the reason the St Magnus Hotel was the only significant hotel in Kirkwall not requisitioned by the navy at the beginning of the war was that the owner was a Great War army comrade of Winston Churchill's. My second-in-command, Lieutenant Commander Michael Dixon, has formed what you might call a close friendship with Betty Swanson, Edward's daughter. Michael said that when he mentioned what the admiral had said to Betty, she'd replied that her father hadn't served in the war because of flat feet. I'm wondering just how Swanson came to retain his hotel.'

'That's interesting.' The inspector looked at his watch. 'Anyway, Mrs Flett will be thinking that something untoward has happened to me, so if you don't mind, group captain, I'll see you tomorrow.'

*

Bob found Monique, Michael and Andrew sitting in an alcove in the St Magnus Hotel bar drinking beers and, he assumed for Monique, a tonic water. As soon as he arrived, they all moved through to the dining room.

Michael had managed to arrange a table in the heavily curtained bow window at the front of the dining room. There were of course no views, but the location did give a little space between them and the nearest other tables. The background chatter was sufficiently loud to give them a degree of privacy when they talked, especially as there were now only four of them sharing a table.

Bob ran through his conversation with the air commodore, except for the closing couple of moments of it. He had to pause while their main course was served, before going on to relate his discussion with Inspector Flett. He'd wondered what to say about Frank Gordon - or Peter Mcilvenny – before deciding to be quite open about what the inspector had said including his possible connection with Edward Swanson.

'Hmm. That could make life a little awkward,' said Lieutenant Commander Dixon.

'Do you mean personally or professionally, Michael?' asked

Monique.

'Possibly both. That Winston Churchill connection and the flat feet did seem odd, but I didn't really think about it at the time. I'll be careful what I say to Betty about what we're doing here. I would be anyway, of course.'

Bob felt it was time he put Michael and Andrew fully in the picture. 'Monique knows, but there's something about Frank Gordon I've not told the two of you that you probably need to be aware of. He's my mother's younger brother, and a long-term enemy of my father's. I think he recognised me on our last visit and searched my room on the morning we left.'

'Ah,' said Michael. 'Does Flett know that?'

'Yes, he does.'

Monique looked around the dining room to check they could still talk privately and then turned to Bob. 'Is this a good moment to discuss what we want to achieve in the morning?'

'As good as any. I believe that Sir Peter Maitland spent a little time this afternoon rattling cages at the Admiralty. Commodore Cunningham told me on the phone earlier that the intention was to ensure that Rear Admiral Kinnaird would this afternoon receive clear orders to cooperate fully with our investigation and to meet with us in the morning. It seems that has happened, because on arrival at the hotel I was given a note telling me that transport has been arranged at 8 a.m. to the admiral's headquarters at Lyness. A car will pick us up outside. It seems that once again, Second Officer Jennings has drawn the short straw and will be our chaperone.'

'How open will you be at the meeting, sir?' asked Michael.

'I'm going to present it as MI11 responding to a request for assistance from the Orkney police in connection with the murder of a man who they believe to have been a lieutenant in the naval provost marshal's office. That will explain in terms the admiral will understand why we have been brought in. I see no need to talk to the admiral about the other matters we intend to investigate at this stage. The one concrete thing I wish to obtain from the admiral is his agreement that we can go anywhere and talk to anyone, with his full authority. I particularly want his agreement that we can talk to the staff in the provost marshal's office at Lyness.'

*

'How do you feel about opening the curtains, Bob?' asked Monique.

'Why not?' The room light was out, and Bob pulled back the curtains and looked out at the darkened harbour below. He remembered that it had been a full moon the previous night and could see a few gaps in the cloud. He could also see movement and the occasional flicker of torchlight around the harbour and occasional vehicles were still passing along the road in front of the hotel. He heard Monique walk up behind him.

'You can share my blanket, if you like, Bob. You'll catch your death of cold standing there naked in this temperature.'

Bob pulled the offered half of a blanket round him, and pressed close to Monique, putting his right arm round her waist. 'Do you think Betty Swanson is going to be a problem?'

'You mean if her father is somehow tied up with Frank Gordon? No, I don't think so. Michael's got his head screwed on and his relationship with her predates the point at which her father might have found us of interest. That suggests it wasn't contrived on her part. It does focus the mind, though. While you were in the bathroom earlier, I had a good look round the room for listening devices.'

'I take it you didn't find any?'

'No. Look, Bob, even with the blanket, I'm getting cold. We can leave the curtains open, but let's go back to bed.

CHAPTER SIXTEEN

Bob shivered as he got out of the car at the landward end of the long stone pier at Scapa. It was just starting to get light and there was a chill wind from the west. He heard crunching from beneath his shoes and realised that puddles formed by indentations in the road surface were frozen over.

A crowd was milling around beyond the naval guards at the end of the pier. Second Officer Jennings had something about a ferry before they got out of the car and it seemed they were having to compete with people wanting to get on to the vessel that was moored at the near end of the pier. Bob could just make out the name *Sir John Hawkins* on the prow of the ship. Further along the pier, beyond the ship, things quietened down, and the WRNS officer led them to a motor gun boat like the one they had used to get to Lyness the previous week.

Once on board the vessel, Bob followed the others down into a tiny, cramped cabin. It was rather too cold to be out in the open air.

'I'm sorry about the crush back there,' said Second Officer Jennings. 'The ferries run two-hourly, and the first in the morning from Scapa to Lyness is always busy. I think she must be running late.'

'It's an impressive operation,' said Bob.

'That's only part of it, sir. The TSS *Sir John Hawkins* tends to be the mainstay of this route. There are also other steamers criss-crossing Scapa Flow between other parts of the mainland and the southern islands, and between the islands, always offering roughly the same two-hourly service. They are mainly intended for military personnel, but they carry civilians without question.'

Bob had always thought of himself as a good sailor, but as the boat picked up speed, he felt more comfortable out in the open air on the bridge, with Lieutenant Commander Dixon and the boat's captain. Petty Officer MacDonald stayed down in the cabin with Monique and Second Officer Jennings. Bob guessed the sun was rising behind the layer of cloud by the time their boat picked its way through others to come alongside one of the piers at Lyness.

As before, they were taken in two cars to the headquarters building close to the harbourside at Scapa Flow. Commander Prendergast was waiting for them in the reception area. Bob noticed there was no delay this time. The commander led them directly to the meeting room they had used on their previous visit.

As they entered, Rear Admiral Kinnaird, who had been standing with a group of officers looking out of one of the windows on the front of the building, turned and walked over. 'Good morning, group captain. Thank you for joining us this morning.'

Bob was looking for signs of stress, anxiety, or anger in the Admiral but could detect none, which he found a little odd. The fact that the meeting had been set up so quickly suggested that whatever the Admiralty had said to Kinnaird had been forceful enough to get him to pay attention.

'Thank you for agreeing to see us at such short notice, sir.'

Kinnaird made his way towards the side of the table he'd sat at before, and Bob took up position opposite, flanked by Michael and Monique. Petty Officer MacDonald sat next to Michael. Bob had asked him to take notes of the meeting. Bob realised that the

WRNS officer was not present and presumed the admiral had instructed her to stay outside.

There was again no tea on offer, but otherwise Kinnaird was courtesy itself. 'As you know, I'm Rear Admiral Kinnaird, Admiral Commanding, Orkneys and Shetlands. On my left is Captain Barnaby Nicholson. Captain Nicholson commands HMS *Proserpine,* the main naval base here at Lyness, and he reports to me. On my right is Captain Paul Cowdrey, who has the titles of "Captain of Dockyard" and "King's Harbour Master at Lyness" and who also reports to me. In effect Barnaby commands all naval personnel who primarily work on land at Lyness, while Paul commands everyone who primarily works afloat, on one of the hundreds of support vessels, tenders, tugs, cranes, depot ships and so on that we need in order to make this place function. He also commands naval operations on Flotta and the other smaller islands.

'To Paul's right, as you know, is Commander Prendergast, who is on my staff. To Barnaby's left is Commander William Napier, who is the naval provost marshal for Orkney.'

Bob looked with interest at Napier. He saw a man of medium build and apparently medium height, in his early forties. Above a black beard that was showing some flecks of grey, Bob found a calm pair of dark-coloured eyes looking back at him. Napier didn't look like a man whose deputy had been murdered and whose own future might be in jeopardy. The commander had medal ribbons suggesting he'd served in the Great War, but none suggesting that he'd seen any action.

Bob introduced his side of the table. He saw a flicker of interest as he said who Monique was. Clearly the three men who had not been present at the previous meeting knew that this was the woman who had bested the admiral and were intrigued.

Admiral Kinnaird leaned back in his chair.

'As you are probably aware, the Admiralty is keen that I offer you my full cooperation, group captain. Perhaps it would help if you could outline why you are back in Orkney. We can then work out how I can give practical effect to that cooperation.'

'Military Intelligence 11 has returned to Orkney at the formal request of the Orkney Constabulary, sir. A body was discovered last Monday in one of the quarries providing stone for the construction of the barriers between the islands on the east side of Scapa Flow. Whoever placed the body there clearly hoped it wouldn't be found. The only distinguishing features were the tattoo of a compass rose on the inside of the right forearm and a set of right-hand fingerprints. The rest of the body was badly crushed by rocks, though not so badly crushed that the forensics people in Aberdeen couldn't work out that the cause of death was gunshot wounds to the chest.

'The particular reason why the Orkney Constabulary has asked MI11 to investigate this case is that they believe the dead man to be Lieutenant Malcolm Rose, who I understand was the deputy to Commander Napier. Perhaps I could start by asking whether you are able to confirm that the police are correct in their belief about the man's identity?'

The admiral leaned forwards in his seat and looked past the captain on his left to Commander Napier. For the first time Bob thought he caught a glimmer of nervousness in Napier's demeanour.

Commander Napier looked away from the admiral and back across the table towards Bob. 'Yes, I can confirm that the body that was found last Monday was that of Lieutenant Malcolm Rose.' Bob could tell that Napier wasn't finished, so didn't break into the pause that followed. 'If I were on your side of the table,

197

group captain, my next question would be why didn't we tell the Orkney police who it was as soon as we knew ourselves.'

'That was going to be one of my next questions,' said Bob. 'The other was: when did you know it was him?'

'I'll take that one first. I was fairly sure whose body it was as soon as I saw the photograph of the tattoo that the police had sent over last Monday. I wasn't certain until we got the fingerprint information from the police on Thursday, which we could check against Malcolm's records, but I was as near certain as made no real difference.'

'Which brings us to the "why?",' Bob prompted. He saw the commander lean forwards to catch the admiral's eye and got the strong sense that what he was about to hear had already been discussed between them.

'Yes sir, and that's rather difficult. You see, I had been investigating the activities of Lieutenant Rose for some time. There were questions asked about his loyalty. His wife's parents were both German Jews who had moved with her to Britain in the early 1930s. I had understood that all their relatives in Germany had either escaped or been killed. In August I was told by someone who knew the lieutenant's family that his mother-in-law still had relatives living in Germany. It seemed to me that this could potentially make him vulnerable to blackmail, using the surviving relatives over there as a lever.'

'You were suspicious that he was a German spy?' asked Monique.

'I had nothing concrete to go on, otherwise I would have involved MI5, but the suspicion was there. In response I tried to keep fairly close watch on what he was doing and who he was doing it with.'

'Let me get this straight. You suspected a German spy at

Scapa Flow, the Royal Navy's most important anchorage and, we've been told, the most heavily defended naval anchorage anywhere in the world, and you effectively did nothing about it? Surely involving MI5 should have been the very first thing you did? We would have been able to offer you support and advice or take over the investigation ourselves. Alternatively, we might have been able to tell you there was nothing to worry about, which would have made your life here very much easier.'

It was the admiral who replied. 'Your points are very well made, Madame Dubois. I first became aware of the suspicions about Lieutenant Rose last Monday, on the day that his body was found, and the day the police passed us a photograph of the tattoo. I share your concerns that MI5 was not involved, and I made those concern very well known to Commander Napier. Indeed, it was because I wished to find out exactly what had been going on that I had to cancel the dinner I was due to host last Monday evening.

'I should perhaps add that I had been unaware that one of your team was seconded from MI5, group captain, and I was only told this on Tuesday morning, when you were on your way over from Kirkwall. I am afraid my ungallant efforts to exclude Madam Dubois from our meeting were a rather irrational response to the crisis I was trying to manage behind the scenes. At the time we were seeking to establish what Lieutenant Rose's movements had been after he was last seen.'

'Were you able to make any progress with that?' asked Bob.

Kinnaird looked along the table again.

Napier coughed to clear his throat, then replied. 'Only up to a point, I am afraid. We were able to establish that late on the Saturday evening, Lieutenant Rose asked to be taken by navy launch to a Portuguese-registered ship at anchor in Kirkwall Bay, a vessel called the SS *Amazon*. The launch took him, then returned to shore without him. This was a ship that had called at Kirkwall several times in the past, though only once since we wound down the Contraband Control unit in May. Its last visit had been in August. Before that it had been here in February. We know that Lieutenant Rose also visited the ship when it was in Orkney in August.'

It was Monique who asked the obvious question. 'You are saying that although you had suspicions about Lieutenant Rose being a German spy, you allowed him to board a neutral ship where he could have picked up instructions or delivered intelligence, or simply escaped?'

'It wasn't as straightforward as that, Madame Dubois. Our efforts to keep track of the lieutenant on Saturday failed.'

'I'm finding this hard to follow,' said Bob. 'When was the lieutenant actually missed?'

'He was last seen in this building on Saturday, in the late morning. On the Sunday morning, he was meant to be duty officer, but failed to turn up. I was contacted, and we immediately started trying to trace his movements. I found out on the Sunday evening that that the lieutenant had boarded the SS *Amazon* 24 hours earlier. Unfortunately, the ship had left Kirkwall early on Sunday morning, bound for Lisbon.'

'Couldn't you have stopped her en route? Her course must have been predictable?'

'She'd have had to take a route to the west of the UK. The North Sea and English Channel would be far too risky for a neutral ship. I did consider asking the Northern Patrol to try to intercept her, but at the time felt that this would be a major over-reaction given that I only had unsubstantiated suspicions about the lieutenant. I also thought it was entirely possible that he'd simply had too much to drink after getting back from the ship and was sleeping it off somewhere in Kirkwall. He did have problems with alcohol at times and that wouldn't have been entirely out of character.'

'But you found no trace of him returning from the ship?' asked Monique.

'No, but if he had returned to the harbour at Kirkwall, it would have been in one of the ship's boats, so that's not surprising.'

'Which means that as well as failing to inform MI5 of suspicions you've had since August, you failed to take the steps necessary to stop the ship you believed the lieutenant was on?'

'I'm afraid it doesn't sound good when you put it like that, Madame Dubois, but that is what happened.'

'Let's move things forward to Monday,' said Bob. 'You knew from the moment you saw the photograph of the tattoo provided by the police that Lieutenant Rose had been killed. What did you do then?'

'I'm afraid that by then it was too late to do anything. My best working hypothesis, given that the SS *Amazon* was probably by that time somewhere out in the North Atlantic and its crew unavailable for questioning, was that Rose had probably been killed on the ship and his body taken by the crew to the quarry where he was found. It seems that the ship left not long after that had been done.'

'Do you have any independent evidence for that?' asked Bob. 'Has there been any trace of the vehicle they must have used, or sightings of members of the crew on Orkney?'

'I'm afraid not, but it seems the only possible explanation.'

'I'm still not sure why you felt it right to cover up the identity of the body.'

'That's my fault, group captain,' said the admiral. 'The

commander informed Captain Nicholson and I of Lieutenant Rose's probable death on Monday afternoon and of his suspicions about the lieutenant. This wasn't long before you and your team were due to arrive in Orkney. I felt, wrongly, I admit, that it would be better to delay our "discovery" that the body was that of Lieutenant Rose until this week. I believed at the time that to do otherwise would expose us to far too many questions of the sort you have very rightly been asking. I had instructed that once you had returned to Edinburgh, we should tell the police that we had identified the body and were seeking to find out who had killed the lieutenant. That would have happened yesterday afternoon. Unfortunately, it seems that the police were ahead of us and I heard that they had identified him from the Admiralty before we had a chance to tell them ourselves.'

'Did you think that delaying telling them would deflect attention and criticism?' asked Bob.

'Possibly not, but it seemed the least bad course of action at the time. I admit it looks very unwise with hindsight. Lieutenant Rose's wife will receive news of his death today. Our delay in informing her has given me more concern than anything else. Do you mind my asking how the police were able to identify the lieutenant without our telling them?'

'I don't mind you asking, sir, but I'm sure you will understand if I prefer to keep that to myself.'

Bob saw a flash of anger cross the admiral's face, swiftly replaced by resignation. Kinnaird clearly understood that his career hung by a thread and losing his temper was not the best way to keep that thread intact.

The admiral sat back. 'Very well. Can I ask what you want of me?'

'Certainly, sir. I would like your explicit approval that my team can go anywhere and speak to anyone within your command and that we can call on any naval resources not needed for operational purposes to assist us with our enquiries.'

'Yes, that's agreed. Commander Napier here will act as your liaison and ensure that everyone affords you complete cooperation.'

'Thank you for the offer, sir,' said Bob, 'but Commander Napier's actions will form part of my investigation. It would not be appropriate for him to carry out the role you suggest.'

The commander stared fixedly at the table in front of him. Bob had the sense of a man on the very edge of complete loss of control.

'What would you suggest instead, group captain?' asked the admiral.

'Frankly, sir, what we need in the way of liaison is someone sufficiently well-connected to set up meetings and interviews; and arrange transport. Second Officer Jennings would be ideal.'

Bob knew he was taking a chance. Jennings could have been assigned to his team in the first place with orders to report back on their activities. He watched the faces of the men opposite as he said her name and was pleased to see the idea wasn't one that they welcomed. That seemed the best character reference the second officer could possibly ask for.

'Very well. I believe she is still in the building, waiting to accompany you back to Kirkwall. Commander Prendergast will locate her. Is there anything else?'

'Yes, sir. I'd like to take the chance to talk to Lieutenant Rose's colleagues in the naval provost marshal's office. I'd like to do so immediately, and I'd like to do so without Commander Napier being present.'

There was a very long pause. The admiral seemed deep in

thought, his elbows on the table in front of him and his hands steepled in front of his mouth. Eventually he looked up. 'Very well. Given all the circumstances, I am with immediate effect suspending Commander Napier from duty and confining him to the officers' quarters here at Lyness.'

Bob saw the shock on Napier's face.

Captain Nicholson turned to the admiral. 'Sir, do you think that's fair?'

'I'm sorry, Barnaby, but it's high time I started doing things properly. I'd be grateful if you could escort Commander Napier to the officers' quarters. You will stay there, Commander Napier, unless given specific permission by the captain or I to leave, for as long as it takes Group Captain Sutherland to conclude his investigation.'

CHAPTER SEVENTEEN

The meeting room was quiet after the admiral and his party left.

'While they get themselves sorted out, we've got a moment to ourselves,' said Bob. 'Do you think this room has listening devices?'

'I doubt if they'd risk anyone listening in on discussions like that one,' said Monique. 'Let's go over to the corner by the window while they find Second Officer Jennings – she was a good choice, by the way Bob, for reasons I'll explain later – and I'm sure we can talk privately there.'

'That went rather better than I'd expected,' said Bob. 'Any quick reactions to what we were told? Monique?'

'The story Napier told was total invention. Nothing really made sense. Surely he'd have involved MI5? And surely he'd have stopped the ship? For God's sake, they've got a fleet based here specifically to control the area the ship would have sailed through. Even the details didn't add up. Wouldn't disposing of the body in a quarry have needed a fair bit of local knowledge? If Rose had been killed on the ship, then it would have been easier and safer for the crew simply to dump his body in the Atlantic attached to a link of anchor chain. No, for me, Napier started with what he thought we knew and fabricated the best story he could manage around it. Besides, I think we can be fairly sure that Malcolm Rose was not a German spy, though as you know Bob, I can't say why. I will, however, pass the story on to my colleagues in MI5 with the request that they check it out.'

'I agree that Napier's story was complete garbage, sir,' said

Michael. 'And I think the admiral had reached the same conclusion by the end of the meeting. That's what led him to take the action he did.'

Bob looked around the room. 'We're agreed, then. The admiral's about-turn at the end was a real shock to Napier. Look, we can talk about this in more detail later, but we need to agree what happens now. As I told the admiral, I want to talk to the staff in the naval provost marshal's office. I have no idea how many of them there are, but we need to check when Rose was last seen and find out anything that they can tell us about him. We also need to take a quiet look at any typewriters in the office. I'm looking for one that produces a barely visible middle leg on the lower case letter "m". That might help us find the person who wrote the anonymous letter that was sent to the police. It goes without saying that we need to avoid exposing the existence of the letter or, if we establish it, the identity of the letter writer.'

*

There turned out to be nine staff working in the provost marshal's office. It was in the same headquarters building as the admiral's meeting room, but on the side facing away from Scapa Flow, where the diagonally cross taped windows gave views of drab rows of wooden huts and Nissen huts rather than of the harbourside and open water.

The staff, all naval junior ranks and all men, occupied an open area that was lined on the wall away from the windows by filing cabinets. Each had a desk and a telephone, and there were four desks with typewriters at one end. At the other end of the area, two offices had been created, both with internal windows looking out into the main office. The slightly larger one had an external window as well, while the smaller one did not. Bob guessed the larger one was Napier's office.

Bob asked Second Officer Jennings to take the staff, who were clearly at a loose end anyway, to wait in the building's canteen until they were called for.

'Andrew, can you look at the typewriters? Monique and I will see if there's anything helpful in Rose's office. Michael, can you have a careful poke round in Napier's office? I'm not expecting to find a .455 Webley revolver with two rounds fired, but it would be very neat if there was one.'

In Rose's office the two filing cabinets were both locked, and at this point Bob wasn't proposing to break them open. Any removal of evidence that was going to happen would already have happened.

There was a knock on the open door. Bob looked up to see Petty Officer MacDonald holding a piece of paper. 'Was this what you meant by a missing middle leg on the "m", sir?'

Bob looked. 'That's exactly right. Whose desk is it?'

'According to the notes I took when we arrived, it's used by a rating called Macpherson, sir. He sits at the desk away from the window at the far end of the room.'

Having confirmed that Michael hadn't turned up a smoking gun, or anything else of great interest, in Napier's office, Bob arranged to have the staff brought in two at a time. He and Monique interviewed one and Michael and Andrew the second. To avoid being too obvious, Bob decided to leave Macpherson until the third pair.

Bob and Monique's first interview went routinely enough. The young man was nervous, but seemed open and honest, if remarkably ignorant about both Rose and Napier. Their second interviewee was an Able Seaman Eric Booth. Bob thought Booth looked extremely young, probably barely twenty.

After he'd accepted Bob's invitation to sit down, the able seaman looked back and forth between Bob and Monique. 'You're here about the letter, aren't you?'

'What letter?' asked Monique.

'The letter I sent to Inspector Flett about Malcolm Rose.'

'That was written on someone else's typewriter.'

'Of course it was, ma'am. I wasn't going to make it that obvious. Malcolm was involved in some murky stuff and I needed to be sure who it was who came to ask about him.'

'Is that also why you phrased the letter as you did?' asked Bob. 'It had a rather childish quality, and you strike me more as a public school kind of boy.'

'Harrow, actually, sir.' Booth smiled. 'If it weren't for this dreadful war, I'd be studying history at Cambridge by now. As it was, I fought off my parents' demands that I apply for officer training and I've spent my time since then finding myself a nice quiet little hidey-hole in which to see out the war. Once it's over I can get back to real life. I was doing quite well until Malcolm was killed.'

Bob bit back his instinctive response to this and then wondered why he disapproved so deeply of the young man's perfectly rational efforts to survive the war. 'Your letter implied that you knew Lieutenant Rose quite well. What can you tell me about him?'

'He was thirty-five, married with no children, and was crooked through and through. He also had a gentle side that no-one else ever saw. No-one in Orkney, anyway.'

'How well did you know the lieutenant?'

Booth looked back at Bob. 'I know the law, sir, all too well. I'm not about to expose myself to a criminal prosecution or a court martial.'

'Look, anything you say will be treated in the strictest confidence. I want to find out who killed Malcolm Rose. I'm not interested in whether you prefer women or men.'

'Very well, sir. Since the beginning of the year, not long after I arrived in Orkney, Malcolm and I have had an arrangement. I met his emotional and physical needs, and he made my life more pleasant and comfortable than it would have otherwise been. He also provided me with an allowance that already means that I can live a little more comfortably when I do eventually get to university. I should add that we were very discreet. As far as I know, no-one here suspected what was going on. He owned a cottage at Scapa, to the south of Kirkwall, and I'd take the steamer over a couple of evenings each week, so we could spend the night together. We'd talk, or read, or listen to the radio. He seemed to crave domesticity and I think I helped him find it. We'd then come back separately the next morning.'

'How did you feel about the fact that Malcolm was married?'

'I didn't feel anything about it, sir. His life with his wife in Hastings was one thing, and our time together here in Orkney was something quite separate. He would talk about taking me away to some paradise island after the war, but we both knew it was only talk. I did, certainly. What we had here worked for both of us. But it wasn't love and I never thought I was in competition with his wife.'

'What makes you say he was crooked through and through?'

'He always carried round loads of cash, sir. And he'd managed to buy the cottage. He never gave any details, but he liked to talk as if he knew things about important people that they didn't want him to know. He sometimes talked of his contacts and his being able to call in favours, especially if he'd had a few drinks. I only ever saw him either here in the office, when we were extremely careful about how we interacted, or at the cottage. For obvious reasons we were never able to go anywhere else, so I never got to meet any of these contacts, and he never named names.'

'You talked of him having a few drinks. It was suggested to us earlier that Malcolm might have had an alcohol problem. Is that correct?'

'Not a serious one. He liked his drink but tended to go for quality rather than quantity. He'd always have top-notch brandy or rum available at the cottage. Personally, I don't drink alcohol at all.'

'This is an important question, able seaman. Did you ever have the slightest suspicion that Lieutenant Rose might have been a German spy?'

Booth looked surprised, then laughed. 'You're joking, aren't you, sir?'

'No, I'm not. The possibility has been suggested to us.'

'Well, I think you can forget it, sir. His wife came from a German Jewish family who left the country years ago. He did tell me once that her relatives who had stayed in Germany had all been killed. I'd say he had a genuine loathing for the Germans. I admit it could have been a cover but if so, it was a really convincing one.'

'Thank you for that. When and where did you last see Malcolm?'

'Here in the office on the Saturday morning. I heard him say something about needing to go to Kirkwall. But as I've said, we didn't really interact here, so I didn't take much notice.'

'We've been told that he boarded a Portuguese ship in Kirkwall Bay that night. Does that surprise you?'

'Not really. As I've said, he never told me much about what he did outside the office or the cottage and I never asked.'

'We've also been told that since August, Commander Napier had been keeping an eye on Malcolm because of his concerns that the lieutenant might have been a spy.'

Booth laughed scornfully. 'He didn't do a particularly good job of it, did he sir? I'd wager that Commander Napier hasn't the slightest idea that I was a regular visitor to Malcolm's cottage. If he'd really been keeping watch on the lieutenant, then he'd have found out about our arrangement and we'd both have been arrested some time ago.'

'Yes, that thought had crossed my mind, too. Is there anything else you think we ought to know?'

'Not really, sir. Malcolm was always very guarded about Commander Napier, but I did sometimes get the impression when I saw them together in the office that they were jointly involved in things they didn't want anyone to know about. They'd have meetings in here with the door closed but forget that there's a window through to the general office. Their interactions sometimes looked quite odd. Remember that at a personal level I know, or knew, Malcolm very well.'

'Can you tell me anything about Commander Napier?'

'Not very much, I'm afraid. I believe he is from Edinburgh, and I get the impression his wife lives there. He comes over as a reasonable man, but distant and stern. Malcolm never talked about him and I never pried.'

'I think that's it,' said Bob, 'apart from the address of the cottage in Scapa and a key if you have one.'

'I can give you the address, sir, but Malcolm never gave me a key. We timed it so he was always there when I arrived. And he always left after me, even if we were using the same steamer.'

'Thank you, able seaman. We'll go and have a look. If you

think of anything else, then I can be contacted at Kirkwall police station.'

*

Although they'd got all the information they'd needed from Booth, Bob felt they had to complete the interviews with all the staff in the naval provost marshal's office, partly to gain others' impressions of Rose and Napier, but mainly to protect the young man's position.

After the interviews were finished, they spent a short time discussing what they'd heard, then went with Second Officer Jennings for lunch in the large officers' wardroom at Lyness, which was set amongst the wooden huts of the officers' quarters, a little inland from the collection of oil tanks that were so obvious in distant views of the base. As agreed between them previously, Petty Officer MacDonald had peeled off the group after leaving the headquarters building and made his own way towards Lyness's bustling piers.

After lunch, Jennings again laid on a fast boat to get them back to Scapa, though this time they diverted via the island of Flotta to allow Lieutenant Commander Dixon to disembark.

Jennings was happy to drop Bob and Monique off at Kirkwall police station before returning to her other duties in the naval HQ in the Kirkwall Hotel.

As they watched the car carrying the second officer pull away, Bob turned to Monique. 'What did you mean earlier about Jennings being a good choice?'

'She talked to me on the boat on the way over. She's got a friend who's got something she wants to tell me. I've agreed to go with Jennings this evening to see this woman at their quarters, in huts built in a park not far from the cathedral. They share a room. I don't know what will come of it, but it seemed to me to be proof that Jennings is on our side.'

'You will be careful, won't you Monique? Once the sun goes down it's bloody dark to be walking round the town on your own.'

'Your concern is very touching Bob but let's remember who you are talking to.'

'Fair enough. Be careful anyway. We really don't know what we're dealing with here, and I have a feeling that this morning's meeting will have caused unpredictable ripples.'

Inspector Flett had been as good as his word and had vacated his office, which was now equipped with a meeting table, four chairs and a lockable filing cabinet. His desk and phone had been pushed into a corner, out of the way. The constable on duty at the reception told them that Flett was in Stromness before showing them on a large-scale map how to get to the address in Scapa that Bob had given him.

Bob and Monique walked to where he had left the RAF car, near the St Magnus Hotel, before setting off to look for Lieutenant Rose's cottage. What they found when they arrived was an attractive building that lay a little inland from the shore and just off a minor road that looped round behind the beach at Scapa.

There was space to pull off the road, close to the cottage, and Bob did so. The cottage itself was the sort a child would draw. A window either side of a front door, with a pair of dormer windows protruding from the roof above. This made it seem small from the front, but as they'd parked, Bob had got the impression there was an extension at the rear.

'What we know about Lieutenant Rose doesn't suggest to me

that he was a "spare key under a plant pot" sort of man,' said Bob, 'but let's look anyway.'

There were pots either side of the door, though with little growing in them in November. As Bob suspected, there was no key in or under either.

'Let's go round the back. I'm sure we can gain access one way or another.' Bob led the way along a path that led down the side of the cottage furthest from the road. 'Ah. It looks like someone's been here before us.' Bob stopped, looking at the smashed-in back door. 'It seems that the locks were stronger than the hinges. I suppose at least it means we won't have to break and enter ourselves. There are no near neighbours, so this could have been done without anyone hearing.'

'We don't know when it was done,' said Monique. 'Let's be careful. I'll go in first, and you keep behind me.' She pulled out her pistol and cocked it.

'I think it's safe,' said Bob. 'The wind's blown in leaves from the garden. This wasn't done today.'

'Let's be careful anyway.' Monique kept her gun in her hand and led the way through the kitchen and into a hall beyond that extended to the front of the cottage, beside a set of stairs leading up from the front door to the floor above.

'Someone's turned the place over very thoroughly,' said Bob. 'That was obvious in the kitchen but it's even more so now.' From where he stood, he could see debris strewn across the floors of both front downstairs rooms.

'The cottage has electric lights,' said Bob. 'Let's turn them on and make a more thorough sweep through each room in turn, to see if we can find anything that whoever's already been here has missed.'

The rooms were small, and Bob and Monique worked as a

team.

'It would be nice to find something that gave us a clue as to how Lieutenant Rose came to be so well off,' said Bob. 'He was obviously involved in something shady. We just have no clear idea what it was.'

Monique opened a cupboard in a sideboard in what would probably be described as the parlour, the best front room. 'I'm surprised this lot wasn't taken. Judging by what's left of the bottles, the spirits that were in here would set you back a fortune, assuming you could find anywhere to buy them in wartime Britain. It looks like someone simply smashed the bottles for the sake of it. That explains the smell in the room.'

Bob looked over her shoulder. 'There's a sense of real anger at work here, but that thought doesn't really get us anywhere. Look, I get the feeling we are wasting our time, Monique.'

'Hang on. When we were upstairs did you see an opening for the loft?'

'No, but with the bedrooms in the roof space, there might not be one. And we know there's no shed out the back either.'

They looked again but could find no way into a roof void. As the light was now fading, Bob led the way out of the smashed back door, and they drove back to the police station.

CHAPTER EIGHTEEN

Lieutenant Commander Dixon and Petty Officer MacDonald were waiting for them in Flett's office. Or perhaps they should now call it the MI11 office, thought Bob.

'How did it go?' he asked.

'Reasonably well,' replied Michael, with a grin on his face.

'What have you got?'

'It's Andrew's story, I'll not spoil it for him. Do you want a cup of tea first?'

They resumed a few minutes later with mugs of tea. Andrew took the lead. 'It was pretty much like last time, sir. I was able to get to Flotta without needing to wait for a ferry. The other ranks' canteen on the island was busy by most standards, though given its size it was far from crowded. I understand it gets busier as the afternoon goes on.

'Anyway, as we'd agreed, I focused on the Crown and Anchor games rather than the trade in beer tickets. I approached one of the Crown and Anchor dealers. I played for a few minutes, and then told him who I was and showed him my MI11 identification. He looked like he was going to run for it, but I calmed him down. Then I told him I was on Flotta because there had been reports of a German spy on the island and swore him to secrecy about that. Word will get round in no time, of course. I said that someone in his position would be very well placed to notice anyone suspicious and asked him to keep his eyes peeled. As we'd hoped, he was flattered. I chatted to him for a few more minutes before asking him what he did when he wasn't running a Crown and Anchor game. It turned out he works on one of the defensive booms that terminate on Flotta. He said he had the afternoon off duty and would be in no hurry to return to his unit.

'That wasn't really of any use to us, so I talked to two more dealers using the same script. As you know, the idea was that if I could find one who was returning to his unit on Flotta this afternoon, then the lieutenant commander and I would drop in on him there and find out the real story behind the economics of the Crown and Anchor games. Again, neither of the next two I talked to was likely to be clear of the canteen, and of watching eyes, until much later today.

'The fourth one I spoke to turned out to be a much better prospect. He'd been running a game since this morning and was on the point of packing up when I sat down. He was intending to leave to return to his accommodation for a couple of hours' sleep because he's due back on duty later tonight. The good news is that he's a member of the crew of one of the drifters that operate the anti-shipping booms and service the ships and do just about everything else on Scapa Flow. His vessel is based at Scapa pier and he was happy to tell me that he's billeted in one of the wooden huts at the camp they've erected nearby. He even agreed to talk to some of his mates to ask them, again in the strictest confidence of course, about whether they'd seen any indication of a German spy, and report back to me before he goes back aboard his boat later this evening. We've agreed I'll pick him up in the car half an hour before he goes on duty. He doesn't know that the lieutenant commander will be with me, or that we'll be talking about the Crown and Anchor games rather than spies. His name, incidentally, is Leading Seaman Keith Corrigan.'

'As a result, it turned out to be rather a waste of time my going to Flotta this afternoon,' said Michael. 'I visited the officers' mess, which is shared by the navy and army officers on the island. The only subject of conversation seemed to be whether they are going to be able to restore a golf course that was used in the Great War. When I met Andrew near the camp cinema as we'd arranged, it was simply to commandeer a lift on a boat coming back to Scapa rather than conduct the follow-up interview we'd been planning.'

'But it does sound as if you've found the man you need,' said Bob. 'Hopefully, we'll know more about who gets to share in the 8% profit from the games when you see him again. Meanwhile, Monique's also going to be out and about this evening, following up a lead with a WRNS officer who wants to talk to her, a friend and roommate of Second Officer Jennings.'

Petty Officer MacDonald placed his mug back on the table. 'Sir, I know we discussed this on the plane coming up, but are we right to be spending our time chasing after the money-making schemes on Flotta when we've been asked to investigate a murder? Shouldn't we focus more directly on finding the killer?'

'That's a fair question, Andrew. Call it instinct if you will, but I'm convinced that Lieutenant Rose's murder is somehow connected with these other things we've turned up. I believed that when we talked on the plane, and after listening to what Able Seaman Booth had to say about the lieutenant, I'm more convinced than ever. I genuinely believe that if we explore our suspicions of wider corruption then, at some point, they will intersect with our search for Lieutenant Rose's killer. Or am I being unrealistic? What do you think, Michael?'

The lieutenant commander looked back at Bob. 'I agree with you, sir. What convinced me more than anything else was that cock-and-bull story we were told today. Napier was clearly trying to cover up the lieutenant's murder, and the only reasons I can think for that would be if he'd done it himself or if he knew it raised questions that he didn't want us asking.'

'What about you, Monique?' asked Bob.

'I entirely agree, Bob. And rest assured, I'd tell you if I didn't.'

Petty Officer MacDonald smiled. 'It's not that I disagree myself, sir. I just thought it worth asking the question. Incidentally, I got the sense that I was being watched on Flotta today. I'd not be surprised to hear that the men I spoke to were subsequently quizzed by others, to find out what I'd been asking about. We can ask Leading Seaman Corrigan about that later. I did tell him not to reveal to anyone that we planned to meet again.'

'It was certainly worth asking the question, Andrew. After Monique and I returned from Hoy we spent some time looking at Lieutenant Rose's cottage, where he entertained Able Seaman Booth. Someone had already thoroughly searched it and we didn't find anything of interest, apart from some very pricey bottles of brandy and other spirits that had been smashed.' Bob looked at his watch. 'Look, it's a bit early for dinner, but should we see if we can get something to eat at the hotel before heading off to our various assignations? While you are all out doing useful things this evening, I'll be back here writing a full report for Commodore Cunningham on how the first day has gone. I'll post it via the RAF secure mail tomorrow morning.'

*

Monique had agreed to wait in the hotel lobby for Second Officer Jennings.

Jennings was ten minutes late and looked flustered. 'I'm sorry, ma'am, one of the patrol's destroyers has reported engine trouble off Iceland and we were trying to make arrangements for her to be towed into Reykjavik. I think we've got everything sorted. The new shift can worry about it now.'

'It's not a problem, Sarah. And please, I'd feel more comfortable if you called me Monique. Where are we going?'

'It's not far. We cut up along Bridge Street and Albert Street. They're Kirkwall's main shopping streets, but you'll find the place is quiet now it's properly dark. Did you bring a torch? Good.'

Second Officer Jennings led the way out of the hotel, then past its front before turning right into a narrow street. The cloud was patchy and although the moon provided some illumination, it wasn't much. The streets weren't completely deserted. They passed a few civilians who seemed to be hurrying home and at one point a group of four naval ratings came out of a side street. They'd apparently been drinking and despite the darkness of the blackout, or perhaps because of the anonymity it offered, two of them whistled at the women.

Monique paused, then half turned towards the men. Sarah caught her arm. 'Leave it, Monique. Don't bother.'

It was light enough for Monique to see the extremely young man nearest her look away from her glare, as if embarrassed. She decided Sarah was right. They continued along the street.

'Who is it we are going to see?' asked Monique.

'Second Officer Mary Chalmers. I'll let her tell you her story herself. It's probably enough that you know she's been on Orkney for about eighteen months. She worked initially with the Contraband Control people who were based in the Kirkwall Hotel. When they wound down in May she was posted to a job looking after the unit who manage personnel records and movements at HMS *Sparrowhawk,* which is what the navy call the Royal Naval Air Station at Hatston, on the west side of the bay.'

'How do you know her?' asked Monique.

'I arrived in Orkney in June. I'd worked previously in the naval dockyard at Portsmouth. Kirkwall was a bit of a culture shock, I can tell you, though as I mentioned, the ready availability of attractive men does help compensate for the incessant wind and the remoteness. When I arrived, I was allocated a shared room in the Wrennery…'

'The what?'

'The Wrennery. It's a hutted encampment that's been built in Buttquoy Park, a little to the south of St Magnus Cathedral. It was built to accommodate WRNS officers and other ranks based in Kirkwall and the surrounding area, including at Scapa and RNAS Hatston. Other ranks have the dubious joy of sleeping in large barrack rooms with closely spaced bunk beds. Junior officers get to share two to a room, which in comparison is real luxury, especially if you get on with your roommate. Anyway, when I arrived, I moved in with Mary, and she's been great. Look, this is the cathedral on our left now. Even in the dark it's impressive. If you get the chance while you are in Orkney, you really should visit. We're passing the west end, and we take a left at the corner ahead of us. We then take the next right.'

'Is that a castle there, on the corner? I've seen it while driving past and wondered.'

'No. The circular tower looks like part of a castle, but I've been told it was built as a palace for a bishop. There are the ruins of another, later, palace hidden in the trees over there. We follow the road that runs between them, Watergate, up past the court and the old police station.'

This part of the walk seemed particularly threatening to Monique, with the darkened road squeezed between stone ruins on one side and railings and overhanging trees on the other. Beyond the court the road opened out and she could make out ahead of them the shapes of wooden huts. The naval guard at the camp gate – a man, Monique noted wryly – studied both their passes in torchlight and then saluted.

'I take it that you don't have many visitors?' Monique asked, as they approached a door in the end of one of the huts.

'No. Men are barred from the Wrennery unless on official business. To be honest, the security isn't oppressive and does give a sense of reassurance. You wouldn't want fools like those we met back there thinking they could come here when the pubs close.'

Monique followed Sarah through one of a series of doors that lined both sides of a corridor that ran the length of the hut.

The room itself was small, with a single bed either side of the heavily curtained window opposite the door. A desk and a chair were placed to Monique's left as she entered and, apart from a chest of drawers and two wardrobes, that was about it.

'I think you'd call it functional rather than homely,' said Sarah. 'Monique, this is Mary.' She gestured towards a woman in WRNS uniform, minus her jacket and tie, who had been sitting on one of the beds reading a newspaper when Monique entered. She seemed to be in her mid-twenties and was a little shorter than Monique herself. She had short tightly curled blonde hair and offered a nervous smile.

'Hello Mary, I'm please to meet you. I'm Monique Dubois.'

'Hello. Can I get you a cup of tea? There's a little kitchen at the end of the hut.'

'Thanks, but I've not long had a cup.'

They settled themselves, with Monique sitting in the chair by the desk while the two WRNS officers each sat on one of the beds.

'Sarah tells me that there's something you want to talk to me about, Mary.'

The woman's face clouded with worry. 'Yes, there is. Is it right that you are with military intelligence?'

'Yes, I'm currently with Military Intelligence 11, which is responsible for military security. I'm seconded to MI11 from the Security Service, from MI5.'

'And is it right that you are looking at the way the navy in Orkney has been running things?'

'That wasn't our starting point. We came here initially to look at security in all three services. But yes, we are back because of concerns about things we've unearthed on the navy side, and to investigate the murder of a naval lieutenant, the deputy to the naval provost marshal in Lyness.'

'If I talk to you now, can you promise that my name won't get back to the navy?'

'Yes, categorically.' There was a pause as Second Officer Chalmers looked down at the bed she was sitting on. 'What is it? Why do you want to talk to me, Mary?'

The woman looked up, and Monique could see a look of determination on her face. 'Something's not right and it's not just something isolated.'

'What do you mean?'

'Until May this year I worked at HMS *Pyramus* in the Kirkwall Hotel, running the administration office for Contraband Control.'

'I've heard the name,' said Monique. 'Didn't they process neutral ships brought in because the Northern Patrol suspected them of trading with the enemy?'

'That's a fair summary. Once in Kirkwall Bay, sometimes under armed escort, they would be checked over. Their paperwork would be looked at, and background enquiries made via the Admiralty in London. Sometimes the ships themselves would be searched, though that could be a very time-consuming process.

'By the time I was posted here, in the early summer of last year, Contraband Control was already winding down. I was told that at its peak, early in the war, there could be up to a hundred detained ships out there in Kirkwall Bay waiting to be processed. There were far fewer when I arrived, though they did form a steady stream. After a while, I started to notice oddities. Some ships you'd expect to have been low risk, given their ports of origin and stated cargoes, could linger here for weeks or longer, sometimes despite the intervention of the relevant embassy in London. Other ships, which you might think were higher risk, could sometimes pass through almost on-the-nod, or after only a very brief delay. It's a pattern that might have been hidden with more ships involved but it became more obvious as numbers dropped. When I asked my senior officer why, I was told in no uncertain terms to mind my own business, that I was at risk of breaching military security, and that I should keep quiet about what I'd noticed if I didn't want to find myself posted somewhere even further from home like Shetland or Iceland.'

'What did you think at the time? What you describe makes it sound like bribes were being paid for early clearance.'

'That's exactly what I thought. By spring this year, with things running down and the unit due for closure, I began to think that there might be even more to it than that. What became clear, and again it became more apparent because the numbers of ships involved was much smaller, was that certain ships, maybe half-a-dozen of them, had turned up in Kirkwall Bay more than once. Some could almost be described as regular callers, every few months, which really didn't fit with what Contraband Control was meant to be doing.'

'Was the Portuguese ship SS *Amazon* one of them?'

'Yes, she was. And because I'm now based at Hatston, which has good views across Kirkwall Bay, I know she's been back since, including quite recently.'

'Why do you think these ships kept calling?'

'With short days at this time of year, you can hide pretty much anything under the cover of darkness but in summer there's daylight most of the time. It never occurred to me when I was based in Kirkwall itself, but from Hatston you get sideways perspective on the bay. You'd expect these ships to be visited and for there to be some coming-and-going. What struck me as odd this summer was that, almost invariably, launches coming out from the harbour or the ship's own boats would always use the side of the ship facing away from Kirkwall, as if trying to minimise the chances of being noticed from the harbour.'

'Why would they do that?' asked Monique.

'I think there must be something underhand going on. Either something is being taken out and loaded onto these ships, or something is being unloaded from them. You can't really tell from a distance, and binoculars are banned by the regulations unless officially sanctioned.'

'Did you raise these concerns with anyone?'

'I did mention them to Sarah after we became friends, but I certainly haven't told anyone else until now.'

'Thank you, Mary. I'm most grateful. What you've said does seem to tie in with other information we have.'

'You've not heard the best of it, yet.'

'There's more?'

'Yes. I command a unit looking after personnel records at the naval air base at Hatston and handling postings in and out. There are vast numbers of military personnel in Orkney. Even though there can be very few safer places in which to spend the war, large numbers of them get so bored with the inactivity or so hacked-off with the weather that they'd prefer to be just about anywhere other than in "Bloody Orkney" as it's often called. In many cases they'd even prefer to be somewhere where they are likely to be shot at.

'Maybe spotting patterns is my thing. It's become obvious to me that there's no consistency in the way requests for postings away from Orkney are handled. I suppose I'd have expected factors such as length of service in Orkney, relevant skills for use elsewhere, or even compassionate or family circumstances to play a part. But nothing seems to fit. I did ask my boss why one young naval officer who had only been in Orkney for three months had his application for a posting away from here approved. Again, I was met with aggression and given no sensible reasons. Again, I smiled and backed off.'

'What does the pattern suggest to you?' asked Monique.

'This time it wasn't the pattern itself that led me to a conclusion,' said Mary. 'Early last month I started going out with a naval pilot involved in training at RNAS Hatston. He'd only been here since the spring and really hated the place. He especially hated the idea of spending a winter in Orkney. One night, in the officers' wardroom at Hatston, he got really drunk and we had an argument. "What was the use of going out with a WRNS officer in personnel if it didn't help get him a posting out of here." That sort of thing. Then he told me that he'd heard that there was a way for naval personnel in Orkney to guarantee a posting away, but only at a price. I told him that was rubbish. He claimed that a friend of his had paid two month's salary, having borrowed money from his parents, and immediately got the posting he wanted to southern England. Again, I told him he was talking nonsense. He stormed out. That was the last time I saw him. He was posted to an operational squadron on an aircraft carrier in the Mediterranean only days later. I then heard that he'd been listed as missing in action within a week of getting there.'

'I'm sorry to hear that,' said Monique. 'If I understand you correctly, you think that someone is selling postings away from Orkney and the going rate is two months' salary?'

'Yes, Monique, and if I'm honest it's a thought I find frightening. If I'm right, and I'm sure I am, then there's a lot of money involved. I dread to think what would happen if whoever's behind this realised that a lowly WRNS officer had worked out what was going on. I've stopped showing any interest in posting patterns and have simply kept my head down.'

'Who do you think is behind it?'

'I don't know. If you wanted to investigate, it wouldn't be hard for someone with the right access to work their way through the posting records and spot the obvious anomalies. The men involved, and all those I noticed were men, would doubtless be able to say who they paid for their postings if the right pressure was brought to bear on them. The thing is, I only see records relating to personnel at Hatston. What if this is going on right across Orkney, where there are many thousands of naval personnel, most of whom would like to be somewhere else? In answer to your question about who is behind it, I get the frightening sense that it's like some sort of secret club, with members drawn from middling to senior ranking naval officers.

Remember that I've now run into the same sort of response to concerns raised in two quite separate parts of naval operations in Orkney.'

'Thank you, Mary,' said Monique. 'I will need to talk to my colleagues about what you've told me. I don't know what we will do about it, but what you've said fits very neatly into a wider pattern we've been seeing for ourselves. I can promise you that something will be done.'

It was very dark as Monique walked back down Watergate, past the ruins of the old palace. The noise of the wind in the trees seemed louder than earlier and at one point she thought she'd heard a shoe scuffing on the pavement behind her. She shivered and looked over her shoulder. There was no-one there. She placed her hand on the butt of the gun under her coat for reassurance, before telling herself that she was simply imagining things.

CHAPTER NINETEEN

Monique found Michael and Andrew in a booth in the hotel bar and accepted Michael's offer of a tonic water.

She looked at her watch. 'We'd better wait until Bob gets back from writing his report to share what we've discovered. Suffice it to say that I think we've opened up a real can of worms.'

'Yes, it is looking that way,' said Michael. 'Look, let's drive up to the police station. We can talk more openly there anyway.'

The constable on the reception desk looked up as Monique entered, followed by the two men.

'We're just going through to the MI11 office to see Group Captain Sutherland,' said Monique.

'I'm afraid you've missed him, ma'am.' The constable glanced at the clock on the wall. 'He left perhaps half an hour ago. He said he'd locked away his report and was walking back to the hotel.'

Monique felt a sinking sensation in the pit of her stomach. She looked round at Michael, to see he'd also drawn some worrying conclusions.

'Perhaps he took a detour on the way,' said Michael. 'Look, let's leave the car here and walk back to the hotel. Sod's law says that we somehow missed him in the blackout, and we'll find him in the hotel bar, getting worried about us.'

Monique smiled in response to Michael's attempt to ease her concern, then walked past him and out onto Junction Road, setting off back towards the harbour on the side nearest the police station.

229

Michael followed. 'Andrew, you stick with Monique on this side. Remember to look in any alleys or over any walls. I'll take the pavement on the other side of the road. We've all got torches, haven't we?'

They hadn't gone far when Monique became aware that Andrew, a little behind her, had stopped walking.

'Look here!' he said.

Monique saw a darker circle against the road surface in the light of Andrew's torch. He bent down to pick it up. 'It looks like Group Captain Sutherland's cap. The braid on the peak is pretty distinctive.'

Monique took the cap off him and shone her torch at the label inside the crown. 'Yes, it's got his name in it.' She looked up and down the empty street. 'I think someone's abducted him. I can't think of any other reason for his cap being here.'

'How would they see him in the dark?'

'I've no idea. Perhaps they identified him as he came out of the police station and followed him.'

'I think we need to talk to Inspector Flett,' said Michael.

It took Inspector Flett no more than fifteen minutes from the time the constable telephoned him at home to get back to the police station, and no more than twenty more for him to have the place buzzing with more police than Monique had seen in Orkney before. The delay seemed an age to her.

Andrew took two constables to show them where Bob's cap had been found, while others set out to scour the quiet centre of Kirkwall.

'I'm not sure there's much more that we can do at present,' said Flett, sitting on the corner of the desk in what had previously been his office.

'I think we should talk to Frank Gordon, or Peter Mcilvenny if you prefer,' said Monique.

'Do you think he's involved in the group captain's disappearance?'

'I can't show you a shred of evidence. But instinctively, I'm sure of it.'

'I've no better ideas,' said the inspector. 'I'll have a constable drive us to the boarding house where he's staying.'

'Andrew and I will come with you,' said Michael.

*

The darkness was disorientating, but Monique formed an impression of a large stone house standing a little back from one of the roads leading out of the southern side of Kirkwall. No lights were showing but in the blackout that was no guide to whether anyone was at home.

It took some time, but the front door was cautiously opened in response to the inspector's repeated knocking and a woman peered round it. The inspector shone his torch on his own face, showing his uniform and cap. 'Hello, it's Mrs Mackay, isn't it? I'm Inspector Flett of the Orkney police. These people are with me. We'd like to talk to one of your guests. Can we come in please?'

'Well, if you must, inspector.' The woman opened the door to let them in, then closed it behind them. Monique found herself standing in a hallway papered with intricate floral wallpaper and decorated by framed samplers of lacework on the walls. Mrs Mackay turned to face them. 'Who is it you want to talk to?'

'Mr Mcilvenny, a gentleman from Glasgow.'

'Ha, he's no gentleman, you can believe me. I can spot a bad one when I meet one. But both men pay their rent regularly, a week in advance, and I've had no trouble from either of them since they arrived at the end of summer. Still, I'm not completely surprised to find you at my door asking after Mr Mcilvenny, inspector.'

'What do you mean by "both men", Mrs Mackay?'

'Mr Mcilvenny and the other man, Mr Walsh. He's Irish, going from the way he talks, and he's the sort of man you'd not want to meet in a dark alley. He's tall, and heavily built. From something I heard them saying one day at breakfast, I think that Mr Walsh worked on the construction of the causeways linking Mainland to South Ronaldsay before Mr Mcilvenny came to Orkney. I don't pry, but from things that Mr Mcilvenny has let drop, I think they spend their time visiting families of Orcadians who have died recently and offering to buy knick-knacks and antiques that the families don't want or don't have room for. It sounds like a grubby business if you ask me. But I suppose I benefit, so I shouldn't complain.'

'Are they in the house at present?' asked Flett.

'No, they both went out a little before it got dark. Mr Mcilvenny has a van that he uses for his business. It's usually parked outside, but they took it when they went.'

'Do you happen to know what make or colour it is, or what the registration number is?'

'I'm sorry, inspector. I think it's dark green. Yes, I'm sure it is. But a van is a van is a van as far as I'm concerned. It's sort of middling-sized, with two front doors, and twin doors that open at the back end. It's the kind of van you often see with the names of merchants painted on the side. There's nothing painted on this one, though.'

Monique, Michael and Andrew were subdued when they returned to the hotel. Flett had promised to maintain extra patrols in Kirkwall overnight, who would now also be looking for an anonymous green van. Additionally, he had stationed a car with two constables where they could keep watch on the boarding house in case Mcilvenny and Walsh returned.

Betty Swanson was on reception and was clearly delighted to see Michael, and then concerned by his lack of response. He looked across at Monique, as if for support. Monique gave him her best 'it's up to you' look before making her way up to bed.

She wondered if she'd be able to sleep but felt utterly exhausted. The irony of Bob's warning about walking alone through Kirkwall at night wasn't lost on her. Then, as a defence mechanism that had served her well at other times of great stress in her life, she simply shut all thought of Bob out of her mind. An unsettled sleep swiftly followed.

*

It was still dark in the room when Monique was awakened by a knock on her bedroom door. She wrapped a blanket round herself before she opened the door. A young police constable with a shocked expression on his face was standing in the corridor. Monique supposed that having a gun pointed in his face by a semi-naked woman was probably a new experience for him.

He recovered well. 'Hello, ma'am, are you Madame Dubois?'

'Yes I am.'

Monique got the sense that the constable was about to ask her for identification, before deciding better of it. 'I've a message from Inspector Flett, ma'am. He says to tell you that Peter Mcilvenny returned to the boarding house he's been staying in a little while ago and has been brought to the police station for questioning. He's locked up in a cell pending your arrival.'

'Have you also told Lieutenant Commander Dixon and Petty Officer MacDonald?'

'I've told the petty officer, ma'am. The lieutenant commander wasn't in his room and the petty officer said he'd find him.'

'What time is it?'

'It's nearly seven, ma'am.'

It was less than half an hour later and still completely dark outside when Monique led Michael and Andrew into the police station. Part of her wanted to be angry with Michael for spending the night with Betty Swanson, but in her heart, she knew that was simply displacement. The fury she felt about Bob's disappearance had no other outlet. Until now.

Inspector Flett met them in the reception area. 'Mcilvenny is in the cells. How do you want to play this, Madame Dubois?'

'You've got an interview room, I believe. I'd be grateful if you could have Mcilvenny taken there, and then Lieutenant Commander Dixon and I will interview him.'

'Do you want a constable present?'

'No, I don't think that will be necessary.'

The inspector looked at Monique. She thought he was about to say something, but instead he simply nodded to a constable standing beside him, who headed off down the corridor to the cells.

'Look, I'll make a cup of tea while they are getting him,' said Andrew. 'We can't start the day on totally empty stomachs. I'll serve it in the office we're using.'

Monique didn't want to delay but could see the sense in what the petty officer said. In the office she stood, sipping her cup of tea, in deep thought.

'What do you want me to do, Monique?' asked Michael.

'Just act naturally and follow my lead. Right, the day's not getting any younger. Let's go and talk to Mcilvenny.'

The interview room was what Monique would have called utilitarian. Plain walls were painted in gloss paint over a far from smooth plaster. The lower few feet of the walls were dark blue, matching the door, with beige above a stark dividing line. There were no windows. The only furniture was a single wooden table that was attached to the floor, and four folding wooden chairs that weren't.

Peter Mcilvenny was sprawled across one of the chairs, which he'd pushed back from the table. His feet were wide apart, and he was leaning back, almost to the point where he was tipping the chair. His hands were behind his head, presumably with his fingers interlocked, and he had a grin on his face.

'Ah, the lady from military intelligence. I am honoured!'

Monique sat down on the opposite side of the table to Mcilvenny and indicated that Michael should sit beside her. 'Would you prefer it if I call you Mr Mcilvenny or Mr Gordon?' she asked.

'Either will do, hen. I don't plan on being here for long. You've nothing to hold me for and you must know that as well as I do.'

'You are here because you are suspected of kidnapping Group Captain Sutherland in Kirkwall last night.'

'I'll bet you don't have a single piece of evidence supporting that suspicion, do you darling? I must say this about my nephew though, he does have a good taste in women. I'm told you're sharing a room this time. I must admit I wouldn't mind giving you one myself. You can take that as a wee compliment if you like.'

'A clapped-out old wreck like you? Do me a favour, Frank. Why would any woman in her right mind come within spitting distance of you? Look at yourself next time you're near a mirror. I'll bet you a pound to a pinch of horse-shit that you'd not be able to get it up even if I gave you the chance.'

The smile disappeared from Frank Gordon's face, and while he maintained his 'couldn't give a damn' posture, Monique could see he was having to work harder at it.

'You arrogant bitch! I'll have you know I've never had a problem in that area, and I get plenty of chances to find out. I test all the merchandise personally and get no complaints at all.'

Monique stood up. 'Let's see, shall we?' She was rewarded by a look of doubt on Gordon's face as he tried to work out what she intended to do.

Monique walked round the end of the table. As she did so, she pulled her pistol from beneath her jacket and leaned forward slightly to thrust the muzzle hard into Frank Gordon's crotch.

'Jesus, woman, what are you doing?'

'Don't move a muscle, Frank. We don't want any misunderstandings, do we? And before the thought crosses your mind, yes, I have cocked the gun and yes, the safety catch is set to "fire".'

Gordon looked at Lieutenant Commander Dixon. 'Are you just going to sit there and let her do this?'

'Do what?' asked Dixon.

'No, that's true, I've not told you what I'm going to do, have I, Frank? The thing is this. I am really upset that you have kidnapped Bob Sutherland, and I am very anxious that you should tell me where he is.'

'Dream on, cow!'

'I thought you might say something like that. Here's what I'm going to do. I will count to three, and then I will pull the trigger and blow your balls off, together with anything else that happens to be loitering about down there.'

'You wouldn't! This is a police station for God's sake! You'd never get away with it!'

'Really? I'd just walk out, and no-one would stop me. I'm the lady from military intelligence, remember. You'd be less well placed, though. There are lots of blood vessels down there, so you'd almost certainly die of loss of blood before the police could get medical help for you. On the other hand, if you were unlucky you might survive and spend the rest of your miserable life pissing through a stump.'

'For God's sake, no!'

'Right, I'm please we understand one another. One…'

Michael stood up. 'Monique!'

'Sit down Michael and stay out of this. This man's kidnapped Bob and I really don't care if I have to blow his balls off to find out what I want to know.'

Michael sat down.

Monique had kept her gaze fixed on Frank Gordon's eyes, which were now filled with terror. 'Where were we? Ah, yes. One… Two…'

'Alright, alright, woman. Don't shoot!'

Monique became aware of a growing damp patch in Gordon's suit trousers round the muzzle of her gun. She wrinkled her nose in distaste. 'We seem to have had a little accident, don't we Frank? You stay exactly as you are, and I'll stay exactly as I am. The moment I think you are trying to pull the wool over my eyes, I'll pick up the count where I left off, and there wasn't much of it left. Now tell me, where's Bob?'

'He's in a tin cottage beside the shore in a place called Hurliness, which is at the head of North Bay, the bay formed by Hoy and the island of South Walls. You can't miss it; it's got a red roof and green walls and it's unlike anything else in the area.'

'Is he safe?'

'He had a knock on the head last night, when we picked him up, and we drugged him when he came round from that. But yes, he's safe enough for now.'

'What do you have planned for him? What do you mean by "for now"?'

Frank Gordon visibly gulped. 'He's going to be put on a boat tonight, one of the converted fishing drifters the navy use on Scapa Flow, and taken out into the Pentland Firth, where he'll be thrown overboard.'

There was a pause. 'Is he under guard? Remember that if I don't maim you now, I can always come back and do it later if it turns out you are lying.'

'Yes, I have two men there. Declan Walsh, who stays here with me in Kirkwall, and Kenny Weir, who normally stays at the cottage. But you'll never get near the place. We've got the navy in our pocket, especially on Hoy. You've no idea what you're up against. Look, I'm trying to help you all I can here!'

'What's the name of the boat you talked about?'

'It's called the *Harvest Moon*. It's based at Houton, along the coast towards Stromness. Declan Walsh and I took Sutherland to Houton last night after we'd picked him up on Junction Road. He was unconscious, and in a crate, so the crew didn't ask too many questions. They took us directly over to the small pier at Hurliness and then brought me back to Houton. I slept for an hour or two in the van, then drove back to Kirkwall, where I found the police waiting for me.'

'Why did you abduct Bob?' asked Monique.

'He was becoming a threat to some people who I count amongst my most important business partners.'

'Who, specifically?' Monique jabbed Gordon with the muzzle of her pistol to remind him of its presence.

'Ow! Alright! Enough! I'm trying to help! I was asked to do something about Sutherland in a message from the naval provost marshal, Commander Napier.'

'Who else is involved?'

'Monique, hang on.'

Monique looked round to see Michael gesturing at his watch. She realised that he was right, and a more thorough interrogation of Frank Gordon could wait. Their priority now had to be rescuing Bob.

*

They left Frank Gordon in the care of Inspector Flett, with instructions that he should be locked up in a cell and kept incommunicado until they returned. They then collected Petty Officer MacDonald and went out to their car.

'What do we do now?' asked Michael. 'We need to do something about the *Harvest Moon,* and we need to get over to Hoy to release the group captain, even though it's possible that the entire Royal Navy on Hoy will be out to stop us, not to mention Frank Gordon's two men. I'm not sure where we start.'

'What would Bob do?' asked Monique.

'He'd probably go and talk to Air Commodore Chilton.'

'True, but while the air commodore might be on the side of the angels, I don't think he's got anyone on Hoy who might be able to help, beyond the crews of the barrage balloons based there. I think we need to go to Stromness and track down Major General Blanch.'

'Do we know we can trust him?' asked Michael.

'No, not for sure,' said Monique. 'But we are going to have to trust someone, because we can't sort this out without help.'

While Andrew drove, Michael told him what had happened during the interview with Frank Gordon.

'Wow, ma'am, would you really have pulled the trigger?'

'Of course, Andrew. If I'd not been certain of that, Gordon would have seen it in my eyes and laughed in my face. As it was, he knew I wasn't bluffing and told us what we needed to know.'

CHAPTER TWENTY

The sky got steadily lighter as they drove, far too slowly for Monique's liking, to Stromness. They parked the car outside the security barriers preventing access to Mackay's Hotel and walked the short distance to the entrance after convincing the sentries to let them past.

It was still before 9 a.m. and the duty officer they found in the first-floor reception area, a lieutenant, was adamant that they would have to wait until Major Gilligan had arrived before any decision could be taken about allowing them to talk to the general.

'But it's a matter of life and death!' shouted Monique. 'Group Captain Sutherland has been kidnapped and we need the general's help to rescue him.'

'I'm sorry, ma'am, I really do expect Major Gilligan to be here any time now…'

'Thank you, lieutenant. Please send Major Gilligan up to join us as soon as he arrives. And get someone to organise some coffee, please. I think we're going to need it.'

Monique whirled round, to see Major General Blanch standing part way up the stairs that connected the first and second floors.

'Madame Dubois, could you and your colleagues follow me, please?' The general led the way up the stairs, then past a sentry and along a corridor to the front of the second floor, where he walked through an open door. 'Welcome to my office. I'll say this for you, Madame Dubois, you certainly know how to make an entrance. Petty officer, would you pull a couple of chairs over from the meeting table, please?'

Monique, Michael and Andrew sat on chairs placed in front of the general's large desk. Monique noticed that this was positioned so he had his back to the bay window. She assumed that this allowed him to enjoy the view to the full by turning round. It also offered plenty of backlighting that he perhaps felt put anyone sitting on the other side of his desk at a disadvantage. It was now almost fully daylight outside, so she could appreciate the effect.

As they settled down, Major Gilligan came in, looking flushed. The general told him to pull over another chair. Gilligan was followed by a soldier carrying a tray of coffee cups.

'Right,' said the general. 'Madame Dubois, could you perhaps explain what you were saying to the duty officer downstairs about Group Captain Sutherland having been kidnapped?'

Monique took a moment to gather her thoughts. Then she swiftly but carefully outlined the events of the past 48 hours, focusing on what Frank Gordon had told them.

The general responded with a series of questions. Both she and Michael provided answers, and Monique could see that the general's initial incredulity was slowly shifting towards concern.

'Very well. As you say, the priority is to ensure that Group Captain Sutherland is safe. I'm not about to engage in armed conflict with the Royal Navy, but I will help you. You must have an idea of what you want from me, or you'd not be sitting there.'

Michael took the lead. 'There are two things, sir. The first is the need to take a navy drifter called the *Harvest Moon* and her crew into custody. She's based at Houton and I hope will be there now, prior to heading back over to Hoy later today.'

'Very well. I will get a contingent of the Corps of Military Police sent down there, strong enough to detain the boat and her crew and dissuade anyone else from interfering in what we are doing.'

'The second thing we need is help in physically releasing Group Captain Sutherland, sir. He's being held at the far end of Hoy, in a cottage close to the causeway that links it to the island of South Walls. That means either a long excursion by boat across Scapa Flow, which is firmly in the grip of the Royal Navy, or a drive along the length of Hoy, passing through the base at Lyness en route, which is also firmly in the grip of the Royal Navy.'

The general got up and walked over to a large map on one wall of his office. 'Can you show me where the group captain is being held?'

Dixon followed him and pointed the place out on the map. 'We must have passed the cottage when we visited Longhope last week, but I don't remember it.'

The general smiled. 'Look, I've got a number of units on Hoy and on South Walls. We can use one of our launches to get you over to the pier here at Mo Ness, near the north end of the island. I'll have men from the Skerry Battery, which helps guard Hoy Sound, meet you there. They are artillerymen but are trained to act as infantry if the need arises. No-one is going to think twice about a group of my coastal gunners travelling to another of my units in South Walls. Only they won't go to South Walls, of course. They will stop a little short of it and release Group Captain Sutherland. Having released him, they will simply reverse the process, bringing you back through Lyness without revealing your presence, or the group captain's, to the navy. You will then be picked up by launch at Mo Ness and returned to Stromness. I've always believed the best plans are simple plans and this one has the benefit of simplicity.

'Major Gilligan will organise a launch to get you over to Hoy straight away and I'll speak on the telephone with the commanding officer of Skerry Battery. I will then speak to the commander of the Corps of Military Police in Orkney, who has an office in this building, and ask him to detain this drifter at Houton.'

*

The crossing of Hoy Sound in the army's launch was a frightening experience for Monique. When she asked the boat's helmsman why the sea was so rough, he explained it was to do with wind and tidal conditions that could set up large standing waves in the sound.

The boat was open to the elements but seemed well built. Monique was less reassured by the unhappy expressions on the faces of Michael and Andrew, who she felt were better placed than her to judge the safety of the crossing.

The far side couldn't come quickly enough, and Monique was grateful to be able to climb up the steps built into the side of the stone pier. Two green lorries were standing at the landward end of the structure. An army captain came to meet them, saluting as he neared Monique and Michael.

'Sir, ma'am. I'm Captain Derek Martin. I'm told that we are going on a rather unusual assignment and that my men and I are to obey whatever instructions you give me.'

'How many men have you got, captain?' asked Michael.

'Twenty, sir. We could all fit in one lorry, but the second is to allow for breakdowns and because I've been told there may be more passengers on the return trip. Are you able to brief me on what you want from us? I've got a map here.'

Michael explained the situation to the captain, emphasising the need for a careful approach when they got to the cottage. He also explained some of the sensitivities concerning the Royal Navy's presence on Hoy.

The captain looked back at the map. 'I've been told to try to avoid confrontation with the navy, but to give you all the help I can. I've been down that end of the island quite a few times. If the cottage you are interested in is where I'm thinking of, then there's a quarry on the hillside to the south of the road. It can't be far from the cottage, and I'm betting it would be a good place to keep watch without being seen.'

Monique, Michael and Andrew travelled in the rear of the front lorry, sitting on a pile of camouflage netting that the captain explained could be used to conceal their presence if needed. It gave off a strong musty smell. The rear flap of the truck's cover was tied down, so they had little sense of their surroundings. The troops travelled in the second lorry.

After what seemed an age to Monique, the truck stopped and the rear flap was lifted.

'We're almost there,' said Captain Martin. 'If you hop out, you can get a sense of the location.'

Monique found they were parked beside a minor road a little above the shore of a bay, and the road could be seen continuing round the head of it in front of them, and then on its far side to their left.

'You can just about make out the cottage on the shoreline, where the road curves round over there, just before it gets to the causeway to South Walls. I've had a look with binoculars, and I think that we should be able to turn up the access road into the quarry opposite without raising suspicions. The cottage's occupants must be used to military vehicles passing backwards and forwards along this road all the time.'

'Fair enough, let's get on with it,' said Monique.

A little later, Monique felt the truck leave the road and climb a rougher track. Then they stopped again.

'We're here,' said the captain, from the open rear flap.

Monique climbed down from the truck, taking the captain's offered hand to help. She was followed by Michael and Andrew.

The captain walked a short distance back, apparently the way they had come, and Monique followed.

'This is even better than I'd expected,' he said. 'Look, we've parked amongst the rock handling and crushing equipment on the floor of the quarry, which forms a sort of bowl. By the look of things, the quarry hasn't been active for a while. I'm wondering if it was used when they built the causeway to South Walls. The lorries are out of sight of the cottage but if you come over this way, carefully, you can see that from the lip of the excavated area you get a perfect view of everything that's happening over there. Even better, we can't be more than two hundred yards away from it.'

Monique looked carefully, as instructed. 'Can I borrow your binoculars?'

The captain passed them to her. Through them she could see that the distinctive tin cottage had a series of white-painted windows looking out towards the road. A little to the left as she looked, perhaps twenty yards from the cottage, was a semi-derelict building that had presumably once been another cottage. Between them and nearer to the shore than either of them stood what looked like a boat shed or store. A track ran from the road to the gap between the two cottages, ending in front of the third building. At its far end a small black van was parked.

'It looks like someone's at home,' she said.

'How are we going to do this?' asked Michael.

The captain had also been surveying the scene. 'It seems to me, sir, that the best line of approach is along the shore, from both directions. I'll get half a dozen men to loop round in each direction beyond the skyline behind us until they can safely cross the road and move down to the shore of North Bay without being seen from the cottage. Once on the shore they can approach from both directions at once. That should bring them to within a few yards of the cottage.'

'That seems good to me,' said Michael.

The captain talked quietly to his men, and then two groups headed off towards the rear of the quarry and the cover of the hillside.

Monique had been keeping an eye on the cottage and saw a large, heavily built man emerge from the front door, which was on the right-hand side of a small porch. 'Look, something's happening.'

Michael and Captain Martin joined her as the man she'd seen leave the cottage got into the van. It then turned round and came back along the track to the road, before turning and heading off towards the causeway. They watched as it crossed, and then drove round the far side of the bay.

'He's on his way to Longhope,' said Martin. 'That leaves only one guard in the cottage if your information is correct.'

'And there's the second man,' said Monique. A man in a dark coat and what seemed to be a flat hat came out the front of the cottage and made his way over to the boat shed or store.

She looked at Michael and Andrew, then at Captain Martin. 'Are your men on the shore going to be in position yet?'

'I very much doubt it, ma'am, they are having to go a reasonable distance to the sides to avoid being noticed as they cross the road.'

'This may not be a chance we'll get again. You said it was two hundred yards, captain. How fast do you think your men can cover that distance?'

The captain grinned. 'Let's find out, shall we, ma'am? If he's the only remaining guard, and if the group captain is in the main cottage, then the worst that can happen is that the guard sees us, and we have to do something about him before he can get back to the cottage.'

'Those are important "ifs",' said Michael.

'Yes, they are,' agreed Monique. 'But as someone once said, "a faint heart never won a lady fair". This may be our best chance. Can you get your men down there as quickly as possible, captain?'

Captain Martin strode swiftly back to where his remaining men were gathered and gestured urgently. The troops set off at a full run down the track from the quarry to the road with Captain Martin in the lead. Monique, Michael and Andrew followed. Monique pulled out her pistol as she ran, cursing the canvas bag slung over her left shoulder but knowing it was too important to discard.

When she thought about it later, Monique remembered that the run seemed to last forever. In reality, it must have taken less than a minute for the first soldiers to reach the main cottage and the shed where the second guard had last been seen. She heard some shouting from the shed but was intent on reaching the cottage. Two soldiers had gone in before her and Andrew reached the door just in front of her. She got the sense that Michael was beside her, also with a pistol in his hand.

Beyond the porch was a stone-floored kitchen, with a door at either end. She heard the shout of 'through here!' come from the doorway to her right. Beyond it she found a filthy bedroom, with a window on the side looking out over the bay and another looking out of the end of the cottage, towards the causeway. There was a fireplace, though no fire, while a few battered items of wooden furniture lined two of the walls. The room felt very cold and it had an unpleasant smell of damp and toilets. Monique's focus was on the ornately iron-framed double bed that stood beneath the bay-facing window. A soldier had laid down his rifle on the floor and was crouched over the bed.

The soldier looked round as she came up behind him. 'He's alive!'

Monique realised that the soldier had been looking at a man, laying under blankets on the bed. When she looked more closely, she saw that the man in the bed was Bob, and he was looking back at her. His eyes had dark rings under them, and he had an unshaven look that in other circumstances she'd have found sexy. Most important of all, however, was the amused expression that crossed his face when he saw the concern on hers.

'Bob, are you all right?' she asked.

'I'd be better if you could do something about these.' Bob rattled handcuffs that attached his right wrist to the near bedpost. 'That way I can get off the bed and away from that horrible bucket on the floor down there. I've been handcuffed to the bed since I came round this morning with a dreadful hangover. I assume I was drugged.'

'The man who was guarding you must have a key,' said Monique. 'Can one of your men relieve him of it, captain?'

It seemed to Monique to take an age to retrieve the key and once Bob was freed it was obvious he was very shaky on his feet. He'd been dressed in a vest and underwear and was shivering. Monique found his uniform bundled up in his greatcoat on the floor beside an old armchair in the sitting room at the other end of the cottage. She was puzzled by a hard lump in the bundle, then realised that it was his shoulder holster, rolled up round his Walther PPK pistol. She wondered why neither of the guards had taken it.

'My shirt could do with an iron,' said Bob, wryly, as he looked at himself in a mirror in the bedroom. 'But I do at least begin to feel a little more human now and a little warmer. It's a shame about my cap. I must have lost it when they jumped me last night.'

'You did, Bob,' said Monique. She unslung the canvas bag from her shoulder and opened it. 'Here you go.' She was surprised to see a hint of tears in Bob's eyes as she passed him his uniform cap. She was even more surprised when, despite the presence in the room of Michael, Andrew, Captain Martin and two of his men, Bob wrapped his arms round her and kissed her deeply. His breath wasn't great, but she wasn't about to let that spoil the moment.

Bob broke the embrace and coughed, clearly embarrassed. 'I'm not sure why they brought me here, but perhaps we should get back to the real world. I was abducted by Frank Gordon and another man, a big bloke. The heavy and a third man have been guarding me here. I heard enough while they thought I was unconscious earlier to know that we're on Hoy and that Frank has some sort of arrangement with the Royal Navy that allows him to feel secure here. I don't know where Frank is, by the way.'

'We do,' said Monique. 'He's in a cell at Kirkwall police station. He was kind enough to tell us where to find you.'

'I'm surprised you got him to talk,' said Bob.

Lieutenant Commander Dixon laughed. 'If you'd seen Monique threaten to blow Frank Gordon's balls off, you'd be less surprised, Bob.'

Bob smiled at Monique. 'What's the plan now, then? How do we get off Hoy?'

It was Captain Martin who replied. 'We've got two lorries nearby, sir. We'll simply drive you, hidden in the back of one of them, to the north end of Hoy and then we'll get you back to Stromness in an army launch. It worked fine on the way down. We've got a prisoner, too. He says his name is Kenny Weir and he's as Glaswegian as it's possible to be. We surprised him in the store they've got down by the shore. It's a real Aladdin's cave in there. Boxes of all sorts of things. Tinned food, brandy, oil lamps, women's silk underwear – yes, seriously – spare parts for cars. And that's what I saw in just thirty seconds. I'd guess a lot of it started life intended as supplies for the naval base here, though I doubt that applies to the brandy or the fancy underwear. I'll get two men to bring the lorries down from the quarry to the road and we can walk up and meet them there. Are you able to walk now, sir?'

'Yes, no problem,' said Bob. Monique wondered how mobile he really was.

A soldier burst into the bedroom. 'Sir, there's a convoy of navy lorries coming round the bay from the direction of Lyness.'

'Damn,' said Captain Martin. 'This could get difficult.'

'If there's a confrontation then I'm best placed to try to resolve things,' said Michael. 'As Major General Blanch said earlier, the last thing we want is armed conflict between the army and the navy. On the other hand, we're not about to hand you over to them, Bob. Your uncle was planning to drown you in the Pentland Firth tonight, so we know there are some very desperate people involved, and some of them wear uniforms like mine.'

The captain instructed his men to keep out of sight. Monique watched from the side of one of the front-facing windows of the kitchen of the cottage as five lorries came into view at the right-hand end of the stretch of road she could see. Bob stood close beside her.

The lorries stopped at the end of the track leading up from the cottage and Monique could feel herself holding her breath. A man got out of the second lorry and walked forward to the cab of the first. There was a conversation, and then the man returned to the second lorry. Shortly afterwards the convoy set off again, before moving out of view along the road to Monique's left. She felt Bob exhale deeply, just as she did so herself.

'Sir!' There was a call from the bedroom Bob had been held in. A soldier came through into the kitchen. 'It looks like they are setting up a roadblock at this end of the Ayre, the causeway leading to South Walls. Two of the lorries have stopped by the old lifeboat station there and navy personnel are climbing out. The other three lorries are continuing towards Longhope.'

'This doesn't have a good feeling about it,' said Captain Martin.

'No, it doesn't,' said Bob. 'I can't make any sense of it, but they must have something to do with our presence on the island. In that case, though, I'm amazed that they didn't check this cottage. If they are associated with Commander Napier or Frank Gordon, they must know that this is somewhere they use, or perhaps even that I'm being held here. I don't understand it. The pieces don't fit together properly.'

The captain went to look out of the end window and then returned. 'The problem we have is that we are in plain view of the navy's roadblock, which is only a quarter of a mile away. If they see any obvious activity here, then they are sure to want to investigate. It's not going to be dark for a few hours yet. The best

I can suggest is that we wait until it is, then cross on foot to the quarry and drive back through Lyness as if nothing had happened. The men at the roadblock will probably hear our lorries coming out of the quarry, but it's the only plan I've got.'

No-one had any better ideas, so they settled down to wait.

It was over an hour later when a soldier stationed at the end window to keep watch on the roadblock called for the captain. Martin went through to the bedroom and returned a couple of minutes later with a worried expression on his face. 'It looks like the other man is on his way back. The one who drove off towards Longhope in a van earlier. The navy have stopped a vehicle that looks like his at the roadblock. I've got men hiding in all three buildings. My guess is that he will park where we saw the van earlier and come into the cottage. We can jump him then.'

After being released by the navy's roadblock, the van did exactly as Captain Martin had predicted. Everyone kept clear of the front windows to avoid being seen.

Monique heard the van's engine just before it came to a halt. Then she heard the van door slam and someone call out, 'Kenny! Kenny! Where are you?' This was followed by some muttering that Monique couldn't catch.

The front door was kicked open and Monique saw a large figure move quickly at a crouch into the porch, a gun raised in his right hand. Perhaps the relative darkness of the kitchen caught him out because it seemed to take him a second to realise the room was crowded with people. Monique saw the gun swing round towards Captain Martin, who was nearest the door. She instinctively raised her pistol but was beaten to it as the sound of two rifle shots rang out almost together. The figure was thrown back by the impact and slid down in a sitting position to the floor of the porch, leaving a trail of blood down the wall behind him, which now had two holes in it. He was very obviously dead.

It was Bob who spoke first. 'Ladies and gentlemen, may I introduce my uncle's right-hand man? I never caught his name.'

'His name's Declan Walsh,' said Monique. 'It was, anyway.'

'And look at his gun,' said Lieutenant Commander Dixon. It's a Webley revolver. There are probably plenty of other identical guns on these islands, but I find Mr Walsh's possession of one significant.'

'Yes, he could easily have been Lieutenant Rose's killer,' said Bob. 'I daresay we'll find out in due course. Captain, would you mind asking one of your men to take possession of the revolver, having wrapped it up in a piece of blanket or something, and make sure it's available for proper examination when time permits?'

Captain Martin had been looking out of the window. 'Yes, of course. Gunner Young, see to it, would you? Sir, I don't want to worry you, but the men at the roadblock must have heard those shots. Even if they couldn't tie down their location exactly, they are sure to have connected the shots to Mr Walsh's arrival at the cottage. I don't think we can afford to wait until it gets dark anymore.'

'What do you suggest?' asked Michael.

'I'll send two men to walk over to the quarry, where they can turn the lorries round and drive them back down the access track to the road. The rest of us will walk, very calmly, up to the road, where we will board the lorries. We'll take Kenny Weir with us but will have to leave the body of this man here, though preferably not where's he's blocking the door. I appreciate we will be in clear view of the men at the roadblock but what I'm suggesting will give them some problems. Firstly, I'm betting that they'd not challenge an army unit based on the island that's simply going about its business. If they did, then I'm betting that the lieutenant commander outranks anyone currently at the roadblock. Remember that once we're on the move we'll be driving away from them, towards Lyness. They'd never abandon the roadblock, so wouldn't pursue us. Which means that my last and biggest bet is that they haven't got a radio there to warn anyone ahead of us what's happening. Yes, they'll have a bizarre story to tell their officer when he gets back and they'll then find the body and an Aladdin's cave here, but we'll be gone.'

Again, no-one had any better ideas.

Two of Captain Martin's men walked casually up the path towards the road, rifles slung and openly smoking cigarettes. Monique thought that was a nice touch.

When the men disappeared out of view into the quarry, everyone else set off towards the road. Monique had been right about Bob's shakiness and held his right arm. She saw that Andrew MacDonald was walking on the other side of him, ready to provide support if needed. She looked across and smiled gratefully at the petty officer.

'Don't react, but I get the impression that someone's taking a good look at us through binoculars,' said Captain Martin. 'Right, that's our lorries on their way down to the road. Shit! One of the naval lorries is on its way too. It's going to get here before we've been able to load up. I suggest Lieutenant Commander Dixon and I walk along the road to meet them, while everyone else proceeds as we discussed.'

Monique watched from the back of the rearmost lorry as Michael and Captain Martin met the naval vehicle twenty yards back towards the roadblock.

A petty officer climbed out of the cab. He looked at Michael and saluted. 'Sir, we heard shots. Is everything in order?'

'It is now, thank you, petty officer. I've been helping the army track down a gang that's been stealing military supplies. There's a dead man in the cottage over there. He pulled a gun on us when he arrived. The building closest to the shore is being used as a store for stolen military goods and equipment. We're just on our way back to Lyness to report what we've found.'

'Can I ask who you are, sir?'

'I'm Lieutenant Commander Michael Dixon. I'm with Military Intelligence 11, based in Edinburgh, and as I say we've been helping the army. Here's my security pass.'

The petty officer looked closely at Michael's pass. Then he saluted again. 'Thank you, sir. You'll understand that we had to investigate what was going on.'

'Yes, of course.'

As Michael turned back towards the army lorries, Monique caught his eye and he winked at her, grinning.

CHAPTER TWENTY-ONE

They tied down the flap at the back of the lorry for the return journey along the island of Hoy, so once again Monique found the outside world closed off to her. She again sat cushioned and supported by a pile of camouflage netting, this time with Bob close beside her. She thought he seemed quiet, then realised that despite the bumps and jerks of the lorry, he was asleep.

She wasn't sure how long they'd been driving for when the lorries stopped. She had no idea where they were.

She could hear voices, though not what was being said. It sounded like questions being asked and then Captain Martin giving answers.

Then the lorries moved off. A few minutes later they stopped again. Again, she could hear questions being asked and answers given. Then there was the sound of lorry doors being slammed. The flap at the back of the truck was pulled up, and Monique reached for her gun.

Captain Martin's head appeared. 'I'm afraid they want everyone to get out, so they can check identities.' He saw Monique's gun. 'It's OK, ma'am, it's not you or the group captain they're looking for.'

'Are you sure, captain?' asked Michael.

'Yes sir, I think it's going to be all right.'

Monique shook Bob awake. She then climbed over the rear of the truck and down to the road, with Bob following. She realised that they had stopped at a roadblock on the northern edge of Lyness, with the huge camp behind them and open hillsides ahead. Several naval ratings were standing off to one side, with their rifles held ready. Captain Martin was standing between the ratings and the lorry's passengers as they emerged. His soldiers were standing in a group beside the front lorry, looking relaxed.

Monique saw that Petty Officer MacDonald was standing beside Kenny Weir and a little behind him. She got the sense that the petty officer had Weir's arm twisted up his back.

The captain turned to a petty officer Monique hadn't noticed, standing beside the rear of the lorry. 'That's everyone.'

The petty officer gestured towards the ratings. 'You two, make sure there's no-one else in this lorry, and you two take the front one.'

He then walked over to Lieutenant Commander Dixon. 'Do you have any identification, sir?'

Michael went through an edited repeat of the spiel he'd given earlier, near the cottage. The petty officer looked at his identification, then looked at Michael and down at a photograph he was holding.

One of the ratings appeared at the back of the lorry. 'There's no-one else.' A similar shout came from the front lorry.

'Sorry to have delayed you, sir. You can get back into the lorries and be on your way.'

Monique waited while Bob climbed back into the lorry. Michael, already on board, helped pull him up, with a broad grin on his face.

'Why are you looking so pleased with yourself, Michael?' asked Monique, as they again tried to find a comfortable spot in the pile of camouflage netting.

'That photograph that the petty officer was looking at. It was a picture of Commander Napier. These roadblocks in Lyness, and presumably the one near the cottage earlier, aren't for us, they've been set up to find Commander Napier. It looks like he's on the run.'

*

The sun had already set as they crossed back over Hoy Sound to Stromness in the same army launch that they'd used earlier.

The crossing was much less bumpy than it had been on the way over to Hoy. When Monique asked why, Andrew had said that the relative directions of the wind and the tide were much more favourable now. She was grateful.

They landed at the same pier they had departed from, at the southern end of the town. Major Gilligan greeted them as they disembarked from the launch. Two military policemen stood nearby. 'It's good to see you safe and well, group captain. Major General Blanch has asked that you meet him at 7 p.m. in his office at Mackay's Hotel. I understand that Rear Admiral Kinnaird and Air Commodore Chilton will be present. I had a telephone call earlier from Inspector Flett at the police station in Kirkwall, asking that Madame Dubois or Lieutenant Commander Dixon get in touch as soon as possible.

'We've got around two hours before the meeting. How long is it since you last ate, sir? How long is it since any of you ate, come to that? The general has suggested that I take you to the Ness Battery, a gun battery forming part of the coastal defences that's located close to here. We also use it as a transit camp for personnel arriving in Stromness from the mainland. You can use the facilities of the officers' mess to get cleaned up and you can eat there.'

'All of us?' asked Michael.

'The petty officer will be able to use the other ranks' facilities, obviously.'

'Look, major, let's keep this simple,' said Bob. 'I'd love to have a quick shower and a shave in the officers' quarters, but is there anywhere we can then all eat together, without offending anyone or tripping over rank distinctions? We've got a lot of catching up to do, preferably before I talk to Major General Blanch and the others.'

'There's a mess hall sir, which is open to all ranks, though officers would normally use the officers' mess.'

'That's settled then. There's one other thing. We've also got a prisoner who needs locking up somewhere secure until we have time to talk to him. His name is Kenny Weir.'

'Yes, Captain Martin warned me that would be the case on the telephone. That's why these gentlemen are here. Gilligan gestured to the two policemen, who moved forward to handcuff Weir's hands behind his back.

They drove to the battery crowded into a single staff car. En route Michael asked Gilligan about the *Harvest Moon* and was assured that the vessel was now moored in Stromness and her crew were in custody. As they drove onto the site, Monique was struck by the dark outlines of two huge guns projecting out over the access road towards Hoy Sound, and then by the shape of a twin-level concrete lookout.

The car stopped amid a group of wooden huts. In the gathering darkness, Monique could see that the area was busy with soldiers coming and going.

Major Gilligan took control. 'I'll take the group captain into the officers' quarters and get someone to organise a shower. There's also an office with a phone there.'

Monique saw Michael look across at her. 'I'll call Inspector Flett,' she said.

'In that case, Andrew and I will sort out a table in the mess hall,' said Michael. 'Where do we find it, major?'

It's the building here, lieutenant commander, opposite the officers' mess.'

Monique was shown into a tiny office in the officers' mess, barely large enough to house a desk and chair. All she was interested in was the phone. It took some time for her to connect to the police station in Kirkwall and then she had to hold for what seemed an age while Inspector Flett finished another telephone call. She was just pleased that he was still on duty.

'Hello Madame Dubois. Were you able to locate the group captain?'

'Yes, he's safe and well, and back in Stromness.'

'That's good news. It's about the only good news we have, however.'

'Why, what's happened?'

'Peter Mcilvenny, Frank Gordon if you prefer, has been murdered.'

'What? How? I thought you had him locked up?'

'We did, Madame Dubois, and we took pains to ensure that he saw no-one and spoke to no-one other than the constable responsible for the cells. I'm sorry to have to tell you that despite our precautions, he was poisoned. The hospital and the doctor we call on for police work both think it was strychnine but that will of course be checked by the forensics people in Aberdeen.'

'How was he poisoned?'

'We were tricked, I'm afraid. I wasn't present at the time, but the responsibility is entirely mine. At lunchtime, Betty Swanson came into the station. She's the girl who sometimes works as a receptionist at the St Magnus Hotel. She's also the daughter of the hotel owner, Edward Swanson. She said that they'd heard

Peter Mcilvenny was in the cells, and as he was a friend of her father's they'd prepared lunch for him. It was in one of those circular aluminium plate covers they use to keep food warm. It never for an instant crossed the mind of the constable on duty that there was anything amiss. I must admit that even if I'd been present, I don't know that I'd have smelled a rat.

'Anyway, the constable took the food from Betty, who left, and then took it to Frank Gordon's cell, along with a spoon to eat it with. He returned a quarter of an hour later, to find Frank Gordon in convulsions on the floor. We got Mr Gordon to the hospital quickly, but he died two hours later from the effects of the poison. The hospital tried to save him, but nothing could be done. The remains of the food will also be examined in Aberdeen to confirm it was the source of the poison.'

'Have you talked to Betty Swanson?'

'Yes. As you can imagine, that was the first thing I did when I was told what had happened. Betty was unaware anything was wrong and appeared genuinely puzzled to be asked about the lunch. It had been prepared at her father's suggestion in the hotel kitchen, and he'd put the plate under its cover. He'd then driven her from the hotel to the police station and asked her to take the meal in.'

'Did you believe what she said?'

'Yes, I did. When I told her that the man she knew as Peter Mcilvenny had been poisoned, and that we strongly believed the lunch she'd delivered was the cause, she broke down completely. At this point he was still alive in hospital, but only just, and it was obvious what the outcome was going to be. I talked to her in a back room at the hotel and one of the older female waiting staff had to comfort her. Her mother died some years ago, I believe of natural causes. I'm not sure what upset her more, the idea that she was implicated in a poisoning, or the fact that she'd apparently been set up to take the blame by her father.'

'What did Edward Swanson have to say for himself?'

'I did warn you I had no good news. Edward Swanson was last seen, by his daughter or as far as we have been able to establish by anyone else, when they arrived back at the hotel after delivering the lunch. He's disappeared. As you can imagine, I am doing everything I can to find him, without any joy so far. His car has also disappeared and we're on the lookout for that too.'

'Do you know how Swanson found out that Peter Mcilvenny was in custody?'

'That's a question that's been causing me a lot of worry. I'm beginning to think that one of my men may have told him, directly or indirectly. I will of course be pursuing that possibility.'

'Edward Swanson isn't the only man on the run in Orkney,' said Monique. 'You should be aware that the naval provost marshal, Commander William Napier, is being hunted by the Royal Navy. Meanwhile we have taken into custody a man called Kenny Weir, a Glaswegian pal of Frank Gordon's, and he's being held by the Military Police in Stromness. Declan Walsh, who as you know was staying with Frank Gordon at the boarding house, has been less fortunate and was shot dead by the army on Hoy earlier this afternoon. What may be significant is that he was shot after waving about a revolver of the same type that killed Lieutenant Rose. I know that's not conclusive, but it seems possible we've found the lieutenant's killer. The army have the revolver so that can be confirmed, or not, by your forensics people in Aberdeen.'

'I'm glad one of us has made some progress,' said Inspector Flett. 'Do you know when you are coming back to Kirkwall?'

'I'm not sure. We've a meeting this evening in Stromness. I'm sure the group captain will want to compare notes with you as soon as we get back, though.'

'Pass on my condolences for the loss of his uncle, will you, Madame Dubois, and my apologies on behalf of the Orkney Constabulary.'

'The information that died with Frank Gordon is a serious loss, but I'm not sure Bob will shed many tears on a personal level. Frank Gordon was planning to kill him tonight.'

*

Monique didn't really know what she'd been expecting from the mess hall at Ness Battery, but it wasn't what she found. The room was much larger than it had seemed from the outside and was brightly lit and rather smoky. It was also busy and quite noisy. Rows of trestle tables filled part of the space, while the end to her right was occupied by a scatter of circular tables. The other end had been fitted with a raised stage that extended across the width of the room, and the wall furthest from the door she'd entered by had a series of hatches that were open to reveal the kitchen beyond.

It was none of this that stopped Monique in her tracks. She'd been intending to scan the room for Michael and Andrew, and perhaps by now Bob. Instead, she found herself transfixed by a series of murals that ran round three sides of the room. The walls had been painted an unattractive brown up to the level of the bottom of the serving hatches. But from there up to the off-white ceiling, every surface on every wall other than the one behind the stage was covered by brightly coloured scenes of countryside, of cottages and villages. The end furthest from the stage seemed to be the focal point, with a fenced pathway leading towards a windmill set on a hill.

As her eyes dropped, she saw Bob, Michael and Andrew watching her from a table in the corner of the room furthest from the stage and the serving hatches. She smiled, then remembered she had bad news for two of them.

'Well, this is quite something,' she said as she sat down.

'I'm told it's all been painted by a harbourmaster from London who's been working with the navy here,' said Andrew. 'It's supposed to show scenes from his native Kent. It certainly brightens the place up.'

'Let's get some food,' said Bob. 'I'm starving.'

'It is over 24 hours since any of us ate anything significant,' said Monique.

Back at their table with heavily laden plates and mugs of tea, Monique saw Bob look around. 'I'm wondering if we can eat and talk,' he said.

'I think we have to try,' said Monique. 'We need to share what we know before we meet the top brass, and we don't have all that much time. I think I'd better start with the bad news I've just had from Inspector Flett.'

As Monique had expected, Bob took the news of his uncle's death in his stride.

Michael was less restrained in his response to news of Betty's involvement by her father. 'What a bastard! I knew there was no love lost between the two of them, or between her mother and father before her mother's death. But you'd have to sink extremely low to implicate your own daughter in murder, then run away and leave her to face the music alone.'

'You'll get a chance to give her your support when we get back to Kirkwall,' said Monique, 'though I've no idea when that will be. Are you all right, Bob?'

'I suppose I'm just coming to terms with the idea of telling my mother that her brother is dead. "No love lost" sums their relationship up pretty well too, as far as I've ever been able to tell, but he was still her younger brother.' Then, to Monique's surprise, Bob laughed.

'What's funny, sir?' asked Michael.

'I'm just thinking that it's going to be a lot easier telling my mother that her brother was poisoned by a crooked business partner than it would have been telling her he was shot by the woman I love.'

Monique was caught off guard by Bob's open declaration in front of their colleagues. Then she smiled. 'Funnily enough, I came close to telling Inspector Flett something like that a few moments ago. I thought better of it.'

Bob looked at his watch. 'What are the headlines that I really need to know before we meet our elders and betters?'

'I think we need to cover three areas, sir,' said Michael. 'The first concerns a couple of things Frank Gordon said while we were interviewing him this morning. We were in a hurry to find out where you were, so left a full interview for another time. But he did talk about having the navy on Hoy in his pocket.' Michael looked at Monique for confirmation.

'That's right,' she said. 'And when I was goading him about his manhood to get him angry, he said that he personally tested all the merchandise. I think this suggests he might have been involved in running prostitutes, even though we've seen no evidence of it anywhere we've been. The most important thing he told us was that he had abducted you having received a message from Commander Napier asking him to do something about you. He described Napier as a "business partner".'

'That's helpful,' said Bob. 'What else? Did you find out

anything useful from the friend of Second Officer Jennings who you were going to see yesterday evening?'

'Yes, I did,' said Monique. She talked them through her meeting with Second Officer Mary Chalmers.

Bob sat back in his chair. 'If I can summarise, Monique, it looks like we've got the possibility of bribes being taken for priority clearance during the time while Contraband Control was in operation and we've got strong suspicions of smuggling or something similar involving the neutral ships that still call in at Kirkwall. The visits by these ships was something you thought was odd after our first visit, Michael. Possibly more lucrative, and more serious, is the suggestion that naval personnel at Hatston, and perhaps more widely across Orkney, can buy postings away from the place at a going rate of two months' pay.'

'I kept the best until last, Bob. When I asked Mary who she thought was behind what was going on, she talked about a feeling of a secret club with membership reserved for middle or senior ranking naval officers. She was genuinely frightened for her own safety.'

'Thanks, Monique. It begins to feel like something out of an Al Capone film. Look, shall we get some dessert?'

After they'd returned to their table with large bowls of pudding cloaked in custard, Bob looked round. 'What have you got, Michael?'

'You know that Andrew and I were going to see one of the Crown and Anchor dealers at Scapa late yesterday, sir. It proved an extremely useful discussion, though given everything else that's going on, I begin to think that what's happening on Flotta is relatively minor. I know we've not much time, so I'll give you the highlights. The people running the canteen on Flotta charge the Crown and Anchor dealers a levy of half of everything they make on the games to be allowed to set up a table. It's all very businesslike. On their behalf, the Ship's Police demand that anyone setting up a game turns out his pockets before play, and then again before they leave. Half of the surplus they make is taken away from them. This is strictly enforced. There's a story that earlier this year a dealer who tried to avoid the system by passing cash to a friend before it was counted when he left was so badly beaten that he spent a week in hospital and the friend was also attacked and badly hurt. No names were mentioned, and I don't know if this was a real event or a story that's been circulated to make men toe the line.'

'How do the dealers find enough time away from duty to make it worthwhile?' asked Bob.

'In the case of Leading Seaman Corrigan, he puts half of what he's left with in a kitty for the benefit of his crewmates and the ship's officers. They help cover for him to give him the time he needs on Flotta to make the whole thing pay. That seems to be a common pattern, sir.'

'Which means that of the eightpence in every hundred pennies that he makes, fourpence goes to the people running the canteen on Flotta, and another tuppence goes to his crewmates, leaving him with just the last tuppence. Does that make it worth his while?'

'Apparently, sir. I also asked him about the trade in beer tickets. It seems to be generally accepted that the traders are working on behalf of the establishment. While they do buy unwanted tickets for a small amount, they sell far more tickets, and for a higher amount. The difference in numbers is made up of previously unissued tickets. It's like printing your own money, really. Again, the house makes a lot from the arrangement. Incidentally, Corrigan confirmed that he had been asked by the

Ship's Police what Andrew had been talking to him about. He said he gave them the story about the spy.'

'Is that everything?' asked Bob.

'Well, there's also the Aladdin's cave the army found in the store by the cottage you were in, sir. To my mind that was a holding point for goods smuggled in through Kirkwall and for stores stolen from the navy on Hoy. Frank Gordon said that the boat he took you to Hoy on last night was going to go to Scrabster tonight, dropping you in the Pentland Firth en route. I'm betting that the original purpose of the trip was to take stolen or smuggled goods from the store to Scrabster for onward transport.'

'Christ, it is difficult to get your head round all the angles, isn't it?' said Bob. 'To top it all, we think that Lieutenant Rose might have been shot by Declan Walsh, perhaps after landing in Kirkwall from a trip to the SS *Amazon*. Who knows, maybe there was a falling out over the latest consignment of smuggled goods?'

'One more thing has a bearing on that, sir,' said Andrew. 'When we saw the landlady at the boarding house where Frank Gordon and Declan Walsh were staying, she said she thought that Walsh had worked on building the barriers before Gordon had come to the islands. That could give him the knowledge needed to try to dispose of Rose's body in the quarry it was found in.'

'Very true,' said Bob, looking at his watch again. 'We really do need to speak to Kenny Weir as soon as we can. I'm hoping he can help us make some sense of all of this. Not now, though. I hope you've all had enough to eat because I think we need to be elsewhere. Let's find Major Gilligan and his car.'

CHAPTER TWENTY-TWO

Major General Blanch's meeting room was on the second floor of Mackay's Hotel, close to his office. As far as Monique could tell, it was on the side of the building, though confirmation was difficult because of the heavy blackout curtains over the windows. The walls were decorated with large military paintings and even larger maps of Orkney.'

Bob and his team sat round one side of an impressive oval wooden meeting table with a fine leather inlay. Monique doubted that it was standard military issue.

On the other side was seated Major General Blanch, with Rear Admiral Kinnaird to his left and Air Commodore Chilton to his right. To the admiral's left was Captain Nicholson. Major Gilligan took a seat nearer the end of the table, with another major she'd not seen before sitting towards the other end. Admiral Kinnaird seemed grey and haggard, like a shell of the man they'd met the previous morning. He was looking at a buff folder on the table in front of him rather than at those he was meeting.

It was Blanch who led things off. 'Thank you for meeting us, group captain. I understand you've had a difficult 24 hours and I should start by saying how relieved I am to see you safe and well. I think you know everyone on my side of the table apart from Major Stewart, who commands the Corps of Military Police here in Orkney. The reason for his presence will become obvious shortly. Would you mind introducing your team for the major's benefit?'

Bob did so.

'Very well. We are here because a quite extraordinary crisis has developed. It seems your investigation into the naval side of things on these islands has triggered a sequence of events that is unlike anything I've ever encountered in my career before. Could I ask you to start, group captain, by giving a very brief outline of your investigation, and what you have found? It would be helpful if you could distinguish between things you know and things you suspect.'

Bob ran quickly though most of what they'd done since returning to Orkney and set out their conclusions and suspicions. 'We will know more when we can talk to Kenny Weir and the crew of the *Harvest Moon,* sir, but for the moment I think that's about all I can tell you.'

'Thank you, group captain. As I said, simply extraordinary. Now I'd like to ask Rear Admiral Kinnaird to speak about developments on his side in the last 24 hours.'

The admiral looked up for the first time. 'I think you are probably aware, group captain, that I found our meeting yesterday morning to be an eye-opening experience. It was also a profoundly distressing one, but that's not relevant now. Until yesterday, I had complete faith in the senior officers reporting to me and at our meeting it became clear that faith was misplaced.

'As you know, at the end of the meeting I confined Commander Napier to the officers' quarters at Lyness and suspended him from duty. Commander Napier was seen at breakfast in the officers' wardroom at about 8 a.m. this morning but then disappeared. He was missed shortly before 10 a.m. when Captain Nicholson went to speak to him in his quarters. Some of Napier's belongings had also gone. Captain Nicholson immediately launched a search and notified me. Given the seriousness of the situation, we put in place measures to try to prevent Commander Napier leaving Hoy, including road blocks and checks on all vessels leaving the island. No trace of him has been found, nor anything else of significance except for the aftermath of your release by the general's troops this afternoon. The cottage you were held in has been put under guard, pending a proper investigation of what was found there and in the nearby store. The body has been removed.

'Although Napier's disappearance was a huge blow, it was not the worst that I have had to deal with today. Yesterday you met Captain Paul Cowdrey, who was responsible for the operations of Scapa Flow as an anchorage and harbour. Captain Cowdray was in his office as normal at first this morning. He then left, telling his staff that he was intending to meet me. Not long afterwards there was a report of a gunshot from his quarters. It seems he had shot himself. He left a handwritten note, addressed to me.'

The admiral opened the folder in front of him and looked down at it. Then he pushed it to his right. 'I'm sorry. Stuart, would you mind?'

The general picked up a piece of paper from the open folder, then coughed to clear his throat. 'The note says: "Dear Hugh. I'm truly sorry. I have let you down; I have let myself down; I have let my family down; and I have let the navy down. I made an error of judgement after drinking too much on a terrible night in January and I have been made to regret it ever since. My actions put me completely in the power of Napier and Rose. Blackmail is a terrible thing, but cowardice is far worse. I know I should have stood up to them, but it seemed better not to at the time; and then the time after that; and so on. If you want to know how things have come to this, you should look in the sick bay of the *Dunluce Castle*. I regret to say that the birds have already flown, but that will allow you to understand the hold that those two men have had over me. You should know that I am not their only victim. I am aware that others, possibly many others, were entrapped in the same way. If I can do one last worthy thing for you, it is to advise you to trust no-one you do not consider to be a close personal friend. Please tell my wife and my sons that I love them and tell them that I hope they can forgive me when they hear what I have done. Yours aye. Paul.'"

The general put the letter back in the folder and closed the cover, before pushing it back towards Kinnaird. He looked up at Bob. 'I should say that his staff have confirmed that the letter seems to be in Captain Cowdray's handwriting. When Admiral Kinnaird was given the letter, he and Captain Nicholson came to see me.'

The admiral looked up again. 'What was most worrying about Paul's letter was his warning about trust. Before you ask the obvious question, Captain Nicholson and I have known each other for many years, and he took up his post in Lyness at my request. He is one of the few people, perhaps the only person, within my command who I can now completely trust.'

There was a pause, which the general filled. 'You will understand that what Admiral Kinnaird had to tell me was chillingly consistent with what Madame Dubois told me this morning. I therefore chose to tell the admiral, in very general terms, parts of what you had said about issues you had uncovered within his command. I also offered him practical support, especially in respect of policing on Hoy and Flotta. Napier and Rose were clearly both criminals, and in the immediate term there could be no question of anyone reporting to them being trusted.

'Earlier this afternoon, a significant party of Corps of Military

Police officers under Major Stewart's command landed in Lyness and on Flotta and have since taken over the duties of the Ship's Police there. I understand you passed back through Lyness shortly before they took over the roadblocks. Major Stewart himself has only just returned.

'Most of the naval police have been confined to quarters until we can find a way of sorting the wheat from the chaff. This is only a temporary measure. The Admiralty are intending to fly up a hundred men who have never been to Orkney before to fill the gap. I hope they will be here within 24 hours. I suspect they may be only the first wave of a wider influx of new blood intended to allow us to understand and resolve the issues in the naval command here in Orkney.'

'Including a new commander,' said Kinnaird. 'I have offered to resign my commission and my offer has unsurprisingly been accepted. My resignation will take effect as soon as a new commander arrives, which might also be as soon as tomorrow.'

Monique realised she'd been sitting forward, concentrating intently on what was being said. She sat back. 'Can I ask what Captain Cowdray meant when he talked about Dunluce Castle? Understanding the hold that Napier and Rose had over him, and apparently others, seems central to sorting this mess out. Where is the castle?'

The general smiled. 'Sorry, Madame Dubois, we were coming to that. You are right of course, except that it's "the" *Dunluce Castle,* and it's a ship rather than a building. Captain Nicholson, could you briefly explain?'

'Of course, sir. The *Dunluce Castle* is a depot ship moored off Lyness. She's an old liner they nearly scrapped before the war. She now serves as transit accommodation for new naval arrivals in Orkney and as a floating uniform and equipment store. She's even got a large theatre in one of her holds, kitted out with seats and dressing rooms salvaged from a bombed London theatre. There are also various offices, including the HQ for our photographic department and the fleet's mail handling centre. I was unaware that the ship's sick bay served any purpose now we have good medical facilities at Lyness and along the coast at North Ness. It was clearly important that we discovered what Paul had meant by his reference to the *Dunluce Castle*, so when Major Stewart and his men landed at Lyness earlier, they boarded the ship.'

Major Stewart spotted his cue. 'You have to think of an old-fashioned liner with a single funnel, built not long after the turn of the century in Belfast for the Union-Castle Line. She was probably beautiful once, but these days she's grey and rusty and has seen far better days. She's moored a little way offshore at Lyness and accessed via a floating pier moored alongside with a gangway that slopes steeply up to deck level.

'I took six men aboard and we made our way to the sick bay, which is in a slightly difficult-to-find corner of one of the lower decks. The main access door was locked, and no-one seemed able to find a key. We had to resort to brute force, which as it was a metal door took a little time. What we found can only be described as a small but well-equipped brothel. There was a reception area, a couple of rooms that were kitted out as individual waiting rooms, presumably intended to avoid clients meeting one another, and four cabins decorated like they were part of an Ottoman harem. There were also three cabins with bunks that looked like any other cabins you might find on the ship, and a lounge, and toilets and a washroom.

'There was no-one there, and it looked like the occupants had left in a hurry. Clothing and belongings seemed to have been discarded. No paperwork had been left. It was perhaps too much to expect that there might be an appointments book listing the names of clients, but I did hope we might find some clues to the identities of the people involved. One interesting find did emerge. Two of the decorated cabins had each been adapted with a sort of built-in wardrobe, fronted by a mirror. It turned out that the mirrors were one-way, allowing someone perched on a stool inside the wardrobe to watch what was going on in the cabin, and to photograph it. We found discarded camera equipment in one of them, without any film, I should add. I sealed the sick bay and placed it under guard until we could check the place more thoroughly.

'Then I went to talk to the ship's captain, who as the vessel doesn't actually go anywhere is a naval lieutenant commander called Saunders. He seemed considerably older than his ship, and it was obvious that when he denied all knowledge of anything going on in the sick bay that he was lying. When I told him that he was looking at a long spell in military prison if he didn't cooperate, he changed his tune. To summarise, the sick bay was operated as a highly exclusive brothel. Four prostitutes lived and worked there for a month at a time, and during that month they never left. The young women seemed to come from Glasgow or southern Ireland. The operation was run by an Irish woman in her forties who he knew as Angela Murphy, though he didn't think that was her real name. Once each month the four prostitutes would depart, dressed as nurses, and another four would arrive, likewise attired. The timing of the changes of personnel seemed to coincide with the arrivals and departures of the SS *St Ninian,* which works for the navy on the Scrabster to Lyness route. The change of shift normally took place at the end of the month but last Friday the current draft left, along with Angela Murphy, and the place has been deserted since.'

'What could he tell you about clients?' asked Monique. 'Finding out who Napier and Rose were blackmailing is central to discovering who can be trusted. Come to think of it, it also might give us a list of men with reasons to want Lieutenant Rose dead, some of whom might have had access to Webley revolvers. Perhaps we maligned Declan Walsh in thinking he was Rose's murderer.'

'It seemed obvious to me that Saunders himself was no stranger to the Ottoman harem, ma'am. He claimed, however, that the many different roles that the *Dunluce Castle* fulfils means there is a huge flow of people coming aboard and leaving, and he had no idea who the brothel's clients might be. I suspect that he probably made a point of not noticing who was visiting that part of the ship. He did say, when pressed, that the arrangement had been established by Commander Napier, who he obviously fears, at the beginning of last year. He also said, unprompted, that there must have been other people in positions of power who knew what was going on, and he offered the thought that simply arranging the permits for the prostitutes to be in Orkney, and organising their passages on the *St Ninian,* would be difficult unless you had levers you could pull.'

'Thank you major,' said Blanch. 'I think that we've now brought one another fully up to date with recent developments. The more pressing question is what we need to do now? Have you any thoughts group captain?'

Monique realised that Bob, like the admiral, was looking at the table in front of him, and wondered whether his experiences over the past 24 hours were catching up with him. She looked across at the general. 'I think there are a couple of obvious next steps we need to take, and there are two overriding priorities we need to tackle. Most immediately, we need to interview Kenny Weir and the crew of the *Harvest Moon*. I suspect they might help fill in the background to what's happened, but I also suspect they may not help us tackle our priorities.'

'And what are they, Madame Dubois?' asked the general.

'The first is to find out who Napier and Rose had in their pockets. Somewhere there must be a client list or an appointments book for the brothel. Let's remember that granting a lonely man access, especially repeated access, to the brothel would be a powerful bribe that could be given to those who were well-placed to do Napier and Rose favours in return.'

'You mean like arranging security permits and travel passes, or selling postings?'

'Exactly, general. But then there's also the blackmail. We know Captain Cowdray was being blackmailed, and we know that the brothel was set up in a way that allowed incriminating evidence to be collected so that others could be blackmailed too. This incriminating evidence probably still exists somewhere, particularly in the form of negatives and photographs of sexual activity. In many ways, information about the clients of the brothel is the most valuable thing in Orkney right now.'

'It may have been removed by the woman running the place when they left last Friday.'

'Yes, that's possible, general. But when Group Captain Sutherland and I visited Lieutenant Rose's cottage in Scapa yesterday afternoon, someone had already thoroughly searched the place. I would place a large bet that they were looking for this client information, which they must have believed was held by the lieutenant before his murder. There's no way of knowing, of course, whether they found it or not. Given that, I would like to ask Major Stewart if it's possible to arrange detailed searches, tonight if possible, of the quarters used by Napier and Rose in Lyness, and of the provost marshal's office. We also need a more thorough searches of Rose's cottage in Scapa and of the cottage that the group captain was held in, though I think that is less likely as a hiding-place for this material.'

'Yes, see to it would you, major?' said Blanch.

'One thing that is very unclear,' said Monique, 'are the relative roles of Rose, Napier and Gordon. We've heard from Major Stewart that it was Napier who set the brothel up, but Frank Gordon said something this morning about "testing the merchandise" that suggested he was also involved. We know he has a background in Glasgow and Dublin, which might tie in with the origins of the women who were working on the ship.'

'That's true,' said Blanch. 'You talked about two priorities and have identified one of them. What do you see as the other?'

'Finding Commander Napier and Edward Swanson. In some ways Edward Swanson is the man who intrigues me most in all of this. It's possible to fit the others into the jigsaw, at least provisionally, but until he killed Frank Gordon, Swanson was very much on the edge of the picture. Until we understand his relationship with Frank Gordon, and their relationships with Napier and Rose, we're never going to get to the bottom of this.

'I can't speak for Swanson,' said Captain Nicholson, 'but thinking through the timing of Napier's disappearance, it is possible he's escaped from Orkney. We've checked all vessels leaving Hoy, and we thoroughly searched the *St Ninian* when she arrived in Scrabster as she'd left Lyness not long before I found Napier had gone. We've also asked that this evening's troop train south from Scrabster is thoroughly searched before it leaves. It depends on how much of a risk he was prepared to take. It took forethought to close the brothel last week. He won't have forgotten to plan for his own escape.'

'Napier is a bit of an unknown in all of this,' said Monique. 'I heard he was from Edinburgh and has a wife there, but otherwise know nothing about him.'

'That's right,' said Captain Nicholson. 'He's 45, he's been involved in naval security on and off since joining the navy in the closing stages of the last war, and he has two sons who I think are at school in Edinburgh. I can't give you a complete run-down, but in the years before the war he was involved in security in some of the shipyards on the Clyde that were building ships for the Royal Navy. He then worked at Rosyth for a while before moving up here as part of the major expansion at Scapa Flow in the months that followed the sinking of HMS *Royal Oak* in October 1939. Others have come and gone, but Commander Napier has been something of a fixture here.'

Major General Blanch leaned forward. 'We know that Major Stewart's men are continuing to look for Napier, but until the Admiralty can get reinforcements here, our resources are a little stretched. I assume the civilian police are looking for Swanson?'

'Yes, they are,' said Monique, 'and he had rather less time to get away than Napier before people started looking for him.'

Blanch looked at his watch. 'Look, it's getting late and I know that some of us have had a very trying time. Let's call it a day, shall we? Please keep me in touch with any developments. If it helps, I will chair another meeting here tomorrow evening at the same time. We can decide tomorrow whether that's needed. I suggest you get the group captain back to his hotel, Madame Dubois. I think he's had about enough for one day.'

'I will sir, but first he and I need to talk to Kenny Weir, and Lieutenant Commander Dixon and Petty Officer MacDonald need to interview the crew of the *Harvest Moon.*'

'Very well. Major Stewart, would you arrange that, please, and then progress the searches we discussed?'

Major Stewart stood up. 'If you would follow me, Madame Dubois, I'll take you to where they are being held.'

Monique helped Bob to his feet. She was relieved when he smiled at her. 'I'm all right, Monique, really.'

As they made their way towards the door, she saw that Air Commodore Chilton, who hadn't said a word during the meeting, had come round to intercept them.

The air commodore patted Bob on the shoulder. 'Good job, Bob. I'm glad to see you safe.' He looked at Monique. 'Look after him, will you?'

*

Monique didn't even feel curious about the time as Andrew drove the car, slowly, in the dark along the road to Kirkwall. Michael sat with him in the front, and Monique sat in the back. Bob was leaning against her, asleep.

Monique looked out of the window. 'Look! That's the first time I've seen the Northern Lights since I arrived in this country. I have a memory of seeing them as a small girl in Siberia, but I've never seen them in Britain.'

'Marvellous, isn't it?' said Andrew. 'Do you want me to pull over, so we can get out and watch?'

'No, I don't want to wake Bob up.'

'How did the interview with Kenny Weir go?' asked Michael.

'It didn't do much more than confirm what we already knew,' said Monique. 'He was on the periphery of things, spending most of his time on Hoy. He was well paid by the man he knew as Peter Mcilvenny and has a nice nest-egg back home that would have allowed him a comfortable early retirement. Mcilvenny/ Gordon – look, I'll just call him Frank Gordon - was brought in a few months ago to replace another Glasgow gangster called Sandy Wilson, who had initially set things up here and who was a great pal of Napier and Rose. Kenny didn't know why Sandy Wilson had been replaced and he claimed he didn't know who Wilson and Frank Gordon worked for in Glasgow. He did hear that Wilson had been found dead in the Clyde not long after leaving Orkney. Kenny had worked for Sandy Wilson since last summer, but Declan Walsh had been recruited by Frank Gordon when he arrived. Kenny got the sense that Frank knew some relatives of Declan's in Dublin.

'In terms of activities, he confirmed much of what we suspected. The building by the cottage was used to hold goods diverted by Lieutenant Rose from the navy's stores supply chain on Hoy, as well as smuggled luxury goods that had arrived in Kirkwall on neutral ships. The merchandise was brought over by the *Harvest Moon* from a pier at St Mary's on East Mainland. Every week or so, the *Harvest Moon* would arrive, usually under cover of darkness except in high summer, and they'd load it up with the contents of the store, both the smuggled and the stolen goods. Even when they did this in daylight, no-one ever questioned what was going on. The boat would then take the goods to Scrabster, from where they would be transported south. Kenny claimed to know nothing about how the stuff was transported, or where to, and I tended to believe him.

'One thing he did say was that tensions had arisen since Frank Gordon's arrival. He pushed Napier and Rose much harder than Sandy Wilson had done and they didn't like it. There were added problems because the supply of smuggled goods through Kirkwall had become more difficult to maintain since the

Contraband Control operation had closed. Kenny had heard an argument at the cottage a few weeks ago between Frank Gordon and Malcolm Rose in which Rose had said that the risk was much higher now the number of ships coming into Kirkwall had reduced. He wanted a bigger share of the profits as compensation for the higher risk.

'We then asked about Lieutenant Rose's murder. Kenny said, and again I tend to believe him, that he wasn't involved. Kenny knew that on the Saturday night, Frank Gordon and Declan Weir had landed goods from a ship in Kirkwall Bay. He didn't know that Malcolm Rose was also involved, though agreed it would have been normal for him to have been. Gordon and Weir had then driven the goods down to St Mary's and the *Harvest Moon* had brought them and the goods over to Hoy. Kenny isn't very bright, but he picked up that something bad had happened from Frank Gordon's behaviour. He didn't ask what. It was Bob who pointed out that St Mary's, where they sailed from, is not far from the quarry where Lieutenant Rose's body was found. Maybe the tensions that already existed boiled over? All three who were directly involved are now dead, so we'll be relying on the forensics people to tie the bullets recovered from Rose's body to Walsh's gun to know for sure.

'I also asked Kenny about Edward Swanson. He knew that Swanson ran the St Magnus Hotel and was a friend of Frank Gordon's, and he said that he'd also been a friend of Sandy Wilson's. But he didn't seem to know anything else. When I asked about Bob's kidnapping, he said that the arrival of Frank Gordon and Declan Walsh at the pier by the cottage last night had been unexpected. Beyond that, he didn't tell us anything we didn't already know. He seemed very scared of something though. I did ask him if Frank Gordon or Malcolm Rose stored any documents at the cottage or in the other buildings there. He said they didn't. Hopefully, the major's searches will confirm that one way or the other.'

'Fascinating,' said Michael. 'We got a largely consistent story from the captain and first mate of the *Harvest Moon*. The crew of eight men were all well paid by Frank Gordon and both the captain and first mate admitted, when asked directly, that they were well acquainted with the sick bay on the *Dunluce Castle*. The vessel has been involved since early last year when the captain was approached by Sandy Wilson. His problem initially was that he thought some members of his crew might not have gone along with smuggling. That problem went away when the navy conveniently arranged a series of postings that meant the drifter had a crew who were all happy to earn a dishonest living. Meanwhile, strings were pulled to ensure that she only did enough "normal" work to avoid standing out too obviously.

'I asked them about Frank Gordon's use of the vessel to transport an abducted officer to Hoy last night, and they seemed genuinely shocked. They were aware of an unusually large crate, but Declan Walsh did most of the handling. They thought it was just more goods, though it was unusual for Gordon to bring stuff that needed transporting to Houton. Normally they arranged to meet at St Mary's. I should add that they were even more shocked to hear that Frank Gordon planned to implicate them in the murder of Group Captain Sutherland tonight. As far as they were concerned, it was to be just a routine run from Hoy to Scrabster with the goods from the store.

'I asked how the stuff they carried to Scrabster was then transported south. They said they were always met by lorries at the quayside and their cargo was moved onto them. They got the sense that the goods were then taken for onward shipment by rail, but that was only from occasional comments that had been made.'

'What about the night of Lieutenant Rose's death?'

Michael smiled. 'Patience, Monique, I was just coming to that. The *Harvest Moon* was due to meet Peter Mcilvenny – or Frank Gordon – plus Declan Walsh and Malcolm Rose at St Mary's as usual. They were two hours late, and only Frank and Declan turned up. They had some story about problems getting the SS *Amazon's* boat to launch, a stuck davit or something, which had delayed Rose bringing the goods back into Kirkwall harbour, where he was due to be met by the other two. Again, it points to a falling-out of some sort. I'm guessing Walsh killed the lieutenant somewhere on the way down to St Mary's from Kirkwall and he and Gordon then disposed of the body in the quarry, which Declan Walsh would have known well given his previous employment. I asked if either the captain or first mate had heard of Edward Swanson. They knew he ran the St Magnus Hotel, and knew he was a friend of Frank Gordon's, but that was as far as it went.'

*

They had to awaken the night porter at the St Magnus Hotel. Bob was mobile, but still seemed groggy. Lieutenant Commander Dixon looked around anxiously as they walked into the reception.

'We're fine, Michael,' said Monique. 'You go and find Betty.'

'She'll be asleep by now.'

'Trust me, Michael, she'll still want to see you.'

'What about Bob?'

'Don't worry sir,' said Andrew, 'I'll help get the group captain to bed.'

CHAPTER TWENTY-THREE

Monique wondered if she was dreaming. Then the knock came again. She reached down under the head of the bed, where she always kept her pistol at night. For some reason Bob seemed to think she went to bed with it under her pillow. She valued her sleep far too much for that. She had no idea what time it was as she cautiously opened the door and looked round it, using it to shield herself from view. She realised that yesterday had started in almost the same way, though this time she had no blanket, as she'd not wanted to uncover Bob.

'I'm sorry, ma'am.' It was Andrew.

'"Monique" is better, especially first thing in the morning. What is it?'

'The hotel stops serving breakfast in half an hour. I thought you'd both need the food more than you need the sleep.'

'We'll be there. Have you seen Michael this morning?'

'I'm afraid I had to wake him up too. Betty was already up and had left him to sleep.'

'You certainly know how to make yourself popular, don't you Andrew? No, seriously, thank you, we do need to get moving.'

Monique closed the door and looked at Bob, still fast asleep. She wondered if she'd ever be able to overcome her deep-seated fear of telling him just how much she loved him. She hoped he knew how she felt without being told.

*

'Bob… Bob… We need to get up. They're stopping serving breakfast soon.'

Bob felt a touch on his cheek and jerked awake, startled. He saw Monique pull open the curtains, careful not to expose herself too openly. From the little of the outside world he could see from the bed, it looked like one of those fine cold days you sometimes got in early winter.

'Come on, sleepy-head. We need to move. We've just about got time to get ready.'

They found Michael and Andrew tucking into plates of fried food in a nearly deserted dining room.

'How are you, sir?' asked Andrew.

'I feel much better, thank you. I'm afraid I was running out of steam by the end of the meeting with the general yesterday and my memory of the interview with Kenny Weir is distinctly fuzzy around the edges. How's Betty doing, Michael?'

'Remarkably well, all things considered. She's angry about what her father's done, and worried about him too. He is still her father, after all. She had a message from Inspector Flett late yesterday that he'd want to talk to her again this morning when we were available to be there too. I think he's looking for background information about her father.'

'That seems sensible,' said Bob. 'We should be there, if only so you can support Betty. Beyond that, though, I'm not sure how much there is left for us usefully to do in Orkney. Napier is being hunted by the Corps of Military Police and the navy, and Swanson is being hunted by the civilian police. Sooner or later, both will be caught. There's only a limited number of places that either of them can run to in wartime, even if Napier did manage to make it to mainland Scotland yesterday. We can also hope for the navy's sake that the records and incriminating material from the brothel come to light. They need to know who can't be trusted. Again, though, that's now out of our hands. I said before we came that it was going to be like fishing with hand grenades. It seems to me that we've killed most of the fish and emptied the pond. It may be time to go back to Edinburgh. I also need to make what I think may be a difficult phone call.'

'It seems a shame to walk away with the job incomplete,' said Monique as their food arrived.

'Yes, I feel that too. Look, as soon as we've finished, we'll drive to the police station. Can you telephone Major Stewart or Major Gilligan from there to find out if there's anything new on their side, Monique, while I make my call? Perhaps, Michael, if you walk there with Betty, we can talk to her when we've finished our phone calls, assuming Inspector Flett is available.'

*

The inspector offered Monique the use of another phone, while Bob used the one in their borrowed office.

'Hello Dad.'

'Hello Bob, where are you?'

'I'm calling from the police station in Kirkwall.'

'I take it you are calling about Frank Gordon?'

'Yes, I am, Dad.'

'Last time we spoke I said I'd see what I could find out. It wasn't very much…'

'Hang on Dad. There's something you need to know.'

'What's wrong?'

'Frank Gordon's dead. He was poisoned in the cells of Kirkwall police station by a meal prepared by a crooked business associate. It happened yesterday.'

There was a pause. Bob wondered whether the connection had failed. 'Dad? Are you there?'

'Yes, Bob. I was just thinking about that. I'm going to have to tell your mother, and I'm wondering how she'll take it. Frank Gordon was a total bastard and a large part of me thinks the world is a better place without him. She's going to be heartbroken, though. Can you explain the circumstances to me?'

Bob talked his father through the background to Frank Gordon's death, how it had happened, and who he thought had done it.

'You're telling me that at the time he was killed he was holding you prisoner on one of the islands, and was intending to kill you last night?'

'That's pretty much the size of it.'

'But you're safe now?'

'Yes, completely. My team released me unharmed.'

'That's good news, Bob. For the obvious reason, but also because it might make it a little easier for your mother to accept Frank's death. Do you still want to know what I found out about him?'

'It might help, Dad. The man who almost certainly killed him is still at large.'

'Very well. I think I said last time we spoke that he'd been released a couple of years ago. I was right, it was in late 1940. At the time Frank had gone inside he was working for a gangster called Clarence Shand. Mr Shand had his fingers in everything nasty happening in Glasgow and for a good distance around it.'

'Yes, I recall the name from my time on the Glasgow force. We never got him, though, did we?'

'No, but tuberculosis did. By the time Frank was released from prison there had been a change of generations, but he picked up pretty much where he'd left off, this time working for Clarence's oldest son, Willie Shand. It may be that your ex-colleagues in Glasgow paid Frank too much attention after his release, or it may have been because Willie Shand was looking to broaden his business horizons. Either way, Frank went off to Dublin not long after he got out of prison. I've not been able to find out anything about his activities or associates over there.'

'That makes sense, Dad. He was engaged in various activities here, under the cover of being an antiques dealer, including large-scale theft, black marketeering and smuggling. He also had links, though they are unclear, with a brothel being run for navy personnel. It seems the girls came from Glasgow and Ireland, and the woman running it was also Irish. It ties in with Frank's time in Dublin.'

'I hope that the limited amount I could add helps.'

'It certainly does, Dad, thanks.'

'You know, Bob, I was quite surprised to find you were calling from Kirkwall again.'

Bob had a sinking feeling in the pit of his stomach. He had an idea what was about to follow. 'Why's that, Dad?'

'Edinburgh can be a small city in some ways, son, as I'm sure you are rediscovering. I had a meeting about something else with a colleague on Tuesday who said he'd seen you over the weekend at the North British Hotel, with a lady.'

'Guilty as charged, Dad. We spent the weekend there after getting back from Orkney. I was going to come and see you and Mum this week, but on Monday I found out I had to come back up to Orkney that same day.'

'Your mother is going to ask who she is and whether we're going to meet her.'

Bob wondered whether his father might not actually be the

more curious of his parents. 'I hope to be able to bring her to see you both, Dad. She's someone I met in Caithness in September. At that time, she worked for MI5, though she has since joined my team in MI11. The name she used in Scotland when I met her was Monique Dubois, and that's the name she's using while on secondment. It's also the name I have for her in my head. It's all extremely complicated, Dad, but it is looking quite good right now.' There was another pause. Bob could imagine his father weighing this up. 'Dad, there is one thing I would ask. Please give Monique a chance to tell you her story in her own way. If I hear you've had your Special Branch people calling in favours from their MI5 contacts to try to dig up her background, then I'll disown you.'

David Sutherland laughed. 'You should know me better than that, Bob. Besides, isn't disownment something parents do to children, rather than the other way round?'

'I'm serious, Dad. Please don't do anything to mess this up for me.'

'I know you are Bob. I won't.'

Bob wasn't sure how much he believed his father.

*

Bob met Monique in the reception area. Seeing he was there, Inspector Flett turned to lead them to the interview room. 'Any news?' Bob asked.

'No,' said Monique. 'They've found nothing of interest in any of the places they've searched. They intend to turn over Swanson's accommodation at the hotel next, though accept that if he had something of value, he'd have taken it with him. There's been no sign of him or Napier. How about you?'

'Dad thinks that the fact that Frank was going to kill me might make it easier for my mother to accept his death. I'm not so sure, but I'm not the one who's going to have to tell her. Look, three of us plus the inspector is going to seem a little heavy-handed, isn't it, for what's really a background interview?'

'Michael will sit with Betty. She'll be all right. The inspector has suggested I should ask the questions if you agree.'

Betty Swanson seemed nervous but composed. Michael sat alongside her. A constable had brought in an extra chair to allow Bob, Monique and Flett to sit on the other side of the wooden table.

Monique sat between the two men. 'Hello Betty. You already know who we are and as this is just an informal chat, I'll not take up your time with introductions. I should start by saying that Inspector Flett has assured me that you are in no way a suspect in the poisoning of Peter Mcilvenny or Frank Gordon. We do desperately need to talk to your father, though, and I'm hoping that you might be able to tell us more about him, to help us work out where he might have gone. Let me start with an obvious question. Does he have relatives in Orkney? Is there anyone he might be staying with?'

'No. Dad was born and brought up in Wick and as far as I know had no relatives on the islands. Mum was the Orcadian. She was an only child, but had more cousins, aunts and uncles than it was easy to keep track of. None of them will have helped him escape. Mum and Dad always argued, as far back as I could remember. She died of cancer in 1938, when I was 19. He showed how deeply he cared by having an adulterous relationship with the wife of a ship's captain while my mother was dying in hospital. It was well known in Kirkwall what was going on. I imagine that the husband eventually found out, because both he and his wife moved away. Dad's been on his own since then, give or take occasional short-term relationships.'

'But you don't know of a lonely widow with a remote cottage somewhere who might be hiding him?'

'Sorry, no. And he's not a very gregarious man. He has a wide circle of acquaintances, but he never seems to have many, or any, close friends. It may help you understand the background if I tell you that the St Magnus Hotel was owned by my grandfather, my mother's father. Dad worked as a shipping agent and came to stay in Kirkwall on business. He met my mother, who was only 17 at the time. This was in December 1918. I arrived nine months later, on the 23rd of September 1919. By that time there had been a shotgun wedding. I think Mum felt that Dad had stolen her youth and saddled her with a child she wasn't ready for and didn't want. He always seemed to feel the same way about her. It wasn't a marriage made in heaven. Mum learned to accept me and was a loving parent. Dad was always distant. They had no other children. The only person who seemed happy about the way things worked out was my grandfather, who lost a daughter but gained a son-in-law willing to take on the running of the hotel. The two of them got on well and when my grandfather died, he left the hotel to my father. That was when I was about 10.'

'Do you know much about your father's early life, in Caithness or elsewhere?' asked Monique.

'I don't know how he got into shipping. We've never really talked much. Mum was born in 1902. Dad is older, obviously. He was 50 on his last birthday, in June, so was born in 1892. I did hear him talking in the bar one night about spending time in Glasgow as a young man, but he stopped when he realised that I was listening.'

'I think Michael's mentioned this, but we did have an admiral over in Lyness tell us that he'd heard the reason why the St Magnus Hotel was the only significant hotel in Kirkwall not requisitioned by the navy at the start of the war was that your father had served with Winston Churchill in the Great War.'

'Yes, I thought that was quite funny. As I've said, Dad never really talked to me. When I was about 10, we learned about the war, which was still very fresh in minds at the time. The teacher showed us a poster produced during the conflict that showed a little girl sitting on her father's knee, and asking "Daddy, what did you do in the Great War?" I've always remembered it because I'd never in my whole life sat on my father's knee.' Betty stopped, and Michael put his hand on hers. 'Anyway, I told Dad about the poster, which I think he was familiar with, and asked what he'd done in the war. He didn't get angry or anything, he simply said that he'd not been able to join up because of flat feet, so had done his bit by arranging shipping to help keep the country fed. I didn't ask where, but I suppose that might have been in Glasgow.'

'If he wasn't an old comrade of Mr Churchill's, have you any idea why the hotel wasn't requisitioned?'

'I've thought about that since Michael told me what the admiral said. After my mother died, Dad did let the place go downhill for a while. I was old enough to know that it had taken a turn for the worse by the time the war started. I think Dad ran into money problems. For a while it wasn't unusual to have single female guests staying for short periods who gave addresses in one of the big Scottish cities. It got to the point where I began to wonder if Dad was supplementing his income by running prostitutes. Very discreetly, of course, I doubt if anyone not directly involved ever knew. Perhaps someone important in the navy felt the hotel was of more use to them operating as it was than if they'd requisitioned it. Things improved after a year or two and you no longer ran the risk of bumping into embarrassed naval officers emerging from young ladies' rooms at odd times.'

Monique turned to Inspector Flett. 'Were you aware of what was happening?'

'No, it's news to me. Given how small Kirkwall is, I'm surprised word didn't get out.'

'The timing is unclear,' said Bob, 'but you could almost think of what was happening in the hotel as a forerunner for what followed on the *Dunluce Castle*. Perhaps one simply replaced the other.'

'I've just a couple more questions Betty,' said Monique. 'Do you know how your Dad knew Frank Gordon?

'No, Mr Mcilvenny, as I knew him, simply appeared a few months ago and was a fairly regular visitor to the hotel, though he didn't stay there. I don't think Dad liked him. Before that there had been a man called Sandy Wilson, who Dad got on much better with. It was him that I heard Dad talking to about Glasgow in the bar.'

'Thank you, Betty, I think that's about it. Does anyone else have any questions?'

'Just one,' said Bob. 'Can you recall hearing of a gentleman from Glasgow called Clarence Shand, or his son, Willie Shand?'

'We get a lot of people passing through, group captain, but I do think I can remember a William Shand staying and meeting Dad and Sandy Wilson once, probably at the end of 1940. This was just before things started to improve at the hotel and the young women stopped staying. I remember it because very soon afterwards, and even though there was a war on, Dad put in place a rolling program of renovations of the bedrooms and public areas. It must have cost a fortune and I've no idea how he got the money or sourced the materials and skilled labour.'

'There's one more thing, Betty,' said Monique. The search for your father is continuing and as part of that, men from the Corps of Military Police are likely to be visiting the hotel to search his private accommodation. I'm saying this simply out of courtesy. Please don't disturb anything there until they've been. I'm afraid I don't know when that will be.'

Michael stood up. 'If it's OK with you, sir, I'll walk Betty back to the hotel.'

'Of course, Michael.' Bob couldn't help thinking that Betty needed all the support she could get.

After they'd gone, Bob leaned back in his chair. 'Perhaps things begin to make a little more sense. Maybe the portfolio of incriminating evidence goes back further than we thought.'

'They might make more sense to you, group captain,' said Inspector Flett. 'I'm wondering if I'm missing some of the important parts of the picture.'

'Yes, I'm sorry.' Bob briefly talked the inspector through what had been happening on the naval side of things over the previous 24 hours.

'Thank you, group captain. For our part, we'll keep looking for Edward Swanson, but so far there's been no sign of either him or his car.'

Monique stood up. 'Come on, Bob. It's a nice day. Let's get some fresh air. Andrew can take any messages that arrive. It might give us a chance to clear our heads and work out whether there's anything left for us to do here.'

*

Monique stopped walking. 'This place felt quite spooky the other night. It looks simply magnificent today.'

Bob thought that the red stone of which St Magnus Cathedral was largely constructed did indeed look magnificent against the wintry blue sky. The centre of Kirkwall was busy on this Thursday morning but the steps leading up from Broad Street to the large west doors were empty. 'You're right. I've never seen anywhere quite like it.'

'Second Officer Jennings reckons it's well worth a visit. Do you fancy going in?'

'Why not?' said Bob.

Entry was through a small wooden door set within a much larger one. After the harsh winter sunlight, the inside of the church seemed very dark and it took Bob's eye some time to adjust to the lower light.

'Wow,' said Monique, her voice hushed.

There were a few people in the cathedral. Two women could be seen kneeling and praying in the nave and a naval officer appeared to be sightseeing in one of the aisles.

'Let's walk along the north side,' said Bob. 'I almost wish Sergeant Bennett were here to give us a guided tour. He did talk about it in the hotel bar on that first night, though. According to him, it was built by a Norse earl in the 1100s to commemorate Earl Magnus, who had been betrayed and killed twenty years earlier.'

'These carved stones are amazing,' whispered Monique. 'There are lots with the skull and crossbones insignia. You'd almost think that Kirkwall was a popular haunt of pirates. Highly successful ones, given how much these stones must have cost to produce.'

'Ah, the joys of the Scottish Reformation,' said Bob. 'Most of Scotland's best churches were destroyed in the Reformation and the old Catholic ways were swept aside by a wave of fervent and deeply joyless Presbyterian Protestantism. In the centuries that followed, symbols considered "Papist" were simply not used and the cross was foremost amongst them. Instead, grave markers tended to be inscribed with reminders of mortality. Often this was explicit. Look, that one has "memento mori" inscribed on it, which roughly translates as "remember that you too must die". The skull and crossbones carvings were intended to hammer the message home, like the hourglass symbols you can also see. You often get angels with wings, too, though I've not noticed any here.'

As they reached the crossing, Bob said, 'I'd thought it was the early date of the church and the relatively small windows that explained the lack of light. That's obviously part of it, but you can see from here that the east window has been boarded up. I suppose that's better than losing it in an air raid.'

Bob and Monique stood beneath the tower and looked up at the four huge columns that supported it.

'What do you think is above the wooden ceiling we can see up there?' asked Bob.

'I don't know, Bob. Looking up is making me feel giddy. Hold my arm, would you?'

'This is beautiful.'

'It is, Bob.' There was a long pause. 'Look, there's something I've been wanting to tell you.'

There was another pause. 'You can tell me, you know, Monique.'

'I know Bob, it's just that...'

There was a bang as the small door they'd entered by slammed shut. They both turned to look down the length of the nave, to see Petty Officer MacDonald walking swiftly towards them. One of the women kneeling in the nave looked round angrily, to identify the source of the disturbance.

'Your timing is impeccable, Andrew,' said Monique as he approached. She had a wistful smile on her face.

'I'm sorry, ma'am. There have been two phone calls. The first was just as you left. Able Seaman Booth from the naval provost marshal's office in Lyness called. He asked if he could come to Kirkwall to talk to you both. He sounded calm enough, but said it was important. I said you'd get back to him as soon as you were back. He said he'd catch the next steamer anyway and try to contact you again when it arrives at Scapa.

'It's because of the second call that I'm here. It was from Major Stewart in the Corps of Military Police. Two naval officers, both apparently lieutenant commanders, have been shot dead at a farmstead on West Mainland. That's bad enough in itself, but one of the bodies had on it two sets of identity documents in different names. One set of documents was in the name of Commander Napier and they think the body is his.' Andrew almost whispered these last words as he became aware of the profound silence of his surroundings.

'Thank you, Andrew, we obviously need to get over there. How did you find us?' asked Bob, wishing that the petty officer had been just a little less efficient.

'A police constable saw you both come into the cathedral. He was on his way into the police station as I came out to look for you. I've got the car outside. I thought we could pick up Lieutenant Commander Dixon at the hotel.'

Bob mentally shook himself, trying to shift his focus back onto the job in hand. 'We'll follow you out.'

As they reached the car Bob said, 'You drive, Andrew. Monique and I will sit in the back. Let's go and release Michael from the arms of Betty Swanson.'

CHAPTER TWENTY-FOUR

'Where are we going?' asked Bob. They'd turned right off the road to Stromness and were driving along a road he'd not been on before.

Andrew looked round from the driving seat. 'The major said that we would come to a village called Dounby a few miles along here. There will be no signs of course but he said we couldn't miss it. On the far side of the village there's a minor road that heads west, not far north of RAF Skeabrae. We're looking for a farmstead on the right, a couple of miles beyond the village.'

'I've got the road on the map,' said Michael, 'I think that must be Dounby in the distance ahead.'

There was no mistaking the farmstead. Several Jeeps and staff cars were parked beside the road, along with a lorry and a navy ambulance.

There was an army guard standing by the archway that led through the front range of the farmstead. He saluted when Bob showed his pass. 'Major Stewart is in the courtyard, sir.'

Bob led the way through. Beyond was a paved courtyard surrounded by ranges of farm buildings that seemed to confirm his initial impression that the farmstead was disued. A Royal Navy staff car was parked on the right-hand side of the area. Major Stewart had been standing beside it, with a group of men. Other men were crouched over something or someone on the ground near the centre of the courtyard.

The major turned. 'I'm glad you're here, group captain, we were just about to remove the bodies. Over here by the door of the car is the body of Lieutenant Commander Peter Lacey, who works, or worked, in the operations wing at HMS *Tern,* which is only a couple of miles away. He was a pilot by training, though was currently flying an office. He was shot in the back, twice. One of the shots passed through him and smashed the window in the car door. We've not done a thorough examination of the scene yet, but it's obvious that there were at least four shots fired at him. There's also a hole in the side of the engine compartment, and another that's hit the front tyre.

'Meanwhile, over in the centre of the courtyard is the body of a man who carries identification in the name of a Lieutenant Commander Flint and is wearing a lieutenant commander's uniform. What's interesting is that he also carries identification in the name of Commander Napier. He was shot once in the face and he isn't wearing identity discs, so formal confirmation of his identity may have to await a check of his fingerprints. However, I do of course know Commander Napier professionally and although he's shaved off his beard and closely cropped his hair, I think it is his body.'

'May I look?' asked Monique.

'Of course, though it's not pretty.'

Monique stopped the stretcher-bearers as they were about to lift the body and pulled back the cloth that was covering its head. She looked from different angles, then stood up. 'I agree with you, major. I only met Napier once but I'm sure that's him.'

'You've had a little time to think about this major,' said Bob. 'What do you think happened?'

'I understand that this place has been deserted for a couple of years, since the farmer who lived here died. His land has since been worked by a neighbouring farmer, who bought those parts of the estate that hadn't been requisitioned by the Air Ministry to form RAF Skeabrae. Although no-one lives here, some of these buildings are used to store agricultural machinery. A little earlier this morning, the farmer who works the place arrived. He parked outside and walked into the courtyard to find this. As he could see they were naval officers, he drove to the guardroom at HMS *Tern* and reported what he had found.

'The naval surgeon commander at HMS *Tern* was here a little earlier. It's complicated by the low temperatures last night, but he thought the bodies had probably been here since yesterday afternoon. We don't have much else in the way of useful information. I have no idea why they came here. Something happened and they were both shot. I've not been able to work that out. Two pistols were found by the bodies, both of which had been fired. One shot had been fired by the pistol by Lacey's body and four by the pistol found with Napier. I can see how Lacey could have shot Napier, who would have been standing facing him, and I can see how Napier could have shot Lacey in the back, perhaps as he was making for the car. I cannot, however, work out how both of those things could have happened.'

'Could someone else have been involved?' asked Bob.

'That could explain how both came to be shot as they were. It could also explain the presence of dried muddy tyre tracks on that side of the courtyard, where another vehicle has brought in mud from the large puddle you might have seen outside the front of the farm. They are similar in character to those left by the car that's still here and the farmer says that nothing he drives into the courtyard would have left tracks like them. We'll get the guns fingerprinted to see if that provides any answers.'

'We do, of course, have another missing man, Edward Swanson,' said Bob. 'As far as I know his car is also still missing.'

'Yes, that thought had crossed my mind too, sir. We really do need to find Mr Swanson before the trail of dead bodies across Orkney becomes any longer.'

*

'I still don't understand why Napier didn't make his escape when he could have done, yesterday morning,' said Michael, in the car.

It was Monique who answered. 'It has to be to do with the incriminating material from the brothel. Perhaps he felt it had long-term value to him, and he didn't want to leave without it?'

'That suggests that Edward Swanson has it,' said Bob. 'Let's assume that yesterday morning Napier disguised himself as Lieutenant Commander Flint and went to Kirkwall to 'see Swanson. He could have got there before Swanson poisoned Frank Gordon. After Frank Gordon was dealt with, the two of them headed off to the farmstead back there, where they met Lieutenant Commander Lacey. Obviously, whatever was planned went wrong. Lacey was a pilot, and although HMS *Tern* is quiet at the moment, they must still have the usual assortment of station aircraft. What if they wanted Lacey to fly them off the islands, and he refused?'

'If Napier had been blackmailing him,' said Monique, 'it's easy to see how they could have fallen out. One thing we have no idea about is how much of this incriminating material there is. The scale and duration of the operation suggests that they could have lots of victims. But does that mean a briefcase full of papers, or a few boxes, or an entire filing cabinet? We have no idea, and it seems to make a lot of difference whether this stuff is portable or not. As things stand, Swanson is on his own, presumably in possession of the material everyone has been looking for.'

'I don't disagree with anything you say, Monique,' said Bob. 'But I really am getting the sense that our role is being eroded as other agencies, quite rightly, take up the running on this.' He saw Michael turn round to speak. 'No, it's all right, Michael. Now we've got this close, I'm not keen to leave the islands until Swanson has been tracked down and caught. And I know you have no wish to abandon Betty right now. I'm prepared to give it another 24 hours to see what turns up.'

'That will give us a chance to find out what Able Seaman Booth has to tell us,' said Monique.

'Very true,' said Bob. 'In all the excitement I'd forgotten about him. Did he say what time he was due to arrive at Scapa, Andrew?'

*

Bob and Monique sat in the car near the landward end of the pier at Scapa and watched the TSS *Sir John Hawkins* make its way towards its moorings.

Monique got out of the car and stood beside it, where she would be seen by passengers leaving the pier.

The young able seaman cut a rather forlorn figure when he approached the car, his slight frame lost in the bulk of his navy blue greatcoat.

Monique held the back door open for him. She smiled. 'Hello, able seaman. Thanks for travelling over to see us.' She followed Booth into the rear of the car.

Bob started the car and drove to a widening in the road behind the beach at the head of the bay, where he pulled off.

'You told our colleague it was important that you saw us,' said

Monique.

'Yes, I did, ma'am. When the two of you spoke to me on Tuesday, you said I should contact you if I thought of anything else.'

'That's right,' said Monique.

'We've had the military police in the office, turning it over and obviously looking for something. Can I ask what they are looking for, ma'am?'

Bob was watching in the mirror and saw Monique glance at him. He nodded.

Monique sat so she was directly facing Booth. 'You told us that Lieutenant Rose was a crook. We've been spending the past couple of days finding out just how right you were. He was involved in a range of activities on the wrong side of the law, including smuggling and theft. What has caused us most concern, however, was his involvement in the running of a brothel for a select group of clients. Part of the role of the brothel was to collect photographic evidence of what the clients had been doing. Lieutenant Rose and Commander Napier used this to blackmail naval officers to help them with their criminal activities. This evidence is missing. It is possible that those running the brothel took it when they left in a hurry last Friday. However, after we saw you on Tuesday, we visited Lieutenant Rose's cottage. Someone had broken in and thoroughly searched it, and that suggests that Lieutenant Rose was the one in possession of the material at the time he was killed, and others have been looking for it since then. We think it possible that the incriminating material is still in Orkney and if it is, then we need to find it.'

'I wondered if it was something like that. That's why I wanted to talk to you. Look, I've got an idea that might help. But first, I want to agree a price if I help you find what you are looking for.'

Bob could see Monique's face in the mirror and could tell she was as surprised as he was that Booth wanted to barter. It seemed quite out of character for the young man.

'Perhaps you should tell us what you have in mind in terms of a "price",' she said.

'When you interviewed me on Tuesday, I very stupidly told you that Malcolm paid me an allowance that I intend to use to help support myself when I finally get to university. I've been kicking myself ever since. If he's as much of a crook as I've always thought, and you also think, then I'm worried that you, or the navy, or someone, will come after the money on the grounds he earned it illegally. As did I, for that matter, given how the law regards homosexuality.'

'Where are you going with this?' asked Monique.

Bob could tell that, like him, she already knew. Again, he nodded as he caught her eye in the mirror.

'I want you both to forget all about the allowance he paid to me and make no mention of it in any reports your write.'

'Yes, I can promise you that.'

'What about him?' asked Booth, gesturing towards the front of the car.

'I think you'll find that the group captain's word is worth rather more than mine,' said Monique. 'Group Captain Sutherland?'

Bob turned round in his seat, so he could look at Booth from his good right eye. 'If you help us find what we are looking for, able seaman, then I give you my absolute assurance that the allowance will simply not register in our investigation. I'd remind you of the "if" at the start of that sentence, though. You still have to deliver on your side of the deal.'

'Thank you, sir. Thank you, ma'am. There is a place where

Malcolm might have stored what you are looking for. You say that his cottage had been searched. Had the flagstones in the kitchen floor been lifted?'

'There was no sign of it,' said Monique.

'Let's go and find out,' said Bob, starting the car.

It took no more than a few minutes to drive round the head of the bay and along the road to where Lieutenant Rose's cottage stood. The back door had been repaired and was closed with a padlock. There was a sign at eye level warning visitors that access was prohibited by order of the commander of the Corps of Military Police.

'Hell,' said Bob.

'Not to worry,' said Monique. She obscured Bob's view, and Booth's, with her body while she tinkered with the lock. 'There you go. Extremely useful things, hair grips.'

Bob couldn't see what Monique had used to open the lock but very much doubted that it was a hair grip.

Inside, the place looked rather more ordered than it had on their last visit. It seemed that the military police had tidied up as they'd searched.

Booth stood in the centre of the kitchen. 'I arrived one evening during the summer to find that the two slabs over on this side, in front of the range, were lifted and laid to one side. Malcolm was embarrassed more than angry that he'd forgotten to replace them. I only got the briefest of glimpses of what was inside, but I got the impression of two brown leather Gladstone bags in the space underneath.'

'Should we look?' asked Monique. 'I don't see any obvious gaps between the flags or scratches on the surface.' She looked around the room, then rummaged through the kitchen drawers. 'Here we are.' She held up a pair of what looked like foot-long steel rulers, only these had no markings and were of thicker steel than any ruler Bob had ever seen. 'If you put them both in at the end of this slab here, then it would be possible to lever it up without leaving obvious signs. Can you do the honours, Bob?'

Bob complied. Monique was right. The end of the slab lifted sufficiently for him to get his fingers under it and lift it to the vertical before moving it to one side. There was an empty space beneath.

'The space continues under the slab next to it,' said Booth.

'I'm afraid you can see there's nothing there either, even without lifting it.'

'Lift it anyway, Bob,' said Monique.

Again, he complied, wondering what she had in mind. This time he pushed the slab across the one next to it, so it left the void beneath almost completely exposed.

Monique turned to Booth. 'Right, that's the space without the slabs in place. Show us where you saw it from and describe exactly what you saw.'

Booth didn't respond.

Bob could see that he looked devastated. 'It's all right, able seaman. No-one will get to hear about your allowance. Any more help that you could give us would be most welcome, though.'

'Thank you, sir. I was there, by the doorway from the hall. The bags were large enough to take up most of the space.'

Monique looked into the void beneath the floor. 'It's completely dry down there, so storing documents or film would have been possible. How big were these bags, able seaman? This big?' She held out her hands, palms facing inwards as she opened them steadily wider in a moving sketch of a bag in the void.

'A bit bigger, ma'am. Yes, that's about right.'

'You could get plenty of documents in two bags that size,' said

Monique. 'They'd take some lugging about if they were full, though. Do you mind putting the slabs back, Bob?'

As Bob moved the one that hadn't completely cleared the void beneath it, something caught his eye, almost invisible in the corner. He reached down. 'Look at this! A leather pouch. It's got three keys in it.' He stood up and held the keys out for Monique and Booth to see.

Monique turned to Booth. 'Do you have any thoughts about what the keys might fit?'

'Possibly, ma'am. I think I told you that we never went out when I was here at the cottage. That's not completely true. One evening, about a month ago, Malcolm said we had to go out for a walk. The weather was reasonable, in terms of no rain and little wind, but it was dark and cold. He had a canvas haversack with him, you know, the sort with a single shoulder strap. We walked down to where the road turns to run along the head of the bay, but went the other way, along a track that runs in front of two cottages before becoming a path that climbs up the low cliffs there. Maybe I've watched too many Hitchcock films, because I began to think he was leading me to where he could push me over the cliff. He was certainly acting very oddly, stopping frequently and looking round, as if to check that we weren't being followed. We probably only walked for a couple of hundred yards along the path, though it seemed much further at the time. Then we climbed over the wall that separates Scapa Distillery from the cliff path.'

'Is that the group of buildings you can see from the pier, over at the west end of the head of the bay?' asked Bob.

'Yes, sir. I'd been aware of the distillery earlier in the year while staying at the cottage. Sometimes you could smell the process under way. When I said we'd be arrested for trespass,

Malcolm laughed. He said that wartime restrictions on the supply of barley for distilleries had been made much more severe not long before our visit, and Scapa had been mothballed. He said that the warehouses were securely locked and there were night watchmen on duty at that end of the site to protect the stocks, but the offices were accessible to anyone who had a key, which he did.

'We walked a little way through the site to what he said was the office. He asked me to stay outside and stand out of sight in a dark corner. He let himself into the office and was in there for fifteen minutes. I kept checking on my watch because the time seemed to pass very slowly, and I was cold and rather frightened. When he came out, we retraced our steps back to the cottage. As I've said, he liked high quality drink and my first thought was that he had gone to collect some Scotch from someone who was still working at the distillery. But that didn't seem to make sense. I got the impression that the haversack weighed less on the way back than it had on the way to the distillery. There was something about the way it swung when Malcolm walked.'

'Do you think he was taking something to the distillery, which he left there?' asked Bob.

'Yes sir. It seemed odd, but as I've said, I never asked questions about anything like that.'

'Thank you,' said Monique. 'If we drive round to the distillery, would you be able to show us where the office is?'

'Yes, ma'am.'

'Good. Help the group captain replace those slabs and then I'll get the place locked up again.'

*

Bob had no problem finding the road leading into Scapa Distillery and followed it as far as a stout wooden gate that firmly prevented access. This was backed up by assorted signs seeking to dissuade casual visitors.

Bob sounded the car horn to try to attract attention but got no response.

They left the car where it was and climbed over the gate. 'Does anything look familiar?' asked Monique. 'We need to be able spot the office when approaching from this direction, and in daylight.'

'I think it's the building on the far side of the courtyard you can see beyond these warehouses,' said Booth. 'Yes, that's it.'

They walked up to the door. As Bob expected, one of the keys fitted the lock. He walked in, followed by Monique and Booth. 'The place has been cleared out.'

'There's a door at the end and another on the back wall,' said Monique.

The door at the end opened into an empty corridor. The one on the back wall was locked. Bob opened it with a second key.

'So far, so good,' he said. The room was dark, and Bob located a switch by the door which he flicked. Slightly to his surprise, the light came on. 'Ah, this is where everything from the main office was cleared to.' He was looking at what might have been a windowless office but was now used as a storeroom. Chairs were piled on top of desks, and access to the cupboards that lined two walls was obstructed by the sheer amount of excess furniture in the room. 'How are we going to find anything in here?'

'Let's think about it logically,' said Monique. 'If we assume the room was like this when Rose visited with Able Seaman Booth then he must have been able to physically access whatever the third key fits.'

'How about this wooden cupboard?' asked Bob. 'No, damn, the third key doesn't fit. Look, there's a metal two-drawer filing cabinet down here, just about within reach beyond the piled chairs. Do you think Lieutenant Rose could fit one of those bags into each draw, Able Seaman Booth?'

'I'm not sure, sir, possibly.'

'The key fits, which is promising. Let me get the security bar off.' Bob pulled open the top drawer. 'Abracadabra!' He lifted out a leather bag. 'It's heavy! Now let's get its companion.'

Bob and Able Seaman Booth carried the bags back to the car while Monique made sure the doors were locked.

They dropped the able seaman off at the landward end of the pier at Scapa, where he could wait for the next ferry back to Lyness.

The young man looked anxious as he opened the car door. 'And you meant what you said about keeping my allowance from Malcolm out of this?'

'What allowance?' asked Bob and Monique in unison.

*

'Why do you think Rose took Able Seaman Booth to the distillery?' asked Bob as he drove back to the police station. 'It seems out of character for him to take a risk like that.'

'Perhaps he had to choose between that or leaving Booth on his own at the cottage, which he never did,' said Monique. 'I'm guessing that he was taking the latest batch of evidence for storage in the Gladstone bags. What puzzles me more is why he decided to move the bags from a secure hiding place in the cottage to one that other people had access to. I'm also wondering how he got hold of the distillery keys.'

'He had a way of getting what he wanted. Perhaps the closure of the distillery seemed like an opportunity to distance himself from the evidence a little. We know that he didn't get on as well with Frank Gordon as he had with Sandy Wilson. Maybe he felt it was dangerous to keep the evidence at the cottage and the risk of leaving it at the distillery was acceptable.' Bob stopped the car opposite the police station. 'Hello, there are military police vehicles outside. I wonder what's happened?'

CHAPTER TWENTY-FIVE

Bob could barely manage the two heavy Gladstone bags, but refused Monique's help carrying them. They entered the police station to find Major Stewart talking to Inspector Flett in the reception area. Both turned as Bob and Monique entered.

'Your timing is perfect, sir,' said the major.

'What's happened?'

'One of the inspector's men has found Swanson's car on Cromwell Road. That's the road that runs round the east side of the harbour. The car was empty, but there was a briefcase containing documents and explicit photographs in the boot.

'I've got a Corps of Military Police tracker dog and handler on their way over from Stromness. We might be able to work out where Swanson went after he left the car, though the vehicle was completely cold, suggesting it had been there a while, possibly since last night. That would make tracking him impossible.'

'I've got every man I have scouring the town for him,' said Inspector Flett.

'Where he left the car isn't far from the St Magnus Hotel, is it?' asked Bob.

'Far enough away not to be obvious, but within easy walking distance. The same thought struck Lieutenant Commander Dixon. He and Petty Officer MacDonald both left a short time ago to ensure Betty Swanson is safe, with two of the major's men. It's difficult to think of any other reason Swanson might have returned to Kirkwall.'

'We'll go and join them,' said Bob. 'First, though, have you got a safe that's large enough to provide a really secure home for these two bags? We've only had a very quick look, but I strongly suspect they hold the evidence used by Napier and Rose to blackmail their victims.'

'We'll put them in one of our cells,' said Flett. He must have seen Bob's doubts reflected on his face. 'Don't worry, I'll put the key for the cell in the safe in the chief constable's office. I promise that we'll keep the bags secure. We'll add the briefcase we found in Swanson's car, which as the major said seems to contain more of the same.'

*

The woman on reception at the St Magnus Hotel directed Bob and Monique along a corridor on the first floor that led to the rear of the hotel. The family's rooms were beyond an anonymous door at the end, marked 'private'. A military policeman stood in the cramped hallway beyond the door, his submachine gun at the ready.

'The lieutenant commander is in the room on the right, sir.'

'Through here, sir!'

Bob followed the voice and found himself in the doorway of a sitting room. A small sofa and a couple of chairs were arranged around a fireplace, while a bookshelf and a bureau stood against the far wall. An upright piano stood against the wall to Bob's immediate left, though there was no stool and the instrument appeared to serve mainly as a stand for family photographs, most featuring a woman and a girl, obviously Betty, pictured at various stages of growing up.

Michael was sitting hunched forwards on one of the chairs while Andrew stood in the corner of the room near the fireplace.

The sofa had its back to the door and Bob could see that Betty was sitting on it. She didn't turn round as he entered.

'Betty's father has been here sir,' said Michael. 'He arrived this morning not long after you picked me up. She thinks he spent the night in an unused staff bedroom and came in via the back door to the family rooms after he saw me leave.'

'What did he want?'

'I don't know, sir. I thought you'd want to ask Betty yourself. She's distraught.'

Bob looked round at Monique, who took the hint. She went and sat on the other armchair and leaned forward to take Betty's hand. Bob stayed out of the young woman's view and saw that Andrew had also moved to the back of the room.

'Are you all right, Betty?' asked Monique.

'It was just a huge shock, with the poisoning and everything. I'd reconciled myself to never seeing him again, and suddenly there he was, as large as life.'

'Why did he come back?'

'He said he wanted to make things right with me. I told him it was too late for that. I told him exactly what I thought of him as a father. He got angry and slapped me. Then he started crying. I'd never seen him cry before. He sat there, where you are now. He said he wanted to explain everything.'

'What did he say?'

'He told me that my mother and grandfather had trapped him in Orkney, that they'd worked together to snare her a husband who could look after the hotel. After Mum had died, Dad had thought that he might make a new beginning, but the hotel was suffering from years of under-investment and his own bad management. When the war started, he hit on the idea of bolstering his income by bringing a few girls to stay in the hotel who were prepared to work as prostitutes. He knew people in Glasgow who helped provide the girls.

'Before long he was contacted by Commander Napier, who knew the same people in Glasgow. Between them they found a way of ensuring that the hotel wasn't requisitioned when others were, which meant there would be no competition for as long as the war went on. But it was still run down. A mutual friend of his and Napier's was a Glasgow businessman who visited the islands in late 1940. It was the man you asked about this morning, Willie Shand. Dad told me that Shand was the son of a man whose life he had saved in a gang fight in Glasgow during the last war. Willie Shand took a quarter share of the hotel in return for the cash needed to do it up. That was when the prostitutes stopped working in the hotel.

'Shand's business interests on the islands had other strands too, which were looked after by Sandy Wilson, who Dad got on well with. A few months ago, Wilson was ordered to return to Glasgow, and he was replaced by Peter Mcilvenny, or Frank Gordon. He caused problems for Dad. He wanted the hotel to perform better and he wanted a cut of the takings for himself as well as the quarter destined for Willie Shand. Dad complained to Commander Napier, who had known Shand since he looked after security for some of the Clyde shipyards in the years before the war. Napier told him that he had his own problems with Frank Gordon, who was taking a much more aggressive approach to the business activities Napier ran on the islands. When Dad went to Glasgow to complain directly to Willie Shand, he got a friendly reception. But then he was beaten up by one of Frank Gordon's men when he got back to Kirkwall. At the time he'd told me that his black eyes were caused by an accident in the beer cellar.

'Dad told me that everything came to a head when Frank

Gordon and this other man killed Lieutenant Rose in an argument about smuggled goods two weeks ago. Then you people arrived, and they realised how dangerous things had become. They thought they'd covered their tracks when you all left, but you came back. Dad said that Napier came to see him late yesterday morning, in disguise. Napier told him that Frank Gordon was being held by the police in Kirkwall and he wanted Dad to poison him. He even provided the poison. Dad said that Napier was worried Frank Gordon would say incriminating things about him and Dad to the police. He also wanted revenge for the death of Lieutenant Rose.'

'What happened after your Dad dropped you off back here, after you'd delivered the lunch?'

'He said that he had driven Napier to West Mainland. Napier knew a pilot there who he could persuade to fly them to central Scotland. They phoned the pilot from a nearby village, then met him at a farm. Dad hid in the back of the car while the two met. There was an argument and the other man shot Commander Napier. Dad said he had no choice but to kill him. He shot him from the back of the car. He then swapped his gun with Commander Napier's, to make it look like Napier had shot the second man. I think Dad was still very shocked by the experience. There was something in his eyes that I'd never seen before.'

'Do you know where he went when he left here?'

'I'm sorry, no. It wasn't long before Michael arrived.'

'I got one of the military police to spread the word that Edward Swanson was nearby,' said Michael. 'I'd imagine that we'd have heard if anyone had found him.'

Bob heard the door to the family accommodation opening, then heard a noise he had trouble placing.

Major Stewart came into the room. 'Miss Swanson, I understand that your father was here not long ago, is that right?'

'Yes, it is.'

'We've got a tracker dog here that can help find where he went. Do you have an item of clothing worn by your father but not washed that we can use to give the dog his scent?'

Betty made her way to the door of the increasingly crowded room. She was back a few moments later with a rolled-up shirt.

Bob followed the major out into the hallway. The dog handler allowed his charge a good chance to smell the shirt, then after a few words of encouragement followed it down a set of stairs and out of a door that led into a yard at the rear of the hotel.

Inspector Flett was waiting outside and took a step backwards as the dog emerged, pulling hard at its leash.

'I suppose we just follow?' asked Bob.

'I suppose so too,' said the Inspector. 'We don't have dogs on the force, so this is a new one on me. There's a warren of streets and paths Swanson could have used, though I hope my men have got them all covered by now. He's not that far ahead of us and he's really running out of options now.'

The dog led Bob, Monique and Flett along a narrow lane that emerged onto a shopping street, then along the street to an open area.

Bob realised where he was. 'This is the cathedral.'

'Yes,' said Flett, 'and it looks like the dog wants to go inside.'

Major Stewart caught up with them. 'It's possible he's got a gun. If we follow him in, he could start shooting innocent people.'

'He told his daughter he swapped his gun with Napier's,' said Monique, 'so he's definitely armed.'

'Let's start by sealing the place off,' said Flett. 'Whatever else, we need to ensure he can't leave. We've got quite a few men here between us now, major. I'll get mine guarding the exits from the cathedral, there are not many of them, and clearing people away from the area. My men should all have been issued with guns by now. Could you find vantage points for yours, so they can provide a second line of defence?'

The major turned and marched off, while the inspector issued instruction to his men.

'What do we do now?' asked Monique. 'I think you're the senior officer present, Bob.'

'Thanks for that, Monique. Rank has its privileges, as I said at RAF Errol. This is the other side of that coin. I don't think we've got a lot of choice. I think I'd better go in and reason with Mr Swanson.'

'You can't Bob. He's a desperate man, he'll kill you.'

'Besides,' said Flett, 'would you know Swanson by sight? He's a civilian and falls within my jurisdiction. I'll go in.'

'Now you're both being bloody silly,' said Monique. 'Let's all three go in, ever so calmly, and see what we can work out.'

Bob felt an overwhelming urge to pull rank and order Monique to stay outside. He knew that if he did, she'd never forgive him. He knew, too, that she'd simply ignore him.

Inspector Flett led the way in, followed by Bob and Monique. All had pistols drawn. Bob heard Flett mutter something under his breath and wondered if he was asking forgiveness for bringing a gun into this place.

It was even quieter than it had been earlier. At first Bob could see no-one. The he realised that a figure of a man was standing, motionless, where the south transept joined the crossing beneath the tower.

The three walked along the south aisle towards the man. As

they came closer Bob could see that the man was elderly and terrified, shaking his head. Then a shot rang out, utterly deafening in the absolute silence of the cathedral. Inspector Flett fell to the floor, clutching his upper left leg. Bob got a glimpse of a figure in the dark of the far corner of the transept, beyond the old man. There was a flash and another deafening bang as he fired again, and then he had gone, through a wooden door Bob hadn't previously noticed.

Monique crouched beside the inspector, removing his tie, Bob imagined for use as a tourniquet. She looked up at the elderly man. 'Get outside, quickly, and tell the police that the inspector needs urgent medical help.'

'First, though, do you know what's beyond that door?' asked Bob.

'Stairs to the upper levels and tower.' Then the elderly man turned and ran towards the west end of the cathedral at a speed that belied his apparent age.

Monique wrapped the tie around Flett's upper leg and twisted it tight. 'You're not going up on your own, Bob. Wait for support to arrive.'

'Sorry, Monique, too many people have been killed since I arrived on these islands. I think it's down to me to bring this to an end.'

'You idiot.'

Bob realised that Monique couldn't move without slackening off the tourniquet on the inspector's leg.

Then she smiled. 'As we're back here, at least I can finish telling you that I love you. Please take care. I don't want the curse to strike again.'

Inspector Flett groaned then spoke through gritted teeth. 'I'm still here, you know.'

'Lie still,' said Monique. 'I've stopped the worst of it, but you're still bleeding.'

Bob's later recollections of the climb were as a fragmentary series of fleeting impressions. He remembered an extremely tight and dimly lit spiral stone stair that led ever upwards. There were confined and claustrophobic passages, and then a sense of almost paralysing fear as he found himself in an open area high in the building, looking right down to the floor of the cathedral. Then he passed through a bell room with a wooden floor. He wondered if this was what lay above the wooden ceiling that he'd noticed in the crossing of the cathedral that morning.

Bob paused. He could hear running feet below him, but also thought he could hear footsteps above him. Yet more stairs. Then a closed wooden door, hinged on both sides and opening away from him in the middle. He wondered if Swanson was waiting on the other side of it with a gun. Bob crouched, then pushed hard against the doors and launched himself forwards. He realised with a sense of sheer terror that he was on a narrow walkway leading round the top of the tower, at the base of the spire. He'd seen it earlier from below, without realising what it was. The stone parapet in front of him was barely waist high. If he'd come through the doors even a little more aggressively, there was every chance he would simply have gone over the top of it.

He realised Swanson must be very near. Bob's right hand felt sweaty as he held his gun. Should he go left, or right? It made little difference in practice, but he decided he'd give himself slightly more chance of seeing round the corners from his right eye if he went anti-clockwise round the walkway.

He found Swanson leaning back against the parapet at the south-east corner of the walkway. He had his gun in his hand, with the muzzle beneath his chin, pointed upwards.

'That's far enough. We meet at last, group captain. You've created quite a stir, you know.'

'There's nothing to be gained from pulling the trigger,' said Bob, lowering his own gun to seem less of a threat. 'You'll just leave Betty without any family at all.'

'Don't you dare bring Betty into this! It's not her fault, but I had a life until I came to this dreadful place and was ensnared by her scheming mother and evil grandfather.'

'But killing yourself isn't an answer to anything.'

'Perhaps not. But killing you first might make my last moments feel a little better.' Swanson pointed the gun at Bob and raised his arm. Bob instinctively closed his eyes and flinched, even before he'd realised the enormity of his miscalculation in lowering his gun.

The last time he'd been shot, a month earlier, he'd heard nothing. This time he was confused to realise that he had heard the shot, albeit oddly removed from reality, but had felt nothing. He opened his eyes to find he was still alive and crouching on the walkway. He stood up and incongruously thought he could hear someone shouting in the street below. The walkway in front of him was empty as far as the corner where Swanson had been standing, though he could see blood on the east parapet. Bob gingerly approached and looked over, careful not to get blood on his greatcoat. He realised that the roof of the choir was going to be far harder for someone to clean than the parapet of the tower walkway.

EPILOGUE

Bob was delighted to find that his Mosquito remained unclaimed by its rightful owners when he arrived back at RAF Turnhouse a little before lunch on the Friday. He smiled when he realised that he was now thinking of it as 'his'. Their flight from RAF Grimsetter in an Avro Anson had been uneventful. The pilot had been happy to sit back and let Bob do all the flying from the co-pilot's seat. Monique, Michael and Andrew had sat in the passenger cabin.

The rest of the previous day had been frenetic. Bob had emerged from St Magnus Cathedral to find Monique hugging Major Stewart on the steps outside. She'd gone on to tell Bob that it was the major who had been on top of the circular tower of the Bishop's Palace, well below the cathedral tower and some distance away from it, who had saved his life by killing Swanson with a single rifle shot. Bob had realised what an incredible, or incredibly lucky, shot it must have been and had shaken the major's hand.

The evening meeting with Major General Blanch had been brought forward to late afternoon. Air Commodore Chilton was also there, together with a replacement rear admiral whose name Bob didn't catch. Bob had briefed the assembled great and good on the developments of the day. Then Major Stewart had talked about how he proposed to process the material Bob and Monique had recovered. Bob hadn't been surprised to learn that the briefcase found in Swanson's car belonged to Napier and contained compromising information about a few individuals, including Lieutenant Commander Lacey, who Napier had presumably felt might help him in an emergency.

Afterwards they'd returned to Kirkwall, where they had visited Inspector Flett in hospital. Bob had been relieved to find that the inspector was not only going to survive, but there was every chance he'd recover sufficiently to be fully mobile again.

There had been five of them for dinner at the St Magnus Hotel. Betty Swanson had seemed to be coping reasonably well with her father's death, but Bob knew it was early days and grief could show itself in odd ways. He had wondered how she'd handle running a hotel that was part-owned by a Glasgow gangster. Then as he watched her with Michael he had begun to wonder if Willie Shand might be persuaded to do the decent thing and pay a fair price for the three-quarters of the hotel he didn't already own. Bob had parked the idea for later reference.

*

Bob knew that his priority on returning to the office was to write a report on everything that had happened in Orkney for Commodore Cunningham. And another about events in Lossiemouth and Wester Ross, he reminded himself. As it turned out, he spent more of the afternoon than he wanted dealing with relatively unimportant but urgent matters that had built up over the week. As it began to get dark, Monique put her head round Bob's office door.

'Do you have plans for the evening, Bob?'

'I can think of lots of things I'd prefer to be doing, especially with you, but it's going to take me hours yet to write these reports. Joyce has said she'll come in tomorrow morning to type them up and see them securely on their way to the commodore.'

'That's fair enough, Bob. The week's catching up with me a little. I'll just grab a bite to eat in the officers' mess, then get someone to run me back to the guest house. I might as well get some value for the money the department's paying for my accommodation.'

'Look, I'll join you in the mess. I could do with something to eat. Then I'll come back and work my way through these reports.'

The meal had been pleasant enough, but Bob got the sense of a distance growing between them. He wondered if Monique regretted what she had said to him in the cathedral. Now didn't seem the right time to ask. He asked about work instead. 'Did you get the chance to talk to MI5 about Dr Taylor from X Base?'

'Ah, yes. It seems I was right about him. He's admitted to telling Helena Berdyaev everything she wanted to know about Porton Down's work on anthrax. He was a founder member of Porton Down's Biology Department when it opened in 1940 and helped establish X Base. He admitted that he's been giving information about X Base's activities and the wider work of Porton Down to the Soviets since the beginning of this year.'

'Why? Money? He didn't strike me as the ideological type.'

'No, it was much more straightforward. Helena Berdyaev recruited him, and has kept him in her pocket, by occasionally letting him into her bed. Not as often as he wanted, it seems, but just often enough to keep him hoping and to keep him betraying his country.'

'What about Leading Aircraftman Murray?'

Monique laughed. 'Dr Taylor is not a fan of Murray's. As far as we can tell, Murray acted on the spur of the moment, and alone, and possibly for ideological reasons. My colleagues believed Taylor when he told them he didn't know Murray before they met at Lossiemouth. They also believed him when he said that he had no idea about what Murray had done until you and I started asking difficult questions. He believes that the Soviets could have warned him that he was about to be exposed because of Murray's actions, but chose not to. That's one of the reasons that he's been so talkative.'

'What will happen to him?'

'I don't know, Bob. It may make a difference that the Soviets are technically our allies, but he was still spying for a foreign power and the information he passed on could be hugely damaging.'

'Did MI5 say if anything has been seen or heard of Michael Murray, in Glasgow or anywhere else?'

'No, nothing at all. I've been thinking about that. I'm wondering if the NKVD had something to do with his disappearance.'

'That's a bit far-fetched, isn't it?'

'Possibly not. We know he contacted them after stealing the anthrax and tried to get it to them. We also know that in the process he became a threat to the much more important operation the NKVD had running with Dr Taylor. Maybe they helped Murray escape, or maybe they simply took steps to silence him for good. We may never know.'

'You and I do have the most pleasant dinner conversations, don't we Monique?'

Monique smiled wearily. Bob could see that the dark shadow behind her eyes was worryingly close to the surface.

*

Bob's secretary, Joyce Stuart, was as good as her word. She had a few queries about Bob's late-night handwriting, and a couple more about his grammar, but by late morning she had typed up his reports. Bob read and signed them, and Joyce then double-enveloped the documents, addressed the outer envelope to Commodore Cunningham, and went off to get them in the confidential mail.

Bob sat back. Joyce had been less successful during the week in her efforts to keep his in-tray as small as possible. Perhaps he was being unfair, thought Bob. Perhaps she had been highly successful, and the small mountain of neglected paperwork she'd moved to his desk from the secure cabinet that morning was just what was left of a much larger mountain. He'd ask her to lock it up again when she got back from the mailroom. It had waited this long; it could wait until Monday morning.

Bob wondered what Monique was doing and thought back to the wonderful weekend they'd spent together in Edinburgh only a week before. He heard the outside office phone ring. Bob knew that there was no-one in the office except him. His army team were on duty, but they were looking at weekend security on a series of army bases in northern England.

The phone on Joyce's desk was still ringing when he got to it. 'Group Captain Sutherland.'

'Hello Bob.'

'Monique! I was just thinking about you.'

'I was thinking about you, too. Look Bob, I've got something to ask you. Do you remember the walk we took along the pier in Kirkwall on our first night there?'

'Of course I do.'

'Did you mean what you said, about finding somewhere in Edinburgh to rent, which perhaps I could then use too?'

'Yes, I missed you last night.'

'Right. I'm calling from the guest house I'm staying in. It's run by a nice elderly lady called Mrs Marsden. Her husband died years ago. The place isn't busy but seems to provide her with a reasonable income. Mrs Marsden has a daughter, Susan Sutton. Susan is a few years older than us and is a widow. Her husband was a captain in an armoured regiment and was killed during the siege of Tobruk last year. They had no children and Susan is going to move in with her mother to help run the guest house and provide company for them both.

'Susan owns a house in Corstorphine, not far from the guest house. Mrs Marsden's brother is a solicitor in Edinburgh and has advised that trying to sell while the war is still on is unlikely to be in Susan's long-term interests. She doesn't need the capital, so has decided to rent it out now and sell it after the war. I've just got back from seeing it, Bob. It's a lovely bungalow with two bedrooms. It's being let fully furnished, so we'll have everything we need. It's in a road called Featherhall Crescent that's close to the western edge of the city and would be perfect for us. I've been honest with Susan that we want somewhere where we can live together, and she has no problem with that. The documents would be in your name. That seems the best bet because you're local, and a senior military officer, and your name really is your name. The rent seems very reasonable. What do you think? Can you come over and see it today?'

Bob had never heard Monique sound so excited. He'd been shocked by his own first reaction on realising where the conversation was going. It had been the same sheer terror he'd felt when emerging onto the walkway round the top of the cathedral two days earlier. There was the same sense of imminent danger of launching himself into space. Then he realised that this might be his only chance of the life he so much wanted with

Monique. Why was he afraid? A simple fear of commitment? There was no time to analyse things now. Bob knew that if he didn't match Monique's enthusiasm, right here and now, then he could easily lose her forever. She'd let her guard down utterly in talking to him on the phone. She'd never forgive him if he betrayed the trust that she'd shown by not responding.

'Bob? Are you there, Bob?'

'It sounds wonderful Monique. I've got one of the cars here, so as soon as Joyce is back from the post room I'll come over and pick you up at the guest house and we can look together.'

'Great, I'll see you then, Bob.'

As he replaced the phone, Bob knew the decision about renting the house had already been made. The suddenness of it was still a little shocking, but that didn't matter because he knew that the much bigger decision, the one he could only make for himself, had also already been made. He smiled.

*

The bungalow had been every bit as good as Monique had said and they were planning to sign the paperwork by Wednesday and move in immediately. As Monique had pointed out, it wasn't as if either of them had much in the way of belongings to transport. Bob realised that it was the word 'planning' that made all the difference. The last time he'd seriously planned anything with anyone had been with Mary Callaghan, a long time and another life ago. That had come to nothing because of his selfishness. He wouldn't make the same mistake twice.

They rented a room in an anonymous small hotel in Edinburgh's New Town for the Saturday and Sunday nights. It had seemed like a good idea at the time and the room was attractive and comfortable. They found out on the first night that while the room was fine, the bed was anything but. It was large enough, and comfortable enough, and there were more than enough blankets. But it creaked, badly, when its occupants did anything more vigorous than rolling over. Their lovemaking on the Saturday night had stopped suddenly after the first two loud creaks, then they had collapsed into giggles.

'I do hope that the bed in the bungalow's not like this one.'

'It won't be, Bob. And even if it is, it's a bungalow so there won't be anyone to hear.'

Bob laughed.

'There something I've been wanting to say to you, Bob.'

'I thought you said it, in the cathedral?'

'Yes, I finally overcame my fear and told you that I love you. I also told you to take care. As you know, I spoke to Major Stewart. He'd been some sort of champion marksman in shooting competitions before the war. When he heard you were going up the cathedral tower, he took a sniper rifle off a policeman – he said he had no idea why the Orkney police had sniper rifles in its armoury – and then he climbed up the tower of the palace across the road, the one I pointed out to you that looks like a castle. He told me that the angle and the parapet only gave him a partial view of what was going on, but through the telescopic sights he could see that Swanson was threatening to shoot himself when you came round to his side of the walkway. Stewart couldn't see you very clearly, but he had a clear view of Swanson when he turned the gun round and raised it as if to shoot you. That's when he killed him.'

'And I'm grateful he did.'

'So am I Bob. What puzzles me is why he needed to. You've got a gun, why didn't you use it?'

'I lowered my gun to appear less threatening when I was trying to talk sense into him. When he turned his gun on me, I had no time to react.'

'Let me make you a promise, Bob. If you ever do anything even remotely as stupid as that again, and survive, I'll kill you myself.'

Bob kissed her, careful not to make the bed creak. 'I promise I won't, Monique.'

*

'You must be Monique! Welcome! I'm David Sutherland. This is Rose.'

Monique could see that Bob was on edge. He seemed to get on well enough with his parents, but she knew he was worried about how they'd respond to her.

'It's a Sunday, so we decided to have a good old-fashioned roast for dinner.'

The roast beef and accompaniments were delicious, and Monique decided it would be ungracious to spend more than a split-second wondering how the meal had been achieved within the restrictions of rationing.

Over dinner the conversation ebbed and flowed round a range of general subjects. The nearest they came to anything personal was when Rose talked about Pearl, Bob's younger sister, who he'd never mentioned to Monique.

'She studied art, but when the war started, she trained to be a nurse. She's working at the Royal Infirmary of Edinburgh in Lauriston Place. She'd be here this evening but is on duty. She sends her apologies. There's something you don't know, Bob. She's been going out with a pilot. He's based out in East Lothian.

He seems a nice young man.'

Monique could see that Bob was at best ambivalent about the idea, but his reply was politely positive. She suspected he'd seen too many young pilots killed to welcome the idea of his sister getting involved with one.

After dinner they sat in front of the fire in the impressive lounge. Bob and David were drinking whisky. Monique had said she was happy to drive afterwards and Rose had joined her in drinking tea. Bob took advantage of a quiet moment to tell his parents that he was planning to rent a house in Edinburgh and that Monique would be sharing it with him.

Neither appeared unduly surprised or concerned, which left Monique feeling deeply relieved.

Rose had seemed very detached since dinner had ended, and Monique wasn't surprised when she looked across at Bob and asked him to tell her about her brother Frank. Monique knew Bob had been steeling himself for this and he replied with a measured and careful explanation of what had happened.

'You're saying that he abducted you and was going to have you killed?'

'Yes, Mum.'

'And he was poisoned partly in revenge for killing a naval officer?'

'That's right. I'm sorry.'

Rose sat back in her armchair. 'I always knew deep down that he was no good, but I always hoped he'd change. He never did and now he never will. Look, I don't want to spoil the evening, but I think I need to go to bed and try to come to terms with what I've learned.'

After Rose left the room, David poured more whisky for himself and Bob, and fetched a tonic for Monique.

David turned to her. 'Bob tells me that you are on loan from MI5, Monique.'

'That's right, David.'

'I think you both met Lieutenant James Bruce not long ago, while tracking down Soviet agents. He's in charge of Special Branch in Edinburgh City Police and reports to me.'

'Dad!' Bob was on his feet. 'I begged you not to use your contacts to pry on Monique.'

'And I didn't,' said David. 'It's just that the colleague who told me he'd seen the two of you in the North British Hotel last weekend was James Bruce. I saw him again on Friday. After we'd covered the ground we needed to cover, he reminded me that you saved the life of the man he called "the idiot major" by shooting that Soviet agent during the raid in Leith, Monique. He went on to say that at the time he'd had a sense of having met you before but had only now worked out where. If he's right, then I nearly met you myself.'

Monique could see there was a twinkle in David's eye and hoped that Bob wasn't about to do anything silly. She had no recollection of meeting James Bruce before her last visit to Edinburgh but had a feeling she knew where David was leading her. 'When was that?' she asked.

'September 1940. I arrested Werner Walti as a German spy when he got off the train from Aberdeen in Edinburgh. James Bruce was involved after Werner's two companions were arrested at the railway station in Port Gordon. He's convinced that you were one of them and that Monique Dubois is Vera Eriksen. Is he right?'

Monique smiled at Bob. 'It's not a problem. I'd have to tell your dad sooner or later. It might as well be now. Have another whisky, both of you, this may take some time.' She could see the twinkle was still in David's eye and realised just how much like his son he was. 'Yes, I was one of the team of three Abwehr agents who came ashore from a seaplane at Port Gordon, and Vera Eriksen was the name I was known by at the time.'

'I did wonder what had become of you. The two men you landed with were executed as spies last year, weren't they?'

'That's right, David. But then they'd not been working for the Secret Intelligence Service, or MI6, for years, even when the White Russians and later the Abwehr thought I was working for them.'

'Good God. How did you get involved in that?'

'It's a long story and it's getting late, David. But I'm happy to give you the headlines.'

Bob sat forward. 'There's no need for this.'

She could see he was desperately uncomfortable. 'Yes, there is, Bob. Your dad's very like you. If I don't tell him, he'll find out for himself, sooner or later.' She turned to face David. 'There are two conditions, though.'

'What are they?'

'That you tell no-one else what I'm about to tell you, and that you make sure that James Bruce tells no-one else what he's worked out.'

'Agreed.'

'Good. I'll leave the story of my childhood for another time. I became a professional dancer when I was 16 and a year later, I was working in Paris. It was there that I met a White Russian count who I fell in love with and married. He had me spy on the communists for the White Russians and introduced me to cocaine. MI6 recruited me when I was 20, after I'd left my first husband, and they helped me kick my cocaine habit. They wanted me to spy on the communists and the White Russians for them, which I did. In 1936, when I was 24, I was recruited by the Abwehr, with the enthusiastic agreement of my MI6 handlers. My first husband was shot as a spy in the Soviet Union at about the same time. A year later I married my second husband, a senior officer in the Abwehr who was nearly 60 at the time. My second husband was killed in a car crash in Berlin in early 1940 and I became a full-time field agent for the Abwehr, again with MI6's blessing. Three of us landed in Scotland on the 29th of September 1940, and the rest you know.'

'Bloody hell! That's incredible.'

'Incredible but true. It seems as well that you know exactly who Bob has got himself involved with.'

Bob had been on the edge of his seat. He now sat back, to Monique's relief. 'There are two more things you need to know about Monique, Dad, before you form any judgements. I didn't tell you the detail at the time, but back in September she saved me from capture by commandeering a Luftwaffe flying boat that had landed on a loch in Caithness. And while this might also be marked up as "incredible", by the same act she also saved King George VI from capture and prevented Britain losing the war.

'More immediately, it was thanks to her that Frank Gordon revealed where I was being held in Orkney. I owe her my life twice over.'

'You know,' said David. 'I thought you slid over that bit of the story very neatly when talking to your mother. Frank Gordon never struck me as the sort of villain who would give anything up easily. How was he persuaded to say where you were?'

Bob told him.

David looked at Monique. 'Really? And he believed that you would?'

'He was right to, David. It saved his life. Only for a few hours, admittedly, but neither of us knew that at the time.'

David Sutherland lay back in his chair and roared with laughter. Monique hoped that Rose was a heavy sleeper. When he sat up again, Monique could see there were tears of mirth in his eyes.

David reached forward and patted the back of her hand. 'Welcome to the family, Monique!'

AUTHOR'S NOTE

This book is a work of fiction and should be read as such. Except as noted below, all characters are fictional and any resemblances to real people, either living or dead, are purely coincidental.

Likewise, many of the events that are described in this book are the products of the author's imagination. Others did take place.

Let's start with the characters. Some of the military personnel who appear between the pages of this book occupy posts that existed at the time, but nonetheless they are all fictional. This is significant because the military commands and units mentioned were usually doing what I describe them as doing at the time the action takes place, though command structures in all three services have been simplified for the sake of keeping the story manageable.

Minor characters are also entirely invented. Some characters could be associated with real people because of their roles in events that took place, such as the senior officers of all three services in Orkney or the scientists at X Base. Again, the characters who play those roles in this book are not based on their real-life counterparts and are fictional. It is worth saying that this is especially true of some of the senior Royal Navy officers in this book: sadly, a world entirely populated by nice, honest and honourable people would be of little use to a thriller writer.

Group Captain Robert Sutherland is also an invented character, though he has a career in the Royal Air Force that will be recognised by anyone familiar with the life and achievements of Squadron Leader Archibald McKellar, DSO, DFC and Bar. Bob Sutherland's family background and pre-war employment were very different to Archibald McKellar's, but the two share an eminent list of achievements during the Battle of Britain. Squadron Leader McKellar was tragically killed when he was shot down on the 1st of November 1940, whereas the fictional Group Captain Sutherland was only wounded when he was shot down on the same day, allowing him to play a leading role in this book and its two predecessors.

And Madame Monique Dubois? She is a fictional alias for a real woman. The real Vera Eriksen, or Vera Schalburg, or take your pick from any number of other aliases, had a story that was both complex and very dark. She disappeared during the war after the two German spies she landed with at Port Gordon on the Moray Firth were tried and executed for spying by the British. One of her two companions was arrested at Waverley Station in Edinburgh, though not by the fictional Superintendent David Sutherland.

There's a flavour of Monique's story in the epilogue of this book but to get a fuller picture you need to read my first novel, *Eyes Turned Skywards.*

Military Intelligence, Section 11, or MI11, was a real organisation which had role in safeguarding military security. Its organisation and other aspects of its operations described in this book are entirely fictional.

The Security Service (MI5) and the Secret Intelligence Service (MI6) both existed, and both continue to exist at the time of writing. MI5 did have a Regional Security Liaison Officer in Scotland during the war but the arrangement with MI11 that underpins the story told here is fictional.

Let's turn to places that appear in this book.

Craigiehall was taken over by the army during the war and later became the main army headquarters in Scotland. It remains an army base at the time of writing.

The North British Hotel in Edinburgh became the Balmoral Hotel some decades ago.

RAF Lossiemouth is at the time of writing the last remaining operational RAF air base in Scotland. The units described as being there in late 1942 were there and were doing roughly what I describe them doing. 46 Maintenance Unit received, finished and distributed aircraft from the factories using Air Transport Auxiliary pilots, some of whom were women. There were times when it had to use fields surrounding the main airfield to store aircraft pending work or awaiting delivery. 20 Operational Training Unit was training young men to fly Wellington bombers at Lossiemouth and was sustaining the horrifying accident rates described. The unit also provided the aircraft that dropped a bomb containing anthrax spores on Gruinard Island on the 26th of September 1942. The idea that some of the anthrax was stolen during this process is my invention.

It follows that X Base at Gruinard Bay and on Gruinard Island was also real, as were the trials intended to turn anthrax into a practical weapon of war. Gruinard House is externally as described here according to online photographs, though the interior is fictional. Today the house seems to be a private residence and that should be respected. Gruinard Island remained contaminated for decades after the war. It was only on the 24th of April 1990 that it was finally declared safe.

Although the activities of X Base are well documented and the film shown to Bob and Monique exists and can be viewed online, the layout and location of parts of the base are more difficult to pin down. The descriptions in this book involve some conjecture on my part.

There is a very real sense in which Orkney has become a major character in this book. Incredible though it seems, all this time later, Scapa Flow was every bit as important to the British war effort as described here and there really were up to 40,000 servicemen and women stationed on a group of islands with an original civilian population of not much more than 20,000.

As far as possible, I have tried to reflect the reality of island life in this book. The Kirkwall Sector Operations Room existed; and continued to do so until fairly recently, when it was, presumably with considerable effort, demolished to make way for a housing estate. The Wrennery also existed, and the name lingered on to describe the post-war housing built on the site of the hutted camp.

It's been said that if you scratch Orkney, it bleeds archaeology. That's true. Much of that archaeology is very ancient. But there is a lot that dates back only as far as the two world wars in the last century, especially the Second World War. There are reminders almost everywhere you look, in the form of concrete gun emplacements, brick or concrete buildings, and more. At Lyness on Hoy many wartime buildings have survived, and there is a museum devoted to the subject (which was being renovated last time I visited).

The Ness Battery near Stromness, which features in this book, is a remarkable survivor. The concrete gun emplacements and lookouts are still there, as are many of the wooden huts, including the mess hall, which comes complete with the magnificent murals that so impressed Monique. Guided tours of the battery are available, and I'd highly recommend one if you are in Orkney. I would like to thank Andrew Hollinrake of

Stromness Tours for showing me round the battery.

Moving on, the St Magnus Hotel is an invention. There is a hotel next door to the Kirkwall Hotel overlooking Kirkwall harbour, but the St Magnus Hotel featured in this book is not based on it – except for a coincidence of location – and is entirely fictional.

The Kirkwall Hotel was used as a naval HQ during the war, while the hotel in the heart of Stromness was the headquarters of Orkney & Shetland Defences, or "OSDef". Almost everyone refers to it being used at that time under its current name, the Stromness Hotel. However, the most convincing source I've seen states that it was called Mackay's Hotel during the war, which is the name I've used for it.

The incident in which Sergeant Peter Bennett stops an army unit driving its Bren gun carriers through the Ring of Brodgar is based on a remarkable wartime photograph showing an army unit doing just that.

The old liner the *Dunluce Castle* did serve as a depot ship moored off Lyness during the war. It provided a wide range of services but the idea that its sick bay was used as described in this book is an invention.

Those familiar with the Hurliness area at the south end of the island of Hoy may have noticed that I've taken some liberties with the local geography. Several other cottages and an old school have been removed to allow the tin cottage in which Bob was held captive to move closer to the end of the Ayre, the causeway linking Hoy with South Walls. Meanwhile the access track to the quarry has been slightly moved. These changes simply make the story work better.

Reference is made in the story to "Mo Ness", near the north end of Hoy. This is called "Moaness" on modern maps, but I've stuck with the name used on the 1948 one-inch Ordnance Survey map and on earlier maps.

St Magnus Cathedral continues to dominate the heart of Kirkwall and should be a part of any visit to Orkney. Tours of the upper reaches of the cathedral, including the walkway round the top of the tower, can be arranged and are highly recommended.

I've noted above that the widespread corruption amongst Royal Navy officers that forms a key strand of this book is fictional. Having said that, at least one real-world account written by a visitor to the huge wartime canteen on Flotta commented on the money being made from Crown and Anchor games and the suspicion that the authorities were taking their cut.

A word about the title might help set it in context. 'Bloody Orkney' is the name of a poem comprising eight (or sometimes nine) stanzas expressing the writer's unhappiness with just about every aspect of being posted to Orkney. It is usually attributed to Captain Hamish Blair, RN. It is said to have been written by him during the Second World War while stationed in Orkney and was published some years after the war. I have used the ninth, often missing and apparently optional, stanza at the head of the prologue. I have also seen a tenth stanza, said to have been written as a riposte by Orcadians: *'Captain Hamish "Bloody" Blair/Isnae posted here nae mair/But no-one seems tae bloody care/In bloody Orkney.'*

Captain Hamish Blair is said to be a pseudonym of the Scottish author and journalist Andrew James Fraser Blair. The odd thing is that he lived from 1872 to 1935. Did he write the poem during the First World War rather than the second as is usually claimed? Odder still is the suggestion he moved to India long before that war began, so it seems unlikely that he served in Orkney then either. Perhaps we'll never know. All that is clear is that the poem is said to sum up the feelings of many who served in Orkney during the Second World War.

To conclude, in my view it is the duty of a fiction writer to create a world that feels right to his or her readers. When the world in question is one that is as far removed in so many ways, some predictable and others not, as 1942 is from today, then it is inevitable that false assumptions will be made and facts will be misunderstood. If you find factual errors within this book I apologise and can only hope that they have not got in the way of your enjoyment of the story.

PRAISE FOR KEN LUSSEY'S PREVIOUS THRILLERS SET IN SCOTLAND DURING WORLD WAR TWO:

EYES TURNED SKYWARDS

'Compelling... extremely enjoyable... The plot is tight and thrilling enough to retain our attention to the end, the detail creating an authentic Britain at war.' *The Literary Shed*

'A winning formula of transplanting a detective storyline into the wartime narrative... makes you want to know what is going to happen to him during the remainder of the war... gripping in its thriller form and wartime context...' *NextToTheAisle*

Readers' Reviews on Amazon:

'Excellent escapist page-turning thriller!'

'A cracking good read.'

'An exciting journey in the search for the truth behind the plane crash of the Duke of Kent.'

'A great insight into one of the greatest stories of the Second World War.'

'For aviation lovers everywhere! A delight to be led gently by the hand into a web of intrigue.'

'I would recommend this to anyone who enjoys a well laid and thought out plot, which combines historical events and locations with great accuracy.'

THE DANGER OF LIFE

'An addictive, action-packed wartime thriller.' *Hair Past a Freckle*

'A fast-paced, cleverly written mystery/thriller that kept me guessing from beginning to end.' *Jessica Belmont, Author & Blogger*

'This is a cracking good World War 2 thriller.' *Alex J Book Reviews*

Readers' Reviews on Amazon:

'A great plot set in WW2 in Scotland. Time and place are evoked brilliantly.'

'The descriptions of Scotland and the restrictions that are in place during WW2 make it seem like another world. Can't wait for the next instalment.'

'A great find. A most enjoyable read. A wartime thriller set in a beautiful area of Scotland, a real feel for the 1940s combined with a familiar landscape, bring on the movie!'